DISCARD

BY ALLEGRA GOODMAN

The Chalk Artist

The Cookbook Collector

The Other Side of the Island

Intuition

Paradise Park

Kaaterskill Falls

The Family Markowitz

Total Immersion

The
Chalk Artist

The Chalk Artist

A NOVEL

Allegra Goodman

THE DIAL PRESS

NEW YORK

Copyright © 2017 by Allegra Goodman

All rights reserved.

Published in the United States by The Dial Press, an imprint of Random House, a division of Penguin Random House LLC, New York.

THE DIAL PRESS and the HOUSE colophon are registered trademarks of Penguin Random House LLC.

Grateful acknowledgment is made to the following for permission to reprint previously published material:

The Belknap Press of Harvard University Press: Excerpt from "There is a pain so utter" from *The Poems of Emily Dickinson*, edited by Thomas H. Johnson (Cambridge, MA: The Belknap Press of Harvard University Press), copyright © 1951, 1955 by the President and Fellows of Harvard College. Copyright © renewed 1979, 1983 by the President and Fellows of Harvard College. Copyright © 1914, 1918, 1919, 1924, 1929, 1930, 1932, 1935, 1937, 1942 by Martha Dickinson Bianchi. Copyright © 1952, 1957, 1958, 1963, 1965 by Mary L. Hampson. Reprinted by permission of The Belknap Press of Harvard University Press.

New Directions Publishing Corporation: Excerpt from "A Virginal" from *Personae* by Ezra Pound, copyright © 1926 by Ezra Pound. Reprinted by permission of New Directions Publishing Corporation.

Library of Congress Cataloging-in-Publication Data
Names: Goodman, Allegra, author.
Title: The chalk artist : a novel / Allegra Goodman.
Description: First edition. | New York : The Dial Press, [2017]
Identifiers: LCCN 2016001270| ISBN 9781400069873 |
ISBN 9780679605041 (ebook)
Subjects: LCSH: Computer games—Social aspects—Fiction. | Video games—
Social aspects—Fiction. | Man-woman relationships—Fiction. |
Interpersonal relations—Fiction. | GSAFD: Love stories.
Classification: LCC PS3557.O5829 C47 2017 | DDC 813/.54—dc23
LC record available at https://lccn.loc.gov/2016001270

Printed in the United States of America on acid-free paper

randomhousebooks.com

2 4 6 8 9 7 5 3 1

First Edition

Book design by Caroline Cunningham
Hand lettering on title page and leaf ornament by Rachel Willey

TO MY TEACHERS

Dana Izumi

June Brieske

Mabel Hefty

Tom Earle

Bill Messer

Liz Foster

Eileen Crean

Leonard Russo

Betty Sullivan

Jerry Devlin

Bill Alfred

Michael Anesko

Larry Benson

Barbara Lewalski

George Dekker

David Riggs

Jay Fliegelman

John Bender

Seth Lerer

Stephen Orgel

The
Chalk Artist

1

Grendel's Den

Her long hair curtained her face as she sat marking papers. Drunk graduate students surrounded her, but she didn't even look up. Rock pounding, dishes clattering, this was Grendel's in winter, the old Cambridge dive, loud, warm, and subterranean, half a flight down from Winthrop Street. A green lamp lit every table, a hundred mirrors hung on paneled walls. Collin watched her reflection from every angle. She looked so elegant and out of place.

She came on Tuesday nights, and sometimes Thursdays too. She would order a Mediterranean salad and start grading papers. She was slender, fair, her eyes dark and shining, as though she knew some secret—she alone. Whenever he got close enough, he looked over her shoulder. Her handwriting was precise, her pen purple, extra fine. Once she glanced up and nearly smiled. You realize, he told her silently, if I drop something it's your fault. If I break a plate, it's all because of you.

He saw guys leering, even if she didn't. "Everybody's looking at her," he told Samantha, the bartender.

Sam said, "Yeah, but mostly you."

Collin was twenty-three, bright, artistic, and unhappy. He had just left college for the second time, and although he had good reasons, his mother was upset with him. His ex-girlfriend Noelle was out of patience. His father was in the navy; he had not seen or even heard from the man in seven years. Collin had thought of enlisting, mostly to travel, but he had grown up on a street where signs in the front yards read WAR IS NOT THE ANSWER. He never did enlist. He didn't go anywhere.

He worked at a bar and went out drinking afterward. Even if he'd enjoyed college and respected his instructors, even if he had excelled at Web design and programming, he didn't have time to go to class. He was busy collecting tips and partying, waking up in other people's beds. Sometimes he despised himself; not often. Sometimes he decided to get serious, but he kept working nights and sleeping in, and hanging with his high school friends, and all of this became a full-time job; youth itself was his vocation.

For this reason, the girl's diligence fascinated him. She sat for hours grading at her table, and she was so young—way too young to be a teacher. She should have known better than to sit alone down there. Few came to work at Grendel's, and those who tried, didn't get much done. They would open their computers and close them gratefully when drinks arrived. This girl did not respond to guys circling her table. She looked royal in her cardigans and trailing scarves and calfskin boots. He sketched her on his order pad. The princess of solitude, with a crown.

One Tuesday, when she started packing up, her coat slipped off the back of her chair, and Collin ran to catch it for her. She stood to go, and he realized how tall she was, almost his height. He was close enough to see the gold flecks in her eyes, the freckles dusting her face. He held his breath as she slipped her arms into the sleeves. Then she thanked him, and rushed off.

"Nice," teased a waitress named Kayte. "Could you catch my coat too? Before it touches the ground?"

Collin watched for the girl on Thursday while he carried out chicken wings and plates of stuffed potato skins. He served foaming Guinness, caught bits of conversation: *Seriously? How much did that cost? I feel guilty but . . .* The Who pounding. Students wailing, *"The exodus is here."* Busy night and no free time, but Collin kept watching until Sam started flicking ice at him from behind the bar. "Who're you waiting for?"

"Shut up."

"So you admit it." Sam was tiny but in your face. She was compiling a book of vintage cocktails.

"I'm not admitting anything."

True, Collin wondered about the teacher. He speculated about her at Broadway Bicycle School, where he taught wheel changing, tire patching—basic repair. She had sounded American, but he decided that she came from Paris. Or London. He said, "Inflate the tube and listen." Maybe Barcelona.

On Monday he colored backdrops for the theater company he had founded with his roommate, Darius. Working with wet chalk on old-fashioned rolling blackboards, he drew slender trunks and arching branches, layered cherry blossoms, white and pink. The edge of his chalk crumbled. He rubbed white and red together with his thumb, and he thought and thought about her. Sometimes she glanced up and she was looking at him, he was sure of it. The next second he would think, No, that can't be true. Daydreaming about her, he felt lighthearted, amused. His fantasies were so chaste and so persistent. She was always sitting at her table, just out of reach, and he liked her there—although he was intensely curious. What was she doing all alone? A girl like that would have a boyfriend. There had to be some story. A long-distance relationship—but she didn't look lonely. He wanted to know her. Or at least to hear her name.

There were days she never even crossed his mind. He spent a weekend with Noelle. They went to a party and stayed out late dancing, and then they went to her place and he began undressing her. She laughed, and he knew why. Now that they'd sworn off each other their bodies were so eager.

Late the next day they woke stale and headachy, annoyed with themselves. Even so, Darius's girlfriend, Emma, had four tickets to Lady Lamb the Beekeeper in Davis Square, and so they went. All that time, Collin didn't think about the girl, until Lady Lamb bent over her guitar, her long hair curtaining her face. Then suddenly he imagined the girl watching him. He saw himself through her eyes and he was cheap, and aimless. He felt poor, as well, although he didn't consider himself poor. He considered himself free.

The next week, he was taking orders for a party of six when she materialized again. He looked up, and there she was, already seated in Kayte's territory. He was not getting off early, but when he saw the huge stack of papers on her table, he made a secret deal with her. If you keep at it until eleven, I'll walk out with you.

All night he watched her table, willing her to stay. When she began to stir, he murmured: "No, you don't. Keep working. You aren't going anywhere."

Ten forty-five, she pushed back her chair. From behind, he saw her shoulders shaking, and thought she must be sobbing, or choking. He rushed over. "Are you all right?"

When she looked up, she was laughing, not crying, and she showed him an essay. Curvy handwriting on lined paper, the title in bigger script: *Juliet: Shakespeare's Heroin.* "What do you think?"

A thousand ideas crowded his mind, none about her student's spelling, as he watched her add an *e.* "Are you really a teacher?"

She said, "I keep asking myself."

"You don't look like one."

She shook back her long brown hair and glanced up at him, amused. "What's a teacher supposed to look like?"

"Old," he told her. "Bitter."

"I'm bitter."

"How long have you been teaching?"

"Three months."

"Your students are that bad?"

She frowned as she looked down at her check. Annoyed? Or just figuring out the tip?

He said, "My friend Darius was thinking of directing *Romeo and Juliet,* but he couldn't find a church."

"He couldn't get permission?" Already she was shouldering her bag, and standing up to go.

"He wanted to do it in a cathedral with stained glass and confessionals, but the only church interested was Unitarian."

"Are you an actor?"

Jean-Philippe, the busboy, was trying to get by, and Collin stepped sideways. "I'm an actor and an artist." He regretted the words as soon as he said them. He sounded pretentious. "Mostly chalk."

She looked puzzled. "On sidewalks?"

"Yeah, but other places too. I do all the art for Theater Without Walls."

"I've heard of them!"

"In the *Phoenix*?" He turned, glancing backward at Kayte. Cover for me, he begged her silently. She was shaking her head, but he knew she liked him. Just five minutes. My tips are yours! "Wait, let me walk you out." He handed the girl a leaflet for *The Cherry Orchard,* a new production at the MIT tennis courts by Theater Without Walls. Art Director: Collin James.

"Tennis courts in December?"

"They're indoor." He led the way upstairs and opened the door for her. The snow around them lit the darkness. "I'm designing the lights . . . and the trees. I'm in it too."

"You perform in Sennott Park, right?"

"We perform all over. We did *The Tempest* on a traffic island."

"That's it! I read about the car accident."

"It was just one guy hitting a pole," he said. "Nobody got hurt."

She smiled.

"Come to *The Cherry Orchard*. I'll get you a ticket. Give me your name and I'll put you on the list."

She didn't say yes, and she didn't say no. She just looked at him, and her eyes were so dark and bright that he drew closer, until she began to laugh.

"Or not." He took a full step back.

"I wasn't laughing at the play."

"Why, then?" He had wild curly hair, black eyes, a quick, athletic body, a defensive look.

"I don't know," she said in some confusion.

"Come if you want," he said coolly.

"Okay," she said, automatically polite.

He didn't ask her name; he pretended she was just a customer. "Have a good night."

2

The Orchard

Collin could not remember why Darius had insisted on the MIT Bubble. Maybe he'd assumed he could reserve all the courts. As it happened, the actors got just one. All through *The Cherry Orchard* they competed with the skid and squeak of athletic shoes, and the *thwack* of tennis balls. Sometimes a stray ball flew over from guys rallying just steps away.

The idea was no chairs. Everyone could walk freely so that, as the play progressed, the audience followed the action, advancing, retreating, and approaching the net. There was no set except for Collin's chalk orchard, his blackboards filled with blooming trees.

The other idea—all Darius—was to stage the play as farce. They had fought about this. "Dude," Collin had told Darius, "the lady returns to where her kid drowned and then finds out she's going to lose her house."

"Yeah, so?" Darius was a big guy, not as tall as Collin, but broader. Smart, and avant-garde, and something of a rainmaker, he came up with grants from the Cambridge Arts Council, permission to perform in public places.

"The play is sad," Collin said.

Darius dismissed this. "Yeah, the sad version is really overdone."

In performance, Darius's girlfriend, Emma, romped across the court, starring as the romantic Ranevskaya, who would lose her childhood home, her past, her everything. Emma was more folk-rock Mainer than Russian nobility to begin with, and when she spun around calling, "Goodbye, old house, old grandfather house," you had the feeling she was excited to move on.

Pouring imaginary tea as the servant, Collin listened to the audience's cautious laughter, and he wanted to dash his imaginary teapot onto the court and smash all his imaginary cups and saucers too. Where was the darkness in the play? Where were the shadows? In rehearsal Darius had conceded that some moments were bittersweet. Now, under rented lights, nothing bittersweet came through. No darkness, except for Collin's seething servant, and Noelle, who played Ranevskaya's daughter Anya.

Everyone wore street clothes instead of costumes, and Noelle dressed in a little undershirt and a pair of frayed jeans that fit her like a second skin. She was an ex-ballerina with spiky hair and a pierced tongue, and she was pissed. She had a lot of anger in general, but she was angry at Collin in particular. They'd had a huge fight the night before, during which she had said, among many other things, "First of all, I hate you. Second of all, you are one hundred percent bad for me, because the only thing you care about is the beginning and the end. You can never be in the middle; you can never actually be with someone or learn something or get something done, because you're always starting and then leaving, which is why I hate myself after I've been with you."

Even now, performing, he heard hostility in every one of Noelle's lines. At the end of the play, she was brutal when she announced in her husky smoker's voice, "The cherry orchard is sold, it's gone, that's true, but don't cry, Mama." Noelle was hard-core for an ingenue.

Collin was glad the girl from Grendel's hadn't come. Her laughter haunted him, because she had known then—she'd known in advance exactly how the play would be. Pretentious and amateurish all at once. Everyone watching related to or sleeping with the cast. After Act II, a couple of strangers wandered in, but they were carrying their racquet bags.

He could see the audience tiring, clustering near the baseline. They perked up when the estate was sold and all the characters said their goodbyes. As soon as Chekhov's characters began talking about the future, everybody started folding camping stools and gathering bags. People were already heading out when Collin flipped his blackboards over, one by one. The audience froze for just a moment as he revealed his chalk drawings on the other side. Jagged stumps, fallen petals, broken branches, a holocaust of trees.

"Don't touch the art," Collin's mother, Maia, told him at the party afterward. "Do you have pictures of that orchard?"

"Darius had the camera."

"Hey," Maia called out to Darius, who sat on a couch overflowing with actors. "Do you have photos of Collin's orchard?" She was unhappy with Collin and also fiercely proud, saving every scrap of art, celebrating each performance, inviting the whole cast to her winter solstice celebration. "That orchard was the best character in the play."

Darius raised his beer bottle.

Collin said, "Good thing he can't hear you."

"I'm your mother," said Maia. She meant, You think I care?

She was tall and young for a mother, darker than Collin, so they didn't quite match. What am I? he used to ask when he was little. Black Irish, his mother said. His father was Irish and she was Italian, French Canadian, and a little bit Native American as well. She worked at the Fletcher Maynard Academy, in the basement therapy room with swings and finger paints, giant inflatable balls. The house was full of teaching prizes, clocks and plaques, two crystal apples from the district. She had posters too. WHAT DO TEACHERS MAKE? I MAKE KIDS WONDER. I MAKE THEM QUESTION . . . Collin had grown up with all these tributes, apples, and rainbows. He had been famous in school as Maia's son, and had played in her therapy room as a small child. There had never been money for babysitters, so he'd attended his mother's afterschool dance classes as well. Jazz, tap, and tango.

Now Maia's colleagues were arriving, and she served them borscht in honor of the Russian play. She ladled the thick magenta soup into bowls, and when she ran out of bowls, she handed mugs to Mrs. McCabe, the librarian, and Ms. Jamil, the occupational therapist. She found a "Mad Genius" mug for Mr. Cooperman, the fifth-grade science teacher, also known as Scienceman.

Yoga friends tramped up the porch of the triple-decker and left their boots in the stairwell. In socks they padded into the dining room, where Maia had covered the Ping-Pong table with rich fabric and flatbreads, quiche, empanadas, latkes.

Upstairs neighbors came in slippers. Lois, the art teacher from the second floor. Sage and her wife, Melissa, who grew tomatoes in window boxes on the third floor. Strawberry-blond Kerry O'Neil came from across the street, along with her twins, Aidan and Diana, suddenly sixteen.

"Can you believe it?" Maia asked Collin.

"How'd you people get so big?" said Collin. "Did I ever babysit you?"

They didn't answer. Aidan wolfed down his food and left, while Diana stayed, nibbling crispy spring rolls.

"Collin!" Lois exclaimed, because she had seen the show. "Your orchard!"

Lois's white hair was short and spiky, her vest hand-quilted, her earrings fashioned of the most precious Scrabble tiles, Z and Q. "When the production ends, what happens to your art?"

"Well . . ." Collin began.

"Don't say it."

Collin enjoyed saying it. Gentle, sentimental, Lois and Maia were crushed when he explained, "I'll wash the boards and start something new."

Lois tried arguing with him, but he couldn't hear. Everyone was laughing over in the living room. Darius laughed so hard that he had to lean over Emma to defog his black-framed glasses.

The actors were talking about putting on a druggier, *Big Chill* Chekhov, like in a big house up in Maine. Meanwhile, the neighbors were discussing snow emergencies and parking bans, and how they were disappointed in the president. Troops still in Afghanistan, prisoners still rotting in Guantánamo. The economy still in the toilet. What good was he?

The battered oak floors thrummed with Crosby, Stills, and Nash. "Judy Blue Eyes," "Marrakesh Express," "Guinnevere." Noelle was flirting with some woodworker named Austin. He was much taller than she was, so she rose up on her toes, *en pointe,* to look into his eyes.

Collin brushed past Noelle and said, "How's the view?"

She ignored him, and he hated her. No, he didn't hate her; he felt nothing. He felt dead.

Darius and Emma started dancing. Maia and Mrs. McCabe joined in, flushed with laughter and with wine, but Collin turned toward the front window to watch the snow. The little street was melting away, all the houses turning to gingerbread, white drifts icing porches and peaked roofs. He wanted to be out in it, away from everyone, especially himself. He pulled his jacket from the pile in the entryway, sat on the stairs and laced his boots.

When he stepped onto the porch he was so lonely he could almost see it like his breath. Impatient with himself, he seized the shovel propped up near the door, and began clearing the front steps. Working fast, he excavated a path to the street and started on the sidewalk. It was still snowing heavily, but he was hot, and un-zipped his jacket.

His mother stepped outside and watched him from the porch. "Oh, come on."

He didn't answer.

She sighed and disappeared into the house. A moment later, she returned in boots. She was holding a glass of wine.

"It's only natural to feel a letdown."

"Letdown from what? The performance wasn't any good."

"So then it's even more natural, because the play wasn't as great as the one in your head. That's art."

"That's life," he said.

"I've seen you and Darius do amazing stuff."

"It's *his* stuff. It's all about him."

"You'll get your chance."

Collin planted his shovel in the snow. "I'm not working with him anymore."

Her temper flared. "Right, that's the answer. Just give up."

"Nobody's interested in theater on traffic islands and indoor ten-nis courts."

"Who's nobody?"

"Nobody in the real world."

"The real world is overrated," Maia said.

"I wouldn't know."

"Your loss."

They stood in silence as the city plow thundered down the street, sparking tiny flames, metal scraping asphalt as it clattered past. Then Collin started shoveling again, heaping snow into the garden.

"Careful," Maia said. "My hydrangeas are somewhere under there."

"They're okay."

"They'd better be." She watched him for a moment in silence and then tried again. "Do you want my advice?"

"No." He didn't want advice. He wanted to escape. He wanted to break away, but he kept coming home, working with Darius, returning to Noelle. What was wrong with him? He could draw, but he drew only for Darius. He was a hired hand. No, just a hand! It wasn't like Darius paid him.

He had cleared the sidewalk and now he carried his shovel up the steps. "It's a play about regret."

"I know." Maia followed him.

"It's about wanting what you can't have," Collin declared under the porch light. "Maybe that's too obvious for Darius. He always gets what he wants, so he can't even see it."

Maia nodded. "I understand."

"No, you don't."

"Mm-hm. What's her name?"

3

Emerson

Loaded down with books and folders, Nina shouldered the heavy school door open. VISITORS REPORT TO THE OFFICE. THIS DOOR TO REMAIN LOCKED. OUR CHILDREN ARE OUR FUTURE. Dreading the day ahead, she backed her way into school.

Dread was not too strong a word for Wednesdays. She had to start with the wild ones, her American lit class. Students came unprepared. (They're kids, said Mrs. West, her department chair.) Some didn't come at all. (It's not about you, said Jeff, her Teacher-Corps mentor.) Nothing worked with these eleventh graders. Her lessons were too difficult, her readings too long, her assignments way too complicated.

"Good morning, Miss Lazare," said Mrs. West as they stood in the glass front office, signing in. All the teachers spoke to one another like that, as if afraid a student might overhear their given names. "Are you okay?"

Nina could only imagine how she looked—pale, sleep-deprived, floundering. Mrs. West, on the other hand, could walk the halls with total mastery, her midnight-blue manicure adorned with tiny crystal stars. Mrs. West was famous for her fingernails, for her languages, French and Haitian Creole, for her gorgeous singing voice, for her in-class performances of *Romeo and Juliet*. Above all, for her way with words. Nina had heard her harangue one boy into submission in the hall. "You can stand there and tell me that's your best work, but you *know* that's not true, so get your butt back in your chair and do it again. The end. That's all!"

"I've got my eleventh graders," Nina said.

"Don't let up!" Part coach, part cheerleader, part preacher, Mrs. West admonished Nina, "If those kids test you—then you test them back!"

A sudden buzz and pulsing orange lights. A couple of boys had set off the metal detector, and the school's police officers sprang into action. "Over here, you guys. Bags on the table. Keep the line moving." Kids continued shuffling in with their backpacks, their headscarves, their puffy jackets, their attitudes. Nina joined them, climbing the chipped cement steps to her classroom, where she opened her desk and locked her purse inside.

Emerson High School was small, diverse, and experimental. There were no exams, only year-end portfolios in which students collected what they considered their best work. The school was open to everyone by lottery, but had a reputation for "out of the box" kids—those who were artistic, or autistic, those with learning differences, or special gifts, or both at once. Each student was required to keep a journal of personal discovery in a marbled composition notebook. Required personal discovery seemed like an oxymoron to Nina, but so did many other aspects of the school. "A community of learners" with metal detectors. A non-linear curriculum in a rectilinear 1930s building. The wiring was antique, the doorknobs brass. The basement flooded during rainstorms, and in places the roof leaked. There were computers in every classroom, but some rooms had no heat. There were no whiteboards, let alone SMART Boards. Blackboards were strictly black.

Nina took a deep breath and picked up her white chalk. *DO*

NOW, she wrote on the board. *List three adjectives Emerson uses to describe* . . .

"Miss?" Students were starting to drift in. "Miss?"

"Get out your packets," Nina announced. There were no textbooks for Emerson's English classes. Humanities teachers had to develop their own materials. "Turn to the essay 'Nature.' Where's your reading?" she asked Xavier.

"I'm not exactly sure."

"Miss." Rakim approached the board. "I think the page was missing or maybe—"

"Let me see," Nina said.

"I think my packet is defective or something like that."

Nina found "Nature" for him. "Have a seat."

"I looked for it," he said.

"Rakim, please sit down."

He raised his hands in mock surrender as he backed away. Two girls started giggling, and Rakim played to the gallery. "Okay. Okay!"

Some people had it—that mysterious rapport, the ability to catch a student's gaze and hold it, to direct without seeming to direct, to take a joke and lob it back. Nina thought of her own high school teachers, charismatic Mr. Kincaid, witty Mr. Rousse. Was it a gift like perfect pitch, or something you could learn? She remembered the silence in Mr. Rousse's classroom, the deliberate way he spoke, the way he made you wait for the next word. You shivered when he called on you.

She had done well in training. For five weeks at Bowdoin College in blackfly season, Nina had learned, in theory, to teach high school. After long days of role-playing, mini lessons, and crash courses in curriculum development, she would sit with other TeacherCorps recruits in a darkened lecture hall to hear testimonies of transformation.

Alumni perched on stools in front of the eight hundred trainees, and, one by one, those alumni stood and walked into the spotlight to tell of raising test scores, breaking through. "Is there anything you can do in this world that's more important?" asked one former fellow, now working at McKinsey. "Is there anything more valuable than the life of a child?"

All the alumni said that their students had taught them lessons they would carry with them their whole lives. Nina never doubted this, but as her own kids came in dancing, slouching, scuffling playfully, she hoped she could teach them something too.

"Miss, could you sign this?"

Leila was holding a pink slip.

"You're dropping language arts?"

"Switching," said Leila, a picture of innocence, framed by her white headscarf. "Mr. DeLaurentis thinks I'll learn better with Mrs. West."

Of course he does, Nina thought miserably. Mrs. West had been teaching almost thirty years. Nina had been trying for thirteen weeks. Mrs. West invented her own acronyms: OWL (Own it, Work it, Learn it). QUACK (Question Underlying Assumptions Critically and Knowledgeably). Nina was still trying to keep her kids in chairs.

She bent to sign her name, and felt for a moment as though she were signing a confession. *I'm a fraud. I have no idea. I've failed to reach you.* Everyone spoke about epiphanies and transcendent moments, the *Miracle Worker* of it all: teacher and student swept up in revelation, spelling into each other's palms—touching the word, grasping the concept, feeling the rush of water. People didn't talk so much about students switching out of your class.

"Okay." She handed Leila the pink paper. "Go for it."

"Thanks." Leila ran out, and Nina shut the door behind her.

"Take out your notebooks," she directed, as she took attendance. Sixteen students, eight absent, including one learning better with Mrs. West. "Write your three adjectives."

"Three adjectives about what?" Rakim asked, and Nina realized that she hadn't finished writing her *DO NOW* on the board.

"Three adjectives Emerson uses to describe . . . nature." She scribbled the missing word.

"Can I borrow a—"

"Can I use a—"

Already two kids were up to sharpen pencils by the window.

A pregnant girl named Brynna asked, "Miss, where's the bathroom pass?"

You just got here, Nina thought, as she searched her desk. "Three adjectives. Faheen, I don't see you writing."

"I'm thinking!"

Squeaking chairs, rustling papers. Always moving, always whispering, the class never settled. As soon as Nina shushed one conversation, another started. She needed to be everywhere at once, but she tried to focus on one student at a time as she walked between desks, reading over shoulders.

"Beautiful, gorgeous, natural. No, that's not quite it. I want adjectives that *Emerson* uses about nature," Nina told Diana, who looked up, insulted.

"Miss?" Brynna asked again.

Nina handed over the restroom key with its big block of wood attached and she began writing on the board the adjectives the students had found in Emerson: *tranquil, perpetual, transparent.*

"Is *theory* an adjective?" Chantal asked.

"Is it descriptive?"

"Yeah."

"Give me an example of *theory* as an adjective."

"Theory of relativity."

"Excuse me?" Nina asked Marisol and Cierra. The girls looked up from their conversation as Nina began walking over, but she got distracted by Rakim writing furiously, filling in some worksheet for another class. Shit. Nina had forgotten to collect homework. "Time out. Please hand in your short responses from last night. Rakim? Marisol? Pass them to the front. Cierra, did you hear me?"

Nine homework sheets came in, accompanied by at least five excuses.

"I was absent yesterday."

"Miss, I didn't get the assignment."

"I never got the questions."

Nina struggled to assert herself. "If you were absent, you're still responsible."

Unfortunately, when she was frustrated, her voice got quiet. Her kids continued writing, ripping pages out of notebooks, sharpening pencils, and talking, talking.

You had to get louder in this profession, not softer. You couldn't just look disappointed. You were supposed to scream to show you cared. Mrs. West would cry out, "Listen up. I'm talking to *you*." Across the hall, Ms. Powers stamped her foot. Mr. Allan could bugle like a moose. Nina's emotions were all wrong, if that was possible. She wasn't angry when kids didn't do the reading. She was crushed.

"If you don't understand, speak up!" she pleaded. "If you never got the questions, then come and get them from me." For a moment, her class looked at her, gauging her annoyance. "I'm tired of excuses," she added, but the chatter had started up again.

"You should all be on page thirteen of your packets. Rosie. Page thirteen?" Once more she walked up and down between the chairs. "Page thirteen," she repeated. " 'Nature.' Faheen, read the second paragraph for us, starting with *'Nature is . . . '* I'm sorry, would you please sit down?" she told Sevonna, who was standing by the windows. She was a big girl scribbling on a tiny piece of paper, which she stuffed into the back pocket of her jeans. "Cierra? Marisol? Sevonna, would you please sit down? Please?" Nina repeated, even as Faheen read slowly, *"Nature is a setting that fits equally well a comic or a mourning piece. In good health, the air is a cordial of incredible virtue."*

The sky outside was bright. From the fourth-floor window Nina could see Lincoln Playground, framed by black trees striped with snow. "Keep reading, Faheen."

"Crossing a bare common, in snow puddles, at twilight, under a clouded sky, without having in my thoughts any occurrence of special good fortune, I have enjoyed a perfect exhilaration."

"Marisol," Nina said. "What does Emerson mean by *exhilaration*?"

"Don't kick my chair, man," said Rakim.

"I never touched your chair." Xavier stretched out his long arms and legs and tilted back his own chair until he sat on a diagonal.

"It was on the homework. *Exhilaration.*" The noise level was rising, but Nina risked turning her back to write the word on the board, along with the words *transport* and *ecstasy*. She drew a line and then wrote SUBLIME as the header for these vocabulary words. "The Transcendentalists were interested in the sublime." She spun around just in time to hear a crash and laughter, as Xavier and his chair slammed onto the floor.

"Ow! Fuck!" Xavier moaned good-naturedly, and took his time getting up again.

"Not in my class," Nina said, and Xavier apologized for his language, but that took more time. Here she was, clock ticking, eight students absent, not to mention one in the bathroom, and she had covered three sentences.

"You deserve it." Diana was talking to Xavier, but Nina thought Diana might as well have been speaking to her.

As a child, Nina had wondered why some teachers were so boring. Now she understood. They were bad actors—terrible at performing what they knew. Everything those teachers said fell flat, every lesson trailed off. First the class stopped listening. Then kids began whispering, laughing, talking openly. Finally, they seized power for themselves. As a student she had seen it happen. Now she watched her students turn on her. Xavier's attempts at comic relief, Marisol's and Cierra's and Sevonna's disrespect. Diana's scorn, Brynna's exit into the real drama of the girls' bathroom. Clear-eyed, Nina watched her class spin away from her.

You don't look like a teacher, Collin James had said at Grendel's. How does a teacher look? Old, he'd said, and bitter. He was a flirt—she'd seen him with the waitresses—but he was right: Teachers had to be hard and spiky, barbed in self-defense. You had to be bitter, to deter kids from eating you alive.

Already the bell was ringing, and she was trying to explain the homework, even though she hadn't finished her lesson. Her class was racing out the door and Nina wanted to run after them. *Standing on the bare ground,—my head bathed by the blithe air, and uplifted into infinite space,—all mean egotism vanishes.* She would carry Emerson to them. Wait! You forgot this! But they were gone. Too late, too late. She'd lost her chance.

4

EverWhen

"Now!" Sword in hand, he ran through tall grass. "Jump!" Together they bounded over rushing water.

The sky was darkening. Smoke clouded the landscape, smudging hills and trees. Faster and faster he ran, and she flew after him, blue hair streaming. No time to talk, no time to breathe. They raced to the edge of the Trackless Wood, which crackled with fire. Danger never stopped them. They kept running, weaving through the burning trees.

She was a Tree Elf named Riyah. He was a Water Elf, Tildor. They came from different realms, but for the past three nights they'd qwested, traded, and killed together. They had hunted basilisks, slain dragons, and retrieved two diamonds, which Riyah carried in the bag hanging at her waist. She was an amazing marksman, and beautiful, even for an Elf, her eyes huge, her body supple. Her breasts swayed as she ran, her quiver bouncing behind her.

Flaming branches crashed around them, the crack of falling trees—then something else—a ripping sound.

They whirled around to face a colossus with jagged teeth and claws, a shifting, seething monster, half man, half bear, tar black.

He rose up on his hind legs to seize them with clawed hands. They slashed him with their swords, but he reconstituted, oozing and bubbling. He snatched up his left hand and jammed it on again. Screaming with pain, he retrieved his severed leg and screwed it onto his own bloody stump.

"Can't finish him with steel," Riyah gasped.

"Shoot."

"Arrows can't penetrate."

"Take a—"

"Let me!" The beast heaved up roaring and she sent her silver dagger into his eye. The colossus melted like a pile of burning tires. "Yes!" Breathing hard, she raised her arms in celebration.

A diamond glittered at the melting monster's core. As Tildor plucked the jewel, a white nimbus glowed around him.

Riyah's voice was hushed. "The third."

Thorny branches overhead turned into talons, flaming twigs to ashen feathers. The forest phoenix woke, and Riyah and Tildor threw themselves onto the bird's back. The landscape shifted under them as they soared into the air. With each wingbeat, the phoenix carried them over smoldering trees and moonlit fields, twisted sunflowers, stubble glowing with white frost. Wind whistled in their ears. "That's the Keep." Riyah pointed to stone towers in the distance.

"And there's the—"

"Aidan?"

"Wait for me," he told Riyah.

He hurried to his bedroom door.

"Aidan!"

He opened the door. "*What?*"

"Take off that headset."

He obeyed and lost the music of the wind and air, the hoots of owls and beating wings, the sound of Riyah's voice. Onscreen the phoenix soared over tangled woods and frozen ponds in the silver winter night of EverWhen. Offscreen, only a computer on a desk, an unmade bed, a backpack open on the floor.

"Do you know what time it is?" his mother demanded. She was home from the night shift at the hospital and he was supposed to be getting ready for school.

Kerry snatched the headset from his hands. "Do you even know what day it is? Aidan? Look at me when I'm talking to you!"

He looked at her. Unprotesting, he sat down on his bed. Lately when his mother screamed at him, he listened. When she said Ever-When was sucking the life out of him, he didn't argue. If she asked for remorse, he showed remorse. If she declared, You're sixteen years old, you're wasting your time, you're failing school, he said he was sorry and promised to do better. He said whatever she wanted him to say, and all the time he kept his computer screen in view. The landscape dark and hidden, stars spelling out the name ARKADIA.

She worked so hard. He said, I know. She loved him so much. He bent his head. She asked what he thought she should do. He couldn't think of anything. She asked whether he thought life was precious. He said yes.

But his mother defined life as singular. He rejected that. He didn't live one life. He lived two. Was it his fault that he preferred the second? In EverWhen he was a healer and an Elvish prince, a leader of his company. He had a pile of gold, and a sword worth eighty marks, a magic ring, a diamond flask filled with a hatchling dragon's blood. He had fashioned his own gear: chain mail, silver helmet, enchanted boots. He'd trained for transformation. If he wanted to run like a deer, he could become one. If he qwested underwater, he could be a beaver, otter, or eel. And now in EverWhen he fought with Riyah at his side. Meanwhile, in the outside world, he was just a skinny kid, blue-eyed, dirty-blond, ignored at school.

His friends were equally unpopular. Jack was a Water Elf, but in real life he took college-level math. Liam was an amazing warrior, but in real life he smoked so much pot Kerry refused to let him in the door.

Aidan's mother worried about drugs, and games, and bad influences—not to mention the transmission on the car, the second mortgage on the house. They lived in a two-family. Priscilla, the piano teacher, paid rent on the other side of the living room wall, but Kerry owned the place. If the roof leaked or the pipes burst, Kerry was responsible. She slept mornings and worked nights, and in her world every day was like the last. No qwests awaited, no treasure maps arrived, no burning trees turned into birds, no cities into stone.

He knew he could outlast his mother because she was so tired. He let her confiscate his headset and joystick. He promised that he'd stop playing; he would get to school. When Kerry dragged herself to bed, he hunted up his other joystick and slipped back into EverWhen.

The sun was rising. Not the sun outside his window, but the sun inside the game, blood orange, melting frost and warming icy air. The colors were so clean and bright it took him a moment to adjust his eyes. Riyah was waiting for him in a thicket. She spoke, but without his headset he couldn't hear.

He typed into the chat box: sorry

After a moment, her answer appeared on the screen. you should be. But she turned toward him, beautiful as ever, in the glowing morning light. more?

cant

too bad.

later? he pleaded.

maybe

wheres the bird?

look

Joystick in hand, he turned his Water Elf around. Pivoting on-screen, Tildor searched the thicket.

Now Aidan saw the phoenix in new form, long feathers changed to white birches marked with what had been the bird's black eyes and claws.

!!!

i know!

His sister's alarm was beeping in the next room. He could hear Diana in the bathroom, flushing the toilet, starting her shower, getting ready for school.

I have togo

Riyah answered, bfn.

wait whats your name?

He waited and waited. He heard the water stop, the shower curtain slide on its metal loops, Diana thumping down the stairs, the kitchen cabinets, the jolt of silverware in the drawer.

Even as he gave up hoping, a word materialized onscreen: daphne

For a moment he just stared. He had never met a Daphne, and assumed the name was another alias. no, he typed, your real name

That IS my real name! Riyah folded her arms across her chest.

He took a breath. i want to see you.

What do you want to see?

He began to answer and then he stopped. Her question confused him. Did he want to see the girl who played with him at night? The one who said her name was Daphne? Or the archer, dagger-thrower, Riyah? It seemed spell-breaking to write, I want to know who you really are—and he wasn't sure if that was true. He wanted to play with Riyah forever. Not his school friends, or his old company. He wanted his headset back. He wanted to talk to her: I need to stay in EverWhen with you.

"Hey, Aidan." Diana was knocking.

"What?" Instinctively he shifted in his chair to block his screen.

She opened his door and stood before him in black jeans and a black sweatshirt. "You never took the recycling out."

"Because it was your turn."

"It wasn't my turn. Check the calendar."

"You check."

"The truck's already coming up the street." She yanked his window shade, but it didn't roll up. She pulled again, harder, and the shade only grew longer.

"Let go. I believe you."

Too late. One final tug and his shade came crashing down. "Diana! God!" he whispered fiercely. "You're going to wake Mom."

Gray sky. Dirty snow. The orange recycling truck lumbered up Antrim Street under a small, cold winter sun.

u there? Riyah's question floated onscreen.

"Are you taking it out?" Diana pressed.

"No! Get out of my room."

The broken window shade billowed on the floor, but Diana did not apologize. She turned on him. "I can't believe you're playing again right after you promised Mom not to."

"I said get out."

"I'm going to tell her," Diana said slowly as she backed away.

"Go ahead," he said, but he knew she wouldn't tell. They were close, or had been. They had a pact, and even now he trusted Diana. He knew his twin would not betray him.

Diana slammed the door, and the house rattled. He could hear his mother's voice, "Aidan!"

He typed, Invaded. I'll comeback.

Would you try another world?

RL???

another game

which one?

can you keep a secret?

"Aidan?" his mother called.

"I'm getting dressed."

huge? Riyah asked.

what????

His screen faded to gray. The network hung. No, it only blinked. He and Riyah stood together as before, surrounded by white birches.

I have UnderWorld beta, she told him.

!!!!!! ru shitting me?

no I have it

noone has it

i do

how???

you want it?

YES

wanna play?

HOW WHERE WHEN?

you need black box

send!

not yet

when??

youwant it?

He pounded out his answer in frustration: Comeon

what can you do for me?

5

Wait for Me

Was he still offended? All evening Nina tried to catch his eye, but he was carrying armfuls of dishes, dashing between tables—keeping his distance. She hadn't meant to hurt him. The play had sounded funny and he was charming and she laughed when she was nervous. She couldn't help it.

She tried to work. *In the play "A Midsummer Night's Dream" by William Shakespeare portrays many characters, all with distinguished characteristics.* She marked this sentence: *In the play "A Midsummer Night's Dream,"* ~~*by*~~ *William Shakespeare portrays many characters, all with* ~~*distinguished*~~ **do you mean distinguishing?** *characteristics.* Then, looking up, she saw him emerging from the kitchen.

He saw her too, and then avoided her.

She couldn't work at all. She waited for her chance when he passed by. "Collin," she said.

Pivoting, he turned toward her.

"How was the play?"

"I'd tell you, but I'd get in trouble standing here so long."

"Oh!" Instantly she turned back to her work, like a kid caught talking during study hall. *Puck is one of the most unique characters who . . .* But this was no study hall, and even with her head down, she felt the warmth of his smile.

"What's your name?"

"Nina."

He bent over his order pad, scribbling, before he rushed away.

A scrap of paper floated down over her student's essay. A drawing no bigger than a silver dollar. Lines quick and confident. Her own face, half hidden by her hair, her chin propped up on her hand. She looked up, trying to find him in the crowded room, but he had disappeared into the kitchen.

Had he really drawn all this just now? His work looked finished, less a sketch than a miniature portrait in black pen. He couldn't have, but yes—she'd told him her name a second ago, and he'd printed in rapid block letters: NINA WAIT FOR ME I'M OFF 11.

That winter was so cold that the drifts never melted, and each storm topped off the one before. Even now, fresh snow was falling, velveting the streets.

They stood in front of Grendel's, facing JFK Street. The park there, colorful in summer with pigeons, buskers, tourists, now pure and white.

"I know where to go," Collin said. "I grew up here, so."

"So did I."

"You did not."

"I went to college here too."

Oh, great, he thought. "Went to college" meant Harvard. If she had gone to Lesley she would have come out with it. If she'd attended Boston University, she would have said BU. Anywhere else, she would have named the school.

"My dad and stepmother still live here," she told him.

"What street?"

She hesitated for a fraction of a second. "Highland."

There were two Highlands in Cambridge. One down near his mother's place, and one west of the Square with spreading trees and Victorian houses layered like wedding cakes. He looked at her and knew which one she meant. I was right the first time, he thought. You're not from here.

Even so, he told her about the play, and he made it sound amazing. Deep instead of flippant, poignant where it had been absurd.

Nina said, "I wish I'd seen it."

You have a boyfriend, Collin thought.

But Nina said, "I'm always behind preparing class."

He led the way between snowbanks as they walked up Brattle. Without asking, he took her bags, two canvas totes filled with composition notebooks. "Where do you teach?"

"Emerson High School."

"No way." He turned around so fast she almost stepped on him. "I went there!"

"Really?"

"Yeah. I know Mr. DeLaurentis."

She could picture Collin in the principal's office. Prankster, troublemaker, effortlessly popular.

"We had these same notebooks." Collin glanced down at her tote bags.

"You kept Discovery Journals too?"

"Mostly I drew pictures of . . ."

"What?" she demanded playfully.

"What do you think?" Collin said.

They went to Café Algiers, with its polished samovars and copper bar, its Egyptian almond cookies behind glass. The red walls were hung with ceramic tiles and antique maps, a framed illustration of "the oriental coffee shop." They sat at a wobbly table and

Collin ordered hummus, pita triangles, bulgur salad, and Lebanese wine. They were the last customers in the door.

"Is this table okay?" He sounded nervous. Actually he sounded like a waiter as he asked, "Do you want to switch?"

"I think they all wobble," Nina said. Her knee was almost touching his.

When the food came she didn't eat anything. "I already had dinner," she explained.

Of course. He had forgotten that. She'd been nibbling at Grendel's all evening.

"Go ahead," she said.

"Okay, I'm starving," he confessed, but he tried not to eat too fast. He tried not to finish all his wine at once. She was just sipping hers. He could see she didn't really drink.

He asked Nina, "Why did you decide to teach?"

She parried, "Why did you decide to draw?"

"For the money."

"Oh, okay. That's why I teach too."

"No, really."

Still, she didn't answer. She turned the conversation back to his own art. "I've never seen anybody draw so fast."

"That's nothing," he said. In the summer he could chalk a whole Van Gogh painting in an afternoon. Sunflowers outside of Faneuil Hall. Irises. He laid down one wet color after another, deep purple, violet, scarlet, gold. Oh, he thought, you don't know what I can do.

"Are you in art school?"

"Well . . ." Collin hedged. "I've been in art school."

You dropped out, she thought, surprised, confused.

He said, "I think, in general, school is overrated. No offense!"

"No problem."

"But you're an educator."

"Not a good one," Nina said.

THE CHALK ARTIST   35

"You look like the sort of person who's good at anything they try."

"Kids hate me."

His eyes were sparkling, full of fun. "Why?"

"My last name is Lazare, so they call me Laser Lips."

"Let me see." He got up and leaned over the table. Her smile was tender, rueful. How would you draw a mouth like that? Ever so slightly, she drew back.

He sat down. "You're strict."

"Well, I want them to learn."

"Yeah, but I mean, do you want them to learn a *lot*?"

"Of course."

"Then obviously they hate you. But that's not bad," he hastened to add. "I mean, sometimes it's good to be feared."

"Nobody fears me. There's always some boy goofing off or fighting or falling out of his chair . . ."

"You're making me feel guilty," Collin said. "Is Mrs. West still there?"

"You had Mrs. West?" She lit up. "Tell me what you did to Mrs. West."

"I loved her. Mrs. West was great."

"Oh."

She looked so disappointed, he wanted to wrap his arms around her. "She's been teaching for like a hundred years. She has all that experience."

"I hate hearing how you need experience."

"Me too."

Her left hand rested on the table, waiting for him. What else could her hand be doing there? He covered it with his. "Real teachers are like fifty years old, and they have a wrinkle right between their eyes. Have you seen Miss Dorfman? Studio art?"

Distracted, she spoke slowly. "Well, I haven't gone around looking at her eyes."

"You should."

"I'm trying to figure out . . ." She wanted his hand back, as soon as he released hers.

"Kids can tell when teachers are trying," Collin said. "It's like how dogs smell fear."

"I have five weeks of training. I'm totally unqualified."

He spoke with confidence. "Real teachers don't worry about that."

"Yeah. Because they know what they're doing."

"No, because they leave all the actual learning to the kids. Like—here's the French Revolution. Just putting it out there. Here's physics. What you do with it is up to you."

"No, I don't think that would work."

"What are you actually trying to do?"

"I want to teach my students to read—not just superficially, but from the inside."

"Kiss of death!"

"I want them to make poetry their own."

"Never ever tell them that!"

"I *know*."

"You told them."

"My students think I'm . . ."

Gorgeous, Collin thought.

"Hopeless."

"They barely know you," Collin said. "They're still watching you."

The restaurant was closing. It didn't feel late, but the whole city was shutting down. There wasn't anywhere to go.

He said he'd walk her home. She said no need, she lived really close. In the end he walked her halfway in the snow-lit night.

"You need a hood," Nina told him, as she pulled up hers.

"I like the snow." He ran his fingers through his curly hair until it looked wilder than ever. Then he shook his head like a dog so that the snow flew off.

"You're silly."

He nodded.

With a hint of regret, she confessed, "I'm not."

He took her arm. "I can help you with that."

6

Snow Day

Fresh snow buried Collin's small basement window. His bedroom was dark to begin with, and he'd painted the walls with blackboard paint. Now his room looked like an ice cave. In the stillness and the half-light he lay in bed remembering the night before. He wanted to hold on to every second as long as possible. And then, suddenly, he sprang out of bed and threw on his clothes.

He stepped into a living room full of salvaged furniture—scarred old tables, mushy upholstered chairs. It was just seven. Darius and Emma were fast asleep, but Collin pulled on coat and boots, swiped a piece of leftover pizza from the fridge, and ran outside. Plunging knee-deep into the snow, he tripped on one of his landlady's scrap-metal sculptures, a sharp-eared cat. He swore and laughed, dusting himself off.

The house was narrow and Victorian, ocher-trimmed with cadmium red. Collin and Darius had painted it over the summer in exchange for rent, while the owner, Dawn, was visiting her daughter in Northampton. Dawn wasn't just a landlady, of course. She was one of the women Collin had always known, drinking coffee in his mother's kitchen, talking about the universe.

Perfect powder, and still falling. Central Square was ghostly white. All but the coffee shops were closed and dark. Teddy Shoes, where you could buy patent-leather pumps with a kitten heel in men's thirteen. Classic Graphx, where you could print one hundred programs cheap for your stealth underground production of *A Streetcar Named Desire*. Collin passed the Seven Stars bookstore, then 1369 Coffee House, its steamy windows already filled with poets, students, therapists. On second thought, he turned back to 1369 and bought chocolate croissants and a gingerbread latte. Then, holding the warm paper cup, he tramped to Antrim Street to find a sled and ask his mother for the car.

"You'll have to shovel out Sage and Lois too," Maia told him, after he gave her the latte. During citywide snow emergencies, the women parked in the one driveway, herding together Maia's ancient Volvo wagon, Lois's Toyota bristling with bike racks, Sage's Subaru. Collin could see three humps of snow through the kitchen window.

"Just give me the keys so I can move them."

Maia shook out the calabash by the front door and tossed each set of keys. He caught them in the air.

"I like you this way."

"Which way?"

"Motivated."

Collin flashed her a smile and headed to the cellar door.

"Hold the railing," she called out as he started down the creaky stairs.

By the light of a naked bulb, he could make out his mother's gardening tools, her leaf bags, damp gloves, and metal rakes, her extra cans of paint and varnish. He squeezed between the rolling blackboards she kept for him. Containers of broken chalk; string bags of sand toys; Cheyenne, the plastic rocking horse galloping on rusty springs and tossing its plastic mane. Lois kept her mountain

bikes down here, and Sage had a dresser she was planning to refin-
ish. He had to search behind a collapsed wading pool, a stack of
cartons labeled CHRISTMAS, and a pair of ratty wicker chairs before
he found the sleds. Two blue singles and a black plastic double. He
dusted off the double and texted Nina, Found it.

She looked chilly waiting in the Square. He opened the car door for
her and apologized for being late. "I had to shovel out three cars to
get here."

"The heat feels good," she said, basking in the car's hot air. She
was wearing a white coat, dark velvety jeans, and black suede
boots.

"Are you going to be warm enough?" He kept looking at her as
he drove, because he had never seen her in daylight. Her eyes were
not dark as he'd thought, but clear gray, like water over river
stones.

The streets were barely plowed, so they had to inch to Danehy
Park. "I'm sorry this is taking so long," he said, although he wasn't
really. There she was, close enough to kiss—but he would wait. He
could be patient sometimes.

As he eased into the parking lot, she saw kids tramping up the
big hill. "I wonder if I'll see my students here."

"We'll mow 'em down." Collin took her gloved hand and led the
way, breaking a path. Her kidskin gloves felt like nothing inside
his, which were puffy, cheap, but insulated. Her clothes were way
too delicate for real weather.

A stand of dwarf pines covered the hill. Little trees bent down
with drifts. Collin held the sled while Nina climbed on, bracing her
feet in front of her. She looked out at red coats and purple mittens,
a black Lab barking, a little girl crying that her sister never let her
steer. All along the snowy slope, she could see children and their

parents, every bright detail. "My father took me here once, and we went down together."

Collin sat behind her and wrapped his arms around her waist. "Like this?"

Her heart jumped, but she had no time to answer. He pushed off with his feet and the sled flew.

The hill was faster than either of them remembered. Nina nearly slipped out of his arms, and he had to hold her tight against his chest.

They skimmed the slope, accelerating into a swoop of snow. Breathless at the bottom, they didn't speak. Her legs felt wobbly, and Collin helped her up, offering his hand.

Again and again they sped down, and trudged back up the hill, which seemed to grow taller as they climbed. She stepped into his footsteps as he led the way, pulling the sled. At the top he looked at her and saw her glowing cheeks, her trailing scarf, her thin gloves soaked through. "Take mine," he said. "They're better."

His bare hands stung with cold, but he didn't care.

Sledding down, wind scoured her nose. Her hood fell back; her hair whipped into his face. He closed his eyes, concentrating on her and not the hill. When they hit a bump they both went flying.

They lay together where they fell, and it was sweet and it was surprising, like waking up together in bed. She turned toward him, drawn by his dark eyes, his laughter, his question, "Are you all right?"

"I'm fine."

"You sure?"

He brushed her hair from her face with his raw hands. "No broken bones?"

"No."

"No sprains?"

She shook her head, even as sleds swerved all around them.

"Not even a scratch?" His lips brushed hers so lightly that she wasn't sure he'd kissed her. Before she could decide, he kissed her for real.

Trembling, she sat up. She wanted more, but he helped her to her feet instead.

Slowly they began walking to his car. She was shivering, but she hardly noticed. He was hungry, but he forgot the croissants flattened in his coat pocket. Already it was afternoon, the sun no longer bright but softer, pale gold. Were the days so short now? Or had they been out so long?

Collin drove with his left hand and took Nina's in his right. He said, "I used to wait and wait for you."

She said, "I know."

They drove to the Brattle Theatre, the classic-movie house, and bought tickets for *The Adventures of Robin Hood* with Errol Flynn, the early show. They had the place to themselves, and they spread their wet coats over empty seats. The Brattle's clock glowed lavender, and they leaned back and ate all their buttered popcorn while they waited for the movie to begin.

"It's warm in here," Nina said drowsily.

"It's quiet."

"I'm starting to feel my toes again."

"Uh-oh." He reached down and slipped off her boots, feeling for her feet. "You're soaked!" He began pulling off her wet socks.

She was startled, and then she let him. "I didn't know the snow would be so deep."

The cartoon was starting, a brief Bugs Bunny called *Rabbit Hood*.

"Didn't your mom teach you to wear good boots for sledding?" He rubbed her bare feet with his hands.

"I lived with my father." She kept her eyes on the screen.

"Divorce?"

"No, they never married."

"So your dad . . ."

"He doesn't really think about boots." Onscreen, with heroic music playing, Bugs Bunny stole a carrot from the King's Carrot Patch, despite warnings posted on stone walls: NO POACHING. NOT EVEN AN EGG.

"What does he do?"

"What's up, Doc?" Bugs Bunny asked the King's skinny sheriff.

"What's up, *forsooth!*" the sheriff retorted, longbow poised to shoot, arrow pointed at Bugs Bunny's heart.

"Whatever he wants."

"Cool. Where does he work?"

She hesitated, even as he rubbed her instep with his thumb.

"Around here?" Collin asked.

"Arkadia."

"Seriously?" As kids, Collin and Darius had haunted Arkadia's message boards for any hint of the next EverWhen expansion. Once they took the commuter rail out to Waltham and walked three miles from the station just to stand in the company parking lot. The two of them streaked with dirt and sweat, two pilgrims at the shrine. "What does he work on?"

Now Nina tucked her bare feet under her. "You're a gamer."

"I used to play EverWhen."

"What level were you?"

"Well . . ."

"Come on."

"Sixty."

"Sixty!" He could hedge, but Nina had played that labyrinthine game. She had wandered the Trackless Wood of EverWhen and qwested in the caves of EverSea. She knew what level sixty meant. He'd claimed five kingdoms, and hunted all twelve dragons to their dens. He had raced from green to golden fields, and lived a thousand years in Arkadian worlds, before he'd met her. He was just getting to know Nina, but he'd already journeyed deep into her father's realm.

Other parents practiced law or medicine; they traded stock, or ran for office, built houses or sold real estate. Nina's father ran a company that produced MMORPGs (massively multiplayer online role-playing games). Millions lived and dreamed inside his virtual worlds. His work was nowhere and everywhere, ephemeral and everlasting.

"I used to play all the time," Collin admitted. "I can close my eyes and see the Keep."

"His Most Royal Majesty cometh! Sound the welcomes and blow the crumpets!" cried Bugs Bunny.

Collin didn't even glance at the cartoon. "Is your dad a developer? Or is he like . . . I mean is he specialized, or more . . ." He interrupted himself. "Is he working on UnderWorld?"

"He works on everything."

In flickering light, Nina watched Collin put the facts together. Her students called her Laser Lips. Her last name was Lazare. Her father was at Arkadia. He worked on everything, including the long-awaited UnderWorld, unreleased, but trending everywhere with its hash tag, #seeyouinhell.

"Is your father . . . ?"

"Viktor Lazare," she said.

"Nina!" Playfully, reproachfully, Collin said, "Your father doesn't work at Arkadia."

"No," she conceded.

Softly Collin said, "He owns it."

7

Dream

"*Having once this juice,*" Nina read to her sophomores, "*I'll watch Titania when she is asleep, / And drop the liquor of it in her eyes.*" She looked up from her book and studied her best-behaved class. "What's happening here?"

"Oberon's going to drug Titania," Noemi said.

"With what kind of juice?"

"Liquor."

"Right. Liquor—which is the nectar of a magic flower. Sean, could you read the rest?"

"*The next thing then she waking looks upon, / Be it on lion, bear, or wolf, or bull, / On meddling monkey, or on busy ape, / She shall pursue it with the soul of love.*"

"So what's going to happen?"

"You're asking me?" Sean looked up with an easy smile.

"Yes."

"She's going to fall in love."

For a second the answer startled her. Then she said, "Who or what will Titania love? Sasha?"

"The first thing she sees."

"Yes!" Silently, for just a moment, Nina celebrated. Her kids got it! Then she thought—three kids got it. She looked at the other thirteen arrayed before her, some whispering, some passing notes. Isaiah sat in back, staring out the window. Anton was drawing Titania—or was it Sasha?—topless. He was smart and tough, green-eyed, Russian. Athletic, but he'd been kicked off the basketball team.

"Anton, why is Oberon going to play this trick on Titania?"

Anton kept drawing.

"Put the notebook away," Nina said.

He did not put the notebook away.

She repeated, "Please put the notebook away so you can concentrate."

At this moment, Jeff, her TeacherCorps mentor, slipped into the room. He found an empty chair and took out his computer. Nina tensed as she stood her ground, confronting Anton.

The class rustled, as trees rustle when the breeze picks up. Jeff watched her, and the kids watched Jeff watching her. For the third time she repeated, "Put the notebook away and tell me about these fairies—Oberon and Titania."

Slowly, Anton closed his notebook, and she could breathe again.

Meanwhile, Jeff was typing rapidly. He had cropped blond hair, a runner's build, eyes Eagle Scout blue. He thought data was the answer. That was why he recorded every bent head in Nina's class.

"I noticed," he would tell Nina later, "that two kids had their heads down on their desks when I came in, and three were missing books. Five minutes after that, we've got three kids with heads down on their desks. Everyone is sitting, which is great, but between the missing books and body language, you had six disengaged when you began your line of questioning." She couldn't stand him. He distracted the class with his tapping on the keyboard, and then he aggravated her afterward. He always said, "Look, it's your call," before he told her what to do.

"What are the fairies like?" she asked her class now. "Are they kind and good-natured?" No one answered. "Are they mischievous? Chandra?" She appealed to her smallest, quietest student.

"Mischievous," Chandra answered in a tiny voice.

"Why is that?"

"Because they're powerful."

"Yes!"

Her response amused the class. Miss Lazare was so intense. She jumped if you guessed what she was thinking—like she was playing Bingo in her mind.

Nina walked to the board. "Does power make you mischievous? Is that true? Who thinks it's true?" She found a broken piece of chalk. "Isaiah, where does power come from in this play?"

"Magic," Isaiah said.

"Good. Where else? Let's list some places power comes from."

"In the play," Isaiah asked, "or in the real world?"

"Both!"

"Money," said Brittani.

Nina wrote that on the board.

"Etienne?"

"Wealth."

"Okay." Nina wrote wealth next to money.

"Politics," said Sasha, who had been nibbling a cookie when she thought Nina wasn't looking.

"Jonee?" Nina tried to call on Jonee every once in a while, but usually Jonee shook her head. Jonee had written permission to keep quiet in class because of a psychosomatic condition that caused her to faint when agitated. Nina found this confusing. She had assumed psychosomatic conditions weren't real. Apparently they were real enough. "Where else does power come from?" she asked.

"Technology," said Chandra.

"Interesting!" Look at us, she thought, as she scribbled "technology" on the board. Hey, Jeff, we're springboarding from Shakespeare to technology. "Where else does power come from?"

No one answered, but she tried to coax the discussion, cup her hands and blow upon the spark. "What about knowledge? Knowledge is power. Francis Bacon said that. What about language? And art? What about poetry?"

Anton was drawing again. Girls were whispering in the back.

"*I know a bank where the wild thyme blows,*" Nina said.

Several kids looked up, startled by her sudden shift to Shakespeare's language.

"*Where oxlips and the nodding violet grows . . .*"

The girls stopped talking. The three kids with heads down began to stir themselves.

"*Quite over-canopied with luscious woodbine, / With sweet musk-roses, and with eglantine: / There sleeps Titania some time of the night, / Lull'd in these flowers with dances and delight.*"

They were all staring. Even Anton stared. Jeff himself stopped typing and gazed at Nina with a mixture of admiration and alarm. She was holding her book open in her hands, but she wasn't looking at it.

Strange and still, the mood inside her room. She felt it happening— she had the kids' attention. If only she could make it last. She wished she could enchant her students with the liquor of a magic flower. Cast a spell so that they would fall in love with poetry.

"How do you know all that by heart?" Isaiah asked.

"Well . . ." she began.

What would she say if she were honest? I memorized almost the whole play in my father's library. *Your father has a library?* her kids would say. I fell in love with Shakespeare when I was eleven. *When you were eleven? Whoa!* I was so lonely. No, she wouldn't tell them that.

"They barely know you," Collin had said, and she felt a rush of pleasure, remembering his dark eyes. "They're still watching you."

"I read the words over and over and over," she told the class. "I kept repeating lines, just the way you learn a song."

"Yeah, but songs have music," Sasha pointed out, "so that's much easier."

Nina said, "Poetry has music too."

She lost some of them then. Once again, the girls started whispering, and Nina thought, as she did so many times a day, How do I lure them back? She opened her book. "Everybody start from *And there the snake*. Read aloud together."

"*And there the snake throws her enamell'd skin,*" the kids read together shyly, some mumbling, some faking it. "*Weed wide enough to wrap a fairy in.*"

"Again."

"*And there the snake throws her enamell'd skin,*" they read in chorus. "*Weed wide enough to wrap a fairy in.*"

"Again."

They glanced up, wondering if she was serious. "*And there the snake . . .*"

She looked at her students murmuring together and imagined the conversation she couldn't have with them.

I grew up in an enormous house. *What do you mean "enormous"?* her kids would ask. Her father's house had carved woodwork and marble floors, a polished staircase, rising and turning like the vortex of a storm. There was a glass conservatory and a library with a gallery. *Awesome!* her kids would shout. *Field trip! Par-tay!*

She hadn't always lived there. As a tiny girl, she'd lived with her grandparents on Evans Road in Brookline. Her grandmother had been pale, with powder in her creases. She set out crystal bowls filled with butterscotch candies. Her grandfather had deep, dark eyes, a raspy voice, a fearsome smile. When he walked, he dragged his feet, because they were so heavy for him. Her grandparents talked to her in Russian and read her Russian books. They beamed at Nina, spending all their warmth on her. Left to themselves, they sat for hours without speaking. They were a pair of armored lizards; they were stone.

Slowly, Nina's grandfather climbed the stairs, and slowly he descended. The stairs were carpeted dark green like moss, the walls papered with lilacs, the soaps in the bathroom carved like cabbage roses. Everything in her grandparents' house looked like something else. The boot scraper took the shape of a hedgehog, the throw pillows were embroidered cats. Even Nina's grandmother began to look like something else, the Blue Fairy in Nina's book. She wore blue quilted slippers and a sky-blue robe. Her eyes grew paler, purer blue. When she left for the hospital, Viktor took Nina to live with him across the river. She was four years old.

"Can I go home?" she would ask her father.

"Later," Viktor said, but she had sensed, even then, that he was powerful and he was mischievous. She saw her grandfather only a few times after that. She never saw her grandmother again.

In her father's house there were no candy dishes. Nina discovered a stone bird, instead, and a gold man sitting in a flower. A giant cartoon hung in the breakfast room. A naked lady lived in the library without arms or nose.

There were other toys, and other women. In the library, her father kept two globes, a green and blue globe of the Earth, and a black globe of the sky. In the hall he kept a grandfather clock. Nina sat on the stairs and studied it, imagining her grandfather rising like the sun painted on the round clock face. She saw her grandmother in robe and slippers, creeping across the sky over days and weeks, growing and then disappearing, like the silver moon.

Now she walked between her students' desks and her class was chanting all around her. *"And there the snake throws her enamell'd skin / Weed wide enough to wrap a fairy in."*

"Stand up," Nina said. The kids shuffled to their feet. Jeff stood too. "Read it one more time *loudly.*"

The kids were almost shouting, *"And there the snake throws her enamell'd skin . . ."*

"Read it one last time, softly."

"And there the snake . . ." her students whispered, rhythmically.

"Good. Now close your books. Everybody close your books."

The kids closed their books like hymnals. "No, don't sit down," Nina said. "Say the lines with me."

Together they recited from memory, *"And there the snake throws her enamell'd skin / Weed wide enough to wrap a fairy in."*

"That's it," she said, even as the class applauded. A couple of kids bowed deeply. They were only joking, but even Jeff was smiling. Ha! Nina thought. She'd engaged every student for at least thirty seconds. Log that!

8

No Moon, No Stars

Saturday night, while Kerry was at work, Diana lay in bed listening to her brother and his friends playing EverWhen. Their deep voices rumbled through the wall as they compared weapons, traded for gold arrows, debated their next move. Tunnel underground? Or fly?

"Hey, Aidan." Diana banged the wall above her head.

Then her brother told Jack and Liam to keep it down, and the noise died away, at least for a little while.

She had no idea how long she had been sleeping when she woke to voices in the hall. "It's still early," Liam was protesting.

Jack said, "It's the weekend!"

"Gotta sleep," Aidan insisted.

His friends clattered down the stairs and barreled through the living room to find their boots. The front door slammed. The storm door snapped shut like a trap. Silence, and then a tapping from Aidan's room. Diana sat up and listened. What was he doing? Texting. Playing with someone else, now that his friends were gone. You aren't sleepy at all, she thought. You lied to them.

He would rather be alone. He would rather play online with

strangers than qwest with friends in the same room. He'd rather live in EverWhen than in this house.

She knew her brother. He might lie to other people, but he couldn't fool her. He was just two minutes older. When they were little they'd played every game together. Hide and seek, tag, and chase. They'd joined forces against big kids who wouldn't let them onto the tire swing at Sennott Park. They had shared a bunk bed at their father's place when he was still allowed to see them. If their dad tried to punish Aidan they would drag that metal bed to barricade the door. They had always protected each other. The year before, when Kerry banned Liam from the house, Diana had lied for Aidan, vouching that his friend no longer came over. In middle school, when someone called Diana fat, Aidan would chase him.

It was true, although her mother never used that word, even to describe other people. Kerry said "plump," which sounded like pillows, or "heavy," which sounded like uranium down at the bottom of the periodic table. Her mother always said, Stand up straight, you're a beautiful girl. She said all this, but even Diana's arms were fat. She hid behind her long black hair and her mother said, Don't do that! Why do you do that? Kerry had read *Reviving Ophelia* and she was afraid Diana would end up starving or cutting herself, or dying, like the original Ophelia, who drowned herself with wildflowers in her hair.

Why do you wear black clothes all the time? her mother asked in her sad, pleading voice. Because I'm in mourning, Diana said. Because I'm Wiccan. I'm practicing black magic. She never admitted the real reason, which was simply that she was trying to disappear. After all, people called her a whale—not to her face, but still. She felt guilty, because she was almost as big around as Brynna, who was six months pregnant. Diana had no excuse, because she had nobody inside her.

She burrowed down in bed. Hibernated in a nest of blankets and limp pillows, along with her math homework and her Discovery

Journal with Miss Lazare's elaborate question. *Thoreau writes: "I went to the woods because I wished to live deliberately, to front only the essential facts of life, and see if I could not learn what it had to teach, and not, when I came to die, discover that I had not lived." What does he mean by this? Why do you go into the woods?*

To this, Diana replied, *We don't go into the woods very much because my mom is afraid of ticks. Also we do not live near the woods, obviously.*

But that night she dreamed of trees. It was spring, and she was running through green leaves. Branches brushed Diana's shoulders as she floated down the street. She was racing, flying to the Charles River, but she didn't stop there. She took the dirt path along the water. She was warm and sweaty as she ran fast and faster. She ran past rowers with long oars, and joyriders in snarling motorboats. Running east, she overtook the sun. She ran with its heat at her back and flung her clothes onto the grass.

She woke with a jolt, heart pounding as she fell to earth. Sunday morning. No oars, no river. No piano lessons next door. Priscilla played organ at church services on Sundays. This was as quiet as it ever got. Aidan sleeping. Their mother home from work, rustling *The Boston Globe.*

In plaid flannel pajama bottoms and a giant T-shirt, Diana padded down to the kitchen, where she ate cereal and chocolate milk and two peanut butter cookies. And then a banana, which was healthy.

Her mother said, "Do you think you should have cookies for breakfast?"

Diana said, "It's more like brunch."

The kitchen was chilly because the windows were old and cost a fortune to replace. Kerry had already bought a new boiler and rebuilt the double porch and patched the roof. Even after the repairs, there were squirrels up in the attic. Diana's mother said that couldn't be, but Priscilla heard them with her keen musician's ears. She insisted, "I hear them trapped inside," and Diana pictured rodents crazed with hunger, eating their own children.

She wished Priscilla would move out. Then they'd have the double house all to themselves. Two living rooms, and two kitchens. Six bedrooms on the second floor! All that space, and no more sonatinas and minuets and little fugues. It was a never-ending guilt trip, sharing a two-family with your old piano teacher.

Diana was not musical, but everyone had been heartbroken when Aidan quit in seventh grade. Priscilla still looked at him wistfully. She would catch him on the porch and say, "I wish that you'd start up again." If Diana was around she'd add, "You too!"

At which point Diana would tell Priscilla, "I heard the squirrels last night."

"Could you start the laundry?" Kerry asked now.

"Could I have some money?" Diana replied.

"How much?"

"A hundred twenty dollars."

"Why? What do you need that for?"

Diana went to the front door and picked up her old silver Nikes.

"Didn't we just buy you shoes?"

"Look." The uppers were splayed open, the rubber heels warped, the laces frayed and broken.

"What did you do to them?" Kerry gazed at Diana's feet, afraid that they were widening with the rest of her. "Let's go shopping this afternoon."

"Maybe." Diana didn't want to hurt her mother's feelings and say she'd already made plans.

When her mother went upstairs to sleep, Diana dragged her laundry bag along with her mother's down to the basement. Two heavy sacks thumping down the stairs. She didn't collect Aidan's. He didn't need clothes, since he lived in EverWhen.

She was afraid of the dank smell and creepy toys. A sophomore at school had been raped in her own basement. A whole gang of boys—guys the girl knew—got in and forced her down. Fast as she could, Diana loaded the washing machine and ran upstairs. Breathing hard, she shut the door behind her.

A heavy step in the living room. She whirled around and saw Brynna. "How did you get in here?"

"I'm doing well," said Brynna. "How are you?"

"Seriously, wasn't the door locked?"

"No." Brynna squeezed herself into a kitchen chair. Pregnancy was good for her skin. Her forehead had cleared up completely. Her green eyes were beautiful to begin with, and she wore her wavy brown hair down over her shoulders, so she looked huge, but gorgeous too.

"I was having brunch," Diana said. "Care to join me?"

"No," Brynna said. "I'm eating right."

"Good for you."

Brynna sat on Diana's bed while she got dressed. Diana pulled an all-black sweater over her head, and when she emerged, Brynna was holding her journal.

"Hey, give that back."

Brynna leafed through Diana's black composition notebook. *One single word to describe myself would be conspicuous. People in the halls are always trying to get around me. If I actually look back at them that's considered rude, like how dare you block my view? Last year I . . .*

"I said give it back." Diana snatched the book from Brynna's hands.

"Okay!" Brynna said. "Sorry! It's not like I was spying on you!"

They took the bus through the slush to the CambridgeSide Galleria on the river at the edge of town. The Galleria would give anyone a headache, but it had a lot of stores.

"What are you going to name her?" Diana asked, as they braved the shiny walkways, all glitter and glass and sleigh bells ringing.

"I like 'Tasha,'" Brynna said.

"Tasha? Is that a name?"

"Yes, it's a name."

"Maybe for a cat." Diana paused in front of Godiva to look at the truffles in the window. "*Godiva* is a good name."

"*What?* My child is not a candy company!"

"Does Anton get a vote?"

Anton was the baby's father, and Brynna didn't even answer that.

They fingered dresses at Motherhood Maternity, but they were so ridiculously expensive that Brynna didn't try on a single one. At Sears, they walked past the baby gear in the infant and toddler department. There were cribs and baby swings and play centers and mobiles with themes like rainbow pandas, or tropical islands. Everything was puffy, soft, and new. Brynna was curious, and at the same time afraid to look.

"Do you want to get something?" Diana asked.

"No!"

"Why not?"

"Because!"

"Okay, let's go home."

"Shoes," Brynna reminded her.

"Later."

"Just get it over with." Brynna steered her toward Lady Foot Locker.

"Don't make me go in there."

"Come on. You said you wanted shoes." It was ironic that Brynna was the pregnant one, because she was so responsible. Maybe it wasn't ironic. Brynna was already such a mom.

Brynna scanned the walls of shoes arrayed for walking, running, cross-training. Diana sat on the polished blond-wood bench. "What about these?" Brynna held up a pair of Sauconys.

"They have green on them," Diana said.

"One little stripe!"

"I don't wear green."

"How about these?" Brynna held up a pair of silver Nikes.
Diana shook her head.

"These are the same shoes you have on," Brynna said. "Look.
They're exactly the same, except they're not falling apart."

"No, I don't think so."

"You're not even going to buy an exact replica of the shoes you
have?"

Diana looked down at her feet. "I hate it here. Let's go."

She was almost out the door when a sales associate in a referee
uniform flagged her down, asking to help. He was dark black, African, and the name on his badge was Joseph. He had an accent and
a nervous look. It was probably his second day. He wanted to know
what kind of shoe Diana was looking for and what sport she played.

"She doesn't play sports," Brynna said.

Joseph didn't give up. "A shoe for exercise?"

"She doesn't—"

"I do exercise," Diana said.

Incredulous, Brynna asked, "Since when?"

The question upset Diana. "I *could* exercise. I might."

Brynna snorted.

"Cross-trainers?" Joseph suggested.

"Something black. Something like this." She pointed to a black
shoe on the wall.

"This one is for running," Joseph said.

That night in her room, Diana opened the cardboard box from
Lady Foot Locker and took out a pair of pure black running shoes.
Black uppers, black heels, black soles, black laces.

One shoe in each hand, she tapped the wall. She loved the new-shoe smell, clean leather and fresh rubber.

"Stop," Aidan said, after a few seconds.

She kept drumming her new shoes at the spot she hoped was just above his computer monitor.

"Stop or I'll kill you."

"He speaks," Diana said. "Hey, Aidan. I got new shoes."

No answer.

When she laced the shoes and walked around her room, she bounced. The floor felt like those giant inflatable birthday party castles. She jumped, and jumped again. Her dresser rattled when she landed. She could hear Aidan shuffling around, her fellow cell mate, self-incarcerated in his room. "I'm going to do something," she told him. "Do you dare me?"

No answer.

"You dare me," she answered for him, but that sounded pathetic. "Okay, I dare myself." That sounded even worse, like she was trying to be inspirational. Even when she was little she had hated anything inspirational, like books where kids saved the day or movies involving wildlife and parents getting back together and slow-motion horse races at the end. She sat on her bed and looked down at her feet in the new shoes. Who are you kidding? she thought. She embarrassed herself, even when she was alone.

Long ago, when she was six and seven, she had swung bar by bar across the climbing structure. As a small girl, she'd gone to GAB, Gymnastics Academy of Boston, which was the only day camp open in the very last weeks of August. At the gym near Fresh Pond, she had practiced pikes and flips on the giant trampoline, hurled herself with all her force up and over the vault. She had been a little gymnast and Aidan had been a swimmer, and they had been a matched pair, wiry and strong. Then at about twelve, he grew tall, and she grew round. The weight came on in cookies and gumdrops, and late-night snacks. Aidan ate too, but it didn't show on him. He was over six feet and growing; she was done at five feet four. He paced the house, while Diana hunkered down. He refueled standing at the kitchen counter, while she curled up with goldfish crackers on the couch. He started killing monsters, and she built up her defenses, practiced her self-doubt.

She was not a small girl anymore, nor was she fast, nor was she flexible. She could barely remember hurtling over anything. For a while now, her tiny pediatrician had been talking about exercise and healthy nutrition. Diana was thirty pounds overweight.

Sometimes she felt doomed. Other times she felt as though she were carrying somebody's lost luggage. When would the real owner come to claim it? She felt disgust, resignation, surprise, but no sense of recognition. She avoided herself. Stayed away from scales, mirrors, bright lights, shorts, and bathing suits.

Kerry could talk all she wanted about standing up straight and being beautiful; she could say it a thousand times. Words could not change anything. "You're a beautiful girl" was like saying God is good. You didn't say these things because they were true, you said them because you hoped the universe would take pity on you.

Diana pounded once more on the wall.

"What?" Aidan shouted.

This time she didn't answer.

"What?" he called again.

When she spoke, she wasn't even talking to him anymore. Thumping down the stairs, she berated herself. "Go. Go. Go. I'm tired of waiting for you."

Near the front door at the bottom of the stairs, she found her broken Nikes, and picked them up by the laces. Outside she flung them in the garbage can and shut the lid.

"Where are you going?" her mother called out from the couch.

"Nowhere," Diana said.

The night was mild, the snowbanks melting, no longer white,

but newsprint gray, the sidewalks cracked, but clear of ice. Diana walked down Antrim Street to Broadway, and she took deep breaths, swinging her arms, speed-walking like the old ladies in the mall. They were probably in better shape than she was. Diana was already hungry after five minutes in the fresh air. At the corner of Prospect Street, she nearly stepped into Tedeschi's market for a bag of chips. The only thing stopping her was Aidan's friend Jack, walking out with two gallons of milk.

He wore glasses, but he had a way of squinting to look at you. He had been the small one. Tiny! Now he was all legs and bony shoulders, incredibly long arms. "Diana." He couldn't wave, because he had a gallon weighing down each arm. "What are you doing here?"

"Nothing." She hated how he examined her.

Since they had known each other since preschool, he thought he had a right to trail after her. He followed her to the traffic light. "We ran out of milk."

"Yeah. I see that." He was heading home to Norfolk Street, where he lived in the Chocolate Factory apartments, so called because yes, the building had been a chocolate factory. She said, "Okay, I cross here."

He knew she lived in the opposite direction. "Why are you . . . ?"

She didn't wait for the light. She dodged cars, crossing Broadway to Sennott Park. Then she checked that he was gone. She didn't want anyone to see her, so she hid behind a tree to touch her toes.

She didn't know the real stretches, the kind they did on teams at school. She didn't know the right way or the fast way, so she just started walking the perimeter of the field. There was no moon; she saw no stars. She wasn't quick enough to pass anything moving, only houses and little stores, and the great silent trees. Her legs were heavy under her, and her sides ached. Breathing hard, she began to run.

9

Drink Me

Now Nina came to Grendel's just to see him. She stacked her students' Discovery Journals on the table and looked up at Collin as he brushed past. He was always hovering near her, or scribbling little notes. His friends thought the situation was hilarious. Not just that Nina was a teacher, but that she'd turned him into such a courtier.

At closing time, Collin and Kayte cleaned up, while Nina waited at the bar.

"You're anomalous," Samantha told her.

"Don't listen to her," Collin said as he wiped tables.

"You aren't a teetotaler, are you?" Sam asked Nina.

"No."

"Because you never even order beer."

"I drink other things."

"Like what?"

Nina hesitated.

"Collin!" Sam cried out as if to say, I can't believe her.

He threw his wet rag and Sam ducked behind the bar.

"Drink me! Drink me!" Sam poured Nina a drop of crème de

menthe. Nina shivered, tasting Sam's strange medicine. She really did look like Alice falling down the rabbit hole. Curiouser and curiouser. Collin had to kiss her.

She went with Collin to Charlie's Kitchen, the almost-all-night diner in the Square. They sat together in a red vinyl booth, and he told her of his days performing plays about nutrition at the Children's Museum, where Darius had worn a full tomato suit.

"Full tomato? Is that like full metal jacket? What were you?"

"A loaf of bread."

She laughed.

"What?"

"I'm trying to picture that," Nina said.

They discovered that they were both turning twenty-four in January. Their birthdays were just a week apart, and they had been born in the same hospital, Beth Israel Deaconess. Strange that they had never met.

She had attended Cambridge-Ellis as a toddler, while he'd spent his days at Aisha's Family Daycare. No chance of meeting there. Ice cream? She had walked to Lizzy's. He'd worked at Christina's. Pizza? She went to The Village Kitchen. He went to Angelo's. Summers she'd interned at CIRCLE, the Center for Information and Research on Civic Learning & Engagement at Tufts. He had taught swimming at the Y. They had grown up two miles apart, but it was as if they came from different cities. He said it was funny. She said, "I'm not so sure."

He caught the guilty note. "That's a West Cambridge thing to say."

He told her about the triple-deckers of Antrim Street. The back porches where you could hang in summers. He told her his old girlfriend had worked as a nanny for a baby named Moses. Noelle would lull Mo to sleep inside and then she and Collin would sit out on the porch and smoke weed until all the trees and green leaves shimmered. He told Nina this, but he downplayed the smoking part. He focused on the trees.

"They're huge," he said. "And people worship them. There was an elm that died and my mom's friend Lois had a funeral before the city took it down."

"What's that like?" Nina asked. "A funeral for a tree?"

"Pretty straightforward. Everybody gathered and Lois said a eulogy."

He described his mother's garden, tiny but so well planted that you couldn't set foot in it without stepping on a flower. There were pale-green hydrangeas, and purple irises, soft lamb's ears, creeping strawberry vines. "You'll see," he told her. "If this winter ever ends."

Nina's stepmother had a garden too. Helen had terraced lawns, and a swimming pool edged with bluestone, and a clay tennis court, but Nina didn't say all that at once. She started with the roses, and the moss on the stone walls.

Each night they stayed out later. They walked to Broadway Bicycle after the shop had closed. Bike seats hung like hunting trophies, the size and shape of deer skulls on the wall. Behind the register, Nina saw hundreds of plastic drawers labeled like body parts: SPIKES, NUTS, SHINS, FANGS.

He took her to Christina's, where he had chocolate-orange and she had gingersnap ice cream. There were no open seats, so they walked up Cambridge Street with their cones past Boutique Fabulous. When they came upon Rosie's Bakery, Collin said, "My father used to take me here before he joined the navy."

"That must have been hard," Nina said.

"What do you mean?"

"Missing each other?"

"They can't get you for child support if you enlist."

They walked down Fayette to the new coffee shop called Dwell-time. "I liked the boyfriends better," Collin said, and he described Maia's main ex-boyfriends: the poet, Greg, who wrote obituaries until he got laid off from *The Boston Globe*. Tony, the chiropractor, who taught Collin how to drive. Best of all was Chris, the guy who'd lived with them until Collin was twelve. "He gave me this," Collin said, showing off an old-fashioned watch with a worn leather band. Chris didn't really work, but he would take Maia and Collin to his parents' farm in Western Mass. They'd drive out in the fall to pick apples and press their own cider. All the ground was covered with peaches, plums, and pears, the fruit ripening, splitting open in the sun, fermenting, so the whole orchard smelled like wine.

They sipped their coffee and she told him about her stepmother. "She's taller than my father," Nina said. "She's tall and jealous."

"Without reason?"

"No, she has reason."

She told Collin how Viktor traveled, and how she had waited up for him. She described his parties and his renovations, his fights with Peter, his younger brother and business partner.

"What do they fight about?" Collin asked.

"Design, schedule, money," Nina said. "But my father always wins."

"Why?"

"Because he's the commercial one."

She told Collin of Viktor's dazzling inventions and the lawsuits afterward. His platforms MORPH and OVID (ocular-virtual integration device). Ideas like comets with long tails. Viktor had invented new ways to use aeroflakes, tiny sensor-receptors that filtered light to construct interactive, immersive fantasies. Aeroflakes drew power wirelessly through walls.

"I want to see that!"

"You will," she told him. "Everybody will."

At work, Viktor was charismatic and aggressive, at home, affectionate and preoccupied, by turns jovial, baffling, furious. Once she had seen her father fly into a rage and smash a table lamp. Another time she'd found him, early in the morning, kissing her au pair. Then Nina ran away to hide. She was the guilty one, terrified he'd punish her.

When Nina told Collin this, he saw her all alone and small, and he wondered what else she'd seen with her gray eyes.

They saw each other almost every night, but she never let him walk her home. Did she think it was too soon? It didn't seem too soon to him. She was so soft, her mouth so sweet. They talked for hours, but she held back. He knew she wasn't teasing; she was a serious person. She didn't take relationships lightly, and that was fine—except he wasn't used to it. He loved the rush, the free fall into intimacy. You had your whole life for conversation afterward.

One night he pulled her close and closer, swept her hair back from her face, and kissed her neck. Serious as you want, he promised silently. Anything you want. "Let me take you home."

"No, that's okay."

"Don't walk by yourself."

She stood there in her white down jacket. "I'm not afraid."

"Yes, you are," he said. "You're afraid of me."

She didn't answer.

"What's wrong? Are you ashamed of where you live?"

"A little bit," she confessed.

"Do you live in some big mansion too expensive for a teacher?"

"No, just an apartment."

"Where?"

"Mem Drive."

She lived in one of those buildings on the river. He had always wondered who lived there. "Show me."

"It's not mine," she told him as they began walking. "My father owns it."

"Okay." He was not surprised.

She looked at Collin earnestly. "Do you know Arkadia's symbol?"

"An ouroboros."

"Right. The dragon eating its own tail."

"And that's your father?"

"That's my family."

"Lots of families eat their own tails," Collin reassured her, but even as he spoke, he realized that she was warning him. Hers was cruel.

She told Collin about how her father married Helen at the Cape. Nina was six and wore green silk, and she cried during pictures on the pier. She'd trailed her hand on the weathered railing and a splinter had pierced her palm.

The weather had been perfect, water glassy in the cove called Pleasant Bay. Barely a breeze ruffled the long sea grass, but Nina's tears ruined the photos and annoyed Helen. Nina's uncle Peter took tweezers and worked the splinter out. "You hate her, don't you?" Nina's uncle said. He was like a magician, drawing the idea out of her. As soon as he said the words, Nina knew that they were true.

She was walking slowly now. Collin waited, but for a long moment she didn't speak.

They were standing in front of Nina's redbrick building, with its bay windows, its faux balconies of fanciful wrought iron.

She said of her family, "I love them. Unfortunately."

He slipped his hands into her coat pockets and felt the rounded corners of her phone, her jingling pocket change. He ran his thumb over the rough edges of her keys. "Why unfortunately?"

"I don't believe in them."

"What does that mean? You don't trust them?"

"I don't trust them—but I can't get away from them."

"Have you ever tried?"

"I'm trying now."

"How? Standing in the cold with me?"

He was impudent and funny, more straightforward than other guys she had known. He spoke without embarrassment about his talents and his difficulties. He loved performing, but he hated computer programming. He drew well but he had dyslexia and didn't like to read. He said that, but he read Nina. He listened intently, and he watched her face. Stories of her family didn't scare him. He kept his eyes on her. It was a simple thing, but it was rare. He really looked at her. "Are you freezing?" she asked.

"My hands are warm."

She felt his hands through the lining of her coat. She felt his warmth and she wanted to kiss him, but he must have known before she did, because he was already kissing her, his mouth softly on her mouth. He hadn't shaved, and his rough cheek scratched her face.

When she tried to make sense of what was happening, she got scared. She'd known him for only two weeks. He had no career. He wasn't even a student. Once or twice she wondered what he might want from her, and then she felt dishonorable thinking that way. She had never known anyone so uncalculating.

Please, his body begged.

"Wait."

"What's wrong?"

"Nothing."

"Should I go?"

"No."

He murmured in her ear, "It doesn't matter who your father is or where you live."

She pulled back, just enough to breathe. "That's not been my experience."

"Try me." His hands closed inside her pockets.

"You have my keys," she said.

•   •   •

From outside, the apartments looked like jewel boxes with their gilt-framed mirrors and carved furniture, their book-lined rooms. Inside, the lobby was dusty and old-fashioned. Chipped plaster-work and scuffed white marble stairs, a squeaky elevator trimmed with brass. The halls were hushed as libraries. Collin pictured old professors tucked away in bed. He smelled wood polish, noticed the umbrella stand inside Nina's door. Who had an umbrella stand?

Her upholstered furniture, her kitchen big enough for chairs, her view, the shining river at her feet. All in an instant, she saw him take it in. Silently she dared him to speak.

He said nothing. He turned toward her instead, his expression rapt, his dark eyes bright. Even so, he waited. Though they stood just a few feet apart, the distance and the silence seemed dangerous to cross. "I'll hang up your . . ." she began, but the coat closet was too far away. When he pulled her in, she let his jacket fall.

As they unwound scarves, unlaced boots, she didn't offer him a drink or something to eat. Undressing, they tasted nothing but each other. They lay down on the couch and then on the carpet. And then they were so warm that they forgot the time, the view, the world outside. They forgot that it was winter.

10

In Her Eyes

Nina still assigned too much homework and popped too many quizzes. She was just as serious in January as she'd been in September—and yet she had changed. She was more relaxed, sitting on her desk or leaning back against the board. Less fearful, less self-conscious, she smiled as she brushed chalk dust from her clothes.

As soon as he walked into her classroom, Jeff noticed her new confidence. Just as he'd predicted, after weathering the first three months, Nina had returned from winter break with fresh purpose. She struggled, but she wasn't nearly so bewildered. At last she understood what she could cover in one period, and arrived at class with two or three main questions instead of an entire lecture.

"Sevonna," Nina said. "Sevonna. Cierra . . ." Nina walked over to the pencil sharpener, where the girls were whispering, and escorted them to their seats. "We were talking about the way Puritans policed one another. Xavier?"

"Courts."

"Peer pressure," said Rakim.

8:20 good intervention / continuity with scarlet letter . . . Jeff typed into his computer log.

"In those days a lot of morality came from peer pressure," Rakim said.

"Say more!"

"Like the stocks," Xavier said. "When you were publicly humiliated."

"But did it work?" Nina asked.

8:25 avoid jumping in too fast

"Obviously it didn't work for Hester Prynne," said Diana, "because . . ."

"Because what?"

Jeff surveyed the class. Only two heads down. Open books on half the desks. One hand raised. Nina waited for Diana, even as she shook her head slightly at Rakim, who was leaning back in his chair again. He landed with a thud, but only a few people laughed.

"Because she had sex anyway, so the peer pressure wasn't working on her," said Diana.

"Exactly." Nina tried not to look at Brynna, who was examining her own long hair, holding up strands as she looked for split ends. Probably lots of pregnant high school girls studied *The Scarlet Letter,* but Brynna was Nina's first, and she couldn't help worrying about what a sixteen-year-old in her third trimester might make of this.

"It's so ironic," Xavier said, without raising his hand, "that usually peer pressure is for bad things, but in this book it's all about morality."

Nina smiled.

Was she really smiling at Xavier? The eleventh graders shuffled in their seats. Oh, my God, Xavier was such a player. The word *ironic* was like crack to Miss Lazare.

good pause, Jeff typed. He assumed Nina was counting silently to ten, as he had suggested at their last meeting, to allow her students more time to answer.

She was not counting to ten, or any other number. She felt delicious, strangely alert, then suddenly sleepy. She and Collin had been together three weeks.

As soon as the bell rang, she rushed off with the students. Jeff tried to catch her with his notes, but she slipped into the windowless, overheated photocopy room and hid behind the supply shelves stacked with paper and toner cartridges. There were several old wooden chairs behind the shelves, and she sat there for five minutes, just to close her eyes. She had to think, she had to dream, but the bell was ringing again. How did it ring so loud? So fast?

At lunchtime, she escaped to the basement, threading her way through tiled corridors, past the cafeteria smelling of disinfectant and steamed broccoli, to an abandoned resource room filled with giant therapy balls. As she leaned against the biggest, the ball deflated slightly, cushioning her body and her sleepy head. There she could rest and feel his hands. Remember him kissing her bare shoulders, burying himself inside her, breath quickening, fingers knit into hers.

She had been in love before. Away at school there had been a boy named Emmett, a runner with long dirty-blond hair, always in his eyes. She would sneak out early before class to find him coming back from morning practice and they would walk together through the Hill School's misty playing fields, to lie down in the wet grass. She had ruined a coat that way, spreading it like a blanket over sticks and stones. Emmett was already warm in his running shirt and shorts; he was wet anyway, his body sleek with sweat. Nina was the one who got suspicious looks at breakfast. Leaves caught in her long hair. She had to carry her black coat to math.

In college she had loved a scruffy literary guy named Jonah who concentrated in philosophy and wrote for the *Lampoon*. Theirs was almost a shipboard relationship; they had lived in such close quarters, studying and sleeping in his narrow bed in Adams House, editing each other's papers, reading poetry.

Jonah had curly hair and wore faded cords and raggedy old sweaters. He had theories about religion and politics and the frayed dynamic between love and friendship. He was interested in transcendental meditation and tech design and stand-up comedy. He wanted to be rich, but, like a juggler tossing knife, tennis ball, and frying pan, he debated management consulting, Hollywood, and graduate school. He never tired of perseverating about his future, or pondering the world. He'd hurt Nina when he began tweeting bits of news she'd told him about Viktor and OVID.

Collin came as a relief. He didn't ask about her father, nor did he talk about the future. He brought takeout to her apartment and he spent the night and they laughed about her students. After bad days he comforted her.

"I could not get them to listen," she said.

"Buy a police whistle," he suggested. "Bring free food."

She leaned against him on the couch. "My students deserve a better teacher."

"Do something else, then. You could do so many other things."

"But this is what I want to do."

"Why?"

"I want to give back."

He looked at her and said in all seriousness, "Why? What did you take?"

She shook her head. He knew that she was rich, but didn't see the rest of it. Her father produced mind-blowing, immersive entertainment. She wanted to separate herself from that. She dreamed of enchanting kids with words instead of optics.

"There are lots of other ways to give back," Collin pointed out. "Homeless people, clean water, the environment."

She was almost too shy to look at him. "I want to teach because that's the real magic."

He nodded, because, of course he'd heard this language before. He'd grown up with his mother's golden apples, her #1 TEACHER paperweights. "Transforming lives."

"I want to give at least a little bit of what my teachers gave to me—but my kids don't even listen."

"I guess you have to be patient."

She tucked her legs under her and considered him. If he'd been patient he would have stayed in college. "Why did you quit?"

He thought of his mother, always hoping he would learn marketable skills. "I hate Web design."

"But you could do studio art."

"Nah."

"Why not?

"I'm not conceptual."

"What does that mean?"

"I'm not big-picture. My art's not deep."

"You're just being modest!" She was thinking of the tiny line drawing he'd given her in Grendel's.

"No, seriously. I have nothing to say. I like to draw. That's all."

"What?" She had never heard anyone admit to such a thing. Jonah had been all ideas; he'd never stopped talking. "That can't be true."

Collin teased, "You think I'm tragic!"

Guilty again. "No, that's not what I meant!"

"I don't need ideas," Collin declared. "I don't need theories in my life."

"What do you need, then?" she asked, partly curious, partly fishing.

Was he supposed to say you? All I need is you? He answered, "Just a box of chalk."

"You're funny."

"I'm serious," he said, as he caressed her hand.

· · ·

The world was brighter now, and strange. She saw rabbit prints on the clean snow, and trees of diamonds glittering. When the last bell rang, kids flooded the staircases, and she could lose herself in the crowd, forgetting books and lessons as her students surged around her. Thrilled to leave, she was becoming just like them.

She took Collin to Burdick's in the Square. He had never had such dark hot chocolate. She took him to Upstairs on the Square just two flights up, but a world away from Grendel's. The dining room all pink and gold, with marble-topped tables and gilt fireplaces.

Every object in her apartment had a history. Her furniture came from the 1950s. The atomic clock on the kitchen wall came from Finland. She had a Narnia chess set—Aslan and his fauns carved of ebony, arrayed against the White Queen and her henchmen cut in alabaster. When Nina was ten, her father had promised her the set if she could beat him, and then relented when she fought him to a draw.

On her bookcase she kept a framed drawing of her father, a pen-and-ink caricature by Al Hirschfeld, an artist Collin didn't know. Collin studied her father's cartoon face, his dark eyes, his curly hair, his exaggerated nose. She told him, "If you look here, you can find my name."

Sure enough, Hirschfeld had hidden the name *Nina* in Viktor's bushy brow.

In the moment, none of this seemed strange. She had beautiful things, but she piled her dishes in the sink like everybody else. When they were together he felt at home. White kitchen, river view, clean sheets. Then he got back to his own place, and he felt like a hobbit living underground. He stood in disbelief on his own threshold, taking in the mousetraps in the kitchen and the dank, shared bathroom. Reentry required several beers. He would sit on Darius's salvaged couch and he would blast Bent Shapes, and draw until he collapsed into his unmade bed.

Never in his life had he devoted so much time to anyone; he barely saw his friends; he abandoned his old haunts—but his behavior didn't seem unusual to Nina. Always, in her quiet way, she wanted more. When she couldn't reach him, she texted, IMY.

Alarmed, he typed, Dont do that!

The next time they saw each other she asked, "What's wrong with saying I miss you? It's just a fact."

But it wasn't a fact for him. It was a demand. He read IMY as "I want more of you." He told her, "This is all the time I have."

"I understand," she said, but she didn't, really.

"I can't be with you every minute of the day," he told her.

She shot back, "I know! I never asked you to."

She got skittish. She needed reassurance—not just words but hours, entire afternoons. Day to day they held each other in suspense. He had to back off and breathe. She wanted to know him better, to unfold their friendship like a map. What else could he give her? Sometimes the question scared him. Sometimes the answer came easily. He would give himself.

On a slushy day in late January he met her after school and said, "I want to show you something."

It was drizzly cold as he hurried her up Cambridge Street, past the fabric store, and the senior center, the Portuguese savings and loan. They dashed across Hampshire in the rain. The trees and bus shelters were dripping. Even the birds hunched up, wet and miserable, on telephone wires.

"Where are we going?" Nina asked.

"You'll see."

"Your apartment?"

"That needs fumigating first."

"You always say that."

"Because it's always true."

"I still want to see it."

"No," he told her. "It's embarrassing. Emma labels all her food with skull and crossbones, and Darius forgets to flush."

"I wouldn't mind."

That angered him. Of course she didn't mind. She didn't live there. "It's a pit."

"But it's yours."

"Exactly," he exploded. "It's *my* pit of an apartment, and I promise you won't like it there."

She said, "But it doesn't matter what—"

He cut her off. "Don't tell me it doesn't matter and you wouldn't mind. Don't be so fucking condescending."

He had never spoken so harshly to her. Maybe nobody had spoken to her that way before. He watched her turn and walk away toward Kendall Square.

She provoked him with her eagerness, her gentleness, her noblesse oblige. After all, what was she doing, spending time with him? He had nothing, he'd done nothing; and when Nina said she didn't mind, she acknowledged it was true.

He watched her figure receding, and he was furious with her and with himself. He'd been planning to surprise her.

"Nina, wait."

She didn't turn.

"Don't go," he called out, as he sprinted down the street, splashing through slush puddles. His shoes were soaked when he finally caught up to her.

She spun around to face him. "I was telling the truth," she said. "I wouldn't mind. And didn't you say the same thing to me about my apartment? It didn't matter where I live?" She had been continuing the argument in her head.

Breathing hard, he took her hands in his. "Let me take you somewhere."

She shook her head.

"I didn't mean to hurt you."

"Yes, you did."

"I'm an idiot."

She didn't contradict him.

"Let me start over. There's something I have to show you."

It was as if they'd never quarreled; his mood changed that fast. She was the one who lagged behind. His anger flared and burned out fast; hers smoldered.

He said, "I'll take you to my place when Darius and Emma are away in Maine."

"No, that's okay."

"I'll wash everything down."

Silence.

He almost coaxed a smile when he said, "I'll cook."

They retraced their steps to Antrim Street, and he led her to a dark-green triple-decker, three Victorian apartments stacked one atop the other with three porches.

Nina turned to him in surprise. "Did you tell her that . . . Shouldn't you call to warn her first?"

"Why would I warn my own mother?"

She hung back. "What if it's a bad time?"

"Sh." He ushered her into the entrance hall and knocked on Maia's door. "There's no bad time."

"Hey," a voice called out. "Come in."

They slipped off their wet coats and shoes and walked into a half-painted living room with all the furniture piled in the center of the floor. "Who is it?"

Collin called back, "Me."

"Hello, you," Maia said, as Collin led Nina into the kitchen.

"This is Nina."

Nina felt flustered, entirely unready. It was just like Collin to spring this on her. Even so, she gazed in fascination as Maia took her hands. Collin's mother was tall, and muscular, a dancer wearing plaid pajamas. She had close-cropped hair, showing off her small ears, her beautifully shaped head. Her almond eyes were dark, and she had a birthmark in one, a sepia ink blot in the white. Nina saw the mark, and immediately forgot it, as everybody did.

Maia ushered Nina in with such warmth that Collin shook his head in silent warning.

"She's so pretty," Maia whispered when he followed her to the hall closet with the coats.

He shot her a look. "Don't screw up."

"That's just what I was going to say to you."

In the kitchen Maia poured them each a glass of wine.

Collin asked his mother, "What are you doing with the living room?"

"You don't like the green?"

"I think it looks like mushy guacamole."

"Okay, thank you, sweetheart." Maia turned to Nina. "I'm not listening to him. Peanut brittle? Caramel corn? Fruit cake?" She covered the kitchen table with Christmas gifts parents had brought her. "Try this." She sliced homemade fruit cake, dark-spiced and walnut-studded, jeweled with candied cherries, carbuncled with pineapple.

"Wow," said Nina. "I got candy canes."

Maia waved her hand over her cards and deluxe candy apples, her mugs filled with gift certificates, and she told Nina, "Someday all this will be yours."

Nina looked doubtful, and Maia laughed.

"Tell her your secrets," Collin said.

"I don't have secrets."

"You know what I mean. Secrets of teaching."

"Well, the first ten years are the hardest," Maia told Nina.

"Come on, Mom."

"It's humbling. I'm not gonna lie."

"Give her something she can use."

"Hmmm." Maia took a long sip and set her wineglass down. "There is such a thing as reincarnation. If you teach long enough, the same kids keep coming back again."

Nina said, "In different forms?"

"Yeah, but they're recognizable—like, Oh, *yes*. I remember you. The ones who can't keep still. The ones who don't listen. The ones who fall in love with you."

"That's not advice," Collin pointed out.

"Advice." Maia pondered. "Be funny."

"I'm not," said Nina.

"Be desperate."

"Okay, I'm good at that."

"See, you are funny," Maia said. "Be surprising. For example, I came in one weekend and painted my classroom purple. It's good to blow their minds."

"She likes paint," Collin said.

"Yeah. If you're wondering where he gets the art from, it's from me."

Maia pulled down Collin's paintings from the refrigerator, his splotchy grade-school pictures of the river. She spread his drawings of ducks across the kitchen table. "The early years. See how he did the webbed feet?"

"I should have warned you," Collin told Nina. "She keeps all my old stuff."

"I'd keep the new stuff too," Maia said serenely. "Oh, wait. You work in *chalk*."

"I like chalk."

"I like a green living room."

"That green is way too blue."

Maia watched Collin pace the kitchen and drink another glass of wine. "Come back and see it in the light."

"It won't work in daylight either." Collin swiped a kitchen towel, soaking it in water.

Maia said, "If you want a rag, look under the sink."

Collin ignored this and disappeared into his old bedroom for socks and shoes. "Come on." He ushered Nina to the entry, where he opened the cellar door and pulled the light string.

Maia called after them, "Careful on those stairs."

Collin ran down quickly and then held out his hand, helping Nina with the last rickety steps.

"Over here." Guiding Nina past the toys and rusty bicycles, he led her to seven rolling blackboards, dark, old-fashioned, like the ones at school. Rising from the basement clutter, they stood mounted in wooden frames with casters underneath.

Quickly, he took the wet towel and wiped the board in front, rubbing the surface clean of every bit of dust and dirt so that it gleamed in the dim light. Then he reached down to excavate a box brimming with chalk. "What would you like?"

"What do you mean?"

"What do you want?" Focused, almost fierce, he picked up a piece of chalk.

She hesitated. "Well . . . what do you like to draw?"

"Everything." Already his hand was moving across the board. "Horses." He found a clear space and drew a horse with mane and tail streaming. "Birds." A pair of white swans glided from his hand, their long necks curving, reflections rippling in a glassy lake. "When I was a kid I liked castles." In seconds he drew crenellated towers and pennants flying, drawbridge opening. "Now I draw people." With one fluid line, he drew a woman lying on a beach—no, on a bed. It was Nina, leaning back, supporting herself with her elbows. That was her hair falling over her shoulders. Those were her arms, her breasts . . .

"Collin!" She had never seen anyone draw so well, so fast. His horses turned their heads to look at each other, his castle stood on foundations of rough stone, his sketch of Nina captured her tender expression, her soft, mussed hair.

He stood back for just a moment to admire his work, and then he wiped it all away. Castle, swans, horses, Nina's portrait vanished, and in their place he drew the hemlock in front of his mother's house. He worked with thick and thin edges, smudging snow onto the branches with his hand, outlining telephone wires in white. "What else?"

What else? She'd like to know how he drew swans so easily. How did he toss off castles in five seconds? He was so quick! He'd told her about his asphalt water lilies and his sidewalk Van Goghs, but she'd been to street fairs, glanced at sidewalk art on Church Street. His work was something else.

His art was quick but never crude or facile. His drawings were lively, streamlined, beautifully observed. As mimics capture gestures in performance, he drew essential details, the curve of a neck, the soft dent in a pillow, the arc of a careening sled. With each sketch, Nina felt a shock of recognition. She forgot the fight, entirely forgot her funk, lost all consciousness of place and time and Maia upstairs. He was drawing the hill at Danehy Park, the dwarf pines weighted down with snow. How did he do it? He seemed to steal from the world.

By now he held four pieces of chalk in his hand. "Tell me what you want."

"A cat."

A white cat capered atop a brick wall, and then a calico on a windowsill, and a dark cat with white feet and white nose crouching in tall grass. "What else?" He never hesitated as his chalk moved across the board. Sometimes he erased a line or smudged it with his hand, but he seemed to have a picture in his mind. Another cat emerged, a slinky, half-grown animal, ginger with green eyes.

"You couldn't learn this in school," Nina said.

"No, but I drew all the teachers."

"You drew the wrinkle between Miss Dorfman's eyes."

His right hand traveled over the board. "Go crazy," he told

Nina. "Ask for furniture." He drew his mother's kitchen table with six chairs. "Or tennis." He sketched himself, long, sinuous, jumping up to serve. He looked at her. "I'm showing off."

"Don't stop." She remembered his words—"I have nothing to say"—but it seemed to her the opposite was true. He had everything to say.

"What else?" he pressed.

"Wait," she said. "Just let me look." He had charmed her, delighted her before. She had enjoyed him for himself. He didn't need to impress her, but to her chagrin, she saw him differently now. It should not have mattered, but it did; she saw his gift. "No!" she begged. "Don't erase your pictures."

With a defiant smile he took his rag and erased his art to start again with a sailboat skimming an imaginary sea.

Her heart was racing, because she could help him if he let her. She didn't tell him, because she was afraid once more he'd take offense. To tell him was to flaunt her own position. Worse than that, to judge him. You're so good. What are you doing with your time? She watched in silence as he drew a sail swelling with the wind. She did not speak, even as the words rushed in her ears. Let me do something for you.

11

Caution

On Sunday Nina met her friends Julianne and Lily at Henrietta's Table. She decided not to mention Collin, because she didn't need her friends passing judgment. The relationship was so new, she wanted to protect it—but they guessed. They knew that she'd been seeing someone. After all, she had been ignoring them.

"He's an artist," Nina said at last. "Sometimes an actor."

"Oh, no," said Julianne.

"What do you mean, 'Oh, no'?" This vehemence surprised Nina, because Julianne was studying to be an opera singer.

"Sometimes an actor?" Lily asked.

"I mean, he's not just an actor," Nina said.

"Uh-huh," said Lily.

"He's smart, and he works hard."

"You're blushing!" Julianne said.

"I'm not."

"Yes, you are."

"Only because you're staring at me," Nina protested, but Julianne had known her since first grade. The girls had grown up ice-skating, scribbling their names inside Nina's closet, pitching tents in the music room of Julianne's stone manor in Milton. This was a house so grand it had its own agent for photo shoots and concerts and commercials. Servants' bells hung in the kitchen. The window seats were deep enough to put on plays.

Nina had loved Julianne's house because it made hers seem more ordinary. There had been something last days of Versailles about the empty ballroom and the vaulted dining room. Gold silverware and crystal filled the butler's pantry, but it was hard to find anything to eat. Hundreds of gilt chairs arrived by truck for chamber music concerts, but couches were few and far between. At night, on the third floor, the girls lay in Julianne's four-poster bed, and they heard distant music downstairs and far away. The house was so big that when Julianne's pet tortoise escaped, he was never seen again.

"Look at yourself." Julianne held up her phone now.

"No, don't!"

Julianne took a picture of Nina laughing and covering her face.

"Is he cute?" said Julianne.

"Is he an egomaniac?" said Lily.

"He has an ego, but he's not a maniac."

"So he's just self-involved."

"No! The opposite."

"But he doesn't have a job."

"He has at least two jobs," Nina said. "Maybe three."

"Hold on." Lily held her hand up. "At *least* two jobs, or at *most* two jobs?"

Lily, Nina's college roommate, had been adopted from China but raised a Klein in Santa Barbara. Her mother was a pediatrician, her father an endocrinologist. She had begun college as a writer and a humanist, comping the poetry board of *The Advocate*, studying folklore and mythology—but within the year, she'd dropped Old Norse and reverted to organic chemistry, dumping her boyfriend from Vermont, along with all his poet friends. In their match-box room in Thayer, she had confessed to Nina, "Student poets suck."

"Didn't e. e. cummings go here?" Nina asked. "And T. S. Eliot?"

Lily said, "Yeah, but he didn't write *The Waste Land* as an undergraduate." Lily had lost all sympathy for literary guys. After graduation, she had crossed the river for Harvard Medical School, leaving Asgard far behind.

"He's talented," said Nina.

Lily said, "Apparently."

"He's a chalk artist."

"Like sidewalk chalk?"

"He can draw anything."

"Okay." Julianne considered this. "He's good with his hands."

"Be serious!"

"I am serious." In her low-cut shirt, Julianne looked like a Renaissance goddess of spring, a buxom mezzo with strawberry-blond hair. "This is your transitional guy."

"What are you reading?" Nina said.

"I'm not reading anything!" The language of recovery came naturally to Julianne, who had been in therapy since she was a child. "I'm just so glad." She'd always said Nina needed to fool around.

But Nina wasn't fooling. "I think I can get him a job."

Lily pounced. "So he isn't actually working."

"He's working, but I have an idea he could do better."

"Doing what?" Julianne asked, because she kept an open mind.

"I thought he could work at Arkadia."

Silence.

"You haven't seen him draw."

Julianne and Lily looked at each other. They knew Nina's enthusiasms and her stubborn resolve. They had seen her disappointed tears.

"Don't you remember Jonah?" Lily said.

Nina quieted a little, even as she said, "He's nothing like Jonah."

Lily said, "You felt used."

Nina told them, "He's an artist, and he's incredible."

"Oh, my God," Julianne told Lily. "She's completely in love with him."

Her friends didn't understand. They assumed Nina was slumming, although they would never use the word. Of course sidewalk art was just as valid as anything else, and joining TeacherCorps was meaningful. It was the kind of thing everyone should try. They believed all this, and then they were startled when Nina actually followed through. She didn't mean it, right? She was just rebelling. This was her version of sex, drugs, and rock 'n' roll—dating a chalk artist, and teaching school.

They were prejudiced. No, that wasn't fair. They just wanted to protect her. They were glad she'd found Collin; relieved that she had slept with him. What alarmed them was her urge to help him. She'd been seeing him for what? Six weeks? Obviously he cared about her, but he knew who her father was.

Julianne said, "I wouldn't help him get a job."

"Why not?"

"You aren't thinking," Lily said.

"I am thinking. I haven't decided anything."

"Good," said Julianne. "Don't!"

"Don't introduce them?"

"Just don't decide."

Nina's friends hugged her after dinner. The three of them stood outside the Charles Hotel and said goodbye and love you. Julianne and Lily were driving back to Brookline. They offered to drop off Nina, but she said no. Are you upset? they asked. Of course not, she lied, and she walked home alone.

She wished she'd never told them. Her desire to help Collin tarnished in the open air. She would not admit that they were right, but their doubts awakened hers. Once she introduced him to her father, there would be no going back. She would be pulling strings, and he would always see her that way. She would be manipulating the situation—giving up any pretense of equality. What would that be like? Risky, Julianne said. Big mistake, said Lily. How can you tell what he really wants? Julianne had asked gently, and of course Nina knew what that meant. You have too many things he needs.

They didn't understand, because they didn't know him. She thought they might change their minds once they met Collin. Then she admitted to herself she wasn't sure.

He had laughed when she showed him her father's house. It was at night and everyone had been out of town. He'd stepped into the hushed foyer and he'd laughed and laughed. "Is this for real?" It wasn't the grand Victorian that flummoxed him, not the gables and turrets and tall windows, but the art inside, the white-flower painting by Georgia O'Keeffe, the eye-popping Lichtenstein of a woman crying on the telephone, the gold Buddha in the dining room.

When Collin saw the statue of Venus standing in the library, he caressed the goddess from her broken shoulder over the curve of her breast and through the folds of her drapery to the hem of her robe. Exultant, he said, "It's like a gallery, but you can touch, and no one's watching!" He seemed to forget that Nina was watching him. He seemed to forget everything.

Sleepless that night, she sat up, marking Discovery Journals.

Q. Why does Hester Prynne conceal the identity of her child? Does her decision make sense to you?

In large, round handwriting, Marisol wrote: *Hester Prynne not revealing the father of her child isn't so impossible to understand. 1. It's embarrassing. 2. In those days it was not appropriate.*

Tiara wrote: *It is dangerous to reveal anything when your a Puritan.*

Dangerous, Nina thought. That was the word. Not the games at Arkadia. The people there.

To me the whole book is ironic, wrote Xavier.

Sevonna said, *Without secrets life would be so blatantly obvious it would be ridiculous.*

Collin might enjoy her help, and he might resent it too. He might be grateful, but she wasn't sure she wanted gratitude. She imagined his mixed feelings, his guilty delight. She considered how he might treat her, as if he owed her something, or as if she'd trapped him in some grand plan.

Diana's entry was an inky thicket. *Everybody's got secrets. Whats more interesting is when you find out other peoples. Then the question is do you tell on THEM? For example my twin and I were like blood brothers only moreso. Now its like he moved away. I hear him whispering daphne daphne.*

Daphne? Nina stopped there, puzzled. Then the word receded into the tangle on the page. *Maybe because he has something to hide, Nathaniel Hawthorne is trying to write in a confusing way. Sometimes its like Nathaniel Hawthorne is trying to be deep.*

Nina imagined speaking to her father. I have to ask you something. It was a big thing to ask—a serious and revealing question.

Go ahead, Viktor would answer, and as he listened, he would jump three steps ahead of her, and he would laugh.

She turned off the light and lay awake in bed. She couldn't keep Collin from her father. Knowing her, he must know Viktor—but not so soon! Coming to Arkadia, Collin would know her uncle Peter too. This gave her pause. Her father was scientific and jovial, devoted to technology. Peter was artistic and perverse.

Arkadia was harsh, fantastical, a tricky labyrinth. She wanted to shield Collin, but that seemed wrong, discounting his independence and his gift. She remembered just a week before, she and Collin had celebrated their birthdays at a little place called Carmen, in the North End. Brown kraft paper covered all the tables, and as they ate, Collin covered the paper in black pen, sketching places they had been—the bike shop, the bar at Grendel's, the stone castle atop Prospect Hill. When the waitress arrived with their check, she looked wide-eyed at the illustrations and said, "Do you want me to wrap that up for you?"

I have to help him, she thought the next morning, as she drove to school. But was there some way she could do it indirectly? She wove through winter streets, looping around the Cambridge Common, dipping into the underpass, and she wished she could help him secretly.

She was not surprised to see police when she arrived at Emerson. She assumed patrol cars meant a safety drill, but then she saw security blocking off the sidewalk, a traffic jam of cars and school buses redirected to the back entrance. She had to circle the block to find a parking place.

Inside the school building, yellow tape cordoned off the lobby, and police officers were directing students downstairs to the gym. CAUTION POLICE LINE DO NOT CROSS. Vandals had attacked the building, spray-painting the entryway.

"Oh, wonderful," said Mr. Allan.

Mrs. West was demanding, "How did they get in?"

The black graffiti extended across the lobby wall in a series of initials over a foot high. The other teachers didn't know yet what the letters meant, nor did Mr. DeLaurentis, who stood outside his office, talking on his phone. Was it a new gang? Or some random prank?

Only Nina understood. She knew instantly, and her face burned. There she'd been, plotting to find Collin a job. Now she wished Arkadia away, along with its obsessive fans. They had tagged her own school with UnderWorld's catchphrase, See You In Hell.

CUCUCUCUCUCUCUCUCUCUCUCUCUCUCUCUCUCUCUCUCUCUCUCUCUCU

12

The Leopard

Across the river, Kerry was catching up on paperwork when she received a text from Emerson. Partial lockdown, vandalism with violent videogame content, classes continuing, increased security, no imminent danger, please wait until dismissal before coming to school. She read all this at once, and then twice, three times, but the only words she saw were "violent videogame content." She hardly noticed signing out, zipping up her coat, shouldering her bag to leave the ICU.

She had no idea what was going on, but her thoughts were all for Aidan, even as she glanced back at patients and parents in their glass-walled rooms. She left—although you could never leave entirely—and took the elevator down to the lobby, which was teeming with families and strollers, musicians toting their guitars, pet therapists leading wise-eyed dogs, hospital ambassadors, costumed clowns.

Kerry hurried past bright murals and saltwater aquariums. Reaching back, she retied her thick blond hair, stuffing the ponytail into her hood. She passed a girl in a wheelchair with head support, then a man-size boy, clinging to his mother. "Bless you," Kerry said, as the boy sneezed loudly, and then sneezed again.

She was a believer. She believed in four-leaf clovers and shooting stars. She believed in Jesus and in angels, although they worked mysteriously. She had seen more of death than most, and she believed, to some extent, in ghosts—not the ghoulish kind, but the quiet ones who come to you in dreams.

She had her superstitions about shoes on tables, and open umbrellas in the house. She had her rituals, and she was not ashamed of them. After all, she worked in a place where knowledge ended and belief began. She got out of bed on the right side, and when she had a chance to swim in the echoing War Memorial pool, she used only a red kickboard—red for happiness—never blue. She didn't think that she could sway the universe, but she hoped that you could nudge it with a prayer.

She prayed now, as she drove through the maze of hospitals— Children's, Beth Israel Deaconess. Her hands were cold inside her gloves, her car's heater was still warming up, and she shivered as she prayed for her own children.

Diana was secretive, but she followed rules; she did her homework and her chores. Trusting Aidan was an act of faith. Some days were easier. He said hello, or washed the dishes. He came downstairs and looked awake. Other days he didn't even glance at her. His games consumed him and he had nothing left. What would become of him? How would he get into college? She berated him and he listened in silence, waiting for her to leave. At those moments she hated home as much as he did. She would drive to the Star Market on Sidney Street, and wheel her cart through the white aisles, and cry.

Driving across the BU Bridge now, she felt a rising dread. The river spread before her, icy near the banks, but lively in the center, gold water dancing in the morning light. She had loved the drive on other mornings. Today her back tightened and her shoulders ached. She tried to breathe and fogged the windows.

Please, she prayed as she wiped the glass with her knit glove. I know you work in your own ways—but could you send me a sign that this year will get better? She didn't ask for a miracle. She'd nearly given up on those, but please, she thought. Just something small?

Slowly, she eased her car between the snowbanks in her shared driveway and picked her way up icy steps. Anxiously, she stepped inside the door. All was quiet; the twins were at school. Of course they were. Even so, she peeked into their rooms. She gazed at Diana's rumpled bed. Briefly, she ventured into Aidan's cave. He had covered his window with aluminum foil so that not a crack of light could penetrate. He'd stripped the walls of posters, and wedged his computer desk into the corner. Kerry reached out to touch the monitor and then drew back. He would know.

Tiptoeing through her own house, she retreated to wash dishes, to take down a load of laundry, to sort the mail, to read *The Boston Globe*. Finally, she took her little photo album to bed with her and flipped through photos of the twins when they were small. She looked at one picture of her children coming down a slide. It was a little slide and they were wearing overalls. She had forgotten about those overalls. They couldn't have been more than two, laughing Aidan first, his hair white gold. Dark-haired Diana peeking over his shoulder, apprehensive, as she slid down after him. Those days had not been easy, but they had been happier. For one thing, Kerry's parents had been alive. She had moved in with them after her ex left. Her parents had watched the children in North Cambridge while she worked night shifts. Her father had built a sandbox for the children, and a little table with matching stools. Later, her parents left her a small inheritance, which she'd used for the down payment on the house.

Now she wished that she could travel back in time. She wouldn't go far. She had no interest in history or adventure—the recent past was all she wanted. Her mother's voice, her father's patient carpentry, the playground with the green slide, the twins at six, learning in school that vitamin A was good for your eyesight. Venturing down to the basement, they held carrots like torches. She had found Aidan and Diana standing in the dark, nibbling the tips.

Hours later, Kerry woke in pale winter light. A creaking, clicking sound, the tick of the gas burner on the stove. "Diana?" Kerry called.

No answer.

"Diana?" Kerry descended to find her daughter in the kitchen. "Diana!"

"*What?*" Diana shouted. "Stop calling me over and over."

"Start answering!"

"I did answer."

"I couldn't hear you."

Diana opened three packets of instant oatmeal.

"It's only twelve-twenty."

"Early dismissal."

"Because of the lockdown?"

"I guess." Diana felt for her mother. Kerry's face looked pallid; even her blond hair was dull and fuzzy, not gold, as it had been. Stand up straight, you're a beautiful girl, Diana thought. It was no use. Exhaustion beat Kerry down. Her delicate features had faded, her hands were raw from washing at the hospital.

"Where's your brother?" Kerry asked.

"Where he always is."

Upstairs, in his room, Aidan was turning a BoX over in his hands. The BoX was black and beautifully smooth, a perfect cube of plastic. He knew what was inside, but he could not find a way to open it.

The cube was compact, small enough to fit into a backpack, but heavy enough to strain the straps. Kneeling, he ran his fingers over the surface, pressing for a secret spring. Gently, he tapped each side. Nothing happened. He shook the BoX, and shook it harder. "What's wrong with you?" He could not open this inert console, although he'd been trying since he got home from school. He'd snatched up the parcel, marked PRIORITY MAIL, and now, like a prisoner, he pried its edges, paced the floor, threw himself down onto his bed, dreamed and despaired of his escape—except that most prisoners imagined getting out. Aidan wanted to get in.

He'd checked the package a hundred times and found no in-structions, no note from Daphne, no code, no Web link. He'd searched online, typing "UnderWorld," "black BoX," "new plat-form." He'd only turned up articles he'd seen before. Now he sat with the BoX on his lap and entered EverWhen, roaming across the screen, sending Tildor over snowfields to search for Daphne.

???, he typed into the chat box.

Nothing.

Gotit now what?

Nothing.

how does it open???

Nothing.

Comeon

Nothing.

Help me open it.

Nothing.

Its fake, he typed in rage and in frustration. soru. bitch.

Watch your language.

The answer came so fast he jumped, and the BoX slid off his lap and crashed onto the floor.

He was afraid he'd broken it. Kneeling, he found a hairline crack, but as he turned the BoX, he saw the surface wasn't cracked at all, but subtly divided. As with a Rubik's Cube, you could twist the top half of the BoX away from the bottom. As with a child-safe medicine bottle, you twisted while pressing down. Oh, I get it, he thought, even as the top popped off in his hands.

The room went dark.

Frantic, Aidan gasped for air in what looked like smoke. In fact, he could breathe easily. The air in his room was just the same; only his perception of the atmosphere had changed. He was crouching in a stream of dust motes. These were aeroflakes, imperceptible on their own, flying together in a cloud.

His room was not his room. His ceiling was dissolving, his walls warping, rippling. A mist rose up around him. Fog that wasn't wet; dry ice that wasn't cold. For a long time he was afraid to stand. Bed, desk, and chair had disappeared, the floor seemed to slide beneath him. Faintly he heard the trickle of water, the rustle of leaves. He imagined a deep forest, but he could barely see. He reached for the light switch on what had been his wall. Aeroflakes shifted and resolved themselves, illuminated by Aidan's ceiling light. He felt for the door of his closet and opened it, groping for the light switch inside. Once more the accumulating mist began to shift and change. Filtering and reflecting light, the particles responded to Aidan's movements and to one another, projecting a multidimensional landscape, deceiving and delighting the eye, coloring the air, even transmitting sound.

Now Aidan perceived bare branches and jagged pieces of blue sky. A forest floor carpeted with leaves, bracken crackling underfoot, trees looming overhead. This was no tableau framed by a computer screen. Without glasses, headset, or joystick, he was standing in a world expanding and deepening every moment.

He tried to take it all in, the piles of leaves and patches of snow, the ancient trees, the bright sky where his ceiling had been. A sunny afternoon, a winter wood. This was where he found himself. Literally found himself, his avatar, a knight in chain mail, taking shape before his eyes, no flat cartoon, but a shifting, sculptural figure cast from his own body, conjured like the woodland from a cloud of dust.

He raised his arm, and the knight raised his in turn. He pivoted, and the knight pivoted as well, so that Aidan couldn't see his alter ego's face. He took a step in place, and the knight began walking through the rustling leaves. As in a dream, Aidan watched himself, his motions fluid, his body long and strong.

Playfully, motes mapped themselves onto the ordinary features of his room. As his knight walked on, Aidan saw his bed take the shape of a great boulder and then a fallen log. Veiled in cloud, illuminating a vaulting winter sky, Aidan's ceiling light shone with the complexity and brilliance of the sun. The knight was just Aidan's height and build, carrying himself as Aidan did. Light-headed, Aidan watched his knight venture deeper. The trees grew closer, stockading against the sky.

Snap of a twig. An animal. No. Something else. He sensed some creature stalking him. Heard it breathing behind him. No, above him. Something in the trees. He wanted to stop, but his knight kept walking. He sensed the creature coming closer. "Stop," he whispered. Then he stamped his foot. His alter ego stopped immediately.

Aidan lifted his arm, and his knight drew his sword. He heard the creature hiss. Snake? Dragon? Spitting monster? He lunged, but he guessed wrong. The thing pounced, screaming, tackling him from behind. Whirling, he fought a leopard, sinuous and dark. He slashed, but could not wound the massive cat. He attacked again, but didn't hit. The leopard sank her teeth into his shoulder, and he saw his own blood showering, drenching his tunic and his arm. Shocked, he fell to his knees and his avatar plunged to the forest floor. The leopard came in for the kill, gold eyes shining, long body undulating. She bit his neck and pinned him down, drinking his blood. She was gentle now, teeth no longer penetrating, claws no longer bared, her tongue almost caressing his raw wound.

As the leopard lapped him up, he felt himself unmoored. He shed his sword and shield, and then he shed his body, legs, arms, head, torso. Whitening like toppled statuary, the corpse of Aidan's knight lay on the forest floor, but the knight's ghost floated free, a weightless spirit-version of his venturing self.

Now the leopard released him. She seemed to purr as she drew back into herself, and he saw that she'd begun to change as well, black velvet lightening to a tawny glow. At first her spots stood out boldly; then they too began to shift and fade; the animal's gold eyes darkened, her head and body turned elfin, white and delicate, claws changing into tapered fingers, great cat changing to a girl in transparent silken robes.

Daphne's voice. "Let's go."

He forgot he'd ever called her fake. He forgot his anger altogether. She was not an elf, nor was she a warrior. She seemed herself, luscious and three-dimensional. She had never seemed so real. "This is the most amazing place I've ever been."

"You haven't even seen the Gates."

"Take me."

"You have to cross the river first." She brushed his phantom body with her hand, and he had to imagine what he could not feel. This world could represent the subtlest exchange, a word, a sigh, even a breath, the smallest gesture, the quirk of an eyebrow, the tremble of a lip—nothing was lost, except for touch.

He couldn't touch her, so he followed her instead. He took the first step, and his knight broke through bracken and forded streams, clambering after Daphne.

Gradually, the river revealed itself. At first he saw nothing more than a shimmer between trees. The shining water unfolded like a ribbon, then a banner. As Daphne led him from the forest, the river opened further, a watery valley, a realm unto itself between steep banks.

Silver, heavy, vast, the river looked like liquid mercury, so slow it scarcely seemed to move. Aidan picked up a pebble and tried to skip it across the surface. The rock sank without a ripple. No birds flew overhead, no fish surfaced, no reeds or plants grew on the dull clay bank. Aidan threw a bigger rock. In this water nothing splashed. Absorbing each stone, the sluggish flow healed itself.

Weird river. Amazing place. Aidan drew his sword and dipped it in the water.

Even Daphne gasped as heavy silver wicked up the blade and continued up his arm as well, cloaking him in metal to his shoulder. He dropped his sword on the riverbank and the liquid metal stopped rising. Ghostly still, he faced Daphne with a silver arm. He flexed his silver fingers, clenched a gleaming fist.

Drumbeats. Thunder. An incessant pounding in the distance.

"What's that?" It took him a moment to realize the pounding was his mother at the door.

"Do you have to go?"

"No," he whispered.

Outside, Kerry watched the strip of light beneath the locked bedroom door. She saw the light brighten, shifting from gray-green to silver, heard her son's whisper and his shuffling feet. No tapping noise. No typing at all. She stopped knocking and stood still, straining to listen.

"Why not?" she heard Aidan say, and then in a louder voice, "I did everything."

Kerry held her breath.

A long pause, and then he said, "I can't."

"Aidan!" Kerry called out. She started banging all over again.

On the other side of the door, Aidan saw a black speck on the water. Slowly, slowly, a boat emerged, an ancient ship with long oars and a black sail. The oars rowed themselves across the heavy river, but hovered mid-stroke just before they reached the bank.

"Stay," begged Aidan.

Lightly Daphne jumped into the boat, which began rowing her away.

"Come back!"

"Let me in!" Kerry called outside his door.

"I need more," Aidan called out.

Now Kerry couldn't make out the words. She heard her own heart beating faster, but she tried to calm herself. Aidan was in his room. He'd gone to school, as usual. Surely the vandalism was some other gamer's work. Aidan had never defaced anything. She took a deep breath and sat down on the stairs.

On the other side of the door, on the far banks of the silver river, Daphne told Aidan, "This time, make it silver."

"I can't!" he answered, but his knight held out his arms to her.

The pull and slap of heavy water, the rhythmic stroke of oars. *Make it silver.* Kerry heard and yet she didn't hear. Sitting on the top stair, Kerry leaned her head against the wall.

At the hospital she had seen parents waiting for diagnoses. Cancer, tumor, genetic disease. When doctors came to speak to them, the parents knew what was coming, but couldn't bring themselves to ask. Kerry had seen mothers do this, holding still, afraid to speak. They weren't cowardly; they weren't lying to themselves. They clung to uncertainty in order to survive. She held still now. She would speak to Aidan; she knew she had to speak to him—but not today. She closed her eyes.

13

Crossing Over

Like a dreamer who didn't want to wake, Aidan played and replayed UnderWorld's opening. The nights his mother slept at home, he slept. The nights she worked, he took the black BoX from his desk drawer under a pile of old school papers. He unscrewed the top, and his room filled with aeroflakes, those lively flecks scattering and gathering into UnderWorld's barren landscape. He played through the night, his movements increasingly fluid, his reflexes faster, his consciousness expanding so that his knight no longer seemed a projection, but a real person. Aidan's ordinary body seemed a dim reflection of his gaming self.

Every morning before dawn, he closed the BoX. He had to put his whole weight into it when he turned the lid. Yielding slowly, the lid attracted aeroflakes. The silver river faded, its barren cliffs collapsed into themselves, as, like metal shavings aligned by a magnetic force, the particles flew in.

He closed the BoX, but he could not shut UnderWorld away for long. He explored the river's edge in every light. Darkness, and pale morning, cloudy afternoon.

Aidan collected stones and threw them in the heavy water. He tried throwing several at once to watch them sink together. Then, with a stick, he dug a shallow trench in the clay at water's edge. Silver oozed up to fill the hole. He was still trying to find a way across, even though he knew there was no way, unless he obeyed Daphne.

He decided to do the thing she asked. Sometimes fear caught him by surprise—a falling sensation, just as he was drifting off to sleep. A sudden chill walking to school. He did not change his mind. Instead, he tried to judge his dread dispassionately. His anxiety, he thought, was superficial, like a nosebleed. He looked down and saw his fear, but hardly felt it. Hour after hour, the river in his room worked its strange magic, inciting him to cross.

Wonderful to await the next installment of his secret life. He became calm, efficient, pleasant, sitting at the kitchen table, catching up on geometry, glancing discreetly at the clock, which looked like a red apple cut in half, with seeds marking the hours. He solved one problem after another, writing out his answers with a sharp pencil. You're so bright, his mother always said. "Now is the time," Mr. Allan had told him at his college counseling meeting. "Your test scores are outstanding. If you do your work, you'll have options. You could compete for scholarships."

As Kerry cooked spaghetti and meat sauce, she turned to look at Aidan. "You see."

"See what?" Aidan asked.

She didn't answer. She was thinking, Here you are, working at the table. Here you are, returned to me. Wasn't that exactly what she'd prayed for? She wished. She hoped—and doubted.

Aidan kept working, and Kerry talked about how he only had to try, and said the thing she always said about how more than half of life was showing up.

"How much more than half?" Aidan asked and she pretended to whack him with her spoon. He looked at his mother with that mixture of love and pity he felt when they were closest, and he had no idea she suspected him. In fact she had spent all afternoon online on gaming-addiction message boards. She had Googled UnderWorld-related vandalism, and found one case in Seattle, one in Austin, in addition to the one in Cambridge.

Now Kerry drained the pasta, and the room filled with steam. She made everyone hold hands to say grace, and that meant Aidan had to reach across to Diana. Kerry bowed her head, but Diana and Aidan kept their eyes on the counter, where the brownies were cooling, half with pecans and half without. "Thank you for this food," Kerry said. "Thank you for our family," and then she added silently, Help me figure out what Aidan plans to do.

"Mom?" Diana asked.

Kerry looked up, and everybody said amen.

Diana had seconds and Aidan had thirds of the spaghetti, although he picked out all the onion from the glistening sauce. Kerry asked what was going on in school, and the twins said nothing, and they said, stuff. It was an ordinary dinner, with Aidan clearing and Diana taking out the recycling, even as Kerry held up Diana's copy of *The Scarlet Letter*, with its cover torn away. "Why do you mutilate your books like that?"

Diana stood in the doorway holding an overflowing bag of newspapers. "They're all online anyway."

Kerry said, "You're mumbling. I can't understand a word you're saying."

Aidan said, "Yeah, Diana," who shot back, "Shut up, Aidan," and their mother looked nostalgic because they were bickering again.

But that night, Aidan lay awake, listening to the sleeping house. He heard his sister snoring in her room next door, pictured his mother buried deep in bed. Fully dressed, he heard dark old beams settling, snow dripping, tiny paws thumping as animals ran across the roof.

He crept downstairs in his socks, and stepped into his waiting boots. Slipped on coat and gloves, collected the bag he'd hidden behind Priscilla's fermenting compost bin. He felt nothing as he walked to the corner, not the slightest apprehension. Like his avatar in UnderWorld, he moved weightlessly, covering the ground with his long strides. Supernatural, he glided across Broadway, ignoring traffic lights and passing cars. Lightly he hopped the low fence and dropped into the field where he'd played soccer years ago.

Except for a few patches, the snow had melted, exposing tangled old grass and spongy ground. He unzipped his jacket and crouched low, shaking his paint can. A metallic clicking like ball bearings rolling around. The can was full, and, finger to the nozzle, he scarcely had to press. A silver stream hissed straight from his hand.

Quickly now, he did his work, keeping head and shoulders down, shielding the spray can with his body as he crossed the field. Looping over the patchy field, his letters gleamed like a skater's figure eights. He didn't stop to watch for passersby, nor did he pause to consider his own writing. He felt, rather than saw, that he wrote elegantly, his CUs smooth.

Any second, a patrol car could expose him with white lights. He was just blocks from the police station, around the corner from City Hall, but he felt invincible, as though he drew his own luck, and painted his own rules. He carried nothing in his pockets. He had no backup plans, or explanations. All he knew was that no one could catch him; he was too fast.

He ran past basketball courts, past the children's playground with its corkscrew slides, all the way to the Koreana restaurant, where he threw the paint can into the garbage bin in back. In the morning everyone would see what he had done, but no would find him. No one could pin it on him. He was long gone. Gloved hands in his pockets, he slipped inside the kitchen door. Athlete, artist, ghost.

"Aidan."

He froze.

"Come here."

Kerry was sitting with her coffee at the table.

"What's going on?"

"Nothing." He glanced at the apple clock above her head.

"What am I going to find out in the morning?"

"I don't know."

She forced herself to ask, "Were you at school tonight?"

He told the truth. "No!"

"Are you involved in this new game CU?"

"There's no game CU."

"UnderWorld, then. Are you playing?" He heard the dread in her voice. She might as well have asked him: Are you using?

"It's not even out yet."

"Don't lie to me."

He looked her in the eye. "I'm not."

Aidan saw her tension ease, and knew he'd won. Exultant and forgiving all at once, he felt a wave of love for his mother. Kerry was too tired to fight on, but he would be merciful. He would protect her, even as he deceived her.

"Don't worry. I'm fine," he told Kerry softly. This was an understatement. He was strong, and he was young. Immortal. He feared nothing as he stood on the threshold of his other life.

Just before dawn, he opened his BoX and saw the river glimmering in darkness. He had already texted Daphne to tell her what he'd done. Now he waited on the bank, expecting his reward. A million stars appeared, more than he had ever seen on Earth. The night opened, unfolding and expanding all around him, a pocket universe.

The sun rose in muted colors and the stars began to fade. A milky fog obscured the water, neither day nor night. What did it mean? Gradually, Aidan realized that his closet light had burned out.

In the half-light at the glowing river's edge, his knight dug up rocks and turned them over, looking for a clue. Some were unyielding; others shattered in his hand. One cracked slowly like an egg. Slime trickled out, and then a ragged tooth emerged, prying the rock open from inside. The hatchling looked like a tiny coiled crocodile, its thorny skin the clay color of the riverbank. Hissing, it uncurled and sprang up snapping, tearing and biting Aidan's spectral self. The monster's little teeth snapped right through Aidan's ghostly form, but could not penetrate his silver arm at all; its teeth clanged instead, metal on metal.

He slashed the creature's throat with his sword, and a red-black ooze pooled under its stony head. Carefully, Aidan laid out the body full-length on the ground. Like a dancer in front of a mirror, he watched himself as he slit the monster lengthwise and peered inside, searching entrails for some clue or sign. He found something hard, a forked rod, a wishbone. Even as he knelt on the riverbank, he felt the bone drawing him toward water with magnetic force. Then again, he really had to pee! He'd put it off as long as possible, but he had to go, and there was no way to pause.

He dropped the divining rod and dashed to the bathroom, but the door was locked. Pounding, he called to Diana, and heard her answer, "Wait." Running down to the bathroom near the kitchen, he tripped and caught himself, cursing the narrow stairs and his own feet. It wasn't just depressing; it was disorienting, emerging from the game to clomp down the stairs or stand at the toilet with no defense against the peeling paint, the sharp corners of the real world.

He dashed back again and saw the upstairs bathroom open and empty. He had left his own door ajar, and on reentry caught Diana standing there, gazing at his river and his sky.

"Out."

"This is so weird," she said. The world was beginning to work on her, the mist of particles, the strange half-light, the slow pull of the river. He closed his door and the game closed around them, the river coming into focus, moving even slower than before, like cooling glass.

"Out," he repeated.

Diana didn't move. She stood there staring at the barren riverbank and shattered dragon egg, and for just a moment he let the game wait. He stood there with her, and they were brother and sister, exploring the basement. They were a pair of eight-year-olds walking to the library. They were the woodcutter's children, and their father had abandoned them.

"Who are you?" Diana asked, as she gazed at Aidan's ghostly avatar.

"I don't have a name yet."

"I thought you pick a name at the beginning when you design your body and all that."

"It's not that kind of game."

"What kind of . . ." Diana began, and then finished her own sentence. "This is UnderWorld."

"Just the demo."

"What do you mean? What demo? Where did you get it?"

"A girl I know."

Diana folded her arms across her chest, and just like that, the spell was broken. She stood there in her black clothes, a wall of skepticism, a frown on her round face. "Daphne."

"You're spying!"

"I'm not! I overheard."

He grabbed her by the shoulder. "What do you mean you overheard? You never heard anything."

She wrenched away. "Let me go. I never said anything. I never did anything to you." Diana didn't care anymore about the river in his room; she didn't look twice at Aidan's ghost, or silver sword, or his divining rod, quivering on the bank. "There is no girl. None of this is real."

"It's real," Aidan told her. "Obviously the game is real. She gave it to me."

"You want that to be true."

"How do you know what's true or not?" Aidan asked his twin, his doubter.

"How do you?"

"Get out."

"Fine." Diana turned to leave.

"You were never here."

Diana shot back, "Neither were you!"

14

The Visit

At first he drew Nina from memory. After seeing her, he came back to his room and drew her on the walls, chalking her shoulders, her breasts, her slender waist. He grew so intent on capturing her that sometimes he felt he had to get away from her.

Over days and weeks, imagination yielded to experience. In February Collin began bringing her to his apartment. He stopped worrying about what she would think, and slept with her in his own bed. Now his blackboard-painted walls were covered with Nina asleep, awake, half dressed, turning her head. She was brushing her hair. She was sitting in a chair with the ribbon strap of her slip looped over her bare arm.

He hardly went to parties anymore. He had stopped drawing backdrops for Theater Without Walls. Darius said, "Who do you think you are, Edgar fucking Degas?" Noelle said—"What? Are you too good for us?" He spent all his time with Nina. Drew her and erased her, studying her every mood.

But Nina studied Collin too. She watched him focus on one aspect of her body and chalk it over and over until he could re-create it without a second glance. He learned to draw her profile, and then he used that view next time, generalizing with slight variations. He was amazing and relentless, developing a shorthand for her body and her face.

He studied shapes and colors the way poets studied words. He kept a bird's nest in his room and a collection of old tools. He had a broken ceiling fan on the floor, a bouquet of shriveled flowers, a crumpled chrome fender, because he liked the way it reflected light. He had a whole library of curling art posters, old masters and fantasy art all mixed together. She saw no books, no tablets, no computers.

One night as he drew her, Nina asked, "How do you learn your parts when you perform?"

With his foot, Collin nudged a tangle of headphones on the floor.

"You just listen?"

"Sometimes I slow down the audio and write the lines." As so often when he was holding chalk, he illustrated his point, writing in fluid script, *We are such stuff as dreams are made on* . . .

"How do you do that?" His words looked like calligraphy. "My printing is so bad half my students say they can't read the homework on the board."

"You're very trusting."

She said quite seriously, "I want to be."

Then he stood back from the board and wondered at her. She was so earnest. "What were you like when you were little?"

"Sad," she told him. "Worried."

"Why?" He sat next to her on the bed.

"I worried I was adopted, and my father was going to give me back. Then I worried I wasn't adopted. I was afraid suicide ran in families, so I worried I would die like my mother did."

He was a little shocked, so he asked lightly, "Oh, is that all?"

She didn't mention that her father had lied about her mother, substituting physical for mental illness. Nina had been almost twelve when she found out the truth. She just said, "I worried about other things too."

She had been afraid of fire, afraid of thunderstorms, afraid of the ocean, afraid of dark, shadowy sharks that could come ripping at her through the water. She had worried about burglars. Distrusting the security system, she had double-checked the doors—all six regular doors and the French doors in her father's house. "I was afraid of my father leaving."

"Poor Nina!"

"Well, I was lucky too."

Money, Collin thought.

But Nina said, "I played my dad's games first."

"Before release?"

"Before everything."

"Which ones?"

"EverRest. EverSea. That's my friend Julianne. That's her voice when all the mermaids sing."

"Seriously? So when you hear the mermaids you're thinking of her."

Nina shrugged. The memory was strange, pleasure mixed with anger. Julianne singing in the studio, Nina aware of Peter watching.

"What's it like to be you?" Collin asked, playfully.

"This is me when I was eleven." Nina reached for her phone and searched for the image from the game. "The girl collecting sand dollars in the sea cave."

Collin looked at a waif of a girl in a green kelp dress. Her hair was long and shimmering, her face serious, her eyes clear gray. "You should tell your students!"

Nina looked at him in disbelief.

"You're like a celebrity!"

"No way!"

"You're no fun." Then again, Collin had always preferred the teachers you could sidetrack: Mr. Dillingham, who talked about running during biology; Mrs. Giannetti, who paused while solving equations to reminisce about her summers with Earthwatch as a volunteer archaeologist. His best teachers had been the most distractible. "When we did Shakespeare, Mrs. West had us perform scenes."

"She still does."

"You should do that! Come dressed as something. Titania." He scrambled to his feet and drew Nina as the fairy queen. His sketch was part Pre-Raphaelite, part 1920s *Vogue,* white chalk and lavender, deep purple, and long trailing wings. He drew a gossamer dress, draped over Nina's naked body.

"I don't think so!"

"Bring props."

"Like ass ears?"

"Let me visit," Collin told her. "I'm a veteran."

"Of what?"

"Veteran dramatic educator!"

She teased. "Full tomato."

"Hey, I played Edward Winslow for two seasons!" He knew his living history. He'd done his time as an interpreter at Plimoth Plantation. Walked up and down in wool breeches and white linen, doffing his hat, cleaning his musket, tending goats, thatching roofs, mending woven eel traps while telling the story of the *Mayflower* to schoolchildren, old couples, tourists from Singapore, Germany, Japan. "We used to do class visits all the time."

Nina tried to picture Collin as a seventeenth-century colonist.

"The voyage was long and stormy," he intoned. "Yet none but a blaspheming sailor was lost at sea . . ."

"But I'm not teaching Pilgrims."

"I could do Shakespeare, no problem."

"My kids are tough," said Nina.

He scoffed. "I work in Harvard Square. My art's been peed on."

"Are you serious?"

"Twice."

"Ohh." She sounded so dismayed. He had to laugh. It wasn't just that she'd never seen such a thing. She had never even thought of such a thing.

The last day before February vacation, he bounded into Emerson, setting off the metal detector. Framed by pulsing orange lights, Collin stood resplendent in plumed hat, brown jerkin and slashed doublet, white shirt with pointed lace collar, sweeping velvet cloak lined with tawny satin, thick brown hose.

"Good morrow, fair lady." He doffed his hat to Nina, as security came running.

"Okay, let's have the sword," the guard said.

Collin's hand tightened on the hilt. "What, surrender my weapon?"

"Yup."

"In death alone," said Collin. "Else forfeit sacred honor."

Nina was laughing. "Stop!"

"Let's have the sword."

"Officer," Nina said, "it isn't real."

"Zero tolerance," he replied.

Nina watched the guard march Collin into the office. "My good Lord DeLaurentis," Collin announced himself to Mrs. Solomon, the principal's secretary. "Is he within?"

"Collin?" Mrs. Solomon strained to recognize the young Emerson alumnus in his Jacobean clothes.

After some discussion, he surrendered his weapon to DeLaurentis himself, and signed the school guest book with a wonderful crabbed hand. Name: *Wm. Shakespeare*. Organization: *The King's Men*.

Then Collin led the way up the stairs of his old school, striding through corridors where crowds parted before him, kids whistling, laughing, calling to one another, "Oh, my God, check this out. Check the boots!" Some thought he was from King Richard's Faire. Others said he was doing the LGBTQ assembly, since he looked like such an amazing queen. Gawkers peeked into Nina's room even when passing time was over. Her students loved it when she closed the door, and William Shakespeare belonged to them alone.

"Today we have a special guest," Nina began, as Collin paced behind her, examining the poster of the old Globe Theatre, experimenting with the light switches, gazing at the ceiling, marveling at the fluorescent glow. "He is an actor, director, playwright, poet . . . the envy of his peers—"

"I have no peers," Shakespeare interrupted.

"Ahem!" Nina shot him a look and the class laughed. "His peers, including . . . Ben Jonson—"

"Prithee," Shakespeare asked the class, "hath anybody seen his work?"

Nobody had.

"Christopher Marlowe," Nina continued.

None of the kids had heard of him. Shakespeare gave Marlowe the thumbs-down.

"Beaumont and Fletcher."

"Boo!" Shakespeare cried, and then to Nina, "Fair lady, I'm the last man standing! They've heard only of me!" Rhythmically, he clapped his hands and gestured for the students to join in.

"He was born in Stratford, and he worked in London," Nina said as her kids clapped along with Collin. "He founded his own theater, the Globe." She looked down at her notes. "He invented the words *radiance, equivocal, lustrous, amazement*. Phrases such as *sea change, all of a sudden, dead as a doornail, in stitches, the game is up, fancy free* . . . "

Shakespeare gestured for Miss Lazare to move along, and the

class laughed as she cut her introduction short. "His plays are still performed all over the world. I give you William Shakespeare."

"Can I call you Will?" Isaiah called out, as the applause died.

Shakespeare raised an eyebrow.

"What do we call you, then?" Isaiah asked.

"The Bard of Avon."

After this answer, bold and pretentious, the class drew back a little. Shakespeare didn't seem to mind. He walked up and down, perfectly possessed, actually enjoying the growing distance between him and his audience.

Nina tried to catch Collin's eye, to remind him of the Q&A they'd planned. But Collin ignored her. He gazed coolly at the class, and, fascinated, they stared back at him. Without a word, he attracted their attention, offering no greeting, no information, nothing but suspense.

"We prepared some questions." Nina spoke as much to her students as to Shakespeare. "Who'd like to start?" She looked out at the students, issuing a silent appeal. Anyone?

Finally, Chandra asked in her small voice, "When did you start writing?"

"When my players needed parts."

"What's your favorite play?" asked Isaiah.

"The one that pays."

Another pause, and Nina gestured to Jonee, who read from her open notebook: "Who did you write the sonnets for?"

"None but you," Shakespeare cried gallantly, and took her by the hand!

The class sniggered. Holding hands with Jonee? She was this large, pale, seriously depressing girl, and there she was, with Shakespeare escorting her to the front of the room, seating her on Miss Lazare's own desk.

Khalil laughed so hard he started coughing. "And you!" Shakespeare added, offering his hand to Khalil as well.

The class exploded with whoops and catcalls, as Khalil shrank back.

Shakespeare knelt down on the spot. *"Shall I compare thee to a summer's day?"* He looked adoringly at Khalil's stubble and his dreadlocks, then gazed into the boy's dark eyes.

No! Nina thought. She hovered behind Khalil's chair, trying to catch Collin's attention.

"Thou art more lovely and more temperate . . ."

"Holy shit!" Khalil interjected, even as Nina gestured for Collin to stop.

"Rough winds do shake the darling buds of May."

The class was in hysterics.

"Back off!" Khalil snarled.

In vain, Nina told her students to settle down. Unheard, her explanation that actually this sonnet was written for a young man. Doubled over, clutching themselves, kids were falling out of their chairs—all but Khalil, who lost his cool completely, and shoved Shakespeare with two hands.

The Bard lost his balance, since he had been down on one knee, but he recovered fast, springing to his feet.

"Let's take a moment here," Nina said, trying to intercede, but Shakespeare waved her off and turned toward Jonee, still sitting where he had left her on Nina's gray Steelcase desk.

"Sometime too hot the eye of heaven shines . . ." he told Jonee. You could see all the blood rush to her face as everyone's attention turned toward her. *"And often is his gold complexion dimmed."*

The class watched in shock. How could the Bard have known that Jonee panicked if you even looked at her? She had a thing where she could hyperventilate at any moment. She could do it now, even as Shakespeare knelt down, velvet cloak streaming around him. He spoke to her as though they were alone. Jonee's eyes widened as he declared, *"And every fair from fair sometime declines . . ."*

Jonee gasped, breathing faster and then faster. Her classmates watched Miss Lazare pluck at Shakespeare's sleeve—to no avail. Jonee's cheeks burned redder than her limp strawberry-blond hair. She swayed.

Miss Lazare tried to stand between Shakespeare and his victim. He waved Lazare away. The guy was hard-core.

Even Anton, who usually kept his head down, was on the edge of his seat. Fully recovered from the assault on his sexuality, Khalil grinned in disbelief. This was going to be the most amazing class in the history of the school; Shakespeare could be causing a medical emergency.

Meanwhile, Shakespeare sounded blissed. *"But thy eternal summer shall not fade,"* he intoned, looking deep into Jonee's eyes.

The Bard got a standing ovation, especially when Jonee flumped off the desk. She would have fallen in a heap, if not for the Bard's steadying hand. Her classmates shouted, "Encore! Encore!" Everybody saw the faint smile on Jonee's face as Shakespeare returned her to her seat.

Nina saw Collin raise a frenzy and then with a flick of his hand, silence the whole class. She watched him and she thought, You should have it all—money, fame, every success.

Collin himself broke into her reverie. He whipped around and bowed to her. Then, right in front of all her students, he took her by the hand. There she'd been, enjoying the show. Now suddenly she was in it. "No. No!" she whispered. Unfair to ambush her like that! "Collin," she begged under her breath.

Her kids thought this was hilarious. "Pray be seated," Shakespeare said, and Lazare was shaking her head, but she had to listen. The guy was a rock star. She took the hot seat atop her desk.

Shakespeare didn't kneel this time. Everybody watched as he looked Lazare up and down. She was so embarrassed she couldn't even meet his eye. Whooo! The guy was her boyfriend. The more she tried to hide it, the more it showed.

With a wave of his hand, Shakespeare signaled his next speech.

"My mistress' eyes," he said, *"are nothing like the sun; / Coral is far more red than her lips' red."*

Oh God, Nina thought, knowing what was coming, but he recited so well. The kids loved him, and loved her embarrassment even more.

Shakespeare took a step back to view her in profile. *"If snow be white, why then her breasts are dun."*

"Owwww!"

"Her breasts are *dung?*"

"If hairs be wires . . ."—Shakespeare lifted a lock of Nina's hair—*"black wires grow on her head."*

"Hey," Nina whispered. She had planned a discussion of playwriting and acting, costuming, performing at the Globe Theatre. "Collin."

Either he ignored her or he couldn't hear. He had galvanized the class, now cheering.

"I have seen roses damasked, red and white, / But no such roses see I in her cheeks; And in some perfumes is there more delight"—the Bard turned away—*"Than in the breath that from my mistress reeks . . ."*

"Ewww!"

"Death match! Death match!" the students screamed.

Isaiah called, "Miss, don't let him tear you down!"

"I love to hear her speak, yet well I know / That music hath a far more pleasing sound."

"Kill! Kill!"

"I grant I never saw a goddess go; / My mistress when she walks treads on the ground. / And yet . . ." Shakespeare paused and looked out at the class and they hushed, wondering what he would do.

He fell to his knees and pulled a single red plastic rose from his

sleeve. "Awwww," chorused the class, amused, but also disappointed to see him cave.

Sean said, "Miss? You gonna *accept* that from him?"

"Reject! Reject!" the class thundered.

Nina shook her head. Her kids cheered as she turned the flower
down.

Despite this, Shakespeare had the last word: *"And yet, by heaven,
I think my love as rare / As any she belied with false compare."*

Applause and cheers and school bells ringing. Wait. Those were
alarms pulsing in the halls. Kids groaned and started shuffling for
the door. As usual, whenever anything fun happened, DeLaurentis
hit them with a fire drill.

15

Open Door

Collin was still carrying the plastic rose when everybody trooped outside. Students and staff gathered in the designated area behind the school, where Mr. DeLaurentis waited, furious, in his charcoal-gray suit. This was not a scheduled fire drill, so either a real fire was raging somewhere in the building, or some kid had pulled the alarm.

"Line up! Line up!" DeLaurentis barked into his electric bullhorn, as students poured out of the building, but no one paid attention. Fire trucks had already arrived, and firemen were tromping into the school with empty hoses trailing behind them. Meanwhile, it was so close to dismissal that the students figured February break had started. *Yes!* The problem was their teachers had rushed them out the door without coats. They had to huddle and hug each other to stay warm.

Like temporary parents, Collin and Nina shepherded their class to the school's spiked black iron fence.

"Yo, Shakespeare," one of the boys called out, but Collin wasn't Shakespeare anymore.

"No reentry," blared Mr. DeLaurentis. "No reentry."

"Bard of Avon," Isaiah asked, "you coming back?"

Collin stole a look at Nina, but she glanced away.

"Did I say you could leave?" Mrs. West was confronting a tall blond kid edging toward the street. "Did I dismiss you, Aidan?"

"Come on, Nina," Collin said, but she wouldn't speak to him where her students could overhear.

"Down. No climbing!" DeLaurentis crackled, even as the student body surged.

Nina saw Aidan close his eyes and lean against the fence. There was something grand about his silent resignation, a royal insolence.

Kids and teachers waited for what felt like hours. In fact, after twenty minutes, the returning firefighters reported no fire, no smoke, no evidence of faulty wiring. The official cause for evacuation was some student, and DeLaurentis was talking about consequences, but no one stuck around to listen, because the fire marshal had just given the all-clear.

In the throng of students racing to empty lockers for vacation week, Collin cleared a path, sheltering Nina with his arm. At last he opened the door for Nina and they took refuge in her empty classroom.

"Phew." Collin tried to keep it light. "Next time we'll do the theater games."

She was picking up stray papers, rescuing paperbacks splayed open on the floor.

"Nina?"

She turned to face him. "I never said you could recite sonnets to me in front of my class."

"I know, but—"

"I asked you to stop!"

"You were laughing." He crossed the room to make his appeal.

"Why didn't you listen?"

"Sorry. I gave you away. The secret's out. You have a crazy boyfriend."

"I wanted this lesson to be about Shakespeare, not you."

"It *was* about Shakespeare," he retorted. "And what's the big deal? The kids already know that you're in love with him."

"You don't understand. They hardly listen to me. I've barely got them sitting down."

He tossed hat and plastic rose onto her desk. "I wasn't trying to embarrass you."

"No. Just having fun at my expense."

"That's not fair."

"Well, what's fair, Collin?"

"I don't know." He took her hands.

He was hard to resist; he was so warm. "I was embarrassed," she admitted. "and I was . . ."

"What?"

"Jealous," she confessed. "You're just . . . surprising. I don't know what to do with you."

He forgot the classroom door was open. He cupped her face in his hands and kissed her.

As if on cue, some kid whistled in the hall.

They sprang apart.

"No more sonnets," he assured her. "No more school visits. I don't want to mess up your life."

Her response surprised him. "I don't want to mess up yours."

"Yeah, I don't think there's any danger."

"I don't want to do the wrong thing."

"Go ahead," he said, not knowing what she meant. "Do the wrong thing. You need the practice."

"You're so talented . . ." she began.

Now his eyes hardened. His body tensed as he guessed where this was going. He had listened to this speech from his mother, from Noelle, from every other serious girlfriend, and he felt a kind of grief to hear Nina start in on him now. Two months before, they had been sledding in Danehy Park. Now the long talks had begun.

She said, "You could do a lot more, and earn a lot more, and have a career if you want."

His voice was cold. "I'm not going back to school."

"It's just an idea—and I keep debating whether to tell you." She took a breath. "I could take you to Arkadia."

"Take me?"

"Well . . . introduce you . . ."

"That's what's on your mind. You want to introduce me to Arkadia."

"I do and I don't," she confessed.

"That's what you're debating. Whether to leave me in my poor miserable life, or invite me to the big leagues?"

"I didn't mean it to come out that way."

"I know!" He almost laughed. "That's the arrogant part. It comes naturally."

"Wait. Let me explain."

"You don't have to explain. I understand."

She persisted. "Listen."

"I don't need you to find me a job. I'm not your charity. I'm not your good deed, okay? I don't want help."

Hands on her hips, she protested, "I let you help me! I let you embarrass me in front of my whole class."

"That was nothing. You're talking about a job. You've got my whole career planned out."

"I don't," she said. "I don't want to change you or mess up your art."

"You've planned so far ahead you're already up to feeling guilty about it."

"Don't tell me what I'm planning."

"Don't tell me what to do."

"I'm not! And don't assume you'd get a job."

She began rubbing out vocabulary words with her felt eraser. "You're the arrogant one."

He didn't answer.

"You don't even listen."

"I'm listening," Collin retorted.

"Is it that hard for you to accept a favor?"

"Stop." He took the eraser from her hand and drenched it with water from the bottle on her desk. Then he wiped her cloudy board until it was sleek and black again.

"You would blow them all away."

"Let's go."

"Okay." She picked up her bag, but then she said, "Just let me introduce you to my father."

"He won't meet with me."

"Yes, he will."

"Because of you."

"Well, that has to be enough."

He shot her a look.

"Can't you just take a chance?"

"You're not offering me a chance," he said. "You're offering a gift, out of the goodness of your privileged heart."

For a long moment she didn't answer.

Young as she was, she understood her position. She could teach for two years or she could quit tomorrow. She could travel, study abroad, go to law school, or do nothing at all. She didn't need to earn a living. Nothing kept her at Emerson but idealism and interest. "It's not a gift," she said at last. "It's not a job. It's just an open door."

"Thanks. I'll open my own doors."

She leaned against her desk. "And how will you do that?"

"None of your business."

Nina thought of Collin's theatrics, and her students' laughter— his crazy visit. "That's what I should have told you!"

"You're right," he said. "I'm sorry. Let's get out of here and have a drink."

Even then, she persisted. "Just think about it."

"I told you I don't want help."

"I know," she said, "but you deserve it."

Those words pierced him. His mother and his girlfriends and his instructors always accused him. He was wasting his time. He wasn't living up to his potential. Nina said the thing he hardly dared to tell himself.

"What's wrong?" she asked, searching his bright eyes.

"Nothing." He wrapped her in his cape.

He held her in his arms and the velvet cape trailed all around her shoulders. Yes, she thought. Yes he would listen to her, but she was half afraid of what she'd done.

In silence they headed out together. Seriously, almost ceremonially, he took his plumed hat from her desk. She turned off the lights and he followed her out into the hall, where janitors roared up and down with vacuum canisters strapped onto their backs.

"I can't program," he reminded Nina.

"That wouldn't matter."

"Yes, it would."

"No, no, no. They'll know what to do with you."

16

The Interview

Collin wore a button-down shirt, blue-striped, clean but wrinkled and papery. Where had he found it? Of course Nina couldn't ask. Her father was sitting next to her, ordering wine, and Collin had been exiled across the table.

They were eating dinner at Harvest, and Collin was trying not to stare. Viktor was fifty-four, but he didn't look old. He looked like a guy who woke at dawn to bike up mountains and ford icy streams. His eyes were black, his nose craggy. His dark hair and bushy eyebrows stood up as if to say, Who're you calling short? He smiled to himself as though delighted with his own ideas—and why not? They were worth a ton of money. Nina's father set Collin on edge immediately. Collin saw the laughing ferocity in Viktor's eyes.

"Nina tells me you act and sing and dance and draw, and I don't know what else," Nina's father said. "Jack of all trades."

Fuck you, Collin thought. "I draw," he said.

"Nina says you're very good."

"Dad!" Nina exclaimed. Clearly he hadn't even opened Collin's portfolio.

Viktor heard the reproach. Nina loved him, but she judged him. Even as a small girl, she'd studied him, until he'd had to look away.

Once, when he was leaving for the airport, he'd knelt down to apologize. "I wish I could stay."

"Why are you going, then?" she had demanded.

Recently, in the heat of argument, she had accused him of ignoring her. "You see," he'd declared. "That proves it. You're my conscience." She had been his family before he had a family. (It did not occur to him to count her mother.) Once it had been the two of them—Viktor and his gray-eyed child, his smaller, better self.

Now Nina drew herself up, as if to say, This is your big gesture? Agreeing to have dinner? And Viktor was sorry. For a moment he felt guilty, but the moment passed.

"Where did you go to school?" he asked Collin.

"MassArt. But I'm still there. I mean technically I'm—"

"Enrolled?"

"Well, not currently, but—"

"The best ones leave," Viktor said. His words were conciliatory, his tone half-mocking. "The best ones teach themselves."

They ate steaks and drank a dark Bordeaux, and Viktor watched Collin. "Did you study game design?"

Slow down, Collin told himself, as he drank his second glass of wine. "Not exactly," he told Viktor, "but I have a long-standing interest in EverWhen, so . . ." The more he drank, the more he found in the Bordeaux. Autumn and dusky stairwells, and dark old jewels and soft lead pencils sinking into blotting paper. He began to feel warm. Viktor was drinking too, but the wine didn't change him; it was Collin who felt overheated, dangerously glib. Pace yourself, he thought, but he kept talking fast. "I was a gamer when I was younger, and I know the monsters. For example, I can draw every major dragon in EverWhen."

"But not the minor ones?" Viktor asked lightly.

"I can draw them too," said Collin. "And the serpents, basilisks, and hydras, Gnomes, Elves, mermaids, bears, wolves . . ." Nina was looking at him anxiously, but he didn't stop. "Birds of prey, owls, phoenixes . . ."

"In other words—" Viktor began.

"Everything," Collin cut him off boldly.

"Excellent," Viktor said, without a flicker of surprise. Some fans were like that. Everheads programmed their own game mods, copied screenshots, directed their own films. Arkadia kept online galleries of their art, thousands of drawings and paintings. Viktor appreciated these tributes, but they didn't excite him. He studied optics, graphics, vision, the interplay of imagination and perception. He lived for innovation, not obsessive imitation. "I'll tell you where to send your stuff."

Collin reminded Nina's father, "I've already sent my stuff to you."

Nina, Viktor thought. What have you been promising this kid?

She shot him a look that meant, Stop! You're overbearing and dismissive.

Viktor was hurt. He wasn't dismissive; he saw through people quickly. He wasn't overbearing; he was busy.

"Can I get you some dessert?" the waiter asked.

Viktor said, "No, thank you."

Collin glanced at Nina, who sat with hands clasped together on the table. So much for her sweet, arrogant idea. She knew her father, but Collin knew something about sending unsolicited portfolios. He might have reached across or smiled to reassure her. I don't care; it doesn't matter. The wine was good and I forgive you for the rest. But at that moment Collin cared greatly. He felt an intense desire to prove himself, as soon as he realized he didn't stand a chance.

"Coffee?" the waiter suggested.

"Just the check," said Viktor.

But Collin told the waiter, "Just a pen."

When the check arrived, Nina's heart stopped as Collin snatched it out of Viktor's hands. Without even glancing at the numbers, he flipped the little paper over and began drawing on the back, working over the entire surface with the restaurant's black ballpoint. The waiter returned long before he finished, and Viktor had to request another check. He said, "We're having this one embellished."

Collin kept his head down, scribing the paper, so small and flimsy, cross-hatching his shadows, exhausting the pen's ink supply. Viktor watched with mild interest. Nina held her breath.

"Here." Unsmiling, Collin handed Viktor his drawing.

Viktor squinted at the drawing, holding it close and then farther away.

Nina plucked Viktor's reading glasses from his breast pocket. "Put these on."

Viktor sensed his daughter's eagerness, her tremendous hope as the drawing came into focus. "Look at that," he said gently. "It's the ouroboros."

Collin had drawn the dragon exactly as he appeared in Ever-When. Slinky, snarky, with evil needle-teeth. Somehow, even in ballpoint, the ouroboros took on a silvery sheen, scales delicately rendered, claws distinct, serpentine body curled around a treasure chest overflowing with gold coins. The dragon's head was long and vicious, jaws bloodied, eyes rolling backward in ecstatic pain as it devoured its own tail. Collin had used every millimeter, puncturing the paper more than once.

Now, as Viktor held the drawing between his thumb and forefinger, he saw Collin for the first time. Here was a young man who could dash off a perfect dragon in five minutes, drunk. This was a prodigious act of illustration—not only lively but anatomically correct. Did Collin have total recall of the dragon's five claws? Had he studied the beast's twenty-one spikes descending in size down his back? Viktor looked over the top of his reading glasses at Collin. "What other monsters did you say you draw?"

"All of them."

Viktor considered his own empire and the myriad creatures in it. No one could remember all of them, let alone draw each one from memory.

Even so, Collin boasted, "I can draw anything."

Viktor smiled as he studied the fierce dragon in his hands.

Come on, Dad, thought Nina. Say it. He's an artist.

Viktor made her wait. He loved pleasing Nina. Pretending he cared about her friends was much less satisfying. Even so, he liked the dragon's looping body—back arching, scales spiking. Collin had caught the monster's self-destroying spirit. "It's good," he said, at last.

Nina was almost too glad. "It would have been even better with a decent pen."

"I don't like pen in general." Collin's face was flushed. "I like to work in chalk. Chalk is pretty much my forte, because you can do so much with dust."

"I can understand that," Viktor said. "I do a lot of work with dust."

Collin nodded. "I like smudging colors, and layering."

"I want to show you something," Viktor said.

They drove out to Waltham in Viktor's little BMW, Nina and her father in the front, Collin folded queasily in back. The car was hardly meant for passengers. Hostages, maybe, with their legs trussed up around their ears.

It was a wet February night, as they sped past glass hotels and low-slung office parks. Viktor was talking to Nina in a low voice and Collin couldn't hear the conversation. He felt like cargo, until Nina turned around to look at him. She looked excited as a child.

When they arrived, Collin saw that Arkadia had grown since he and Darius had visited as kids. Like a space colony, its polygonal buildings extended on and on into the night.

There were the usual glass doors and guards. There was a guest book, and Collin got a sticky name tag printed VISITOR. There were desks and workstations. There was a glass atrium set up as a café. However, on examination, every ordinary feature seemed a little strange. Glass doors darkened as visitors passed through. A life-size sculpture of Toth, the mountain king, loomed over the salad bar, commanding attention with his bear's head and great clawed paws.

Viktor led the way through clusters of cubicles. Corporate enough, but as they walked, the cubicles grew larger, and their gray walls taller. It was like entering a forest. With each step, Arkadia grew darker. Programmers clustered at monitors like moths to flames. As his eyes adjusted, Collin saw bits of EverWhen on each monitor, fragments of the Trackless Wood, Elves battling tarry monsters.

"Where's Peter?" Viktor asked. Despite the late hour, Arkadia was full of people. It might have been the middle of the day. "Anyone seen Peter?"

Employees looked up, startled by the sudden visit. They seemed almost afraid to answer. "I saw him heading over there," one woman ventured.

"Hello?" Viktor was standing before a self-contained room, a windowless cabin in the darkness. He opened the door to a cube insulated and baffled with wavy black foam, a music studio dominated by huge black speakers. There were multiple electric guitars, black piano keyboards, giant computer screens. A burly, bearded man was sitting there, reading a printed book to a little boy in pajamas, visible on his monitor.

"That's Nicholas," Nina whispered to Collin. "He's a sound engineer."

Nicholas spun around in his swivel chair to greet them. He wore a Jerry Garcia T-shirt and his voice was husky. He looked like a retired football player, and he sounded like a rocker before his first cup of coffee. "Bedtime story for my kid."

"Go on, go on!" Viktor encouraged him.

"Of course the Neverland had been make-believe in those days," read Nicholas, *"but it was real now . . ."* He waved as his visitors backed out, shutting the heavy door behind them.

Stranger and stranger, Arkadia glowed with Whennish light. Viktor led Collin and Nina into a misty corridor. Ethereal shapes appeared, insubstantial from a distance, overwhelming up close. Collin flinched as a dark leopard approached with golden eyes. A few steps farther, he nearly tripped over a bloody giant lying at his feet. Craggy mountains rose up in the distance. He could see an EXIT sign and then the outlines of a door embedded in the rock face, but the door itself was bursting into flame.

"Nina," Collin whispered. Dazzled, he was looking everywhere at once, but she looked at him alone.

"There's so much more," Nina told him.

Collin watched in awe as Nina walked through each illusion. She was the magician's daughter, and mountains shattered, dragons shrank before her. Monsters turned to dust motes in her wake.

They walked into another dark space, a labyrinth of tall black walls, each workstation a peephole, a glimpse of river, a dark cavern, or white bats. Curious, the nearest animators glanced up at Viktor. "These are our hellions," Viktor said. "And this is Peter, their developer."

A tall man pushed his swivel chair away from his desk.

Peter was ten years younger, his brother's partner, but not quite his equal. Viktor's technology drove the company and much of the marketplace as well. Peter's role as developer, scheduler, manager, and coordinator of every team at UnderWorld was secondary. Nevertheless, Peter had powers of his own. Storyteller, Gorey winner, he was Arkadia's chief geographer, historian, world-builder. The press called him the Dark Lord, while Viktor was simply CEO.

Collin was amazed by Peter's height, his leonine body, his long dark hair and glowing eyes, more gold than brown, like liquid amber. Collin couldn't help staring, but Peter looked at his niece alone.

Viktor said, "Here's our artist, Nina's friend."

"Any friend of Nina's," Peter said.

Nervous, Nina tried to read her uncle's face, and he gazed back, amused. He was mesmerizing, strange. He had performed card tricks for Nina when she was small. Coin tricks, sleight of hand. He had told stories of blood and magic, seven brothers sewing wings into their flesh as they turned into swans, princesses dismembering frogs. He had taught her the violence in fairy tales, and the cruelty of dragonflies. If he built a sand castle with Nina, he'd show her how to build a siege ramp too. And then there came a time when she rejected him. She had watched him enchant young artists and then throw their work away. She had seen him in the recording booth with Julianne. He had never touched her friend, but she'd caught his predatory gaze.

"He's not just any artist," Nina said, and Peter heard the warning in her voice: Don't hurt him. Don't dismiss him.

Peter turned to Collin. "What kind of artist are you?"

"Any kind you want."

You're cute, Peter thought. Eager, insubstantial. "What if I want Rembrandt?"

His questions nettled Collin. They were insistent, but idle as well. Peter leaned back against the edge of a cubicle and his whole body seemed to say, I'm already bored with you. "I couldn't *be* Rembrandt," Collin said, "but I could draw a Rembrandt."

"So you're not an artist. You're a copyist."

"I'm both." Asshole, Collin added silently.

Peter led the way to a huge whiteboard. Covering half a wall, its surface was adorned with diagrams and flow charts, doodles and sketches.

Collin frowned. He hated dry-erase markers, their scanty ink, their faded colors and anemic lines. He was up for anything—but how could he show Peter what he could do?

Peter seemed to read his mind. He dipped his finger in the aluminum chalk tray at the bottom of the board, and the white surface, along with all its graffiti, disappeared, changing to pure glossy black. Then he handed Collin a pair of plastic styluses, one thick, one thin. "You've got your colors here." Peter showed Collin the array of colored squares in the chalk tray. "Just dip the stylus." Peter demonstrated with a quick sketch of the girl from EverSea. Collin recognized Nina immediately, ten, maybe eleven, with her hair falling over her shoulders.

Nina had never told Collin that Peter could draw. The sketch was simple and unshaded, just a line drawing in silver, and yet it conveyed a kind of magic. Peter's hand was so light, the expression on Nina's face so tender.

Peter cleared the board with a brush of his hand. "Okay, let's see what you can do."

Tentatively, Collin touched the electronic chalk tray with the thin stylus and saw the tip turn green. He touched the board and left a dot. As he applied pressure his dot expanded into a green pool, a lake.

He had never played with an electronic board like this. He drew one line and then another. He scribbled with the wireless chalk, and the board picked up his slightest gesture, responding to his every touch. He could dip into any of a hundred colors, and try a thousand shades. He met with no resistance, and no crumbling. With ordinary chalk he would layer, fuss, and wet his sticks to produce saturated color; here his tints were luminous each time.

Lines came fast; color flowed endlessly. The trouble was the surface felt so slick. He was like a runner trying ice skates for the first time. He could not control his strokes. Every time he tried, his stylus glided out from under him. He had to erase, brushing away his blunders with his hand. "Shit. Sorry!" he murmured. "I'm not . . ." He tried again, and then again, and all the time he sensed Peter growing colder.

Nina turned on her uncle. "Why can't he have pen and paper?"

"What are those?" Peter replied.

"Take your time," said Viktor, enjoying the sport.

Collin knew he couldn't take his time. He had to figure this out *now*. He had about half a minute before Peter lost interest altogether.

Shut them out, he thought, as he glared at the glossy board. Viktor, Peter. Even Nina. He had to forget her hopes for him. Lighten your strokes. Limit yourself. Keep the stylus under you. Don't overdraw.

He began an easy dragon, an ordinary fire-eater with rolling eyes and iridescent wings. He drew the dragon big, working its undulating body across the length of the board. Then he drew a dragon's nest. He didn't try for every detail; he practiced with the thick stylus until he had the nest just right. Now he drew a dragon with its breath aflame. With his thin stylus he added scales and claws, jagged, sooty teeth.

Building confidence, he drew faster. A phoenix swooping through the air. A silver falcon. Then, tiring of birds and flying monsters, he brushed them away with his arm, erasing with his shirtsleeve.

"Oh." Nina sighed. Collin's drawings bloomed like fireworks, dazzling and brief.

"Don't worry," Viktor said, because the board saved each image, captured every stroke.

Collin drew Gnomes and Fire Elves, forest creatures, deer camouflaged in trees. He still slipped, but he corrected quickly. He understood the surface now. With each drawing, Collin grew bolder; his work grew more precise. The board changed into a shimmering landscape and the room began to change as well. He sensed hellions gathering to watch.

Peter stood among them and he felt a rush of jealous pleasure—surprise at Collin's skill, admiration of his line. When Peter glanced at Nina she met his eye as if to say, You see?

Hellions stood in silence as Collin drew a riderless horse, a stallion tossing its long mane and tail. He didn't know there was a horse in UnderWorld. He only knew he had an audience.

He drew the horse huge, devouring the wall. He was working freely now with his whole arm. Galloping across the blackboard, Collin's horse was fearsome, and also strangely beautiful. In silver lines alone, in two dimensions only, Collin animated the horse's corded muscles, its powerful legs, and flying feet. Intent on his work, he couldn't see Nina's rapt expression or Viktor's triumphant smile. He saw none of this, but he sensed Peter drawing closer. Now I have you, Collin thought.

When Collin finished he stepped back amid a rustling, a whispering from the crowd. A mix of admiration and foreboding, because Collin's horse was better than the one in UnderWorld. More powerful, more dynamic, and subtler too. The horse they had appeared cartoonish in comparison. The hellions knew, before Peter said a word. They saw fresh art coming, long days and sleepless nights ahead. They saw it all, even before Peter pointed to Collin's stallion and said, "I want that."

17

Arkadia

When Collin started working at Arkadia, he collected enough company T-shirts, caps, ear warmers, and fleece vests to outfit everyone in Theater Without Walls. He got his own Arkadian backpack and water bottle and high-fidelity headphones for blasting music late at night. He had never seen so many gaming toys—not just electronics, but miniatures of every beast and warrior. He could have played for hours with the Elves, no bigger than toy soldiers, but far more beautiful, with their blue hair and meticulously painted clothes. Some carried longbows, some knelt to shoot atop computer monitors, some guarded keyboards, brandishing their needle swords. Once, at night, he stumbled upon an entire squadron lined up in formation on the floor.

Each day, Collin discovered something new, a funhouse mirror, a hall wallpapered in a skull print. Ping-Pong, foosball, mini basketball. He found a cache of real skeletons, an art book on Michelangelo, a war room with a map of the world projected on the wall. In this map's glow, a handful of troubleshooters manned workstations, watching for power outages and natural disasters that could short-circuit Arkadia's network and interrupt players' negotiations and alliances, their qwests and feuds.

The place was scientific and theatrical. Meetings addressed the physics of an avalanche, the look and feel of UnderWorld's caverns, the speed of flaming arrows, the way a castle might explode. Testers reported back on lags. For example, when you were mowing down your enemies in battle, you wanted them to fall before you instantly. Death throes were fun to watch when you were fighting one-on-one, but in the aggregate they dragged. Speed, fluidity, efficiency: These weren't just computational problems, they were artistic problems too. You could accelerate a war with visual shortcuts. "Know your history," Peter said, and he showed classic sequences from World of Warcraft and Call of Duty and Grand Theft Auto.

A long-haired archivist named Robbie presided over a cache of antique Game Boys, X-Boxes, and arcade consoles. He told Collin, "I played Pong before you were born."

Tempted, Collin studied the library of boxed classics, everything from American McGee's Alice to the Bitmap Brothers' Z. Myst, with its subtle island veiled in cloud. Reluctantly, he turned away. He saw how people worked, watched Peter deliver schedules and agendas. UnderWorld was a vast construction project, a virtual cathedral. Animators, modelers, and programmers all scrummed together in small pods, and together the pods built up the game.

He had signed and initialed a thirty-page contract filled with references to company ownership, licensing, and intellectual property. He had taught his final class at Broadway Bicycle, and waited his last tables at Grendel's. Samantha presented him with her bartender's business card. "Hey, think of me for parties."

Parties! He wasn't thinking about parties. He was living, breathing, dreaming horses. He drew them in silhouette, in small black thumbnails, racing, turning, leaping on his slate. Peter judged each variant—one small and muscular like a mustang, one massive, one slender, built to run. He chose elements he liked and Collin worked up a detailed study, a horse noble but also wild, with dark, rolling eyes, broad shoulders, nervous ears, rough mane and tail.

If Peter approved an image you were golden. More often, he dismissed his artists' work. These were not quiet critiques, nor were they cushioned with encouragement. Peter used group meetings to tear into artists, ripping them apart. Hellions called it getting drawn and quartered.

"I didn't think this could get worse," Peter told an artist named Akosh. "Somehow you found a way."

Collin watched with twenty others as Peter stood at the whiteboard and destroyed an entire winter landscape, gorgeous trees knee-deep in snow. He slashed the forest through with one black stroke.

"It's pale, it's soft, it's *pretty*," Peter said, and Collin saw that "pretty" was a felony.

"As for you . . ." Peter cleared the board and brought up a sketch by an artist named Obi. "You call this a knight? I asked for rust. I told you his sword is filthy. What is this shit?" With his stylus Peter roughened armor, bloodied the knight's gleaming weapon.

"I'll change it," Obi said.

"Don't change it. Start over."

"Okay."

Obi's conciliatory tone only irritated Peter further. "Okay. Okay, I'll change it. *No.* Don't tell me what you think I want to hear. Do it right the first time."

Obi ventured, "I thought you wanted the knight first and then we'd modify it."

Peter didn't answer this. He stood there staring at Obi until the hapless artist had to look away. "I'm not interested in what you thought," Peter said at last. He seemed at that moment a monarch, denying all history and memory. Nothing mattered but his current inclination.

"He's harsh," Collin told Nina.

Her reply surprised him. "That's good. You know where you stand."

"Have you ever heard him?" Collin asked in disbelief.

She nodded. "Praise is worse."

"Why?"

"That's where he messes with your mind."

In fact Peter had singled Collin out for commendation. "Okay," he said when Collin showed him his new horses. Collin could scarcely believe it. Compared to what he'd heard, "okay" seemed a precious gem. He treasured that single word for days. "Could be interesting," Peter added on another occasion, and Collin wanted to leap with joy. He remembered Nina's words, but Peter didn't lavish praise on Collin. Instead, he lavished time.

Peter began watching Collin work, and even guiding Collin as he drew. "More sinew. Ears back. Neck outstretched," he directed, as Collin made mid-course corrections.

Other hellions watched Peter work with Collin. True, Collin stood out as a draftsman. Some artists could talk about procedural shaders and facial animation systems. Some could sculpt a gorgeous scene with aeroflakes. But nobody could draw like Collin. As Peter's favorite, he didn't win friends, but gradually he earned respect. Arkadians would crowd around at lunch to see his horses, and he began posting sketches on his cubicle walls.

In those early days he took his slate and stylus everywhere. He worked at home and at lunch, and even on the company shuttle bus. In the seat next to him, Collin's Brazilian scrum master, Tomas, watched a horse emerge white against the black surface of the slate. Behind them, Akosh leaned over the back of Collin's seat, as did Obi, whose chestnut hair flowed almost to his waist, in the style of the Elvish kings. Only one person on the shuttle held herself apart. It seemed a matter of pride. She wouldn't let Collin catch her watching.

Her name was Daphne. She had just graduated from Full Sail

University, and she worked in marketing. Her face was impudent, her dark hair cropped short. Her eyes were pure blue, her expression mocking. She wore black jeans and a CU sweatshirt, so she was all covered up, whether at her desk, or gaming late at night. Only her hands showed, and Collin found himself gazing at the flowers tattooed on her wrists. The petals were finely drawn, as if they'd been scribed in India ink. He wondered who had done the work, and if the design continued up her arms.

Daphne wasn't a programmer, and she wasn't an artist, and she wasn't really a tester, but she was a brilliant gamer. Like a chess master, she could play multiple games at once. She would stand in a pool of light with her avatars lit up around her as she showed off unreleased UnderWorld to the select few—those beta gamers she found most extreme, all kids, all boys.

Fluid as a dancer, she darted in and out of worlds. No hellion could beat her in a duel. Nobody even came close, and Collin loved to watch her take her colleagues down. She took such pleasure in it; you couldn't begrudge her gloating. Sometimes she would take a bow. Peter liked to watch as well, and this was the other thing that fascinated Collin. Peter was the only one who rattled Daphne. In his presence her whole body tensed. She shot her virtual arrows and she missed. No one was immune to Nina's uncle. No one except Nina herself—but then she didn't work for him.

Hellions feared Peter, but they also worshipped him, waiting for him as he strode the halls, following him with questions. They competed for answers and decisions, but most of all for Peter's sketches. His vision was dark and strange and always new. He never developed drawings; he left his sketches bare and suggestive, a landscape ever so subtly wrong, an imminent nightmare. These were the challenges he set his artists, and then he wondered why they couldn't read his mind.

Collin began to see what Peter was about. Nina's uncle detested all things shiny, perfect, new. He was building a world of darkness, decay, infection, and Collin adapted quickly to this vision. He drew Peter to him with his facility and speed, and soon Peter was thinking out loud while Collin took down ideas on his slate. "A white dragon," Peter said. As Collin sketched, Peter ordered, "Keep the wings and lose the scales. No. Scales on the body. Open wings. Keep opening." Collin drew wings opening big enough to fill a room. "Bigger," Peter said. "Wings big enough to block the sun." An hour passed, but it felt like just a minute. Collin's drawing evolved that fast.

Then Peter lost interest and demanded something new. "Two horses," he said, as though he were ordering at a restaurant. When Collin drew the horses, Peter rejected them instantly. "What are they, twins? Nobody can tell them apart. Again."

Collin looked up, startled.

"I said draw them again."

Peter never let up, but Collin realized this was a sign of favor. He had won Peter's attention.

All the others noticed. Jealous, they watched Collin draw for Peter. Even Daphne gave up acting cool and hovered, challenging Collin for Peter's time. She caught Peter's attention when she reported news of her campaign. "We've got CU trending now." She held up a tablet, offering him fresh numbers.

Whenever Peter worked with Collin, she waited on the periphery. Eventually she began looking at Collin's work. She started glancing and then she began watching him at night when she thought he wasn't looking. At last she scooted her swivel chair to his workstation to gaze at the horses on his monitor.

"Seriously?" she said under her breath.

"What?"

He watched her struggle with herself. She wouldn't compliment him. No, she would not give him the satisfaction. "Is that all you can do?"

"Jealous?" Collin teased.

"You wish!"

He didn't know Daphne, but her trash talk amused him. He felt chosen by them both—Peter the master, and Daphne the marketer. But they were different. Peter demanded while Daphne teased. Peter pushed while Daphne bantered. There was something hard about Daphne, and also sweet. He felt at ease with her, and confused by her as well. He couldn't tell what she really thought of him.

Almost unconsciously he began sketching Daphne on his electronic slate, covering the surface with her clever face, her cropped hair and wide blue eyes. He drew Daphne working at her terminal with her legs tucked under her. He drew her in Elvish guise, delicate in thin draperies, and then he sketched her gaming like a boy, brandishing an imaginary sword.

"What are you doing?" she said.

"Nothing. Drawing you."

She drew close and closer. He could feel her quick breath. Then she brushed his slate clean with the cuff of her sleeve. "I never said you could."

"I didn't know I had to ask!"

"Yeah, I'm copyright."

"You can't copyright yourself."

"Well, you have to ask permission."

"Why? I don't need permission to look at you," Collin pointed out.

"Yes, you do." For just a moment, she covered his eyes with her small hand.

He laughed.

"What?" she demanded, mock seriously.

"You really want me to stop drawing you?"

She had a smile too quick to capture. Her eyes shone with fun. "I want to play with you."

The first time they fought in EverWhen, she was a Fire Elf and

Collin was a Forest Elf. They fought with spears, and in two blows Daphne cut Collin down, dismembered him, and left him for dead.

"Once more," Collin said.

They fought with cudgels and he landed only one glancing blow before she knocked Collin to the ground and brained him.

The third time they clashed swords. They stood on the banks of a crystal stream, and Collin forced Daphne into the water, but once again she was too fast for him. In one swift move, she slashed his arm and then drove her blade through his Elf's chest. The purling water turned blood red.

"Just one more time," he said.

"Go practice."

He felt a flash of anger, but it lasted only for an instant. Luminous in the Arkadian darkness, she disarmed him.

Daphne was like girls he had once known. A little selfish, a little dangerous. She liked to play; she liked to drink. After long days, Obi and Akosh and Collin and Daphne would go out drinking after work. "The bars of Waltham," Daphne intoned. They would sit together at O'Riley's, joking, and it was like the old days, when he could leave his work behind, and no one wondered where he was at night. Not that he wanted his old life. He knew the difference between odd jobs and full employment. He understood the difference between lust and love, and he wanted what lasted. Of course he did. But the "of course" part rankled. How strict and narrow real life turned out to be. Of course you wanted a career. Of course you wanted to be with the girl so much better than you it wasn't even funny. But he missed being funny and stupid and irresponsible.

He was Collin, even in Arkadia. Especially in Arkadia. He got drunk enough to flirt with Daphne. He drank enough to be himself, pushing her sleeves up off her wrists, catching a glimpse of ink. Most people flaunted their tattoos. Strangely modest, or perversely teasing, Daphne kept hers covered up.

"What kind of leaves are these?" He studied her forearms.

"Laurels," she said. "Duh."

"Show me."

She slipped off her barstool and said, "You'd have to beat me first."

Then Obi and Akosh were laughing as though she'd said something witty, but she meant it, and handed Collin a pool cue. He wasn't bad, but she was lethal with her angles, maddening, and also cute, undeniably funny when she triumphed over him. "Ha!" She raised her cue like a Whennish spear. "I'm so much better than you!"

Over days and weeks, Collin drew a hundred horses. Hoofbeats thundered in his ears. Even when he closed his eyes for a few minutes, he dreamed of horses. He slept on the hellions' black leather couch and saw his horses racing on the beach, kicking sand in the salt air. Then he dreamed of Daphne—a strange Arkadian dream. Leaves unfolded on her slender arms, stems and tendrils crept over her neck. Shocked, he watched her disappear. Her ears changed to budding twigs, her nipples hardened into berries. Her limbs were smooth and silvery, her toes rooted to the ground. Those were not her eyes anymore, but birds sheltering in her branches. That was not her mouth, but a dark nest with fledglings where her tongue had been.

Gradually Nina saw a haze come over Collin. That spring he was exhausted. Not just a little sleepy, spent. Often when they met for dinner he was too tired to talk, certainly too tired to draw on kraft paper. Sometimes he was too tired to eat. They met at Grafton Street and ordered a Margherita pizza, but his slices grew cold.

"How's your hand?" Nina said.

"It's fine. It hurts."

"Is it hurting now?"

"No. It's not too bad."

She said, "We've got spring fever at school." She had been teaching William Carlos Williams to her eleventh graders. "This Is Just to Say" and "Burning the Christmas Greens" and "Spring and All." "My student had a baby," she told Collin. "Brynna had a baby girl."

Collin smiled. Nina was so beautiful and he was so relieved to see her. She was like home; she took him back.

"Collin?"

He'd drifted off only for a moment.

Nina said, "You can't work all day and all night too."

"I don't."

She leaned across the table. "Don't let them wear you down."

"Don't lecture me."

That offended her, not just his words, but his cold tone.

In silence, he paid for dinner. In silence, Nina handed him the leftover pizza in a box. When they walked outside the night was misty, fogging the windows of Harvard Book Store. The spring air woke him, but Nina was angry. He knew it, even though she didn't say it. He knew because she didn't speak.

"I wasn't lecturing," Nina said at last.

"Yes, you were. That's what you do." He had to get away; he had to rest. He would have canceled dinner, except that he'd have disappointed her.

She looked at him and sensed something was wrong. "You never draw anymore."

He said, "I draw all day."

"And you're tired of it now."

"No, I'm just tired."

"You should have said you were too tired to meet me."

"You'd be upset."

"Like I am now?"

"Yeah, because I never see you anymore, or I'm working so much that I ignore you."

"I never said that."

"That's what you were thinking."

"Don't tell me what I've been thinking."

"Don't make such a big deal out of everything."

Tears started in her eyes.

What am I doing? Collin thought. Why did he want to hurt her? "No," he said softly.

"No what?" Nina asked.

"Just don't cry."

She took a long breath.

"I don't forget you. I could close my eyes and draw your face." With his finger he traced her profile on the frosty bookstore window. With one curving line he captured her forehead, her straight nose, her decided chin, her long neck. In one more stroke he drew her hair flowing down over her shoulders. "You're the one who can't remember."

She gazed at her image, a portrait in two lines, the work of a moment, subtle, ephemeral. Collin had caught her likeness, but she found him in the glass as well. She saw his easy grace, his quicksilver imagination. "I do remember," she said. "That's why I miss you."

18

The Gates

Now he was creeping closer to the Gates. Digging into sludge with dragon's bone, Aidan's knight caught a glint of gold. He knelt to unearth a token for the ferry, which began gliding toward him, drawn by the bright coin. At last he boarded, crossing to the darker shore.

Daphne didn't show herself, but he heard her voice as he jumped off the boat into thick mud. "Look down," she called. "Look down."

Aidan stared at his knight's legs. Leeches, long, black, and gelatinous, had torn his leggings and his boots away. He pulled them off, one after another, flung them away, but they snapped back, wrapping themselves around his arms and neck. Each place they sucked, an ooze of silver flowed and blackened. He dripped with tarnished phantom blood.

Invisible, Daphne laughed as he finally threw the suckers off. He slashed them with his sword and they fell, curling like dark ribbons at the mucky river's edge.

She taunted him, but he was strong. Furious, he charged ahead and destroyed the next monster he saw, slaughtered a double-headed dog, slashing two throats with one stroke.

"Where are you?" he called out to Daphne.

"Inside."

He stumbled through a marshy swamp, tripping over rocks, and roots, and fallen trees. He cut a path before him, but his sword dulled and slowed as he fought onward. In EverWhen you got stronger, earning more power and collecting more weapons in a qwest. In UnderWorld, you struggled as you advanced; your weapon failed you. The silver blackened on his blade, and his silvered arm tarnished as well.

Light-headed, he played on, late into the night. His schoolbooks lay forgotten in the mud. Jack and Liam wanted to come over, but he told them no. Messages from his company in EverWhen remained unread.

Smaller and smaller in the distance, the people he had known in real life. It was as if he'd left them on the riverbank. Their faces became indistinct and their voices died away. Diana was the last one he could hear. She threatened to tell their mother that he played all night, but he knew she wouldn't. Week after week she kept his secret. Their pact held, even as the wall between them turned to stone.

He battled demons while his sister slept and his mother worked her night shift at the hospital. He traveled leagues, and it was morning when at last he saw UnderWorld's horizon glowing red, a smudge of fire in the distance. Then, with new strength, he rushed through bog and bracken to arrive stunned, breathless, at massive gates with runic messages forged in iron. ABANDON HOPE he read, and pumped his fist. Yes! He had reached the gates of hell.

Springtime was an old movie outside. Loud daffodils and bright birds singing. Junior year was a recurring dream. For months he had done the minimum to avoid calls home. Dashed off lab reports, polished off math problems, filled bubbles on answer sheets. He learned the way he ate—gulping down enough to get through the day. School was a holding pen, home a portal for the game.

"When can I see you?" he asked Daphne the next night.

"Inside."

He pulled at the Gates' iron bars with no success. The metal warped and bent, refashioning itself into a massive Iron Man with slits for eyes. The Iron Man was twice the size of Aidan's knight. Under iron feet, the earth resounded like a drum. Aidan tried to fight, but with one blow, the Iron Man knocked him down and snapped his sword.

"Daphne!" Aidan dropped his stump of a sword and struggled to his feet.

The Iron Man had no weapons. He killed with his body and his claws. Without even bending, he kicked Aidan's chest in.

Aidan could not recover from that blow. He watched the Iron Man pound his gaming body again and again. Black blood trickled from Aidan's mouth. "Daphne," he called again. As if to silence him, the giant kicked Aidan's head off, and with a surge of nausea, Aidan watched his avatar's staring eyes freeze and his hair blacken in a fountain of blood.

The world went dark. "Daphne!"

No answer.

"Where am I?"

"Inside." Her voice was hollow, echoey, as though she were hiding in a deep cave underground. Then he saw that the game was not altogether dark, but shadowy. He found himself in a new place, vast and wet. He heard the drip of water, and he began to make out the contours of cavern walls. He was ashen, from his bloody hair to his torn leather boots. With his two hands he tried to lift his head and screw it back in place. He got it on backward at first. His gaming vision blurred, and he almost lost his balance. He reached out with an arm to steady himself, and the stone walls buckled for a queasy moment before he got his head on straight.

"I'm over here."

He whipped around, starting a small avalanche of pebbles. He heard them pinging far below. Looking down he could not see the cavern floor, only ledges upon ledges, piled with guano.

"Careful."

At last. She leaned against the cavern wall. Her hair was white blond in the darkness, her leather bodice half unlaced.

"Who are you, really?" he demanded.

"Daphne," she told him, for the thousandth time.

"Where do you live?"

"Close."

For a moment he couldn't speak; he could scarcely breathe. He played with people from all over the world, and took huge distances for granted. He had never pictured her nearby. "Please." He had to see her; he had to touch her; he couldn't wait.

Slowly he stepped closer. Ever so slowly, he pulled the laces on her bodice, so that for an instant he saw her breasts, or at least the swollen image of her breasts exposed.

He heard a car and froze. Footsteps on the porch, a door opening. No, that was the other door. Priscilla, not his mother.

In that instant, Daphne turned away and laced herself up again.

He lifted his hand and watched himself touch her shoulder. She almost smiled as she looked back at him. He reached, but she escaped again. Sure-footed, she ran down the narrow ledge and vanished.

Scrambling after her, he found a long fissure in the rock, an entrance to another cave, not vast, but intimate, a cavern flickering with candles set into the hollows of the walls. He edged inside. "Which way?"

"Right in front of you."

He found her blocking the entrance to a tunnel absolutely dark.

"This is the way to the First Circle."

"Let me in."

"Why?" she asked lightly. "What's in it for me?" Her teasing voice hurt after all this time qwesting.

"Nothing," he said.

"Then you can't go on." She sealed the entrance with a boulder, easily rolling the gigantic rock. "You can wait for the release like everybody else."

"Don't go."

In his dreams she struggled, but she couldn't get away. Then he devoured her, ripping off her clothes, pushing himself inside her, biting her nipples until they bled. His dreams throbbed fast and hard as he licked her white skin and tasted her blood, sweet as metal. In his dreams she belonged to him, but in the game, he couldn't catch her.

Caverns and candlelight disappeared. When she materialized again she was standing on a stone bridge, still out of reach. In Ever-When they'd played together. Now she played against him, toying with him, and he was confused by how much he wanted her, and how much he hated her. He sensed that she was using him, but he could not break free.

"Fight me." He bounded onto the bridge, brandishing his broken sword.

"You know what I want." Her voice was close, and slightly agitated, tempted by his intensity.

"You want me to paint." He watched her materialize, holding two weapons.

She tossed him a new sword, but before he could get a grip, she lunged and sliced his shoulder.

"See you in hell," he said.

"Write it out."

"If you win," he said, parrying her silver blade, "I'll write it out. But if I win . . ."

She grazed his ear with the knife edge of her blade.

"I get to see *you*." He slashed and severed her wrist. Her left hand fell to the cavern floor.

She kept her eyes on him as she bent to pick it up, but he was quicker, and he got there first, pocketing her white hand as his prize.

Stroke and counterstroke, they watched themselves bleed, clanging swords and breathing hard. They couldn't feel a thing, but they were gasping with each blow. "See you . . ." He pushed hard, driving her back against the wall. "In real life."

She parried, but he cut her thigh in the gap between her leggings and her tall boots. Then in one fluid motion, he knocked her sword from her hands. "I get to meet you," he said, drawing his dagger, plunging the point deep into her heart.

19

Deer

In the next room, Diana typed with books and papers spread out on her bed. *In my opinion Huckleberry Finn is a character whose morality is different from society but in a good way.* She picked up her paperback and leafed through it, looking for a quote. Lazare loved quotes, so Diana used as many as possible. The trouble was Lazare expected a lot of other things too. She had written out a rubric, also a series of step-by-step instructions, starting *1. Write with a sense of purpose.*

As usual, her mother was knocking on her door. "What?"

"Hey, it's Aidan."

Diana was so surprised she lost her place.

"Can I come in?"

"I guess."

He closed the door behind him, even though their mother wasn't home. She stared as he took a seat on her desk chair, straddling it backward. "I have to ask a favor."

"No."

"Wait, listen to me first."

"No," she repeated, just to annoy him. She missed him so much.

There were days Diana didn't talk to anyone at all. She woke and ate breakfast alone, walked to school alone, kept her head down in the halls. Brynna was still home with her new baby, and she was coming back to school at some point, but even when she talked about returning, she seemed far away, like a girl who'd died, promising to visit Earth again. Brynna had changed forever, no matter what she said. She was living this strange afterlife, sequestered with her parents and her newborn and a million stuffed animals and white china picture frames with wings and halos. She'd even named the baby Angela.

"Are you writing your paper?" Aidan cast his eyes over the papers on Diana's bed.

"Obviously."

"When you finish, can I copy you?"

He spoke without hesitation, but when Diana looked at him, he quavered just a moment. He'd left her far behind, but he still needed her. He ignored her, but she knew his secrets. She'd heard him whispering Daphne's name and talking about tagging walls at night. She'd listened as he crept downstairs. She'd seen his graffiti, the long chain of letters CUCU tagging the lobby of the school.

Naturally, Diana had heard DeLaurentis lecture about defacing public property. She'd scrunched down in the auditorium, knees up on the seat back in front of her, and watched the principal exhort students to come forward with information. Diana had not come forward. That wasn't even a question in her mind. As far as property went, she hated school. As far as Aidan went, he was no criminal; or if he was a criminal on occasion, he was also a genius, mastering everything he tried. He had been the musical twin, the academic twin, the fantastic test-taking twin. He got the highest scores and he got into the worst trouble. When teachers talked about not fulfilling potential, they were just a little worried about Diana; Aidan was the one who really scared them. The gap between his performance and abilities was so huge.

"Can I?" Aidan asked again.

"No! We'll get in trouble."

"Why? We're not even in the same class." Diana had Miss Lazare and he had Mrs. West.

"What are you talking about? We'll get caught and fail English. I'm not taking summer school."

"We won't get caught," Aidan insisted. "And if we do, I'll take the blame."

"Don't you think Lazare and West compare their students' work?"

"How would they have time for that?"

"What do you mean? That's like their job. That's what teachers do."

"I always let you copy me," Aidan said.

This was true. More than once in elementary school, when Aidan had finished homework first, he'd handed over his word searches or long-division worksheets to Diana. "Why do you want my paper now?" she asked. "You never asked before."

"I have to turn something in tomorrow."

"Just do it."

"I haven't read the book. I don't have time."

Diana thought about the silver river in her brother's room. "You've been playing that imaginary girl."

"She's not imaginary."

"You have an imaginary friend in a totally imaginary place." She spoke mockingly, but she also envied him. She wanted what Aidan had, crazy as that seemed. All through the winter she'd walked and run along the Charles. Panting, she had slogged through snow and ice, and now, in spring, through mud. She ran until her breath came hard and her feet ached, and sometimes even then, she could not outrun her loneliness. "Let me play," she said.

"No way."

"Let me try."

"You've already tried EverWhen."

"No, the new one."

"I can't. It's secret. It's not even on sale."

"I want to see it."

"Why?"

She sprang off her bed. "I want to see where you live. Come on."

"I can't."

She loved that she could make him nervous. "I'll let you copy, if you let me play."

"You can't tell anyone about it," he warned, as he led the way into his room. "And you can only play a little bit. You'll have to use my avatar. I can't give you a new one. Stand here. Just wait. Stand still."

Diana wasn't listening. She was watching the game rise up around her. Great caves shadowed Aidan's walls, dark passageways came into focus, and suddenly a flight of tiny animals. She sprang back as a thousand white bats swooped down upon her.

"That's you," said Aidan, pointing to a ghostly knight, ducking and weaving in the onslaught. "You can fight off these bats with your sword. Lift your right hand."

She lifted her right hand and saw her weapon. When she slashed her sword, the bats screamed around her, and their red blood spattered. Startled, she stopped moving, and the creatures swarmed her ghostlike body, biting and ripping at her neck, arms, and face. She covered her eyes as Aidan warned, "Don't drop the sword."

Too late. More and more bats attacked her, flying mice with tiny vampire fangs. They covered her entire body. Whenever she moved, the creatures moved with her, a mass of squirming bodies and red eyes. She swatted at her face, and watched herself knocking bats away.

Her stomach lurched when she saw what was left of her avatar.

The bats had eaten half the knight's flesh away, but they had not exposed muscle or bone. No, their attack revealed something else, another creature, an elongated nose, black eyes, wide-set, rolling independently. An ear, unfolding like a leaf from the raw patch where the knight's ear had been, and from his forehead, nubs of horns. Doubled over now, she heard Aidan calling to her.

Her image doubled over too, and shook the bats away as human limbs morphed into four legs. She was changing into a deer. She could reach out and almost touch her other self, the doe hovering before her, pale flanks foaming, ears twitching, body quivering with a strange, borrowed life.

Aidan said, "Don't throw up in my room."

"I won't!" She felt hot and tearful all the same. As she tried to catch her breath, she lifted her head, and saw the deer prick up her ears. Her head was small, her neck long and delicate, her legs slender. How beautiful she was. Heart pounding, adrenaline racing through her body, she couldn't take her eyes off her deer-self.

A clanging echo in the cavern, great footsteps like giants walking. A jolt of fear. How could she escape?

"Aidan!" she pleaded.

He knelt and closed a black box, a console without buttons. As he screwed top to bottom, the deer vanished, along with swirling bats. The bloodstained cavern melted, and Aidan's walls emerged again, his foil-covered window, his bookcase, his floor strewn with dirty clothes.

Diana sank onto the bed.

He looked at her anxiously. He couldn't copy her essay if she couldn't write. "Are you okay?"

"That was sick."

"I know."

She closed her eyes and leaned back against the wall. "I'm seeing spots."

"They go away."

"I can see them with my eyes open." The spots were small and bright like fireflies, but they didn't last.

She had a strong stomach. She could read on long car rides. She did fine in boats. After a few minutes, Diana sat up on the edge of his bed. "That was seriously the most nauseating thing I've ever seen. Can I play again?"

"You promised. You can't change your mind now."

"I was kidding. God!"

He didn't see the joke. She didn't care about the game, she didn't care about the copying; she cared about him.

"It's late," he said.

She asked, "Is this like the first thing you're going to turn in all year?"

He opened the door. "Get started."

"Stop panicking!"

She returned to her room, gathered up computer, rubric, paperback, and descended to the kitchen. There, beneath the apple clock, she ate half a bag of pretzels as she pounded out three pages. She was writing with a sense of purpose now, and words came easily. She laid on the quotations. She expatiated on Huck Finn's personal morality. She even threw in Lazare's favorite word, *ironically. Huck Finn decided to go to Hell but for a good cause which ironically shows some things are more important than what you believe society wants you to do.*

20

Very Close

That year school went on almost forever. To make up for snow days, the district mandated extra class time straight through the end of June. Kids pulled together their portfolios, and, without warning, the weather changed from cold to scorching. Bees flew in through the open windows of Emerson's un-air-conditioned class-rooms. Kids brought miniature spray-bottle fans, and Mr. DeLau-rentis had to announce that these devices were for personal use only, which caused some snickering. You could spray yourself, but not your girlfriend.

Then, just when it got too hot to do anything, it started pour-ing. It rained so hard the morning of the annual Antrim Street Block Party that the yard sale had to move indoors to the Pres-byterian church. It was still drizzling a couple of hours later, and people carried umbrellas for the garden tour. Maia led neighbors through Antrim's secret gardens, lush oases behind closely built houses.

Gazing at her neighbors' crimson roses, their hidden lawns, and flowering ginkgos, Kerry wished that she had time to tend her own overgrown patch, or money to afford a gardener. Long ago she had imagined that her children would help her. Together as a family they would clear away the dead branches and the big weeds and sow new grass. "Apart from seeing friends, no teenager will go outside," Maia had warned her, and Kerry understood that now, as she did so many other things.

When evening came and neighbors cordoned Antrim off with orange traffic cones, the street began its transformation. Lois strung sparkling lights through oak branches. Sage set up camping tables. Neighbors carried out their lawn chairs and their salad bowls piled high with fruit or pasta, watermelon slices, bulgur wheat. There were casseroles, and bags of pretzels, and roasting pans filled with deep-fried cauliflower. Greg played his banjo, and his new girl-friend, Nella, joined him on her flute. Preschoolers ran in a pack and were thrilled to draw chalk pictures where they couldn't play on any other day, the middle of the street.

Like moths Aidan and Diana materialized, pale, in the fading light. Diana hovered near the grilled portobello mushrooms and listened to her mother and Maia go on about the year the whole street flooded. Remember that?

"You and Aidan were just two years old," said Kerry. "The base-ment filled with water."

"That was the worst flood I've ever seen," said Maia. "That was build-an-ark-type rain. Collin and Darius took a kayak and pad-dled down the street."

Lois was testing out her photos for the slideshow, even as Greg fixed the screen, a white sheet strung from the great branches of a maple. "Oh, God," said Diana, because there she was at four, rid-ing her tricycle in a purple satin cape and a gold crown. "I had to run behind you," Kerry said. "I had to lift your cape, or it would get caught up in the wheels."

"And there's your brother, and there's Liam, and who's that? Jack?" The boys must have been in kindergarten. They looked so small and delicate, standing shirtless, holding water balloons.

"Yeah, that was me," said Jack. He was helping his father, aka Scienceman, set up a giant gyroscope.

"I can't believe you still do that," Diana said.

"This is my community," Jack told her. "There aren't a lot of block parties anymore."

She just stared. There was something so horribly sincere about him. She remembered her mother dragging her along with Aidan to watch Jack and his mom perform in the North Cambridge Family Opera as singing insects. What had he been? A dung beetle? Cricket? She concluded, "You're just weird."

Jack told her, "You're just mean."

His directness startled her. When he narrowed his blue eyes to look at her, she wanted to hurt him. "My brother is completely bored with you," she blurted out.

Coolly Jack said, "Then you and I have something in common," and he left her standing there.

Pictures in the trees of Lois and her godchild from Uganda, the water fight when five boys got ahold of the Mednicks' garden house.

"Hey, baby! Hey, Nina," Maia called out.

Diana turned to look, and then she looked again at Nina. Of course teachers had first names and didn't live at school. Miss Lazare didn't sleep under her desk. Diana knew all this in theory, but it was a shock to see her teacher there.

Instinctively, Diana shrank back as Nina and Collin approached the table for their drinks.

"Hi." Collin breezed by, but Miss Lazare gazed into Diana's eyes as though she could see inside of her.

What? Diana demanded silently. Instantly she felt huge and guilty.

She knows, Diana thought, even as Lazare walked on. She knows!

Diana scanned the crowd. Old guys, couples drinking hard cider, mothers nursing babies in lawn chairs. Kids rumbling up and down in Big Wheels. There he was, sitting alone on their front steps.

"Aidan." She ran up to him.

"What?"

"Lazare knows we cheated."

"No, she doesn't."

"Yes, she does."

"What did she say?"

"Nothing. She just looked at me. It's obvious. They're all sitting at school comparing end-of-year portfolios."

Aidan dismissed this. "Yeah, I don't think so."

"I'm serious."

Aidan stood up. "You don't have to do anything. I take the blame and say I copied you."

"They're not going to believe that."

"They will if you let them."

Walking down the street with Maia, Kerry saw her children standing in the soft light of her porch. "They're really very close," she told Maia. She saw the conversation, but she couldn't hear the words.

Maia said, "And there you were, worrying all winter."

Quietly Kerry said, "You would have worried too."

"They come out of it. They start growing up eventually. Look at Collin!"

Kerry flushed under her freckles. She could not share Maia's joy—not while Collin worked at Arkadia. Yes, it was a full-time job. Yes, he had benefits. Yes, he could earn a living making art, but the thought sickened her. "It's like working at a munitions factory."

"Kerry."

"I'm sorry. It's true." Kerry had known her neighbor almost fifteen years. Maia was just about her closest friend, but she spoke out anyway. "It's like building bombs."

Maia's temper flared. "First of all, as you'll find out, you don't tell your twenty-four-year-old son where he can and cannot work. Second of all, games aren't bombs."

"Yes, they are. They are! They're weapons of mass destruction," Kerry burst out. In cloud, in smoke, in myth, Arkadian games were detonating in a million minds. She had been following the news. She'd read about the kid in Austin caught defacing public property, the kid in Seattle charged with hacking his school website so the banner read cu.

"Hey, are we fighting about this now?" Maia asked gently.

Kerry was too upset to speak.

"They're pastimes," Maia said. "They're part of life."

Death is part of life, thought Kerry. Maia's words reminded her of chaplains and hospice nurses at the hospital.

Maia said, "Games are just like music and art and dreaming."

"Whose dreams?" Kerry demanded. "Not *my* dreams for my children!"

Meanwhile, on the porch, Diana asked Aidan, "What are you going to do when they say they want to talk to you?"

"If that ever happens I'll just sit there," Aidan said.

"And you'll admit you cheated?"

"Yeah."

He opened the glass storm door.

"But what about Mom?"

The question pierced him. If Diana was right and they got disciplined, Kerry would search his room.

"We have to think." Diana followed him inside the house.

But he was thinking of himself. He had to hide his BoX. "I want you to do something," he told his sister.

"No," Diana said, but she trailed him upstairs to his room, where he rooted in the closet under laundry, worn-out shoes, old schoolbooks, a pair of hockey skates. From the depths he pulled out the scuffed black BoX.

"It's heavy," Aidan warned.

She started back as if he'd handed her a loaded gun.

"Don't drop it."

"Your game? You're giving me your game?" she asked, incredulous.

"Just hide it for a little while."

"I'm not keeping this in my room."

"Hide it somewhere else, then."

"Why?"

"So I won't play."

"You're going to stop?"

"Just hide it and don't tell me where it is."

He saw her wavering.

"I'm taking the blame," he reminded her. "Just keep it somewhere."

The BoX was cold and smooth. She was afraid of it, and at the
same time she thought, But he won't play. He's going to stop.

He looked at her with trust, with urgency. "Hide it."

Don't even touch it, she thought, but she took the BoX.

He promised, "You don't ever have to tell me where."

And she accepted this fiction; she took this lie to heart, even as
she said, "Yeah, so you won't know where it is when Mom comes
after you."

On the Monday after the block party, Aidan and Diana faced Miss
Lazare and Mrs. West and Mr. DeLaurentis and their mother. It
was two-fifty in the afternoon, and the last bells had rung. DeLaurentis's first-floor office vibrated with students' feet.

Mr. DeLaurentis hung his suit jacket on the back of his chair,
and all Diana could think was it took a lot of cloth to sew that blue
dress shirt.

The principal had a whiteboard covered with a grid for days of the week, a poster that said BE THE CHANGE YOU WANT TO SEE. Binders filled his bookshelves, and his phone lay on the desk, along with twin essays on morality in *The Adventures of Huckleberry Finn.*

"It's my fault," Aidan confessed immediately. "I stole her paper without her knowledge."

"You expect us to believe that?" DeLaurentis asked, and he turned to Diana. "You had no idea this was happening?"

She shook her head.

"How do you steal a paper from your sister? You found it? You just saw it lying around? What?"

"I took it from her computer," Aidan said.

"You just left it there on your computer?" DeLaurentis asked Diana.

She nodded. "That's where I wrote it."

"Don't you have a password?"

"Yes."

"But I know it." Aidan was way too calm, taking all the blame.

Mrs. West said, "Aidan, this was cheating. You get that, right?"

He didn't even blink.

Miss Lazare started talking about what would happen if they were at college, but DeLaurentis cut her off and said, "Excuse me, one step at a time. The goal is getting into college. Let's get there first."

Lazare looked hot and flushed, all You can do better, and you know it in your heart. Kerry's eyes filled with tears, and DeLaurentis reached behind him for his box of tissues, but even then—especially then—Aidan sat unmoved.

He betrayed no emotion as DeLaurentis talked about the Honor Code and pride in end-of-year portfolios and summer school. I knew it, Diana thought; and she was scared, not so much by the situation as by her own psychic powers, the whole thing playing out as she'd imagined.

She held still, afraid of crying, but Aidan radiated confidence. He was a beautiful liar, his voice unwavering, his details bold and magical, conjured up as though he were remembering. *She was sleeping with her head down on the kitchen table and her computer open.*

Diana listened in awe. Her brother was so smart. Nobody, not DeLaurentis, not Lazare, not even their mother could trip him up or force him into inconsistencies.

Except that his teachers had caught him copying. DeLaurentis would not allow Aidan to forget that.

"So you're admitting that you plagiarized," DeLaurentis said.

"Pretty much."

"Excuse me?"

"I did it."

By the time the meeting ended, the building was deserted. The twins followed Kerry through dank tiled halls. Outside, the field was empty. Kerry led the way and unlocked the car. She said nothing. She let herself in and just stared out the dirty windshield. She wasn't crying anymore. Her eyes were blank, and that was almost worse.

The twins exchanged glances, and for the first time Diana saw regret in Aidan's eyes. A touch of sadness and embarrassment. Poor Mom. Poor us. Wordless, like little children, they piled in back with all their stuff. Neither would brave the front seat. Diana felt miserable, but more than that, a sense of solidarity, as Aidan untangled his seatbelt from hers.

How angry was their mother? White-hot. Incinerating. She marched up the porch steps, unlocked the door, and threw her keys down on the kitchen table. In silence, Diana and Aidan watched Kerry open mail, ripping envelopes, tossing junk into the brown paper recycling bag. In silence, they saw her pile up breakfast dishes in the sink, scummy cereal bowls sitting out since morning. Then up the stairs she went, but not to her own room. They heard her slam Aidan's door behind her.

Diana retreated to the living room couch and considered her brother leaning in the kitchen doorway. "What now?" she said.

"What now?" Aidan echoed, mockingly. He could be so warm. He was brilliant as the sun, and then the next moment he turned his back on you.

"I feel like we should do something."

Aidan lashed out. "You mean like make a card?"

There had been a time when the two of them gave Kerry cards after they did something wrong. A drawing of a heart, a portrait of the stray cat they'd adopted. A rainbow and the single word SORY. That wasn't happening now. Kerry was ransacking Aidan's room. Aidan had predicted this, but he was furious at the invasion. He had never been sorry for what he'd done. Now he wasn't even sorry for his mother.

Upstairs Kerry collected two joysticks and a headset. Pawing through his laundry, she searched for more. She would do better. She would be stronger. Take Aidan's games away, cut him off from his computer. She had to find a way to punish him—and not just for cheating. He'd dragged Diana into trouble. This was the hold Arkadia had on him.

She emptied Aidan's closet, piling the floor with childish things, old Legos, outgrown clothes, broken toys. She would fumigate. Burn all his stuff. Attack his computer with a baseball bat. If only it would make a difference. If only she could drown his phone.

Stripping his bed and peering under it, she excavated dirty T-shirts and twisted jeans. She dumped all the old papers and candy wrappers from his desk drawers, riffled through the binders piled on the floor. Just two years before, Aidan had blazed through

homework every afternoon. He'd aced his tests and writing assignments too. Didn't she have his A paper on the battle of Vicksburg?

Jostling his monitor, Kerry saw his screen glow and darken. A
silvery pattern, the sheen of water, shimmered and rippled eerily,
but she didn't know how to break into his machine.

She knelt down, peering under Aidan's desk and touched a scar
on the wood floor, a deeper gash than other scratches. For a moment she paused, tracing the raw place, but she didn't know the
cause.

Feeling for his surge protector, Kerry unplugged the black cord.
She had done it before. Now, once again, she would pull up her
son's computer by the roots, discontinue cable service, disable the
house router. She would stanch the electric river through which
games flowed. None of this would frighten Aidan. Last time, he'd
simply walked away, surfacing days later at Liam's house. Panicked, Kerry had come running after him. This time she would not
negotiate. Don't give in, she told herself, although her child was
almost seventeen, and more than six feet tall.

She sat back on her heels, and sadness overcame her as the monitor went dark. Other kids enjoyed games for a weekend. Jack
would play, but he went to Math Circle and competed on the ro-
botics team. Even Liam had his band. Aidan was the one who
couldn't stop. For this, she blamed herself.

She had a good job, but it wasn't good enough. She earned decent money, but not enough. She loved him, but that was not
enough. She could not afford a mountain program; she didn't have
the cash to send him to some snow-capped wilderness where he
might waken from his soul-sucking dream. If she took him to the
police, maybe that would scare him. If she found explosives in his
closet, if she discovered drugs, or caught him dealing, then she'd
have some leverage. What could she do with a son whose drug of
choice was legal? Whose weapon was his own imagination?

21

Face-to-Face

Just as Kerry despaired of Aidan and his future, he grew quiet, almost docile. He accepted the loss of his computer, along with being grounded every afternoon and weekend. He accepted that he had failed English and would repeat the class next year. He accepted that he had failed biology as well. After the term ended he would return for summer school. When Kerry asked him to wash dishes or take out garbage or bring up the laundry, he did it instantly.

At first, his compliance made her nervous. She had prayed, but this was more than she had hoped. Aidan returned from school to do his homework. He ate dinner. He even slept at night—he really slept. When Kerry returned from her night shift, she didn't hear a sound. Aidan's behavior seemed to her too good too fast, and yet she wanted to believe in him. Maybe it was true, as she had read, that deep down teens craved structure and authority. Confiscating Aidan's electronics may have been his secret wish!

Aidan never asked for his computer and his games. Nor did he run away to play with friends. Day by day, he worked to earn his mother's trust. He held out his open palm for Kerry, and, like a hungry woodland creature, she watched him from a distance. Steadily he made his offering. No sudden movements, no threatening gestures, as Kerry crept closer. Trembling, she circled hungrily. She knew better. Experience told her otherwise, but need trumped fear as she began grazing from his hand.

Kerry re-established Sunday breakfast, which she prepared after her Saturday-night shift. She made the children French toast as soon as she came home, and they ate together at the kitchen table, their plates drenched with syrup, their glasses filled with fresh-squeezed orange juice. Aidan was quiet, but his mother didn't mind. Just two weeks after she had confiscated his computer, she saw a calmer manner, a steadier gaze. No longer did he fidget at the table and race away to play. To her mind, he'd hit rock bottom, and now he was rebuilding. She rejoiced, but tried to temper her excitement. On Friday morning, when he said he wasn't feeling well, she took his temperature. Trust but verify. He had a fever of 101, and she allowed him to stay home from school.

"You rest," she told him as she hunted for ibuprofen. "Take these, and I'll check on you when I wake up." Then gratefully, she lay down in her own bed.

Coming down with a cold that morning wasn't planned. Aidan's body ached, and his throat hurt when he swallowed, but he didn't care. His heart pounded as he listened to Diana leave for school. Then, when she was gone and all was quiet, he slipped downstairs, supporting himself with his arms on wall and banister, so that his feet scarcely touched the creaky treads. Softly he escaped through the kitchen. Gently, he shut the back door.

Great trees canopied his street and Maia's roses were all blooming luscious red, but Aidan didn't stop to look. He ran to Central Square to catch the T inbound. Plunged, with his student CharlieCard into dank tunnels and took the rattling train to Boston.

He had never been to the Seaport World Trade Center. He had hardly been to Boston Harbor except on trips to the Children's Museum when he was small. Now he saw the ferries and the sailboats, the rusty fishing boats, and all the people swarming the gray convention center on the water. A friendly mob had gathered even before doors opened, gamers in costume, entire companies brandishing their spears like shaggy Vikings at the harbor's edge. Hand-sewn Elvish shoes with turned-up toes, custom knives and swords, the glint of chain mail in the sun—this was EverCon.

"Yo, why aren't you dressed?" demanded a blue-haired Fire Elf.

She was a girl from Kansas City traveling with three friends from her company, all dressed in black leather bustiers and thigh-high boots.

Aidan did feel undressed in ordinary clothes. He was relieved to see that some Everheads had come in jeans—the buskers selling ouroboros T-shirts, the guys scalping tickets to the evening show. There were jugglers and musicians crowding the door. A man entertained the crowd with a Whennish lute he'd built himself, a seven-stringed instrument inlaid with mother-of-pearl and a twangy sound like a medieval banjo.

The crowd was joyous. Everheads were eating breakfast harborside in folding beach chairs, trading tips and telling war stories, reuniting with their companies, donning matching T-shirts. After campaigning together for months and years online, qwesters embraced, many meeting in person for the first time. They were college kids and couples, and hordes of hard-core single gaming geeks. They were men and women, Elves, and Gnomes, masters and journeymen. My people, Aidan thought. Arkadian nation.

Even so, he hesitated at the Trade Center doors. At least twenty protesters stood right in front, flanked by police. Christians Against Gaming Exploitation wore matching CAGE T-shirts, and brandished big hand-painted signs for the cameras of Channel 7 Eyewitness News.

CU IN HEAVEN!

BE A PRAY-ER, NOT A PLAYER

HELL NO: DON'T GO

"What are you doing here, son?" one Christian asked. The man had a round, friendly face, and he wore round, friendly glasses. "Shouldn't you be at school?"

Aidan flinched, nervous about the cops.

"Won't you join us?" a second Christian asked. She had long blond hair, and she wore a little gold cross on a chain. "Won't you consider reading this?" She held out a leaflet printed:

YOU AND CHRIST: WIN WIN!

Keep walking, Aidan thought. He wouldn't take the leaflets offered him.

"God has other plans for you!" the picketers called after Aidan as he hurried toward the World Trade Center doors. "Jesus is waiting, if you let him in!"

What a relief to dash inside without anyone chasing or reporting him. Aidan presented his school ID at the registration table and no one questioned him. His name was on the master list, and he received an all-access pass to wear on a chain around his neck. He fingered that strand of tiny metal beads as though it were a chain of Elvish gold.

"Straight ahead," one of the EverCon staffers said.

Aidan entered the blue-carpeted Commonwealth Hall, and it was dark after the June sun. Vast as a theater, dim-lit, draped in black. For a moment Aidan stopped in awe. Thousands of gamers had brought their home computers and powered up, logging in to play EverWhen, together and apart. Rustling, shuffling, clicking, the assembled armchair heroes sounded like cicadas on a summer night as they slayed dragons with trackballs and joysticks. Above them, banners hung from the vaulted ceiling, pennants floating over the virtual fair. There were monitors pimped out with flashing police lights, computers bedazzled with crystals. Aidan saw a PC transformed into a steampunk masterpiece of cherrywood, antique typewriter buttons, and polished brass.

There were girls dressed like cheerleaders walking the aisles to toss out T-shirts, bumper stickers, free download codes. There was the blue-haired Elf from Kansas City, who had followed him inside. She told him she had legally changed her name to Kalinda, but he had someone else in mind.

Daphne was here somewhere in this mass of people, and she'd promised, after his long days and dangerous nights, after a million refusals, that he could meet her face-to-face. She had arranged his all-access pass.

Curtained off from the gaming hall, vendors sold costumes, crystals, dragon masks, silver ouroboros bracelets, and pendants of amethyst. Some wares were silly, like needlepoint phoenix pillows, or hand-painted eyeglass cases with your company's insignia. Some exquisite, like the swords of tempered steel. You could buy anything, from Elf-inspired candles to prosthetic noses, humps, and wings. At the Arkadian brokerage, you could sit at a bank of computers, log in, and bid real money for an imaginary jewel or weapon or gold ring. You could buy an enchanted sword that would take months to earn in EverWhen—or you could sell your hand-forged virtual armor in an instant.

Daphne had promised Aidan that he'd find her, but the convention was even bigger than he'd imagined. He watched early-round tournament play on giant screens. He saw Viktor Lazare speaking to a thousand Everheads about UnderWorld and its new platform. "This is official," Lazare announced. "Everything you've heard is true. We're launching in December." But even Lazare's keynote couldn't hold Aidan for long. He searched every hall, texting, **where ru?**

Daphne did not reply, and yet he scanned the crowds. Every blond girl in black leather startled him. He texted again, but his phone didn't even blink. He remembered Diana's words—"There is no girl."

But his sister was wrong. Daphne was real. She had to be. He had traveled with Daphne; he had fought with her and against her. She had been his guide, his companion, and his closest friend. Even without his headset, he heard her throaty voice, her whisper, and her laughter in his ears.

He hadn't eaten, and after several hours his body ached in the highly air-conditioned hall. The place began to look fake, with its black drapes and kitschy painted booths. He kept looking for Daphne, but he moved slowly now. He saw spectacular costumes, but others seemed hokey and embarrassed him. So many girls fell short compared to Elvish women. Their arms were flabby, and they were always tugging at their bodices, afraid they would fall down. So many guys were old and bald. They didn't have the physique or hair of warriors. Everheads could not live up to the real thing.

Discouraged, he drifted through the demo booths, with their banks of computers set up for free trials. EverHeart. EverFlight. He sank into a swivel chair, and a black-shirted Arkadian staffer offered him a headset to play EverSea.

At first he said no, because he wanted to keep searching, but after a few minutes he slipped the headset on. Logging in as his old Elf, Tildor, he found himself in the Golden Islands, where he came upon a skiff beached on the shore. A fair wind was blowing, and the tide began to rise. The golden ocean swelled, murmuring around him, and he leapt into the skiff and began to play.

The wind whipped up. Salt spray flew into his face and water roared in his ears, along with the pure voices of mermaids singing on outlying rocks. The mermaids' breasts were full and lovely, their hidden tails serpentine, deadly underneath.

"Hey, buddy." A male voice broke in. "Five-minute warning before we have to shut this thing off."

"Okay." Aidan kept his eyes on the screen.

Quickly, nimbly, he tapped and clicked, approaching the mermaids, but keeping his skiff just out of reach. He kept his distance as each mermaid questioned him in turn.

"Who are you?"

"What are you doing?"

"Where have you been?"

He froze when he heard the last mermaid. Daphne.

"Listen, I've really gotta shut you down," the EverSea demonstration supervisor said apologetically.

"Just one second," Aidan pleaded as he scanned waves and rocks. Then into his headset, "What do you mean where have I been? I've been looking for you everywhere."

Daphne laughed.

"You said you'd come here as yourself," he said.

"I *am* here as myself."

"Yeah, right."

The islands vanished; the singing ended.

"Sorry." The supervisor started packing up the monitor and CPU.

Aidan took off his headset, but, strangely, he could still hear Daphne's mocking voice. It took him a moment to realize she wasn't speaking to him from inside the game. "I'm standing right behind you. Turn around."

22

Pursuit

He spun around in the swivel chair and there she was, looking nothing like Riyah. No flowing locks, no leather bodice, no heaving breasts. She wore black jeans and a black sweatshirt. She was so covered up, he could barely even see her hands. When she pulled up her sleeves, he saw indigo flowers tattooed on her wrists.

"What?" she asked playfully.

"Nothing. You look different."

"From what you expected?"

He looked down, embarrassed. "I probably look different too."

"No," she told him. "You look exactly the way I imagined you."

Her voice was just as he remembered—knowing, teasing. ARKA-DIA was the word on her hooded sweatshirt.

"You work here."

"Yeah," she said. "Of course I do."

She wasn't Elvish but elfin, with her slight frame, short hair, and huge blue eyes. The object of his obsession was not an object at all. She was bright, her expression lively, her smile incandescent. He had no idea how old she was, but he figured at least twenty, college age or more. Her voice was condescending, her expression curious.

"What do you want to play?" she asked.

"Nothing. I want to talk to you."

"I don't like talking."

His throat was dry. "What do you like instead?"

She took him upstairs to the Harborview Ballroom, where several hundred champion qwesters were playing EverWhen.

Aidan said, "I thought you have to register for the tournament to play."

"Not if you're with me."

She commandeered two Arkadian workstations, and they sat in swivel chairs across the table from each other. A strange place for gaming, with its sea-green corporate carpeting, but once you started, you didn't notice anything.

Charging on horseback, fighting with broadswords, shooting arrows, casting spells that rained down sparks like fireworks, she played well, but he played better. Trembling, feverish, his reflexes were faster. Jousting, he unhorsed her. He thrust and parried, forcing her down on the leafy forest floor. Again and again he vanquished Daphne. He frustrated and dazzled her. He fought brilliantly, but she would not admit defeat. She sprang up, challenging him in archery. Together they sent arrows flying after moving targets, gold birds darting and wheeling in the bright sky.

"Once more, once more," she urged him on.

"I won," he said. "Admit it."

"One more round."

"No." He scooted his swivel chair to her side of the table.

Reluctantly, Daphne turned away from the game.

Once again he said, "I need to talk to you."

She felt a prick of fear when she saw Aidan's face, because he looked so serious. To tell the truth, she had considered standing him up. All day she had ignored his messages, and when he texted that he was playing EverSea, she had circled for a long time, watching.

He was too involved with her. He had revealed way too much about himself. His name, his school, his loneliness. Sad Aidan was sadly predictable, because, of course, Daphne knew exactly what he was going through. Once upon a time she'd been a miserable teenager, shutting herself up and gaming for days. She didn't need to hear about it when she'd lived it. Even so, he'd won the chance to see her. He'd stabbed her through the heart, and she played fair. "What do you want to talk about?"

He was practically shaking, meeting her like this. He had no weapons; he wore no armor. Even so, he forced himself to speak. "I want to know you."

"You're a kid," she said, as much to reassure herself as to remind him.

He wouldn't let her put him off. "Who are you?"

"I'm exactly what you see."

"No, you're not."

"Stop!" She brushed his hand with hers. The brief contact, meant as friendly and dismissive, shocked them both. Her touch surged through his body. She felt his heat. "What are you on?" She was only half joking. "I want some."

"I'm not on anything."

"I was kidding!" Then she added, "You don't get to know me."

"Why?"

"Because it's not good for you."

"How do you know what's good for me?"

"Okay, we're done now." She sprang out of her chair and began walking.

He hurried after her. "Why are you, of all people, talking about what's good for me?"

She walked faster. She was nearly running to the mezzanine.

"Daphne!"

She slipped into a crowded elevator going down.

"Wait!" Aidan called out as the doors were closing.

She might have escaped then, but a friendly Water Elf held the door, and Aidan squeezed in with a crowd of costumed Everheads.

"Going to the show?" the Water Elf asked Daphne.

She answered, "Absolutely."

Aidan tried to edge closer, but too many sweaty bodies blocked him. Last in, first out when the doors opened, Aidan tried to catch Daphne leaving, but other elevators were opening too. Streams of Everheads were exiting, and she slipped into the crowd, ignoring him, as she race-walked to Commonwealth Hall.

He followed Daphne into a conference venue transformed into a rock concert. Sparkling light rained down, as Aidan plunged into a sea of bodies. For a moment he couldn't even see. He almost lost Daphne in the darkness and the virtual fireworks, the huge reverb, the thunder of Arkadia's house band, the Velvet Pixels, rocking out onstage, the roar of a thousand Everheads partying. Half blind, he reached out and caught the hood of her sweatshirt.

She glanced over her shoulder, amazed at his tenacity. Her eyes were mocking; her whole body told him, Catch me—I dare you. Her hood ripped as she tore away.

"Stop," he called. She paused for just a second, and then she raced off again.

He pursued her from the dance floor to the great hall of gamers, with their glowing monitors. Security tried to block him, but he hardly noticed. If Daphne had stopped here, guards would have caught him, but she kept running through the hall. She tried one door, and then another. When she hit an unlocked exit, he was right there after her.

Gasping, laughing, she sprinted down two flights of stairs. His speed was thrilling, actually Elvish. His legs were longer than hers and he jumped the last four stairs at the exit to the parking lot.

"Okay," she said.

"Okay what?"

She kissed him on the lips.

He was already light-headed, and now he felt like he was float-ing. For a long moment he was dreaming, flying! But no, he was really standing there with Daphne. That was her tongue pressing against his.

His hands spread over her shoulders. Still kissing, he unzipped her sweatshirt. He touched her through her ribbed undershirt as he kissed her neck, her collarbone. Then, opening his eyes, he saw her ink. Thick twigs and flowers covered her arms and shoulders, climbing over her shoulder blades. For such a long time he'd fanta-sized about her Elvish flesh, her pure white character in game. He'd imagined her softness and her nakedness, but she had clothed her-self in intricate designs. Black branches, berries, thick leaves tat-tooed her entire torso.

The instant he paused to look, she pulled away.

He reached for her. Just wait, he pleaded with his eyes.

She glanced at him with a hint of sympathy. "Ohh," she said, as she might speak to a small child. Then she ran upstairs.

He couldn't follow. His head was pounding. His muscles throbbed. With sheer adrenaline, he'd chased her down, but he had nothing left, and he sank back against the wall. He was so sick, his mind and body racing. He thought his heart would burst. It wasn't fair. He'd caught her, touched her, half undressed her, and still she wasn't his.

Upstairs, the Velvet Pixels were performing and the audience was belting out the chorus. *"Reality! Reality!"* Grateful, Daphne slipped into the crowd. People were singing, and they were swaying, and they were holding light sticks. The darkness and the mayhem com-forted her. She loved crowds because you had strangers to fall back on when you were bruised and rattled, out of breath.

She hung back when the Velvet Pixels took their bows and walked offstage, changing from rock stars to programmers and engineers. She did not join her colleagues as they met the band out-side to head to Viktor's after-party at the Institute of Contemporary Art.

Obi saw her and called, "Come on." Arkadians had been work-ing the conference all day, answering questions, demonstrating fea-tures, mingling with fans, and they were ready to escape and celebrate.

"Later," Daphne said.

Her colleagues left without her. All the Arkadians had changed their clothes, because the invitation had suggested evening dress and vintage gowns. They stuffed their jeans and T-shirts into back-packs or trunks of people's cars, and trooped outside into the warm summer night.

Collin wondered where Daphne had gone, and then he thought, She's way too cool for this. Leaving with the others, he thought the hellions betrayed their name, dressed up like a bunch of kids at prom. Even so, his heart beat faster as the group crossed parking lots and wove between construction sites to reach the ICA, glowing like a square-cut diamond on the water.

How strange, coming to a museum as an invited guest. Collin wore a used tux from Keezer's in Central Square, and his black dress shoes echoed on wood planks so that arriving felt like board-ing ship.

Arkadians had gathered on the deck outside with their guests. Scanning the crowd, Collin saw Akosh's wife, Meta, in a sari of gold silk and Obi with a Russian graduate student dressed in a ballroom dancer's plunging evening gown. There was Viktor, hold-ing forth with his six-foot wife, Helen. There was Peter, with his amber eyes. But where was Nina? It took Collin a moment to rec-ognize her, even as he kissed her. She was wearing a silvery-blue sheath, the lightest, smoothest fabric rippling over her body. A diamond clip was shining in her hair. "They're just rhinestones," she told Collin, but she looked so elegant, he only half believed her.

For a moment he felt like a stranger. He thought, No way; I don't belong here with Nina and her uncle and her father. Martinis helped. He finished his first and had another. The evening shimmered; the warm summer night caressed him. When Nina introduced him to her stepmother, the museum levitated on the water.

Helen stared at Collin as she offered her cold hand.

Collin gazed back at the dark-eyed, dark-haired woman in her tight dress. Tall as she was, she wore stiletto heels. She enjoyed her height.

"Good evening," Helen said in accented English.

"Where are you from?" Collin asked, a little louder than he'd intended.

"I come from Greece," said Helen. Her voice was courtesy itself. Her eyes said, Who the hell are you?

Viktor told Collin, "Now you know what I mean when I say that I'm a Hellenized Jew."

Collin smiled, pretending he knew what Viktor meant.

"Collin draws horses," Peter was telling Helen.

"Oh, good," she said.

"He's better than good," Viktor said. "He's insanely great." Showman, technocrat, Gatsby without tears, he told Collin, "Someday you'll develop games for us."

Helen warned, "My husband likes making promises."

"Predictions!" Viktor corrected.

"They're easier," Peter pointed out.

Viktor waved all this away. Partly flattering, partly self-satirizing, he told Collin, "We'll make you a star."

"Don't believe him," Helen said. "Don't trust anything he says."

"You're beautiful tonight," Viktor told his wife.

Helen was not amused, but Viktor didn't mind. He entertained himself. He was fierce and jovial, voracious and self-satisfied. Announcing UnderWorld's release date in December, he had chosen an audacious path, accelerating development to the deadline. Peter had worried about rushing, cutting corners, cheapening the game. He had protested, "Don't sacrifice the story for effects. Give us time to build the myth." He'd made his case, but Viktor chose December anyway, high risk and high reward. OVID couldn't wait. Arkadia's rival, Urania, was building its own platform for gaming in the round.

Others called him ruthless, but disruption, quick reversals, and bold decisions spelled leadership for Nina's father. By the same token, escapism and delusion were not problems but products in Viktor's lexicon. He never doubted his profession the way some of his colleagues did. There were those at Arkadia who had trained as researchers—not just computer scientists, but biologists and physicists. There were those nostalgic for their old disciplines and their youthful goals. Once they had studied structures of living things, and pondered laws of the actual universe. Now they spoke wistfully of science as their homeland, and their old religion. Viktor was not among them. He had been and remained a scientist, investigating vision—fundamental questions of perception. Applying his research to gaming did not disappoint him. Consummate player, joyful inventor, he never apologized for the diversions he marketed. Not at EverCon, where players thanked him for bringing them together and granting them such pleasure and such power. Not after that morning's symposium on role-playing as therapy for autism, not after the Q&A, where a gamer in a wheelchair told Viktor, In EverWhen I run, I swim, I fly.

"Am I glib?" Viktor asked Nina.

"Sometimes."

"I thought so." Viktor spoke with such satisfaction that she laughed and Collin laughed with her. Even Helen smiled. With few exceptions, Viktor captivated people. When he was happy the whole world glowed. That very moment the sky was deepening from lavender to violet. He might have cast that sunset over his shoulder; it would have been just like him.

Peter was one of the exceptions, and he kept quiet as he watched Nina and Collin basking in his older brother's praise.

"The point is, you'll go far," Viktor told Collin.

"Promise or prediction?" Peter asked.

The question startled Collin, but Viktor was whispering to Nina. No one heard, but she was glowing with her father's words.

She knew flattery came easily to Viktor. He didn't just say what you wanted to hear. He said what you hardly dared to hope. Even so, he loved talent. He loved youth, and he appreciated art. Nina could have kissed him when he praised Collin.

She had been to parties at the ICA before. She had watched the waves framed by the glass window on the mezzanine, but when she stood with Collin, it was like holding the ocean in your hands, studying the weave up close, the warp and weft of water. The glass galleries seemed stranger, funnier, far more beautiful. A sofa sank under papier-mâché lovers. A woman in a video installation stood gazing out at shimmering water from her balcony. Collin sat on a marble bench, chaste white, funereal, carved with the words PROTECT ME FROM WHAT I WANT. When he opened his arms for Nina, a guard hurried over. "Sir! I'm sorry—you can't sit there!"

"See, that's the big-picture stuff," Collin told Nina. "Guards coming over and acting out the message of the piece! I would never think of that."

They took the glass freight elevator to view a three-story paper pagoda from above. They ate oysters. They drank Champagne. They listened to the jazz trio and they danced together. She didn't know the fox trot or salsa or tango, but Collin whispered instructions in her ear. "One, two, onetwo, one two onetwo. Look up. Just look at me."

He had told her that his mother taught dancing, but Nina had always imagined him watching the class. Now she realized that he had learned as well.

He said, "I had to dance with all the girls who didn't have a partner. I'd be the youngest one, and I was like a foot shorter, so I was staring straight at all these eighth-grade breasts."

"Sh!"

"What? It was like the highlight of my childhood."

She was laughing as he spun her out. "How do you think those girls felt?"

"You need more Champagne," said Collin.

"Oh, I don't think so."

"I think you do."

They walked outside to the bar and got two glasses, but she didn't drink from hers.

"Do you think there's such a thing as too much fun?" He set his empty Champagne flute on the railing.

"Well, it depends . . ." she began.

"Okay, just by that answer I can tell you aren't drunk enough."

Already he was more at home than she was. He seemed born for music and Champagne and black-tie parties. He looked danger-ously handsome, not tamed, but liberated in formal clothes.

He was leaning back against the railing and Nina was facing him. This was how Daphne saw them as she walked up the stairs to the deck. Her first thought was, Look at you, Collin, with your tuxedo and your girlfriend. Her second thought: You know I'm here but you're pretending you can't see me.

She had come only for a quick drink. That's what she explained to everyone who asked. She was still wearing her black Arkadia sweatshirt with the ripped hood.

"What happened to you?" Tomas asked her at the bar.

She said, "I got held up at EverCon. I had to tear myself away."

"It's almost ten," Peter pointed out.

She shrugged, trying to seem nonchalant, even as he studied her. "I wasn't going to come at all."

Drink in hand, Daphne made her way to the dessert table, where she surveyed lemon tarts the size of silver dollars, chocolate mousse in shot glasses, marzipan fruit, petits fours adorned with candied violets. Collecting one of each, she looked up to see Collin and Nina just ahead of her in line.

"Is that your dinner?" Collin asked, and he was not avoiding her. He was expansive, and a little drunk.

"Definitely."

It was dark now, and they stood in candlelight. Collin with his princess at his side. All around them Arkadians were plucking petits fours like flowers. "Nina, this is Daphne."

Daphne lifted her glass in greeting. "Hey."

Nina was confused. She'd heard Daphne's name. She was sure she'd met Daphne somewhere before—but Collin was the one who knew her, demanding playfully, "Where were you?"

"Working! Did you like our protesters?"

"What do you mean?"

Daphne smiled.

Nina said, "You hired them."

"They got great coverage! They were on the news at six, and again at ten. Wait." Daphne checked her phone. "They're on *now*. Look."

Nina watched Daphne and Collin exclaim over the unfolding newscast on the phone, and the whole evening began to change. She watched the two of them together, and their conversation, spoken and unspoken, seemed familiar. Collin had never mentioned Daphne, but she was not simply an acquaintance. She was his close friend.

Daphne was explaining, "I had to coordinate the protest, and

then I did the giveaway at eight, but the worst was I got chased!"
She rolled up her sleeve and showed off the purpling bruise on her
wrist.

"Who did that?"

"A rabid fanboy ran me down. He had me cornered in a stairwell." Daphne spoke ruefully, but her eyes were mischievous as
Collin examined her. "And he was *big*. At least sixteen."

"Why would he chase you?" Nina asked.

"You need ice." Collin pressed his cold glass to Daphne's wrist.

Surprised and hurt, Nina turned to look at him, although he was
just being Collin: friendly, flirtatious, drinking too much.

"Occupational hazard," Daphne said.

"What does that mean?"

"It's like sometimes you get bitten. I feed new games to hungry
kids."

"Why do they bite?"

"Because they get wild."

"Is that the plan?"

"No!" Daphne protested. "I just want them a little bit obsessed."

Collin chided, "You can't just tell people where to find you."

He was so warm, so playful with Daphne, that Nina took a full
step back. He didn't even notice. His concern was all for Daphne as
Nina walked away.

She drifted to the dessert table, then to the bar. The glass freight
elevator descended gently, and all the music and all the art and all
the laughter of the evening seemed to sink slowly, noiselessly. All of
it seemed joyless now.

Idly she watched the waiters carrying their trays. Champagne
flutes by the dozen. Chocolates decorated with gold leaf. Nina
wanted nothing but to get away. She had nearly disappeared down
the wood stairs when Collin caught up with her.

"Stop and tell me what's wrong."

She kept walking to the parking lot. "You have to ask. That's what's wrong."

"Daphne offended you."

"No, you did."

"Why?"

"Because you were defending her!"

"She's the one who got hurt."

"Do you know that?" she demanded. "How do you know that? You aren't thinking about that kid."

"This isn't like you," he said.

"Really? How am I supposed to be?"

"I don't know. I don't go around telling people how they should be. I know how you are."

"You don't know anything."

He looked into her hurt eyes. "You're jealous."

"Not true!"

Nina turned her back on him, unlocking her car. She slipped inside and slammed the door. Then she opened the door again because she'd caught her dress.

Collin said, "Wait—let me come with you."

"No."

She could be so lovely and so delighted with the world, and then she doubted everything. All he wanted was to see her happy, to make her laugh, but she had to find some catch. He could be moody, he had a temper, but hers had this weight, this crushing moral force. Nina wasn't just angry—she had to drag in the whole universe. "Don't be like this."

What did that mean? Was she too serious? She couldn't help it. She was serious the way she was left-handed, and she couldn't change. She had been raised on lies and fairy tales, and she hated deception and excuses. She had grown up with games, and she craved truth.

He repeated, "Let me come with you."

"No, stay. You want to." She nearly caught his fingers as she closed the car door.

"You know what your problem is?" he called out as she started the engine.

"My problem is you," she called back. "My problem is that I'm in love with you."

23

Admission

He could hardly see when he got home that night. Body shaking, teeth chattering with fever, Aidan collapsed inside the door. His mother said, Oh, my God, what happened to you, even as she asked, Where have you been, what did you do? At first he couldn't answer. He was throbbing with pain. He lay on the floor, and when his mother tried to help him up, he vomited. Oh, my God, his mother kept saying. I'm taking you in.

"No," Aidan groaned.

"Diana!"

"I'm right here." Diana hovered near the kitchen door. Whenever Aidan got sick, she had a sinking feeling she would be next.

"Get me the thermometer from my bathroom."

Diana raced up the stairs.

"Don't bite," Kerry told Aidan. "Don't break the glass." A moment later, she turned around and told Diana, "Help me get him to the car."

"Isn't the doctor closed?"

"We aren't going to the doctor's office."

He thrashed and fought as they tried to move him.

"Ow!" Diana turned to her mother. "He scratched me!"

"Come nicely or I'm calling an ambulance," Kerry said.

Diana turned on Aidan. "What is wrong with you?"

They were trying to pull him through the front door, but he clung to the doorframe. "Let me go! Let go!" he screamed, and it took all their strength to hold him, even in his weakened state. He demanded, "Give me my sword."

"Is he high?" his sister whispered. His eyes were glassy, his face dead white.

"Hold his arm back," Kerry ordered. "His left arm. I've got his right." Pinning his arms back, holding him on either side, they got him through the door, and all the time Kerry spoke to Aidan. Her voice was stern and quiet in his ear. "You're sick. You're delirious. You're fighting a hundred and four fever and you might have a bacterial infection. I'm taking you to the ER."

Step by step, she talked him down the stairs into the humid night. She never took her eyes off him, so he felt her gaze, even though he wouldn't look at her. "Now we're going to the car," she said, for Diana's benefit as much as for Aidan's. "We're going to the car. I'm going to strap you in."

He stopped fighting. They couldn't tell whether he went limp from exhaustion or in protest, but they knew better than to let go. Half carrying him, they edged into the driveway.

"Get my purse," Kerry told Diana.

Now Aidan cried out and tried to wrest himself away again.

Kerry pinned him against the old Subaru. Diana opened the passenger-side door, and he closed his eyes as Kerry strapped him in.

"Am I coming?" Diana asked.

"No, wait here."

Kerry was already starting the car. She had to concentrate on Aidan. "You'll be all right," she told him as she reached over to adjust his seat, sliding and tilting so he could lie back.

She touched his burning forehead, and he couldn't move his

head away. His neck was like a superheated steel rod. He couldn't bend; he couldn't turn without bursting into flame.

You can do this, Kerry kept telling herself, as she drove through the night. You can do this. But when she began threading through the maze of Longwood's labs and hospitals, Beth Israel, Joslin, Dana-Farber, she began to cry.

She pulled up in front of Children's, her own hospital, and she got help with a wheelchair and rushed Aidan inside.

How many times had she met parents as they rushed in hyperventilating, sick with fear? Take a breath. Sit for just a second. Let me get you a cup of juice. Try to drink this. Just take a little sip. All those years, all the waking hours of her working life, Kerry had nursed other people's children. Now she was the one wheeling her son past fish tanks and patient art, doves and rainbows, painted words: DREAM! HOPE! LOVE! She was the mother printing Aidan's birth date, affirming no known allergies, as children's cartoons laughed, wheezed, screamed. She was like everybody else who came in with a sick baby. The only difference was that Kerry didn't have to wait.

"I'm taking you to see the doctors," she told Aidan, unconsciously simplifying her language. "They're going to look at you."

He was unresponsive when the nurse spoke to him. He knew vaguely that he was in the hospital, but the voices were too loud, the walls too bright. Docile, he gave over his body, submitting to the doctors' tests. He wasn't trying to cooperate; he was too sick to object.

Everyone was explaining what would happen. Some tests, some blood, some time to rest, some spinal fluid to see if he was cloudy. He knew the answer. He was so cloudy that he couldn't see. A dark moon blocked his vision, but he could hear and he could feel. Jackhammer pain, sharp needles in his neck, and in his head, behind his eyes. Dry heaves and distant voices. A lurching, sickening puncture in his back.

"They're going to admit you," his mother told him, and he thought, Where did I get in? "They're going to help you heal," she said. "That's why you've got the IV. That's for your antibiotics. Don't pull it out." He had not been aware that he was pulling. Those were just hands. Nothing to do with him.

Kerry called Diana and told her that Aidan had to stay the night.

"Okay," Diana said.

"They're doing some tests," Kerry said. "He has an infection." She couldn't bring herself to say "meningitis."

"Okay."

"I have to stay."

"When's he coming home?"

"I don't know."

She took this in. "Could he die?"

For a split second, Kerry hesitated. Then she said, "No!" as if the very question were offensive, as if from that day forward nobody would ever die again.

A muffled sound at the other end of the line.

"I need you to stay calm."

Long pause. "Okay," Diana said.

All that night, Kerry stayed with Aidan in the ICU. She envisioned his recovery. She had seen it happen. At the same time, she could imagine losing him; she'd seen that too.

She watched him in the darkened room; she just sat and watched. She tried to pray, but fear silenced her. The enormity of the situation smothered her. Every thought flew to Aidan. He looked so still, so straight, so narrow, like a beautiful felled tree. His hair stuck out every which way, and Kerry thought, You need a haircut. What a strange idea, when he needed so many other things first. His hands lay quiet on his blanket. Beautiful fingers, long and tapered. Piano fingers, Priscilla always said. Piano fingers, gaming fingers, lightning quick.

"You were hardly ever sick," she told him. "When you were little, you barely had an ear infection. If you and Diana came down with something you'd be sick for just a day. That's all."

He breathed evenly, but his eyes were only partly closed. She always told parents to assume their child could hear them.

"You're strong," she told him. "You're very strong, and you're in the right place. This is the place . . ."

He stirred and cried out softly.

"It's me. It's just me," she told him in her low, urgent voice. "I know we've fought. It doesn't matter now. It didn't even matter then. I love you just the same as I did when you were born. I'm with you now, just the way I was then."

Nurses came to check on Kerry and Aidan. Robyn, the duty nurse, came in to work, but she and others also came to clasp Kerry's hand, to bring her tea, to promise, I'll watch him if you need to sleep. I'll sit here for you. No, no, Kerry said. I'll stay. But all that long night, as Kerry watched over Aidan, her friends watched over her.

24

Discovery

While Kerry sat with Aidan in the hospital, Nina paced her apartment. She had changed from her silk dress into a cotton nightshirt, tossed her hair clips onto the dresser. She tried watching a movie on her computer. Then she tried to read her battered Thoreau. She leafed through her students' papers, but all she saw was Collin holding his cold glass to Daphne's wrist.

She tried to stifle jealousy, or at least outwork it. Sitting on the couch, she stacked and restacked her students' end-of-year portfolios. One by one, she opened composition books. She stared at Brynna's perfect, even printing, Marisol's huge letters, ballooning in blue ballpoint, every *s* a sail, every dot a circle, round as a full moon. She opened Anton's journal and saw anime drawings, spiky-haired punks with evil grins and inky eyes.

The sun was rising when Nina fell asleep with her computer and her headphones and her students' journals on the couch. She woke hours later in a jumble of composition books and wires. Bleary, barely conscious, she thought of Collin and she missed him, even as the events of the evening came rushing back to her. Half dreading, half hoping for a message, she checked her phone and found a medical alert from school: ONE OF OUR STUDENTS WAS ADMITTED LAST NIGHT TO CHILDREN'S HOSPITAL. AIDAN O'NEIL IS IN SERIOUS BUT STABLE CONDITION WITH A DIAGNOSIS OF MENINGITIS.

Now she was awake, startled from her own unhappiness. Aidan? She thought about the disciplinary meeting—Aidan's performance in DeLaurentis's office. SOME FORMS OF MENINGITIS ARE CONTAGIOUS. WE ARE WAITING TO LEARN WHETHER . . . What was it about him? A kind of chivalry as he took the blame, a strange protectiveness, although he had dragged his sister into trouble, copying her work. There was something brilliant and dangerous about Aidan. "I've had kids like him before," Mrs. West had told Nina after the plagiarism meeting. "I taught a kid named Daniel with an attitude like that. You know where he is now? In jail."

Alarmed, uncertain, Nina sat up. She remembered that Diana had written about her brother. He was a liar or a stoner. Diana had written unhappily about him.

Nina began searching for Diana's Journal of Discovery. She sifted through her composition books, and eventually she found it in an unread pile in her bedroom. Nina sat in bed and returned to the black-ink thicket of Diana's writing. Entries on *The Scarlet Letter,* entries on Thoreau. When she'd marked the journal the first time, Nina had been checking to see that Diana had done the reading. Now Nina skipped over Diana's analysis, such as it was, and searched out the places where Diana digressed or misinterpreted or ignored the question.

Q. How would you characterize Hawthorne's ghost stories? How does he use ghosts to represent the past?

Living with my brother its like living with a ghost. If you leave out a sandwich it might not be there later but you won't see him, only his shoes. When I see him

Nina turned the page.

. . . I'm like who are you because he is inside his game. He is obsessed with this game like he prefers to be there—even though he

is not allowed. Hes not supposed to play but he always finds a way to get inside.

Q. How would you characterize the mood in Whitman's opening line: "I sing the body electric"? What do you think about when you read these words?

Danger. High voltage! People turning into machines. Instead of blood vessels wires instead of brains circuits chips etc. Or machines turning into people inhabiting people infecting their brains, controlling them so they do whatever the machine wants them to.

Or what would it be like if a machine controlled the world instead? Like the world is a game and you just live in it? You think you're a player but actually you're getting played?

Once again, Nina remembered Aidan in DeLaurentis's office. Clear-eyed, he had countered every question. Such was his confidence. He might have been a patriot captured and questioned by the enemy, or a young saint who heard angelic voices.

Q. Consider Bartleby's famous line: "I would prefer not to." What is he rejecting? What do those words mean to you?

I would prefer not to wake up in the dark that really sucks. I would prefer not to go to school. I would prefer not to be seen. I would prefer not to enter the cafeteria. I would prefer not to eat lunch. I would prefer not to care what anybody thinks. I would prefer not to do my homework. I would prefer not to take out the recycling. I would prefer not to hear squirrels in the attic. I would prefer not to go down to the basement (mice). I would prefer no games, no paint, no lies. I would prefer you to leave since your gone already. CU Aidan. CUCU

Nina stared at that chain of letters linked together. No paint. No lies. He had tagged the school. Diana had confessed it.

Everybody's got secrets. Whats more interesting is when you find out other peoples. Then the question is do you tell on THEM? For example my twin and I were like blood brothers only moreso. Now its like he moved away. I hear him whispering daphne daphne.

No, it couldn't be. It was too strange. She reread Diana's words, expecting them to change—but they did not. This was where she'd seen Daphne's name—in the Discovery Journal. And this was how Daphne did her work. Aidan was Daphne's rabid fanboy. Nina could see it even now. Daphne had led him on, although she had not mentioned where she'd led him.

Don't panic. Think. There were rules. There must be rules for this. The school had guidelines for red flags and danger signs. In her capacity as Language Arts Team Leader, Mrs. West had briefed new teachers on calls for help. I think I'm going to drown myself. I fantasize about shooting my parents or my teachers or my class-mates. I'm going to set myself on fire in the gym. That kind of thing. "You'll know it when you see it. And if you see it, report it," Mrs. West told the assembled faculty at orientation. "Do not hesi-tate!"

What should she do? Go to Mrs. West? Run to Miss Sorentino, the school psychologist? Diana's journal was neither hate speech nor suicide note, but suggested Aidan had committed a crime. The diary revealed this—but could anybody apart from Nina see it?

Her mind raced on, and she imagined Aidan with a new can of paint, then with a dagger, then a gun. Millions play, her father al-ways told reporters. In every population of this size you'll find a couple of crazies. That was what her father said after the mall shooting in Connecticut, the massacre in Norway. Gaming is like the world. No one can prove gaming causes violent crime. It's not what gaming does to you. Gaming is what you bring. Despite this, she imagined Daphne enticing Aidan. She imagined EverCon, and beyond that a bigger marketplace, and she felt responsible—not theoretically, but personally, responsible. Arkadia was not simply property of her father and her uncle. Viktor had given her a share of the company when she was a little child. Nina was a silent part-ner in more ways than one; she never spoke of this.

She was implicated. She had not divested herself, but had maintained her position. She had been practical, imagining she could use her money to do good work. She had been loyal to her father's enterprise, despite her doubts. What a hypocrite she'd been.

She threw off the covers and snatched up Diana's journal. Took the composition book to her desk in the living room and began scanning pages, one after another.

Nina? Collin texted Nina on her phone. u there?

no, she typed back.

can you talk?

can't.

cant or wont?

we'll just fight.

A moment later, phone in hand, he was standing in her doorway. "Let's fight, then."

"You scared me!" She was pale, exhausted, her hair rough, unbrushed.

"What are you doing?"

She cut him off. "There's just one thing I want to say to you."

"Say whatever you want." He meant, Say you hate me. Say I drink too much. Say that I was out of line.

But she said none of those things. She stood in front of her scanner and told Collin, "Daphne can't play with kids. It's wrong, and if you don't see why, then I can never, ever be with you."

"Why don't you just admit you're angry at me?"

"You're not thinking what Daphne does to people."

"She's never done anything to me."

"She plays kids. She played Aidan and he chased her and now he's in the hospital."

"What? Slow down! Aidan O'Neil? Kerry's kid?"

At last Nina had startled him. She showed Collin the medical alert from school and he said, "What if he got Daphne sick?"

"That's what you're worried about?"

It seemed obvious to Nina that nothing bad would ever happen to Daphne. She was the perpetrator, not the victim. "She led him on. That's her test marketing."

"With one sixteen-year-old. Who could be anyone!"

"She uses him to get the word out."

"How would Aidan get the word out?"

She spoke with fevered intensity. "In pranks. On walls."

"What are you talking about?"

"He tagged Emerson."

"Prove it."

She almost showed him Diana's journal. She nearly opened to the page—and then she held back, afraid of making a mistake, betraying student-teacher confidentiality, exposing Aidan, helpless in the hospital.

"You're imagining what *could* happen," Collin told her.

She took a deep breath. "I'm not imagining. I know."

"You know for sure? You can say without a doubt?"

"Yes."

"How?"

"I can't tell you."

"So I just have to trust you."

She nodded.

"Then can I ask you something?"

"What?"

"Why can't you trust me?"

25

Lucky

Diana slept on the couch. The air conditioners were too heavy to carry from the basement, and without them, it was too hot to sleep upstairs. Monday morning, she padded to the kitchen and listened to the house creak. The phone rang, and people left messages. Mrs. Solomon called to inform Kerry that Diana was absent from school.

Maia came over with a casserole of vegetarian enchiladas, and Diana said thank you very much, but as soon as Maia left, she slid the whole thing into the freezer. She was too hot to eat. Too hot for anything. She took off her shirt and lay on the living room rug. Then she took off her shorts. Her long hair smothered her neck and shoulders.

When her mother phoned that afternoon, Diana roused herself to answer. "Hello."

"Diana?"

"No, this is a robber," Diana said.

"What?"

"Yes, Mom. It's Diana. Who else would it be?"

"How are you, sweetheart?"

"I'm fine," Diana said.

"He's sleeping now. He's stable," said Kerry, although Diana hadn't asked.

"Okay."

"You can see him. I can't leave, but Priscilla says she'll drive you."

Diana didn't answer.

"Are you there? Diana?"

"What?"

"Just go next door and ask. She's glad to take you. She has to finish a lesson this afternoon but then . . ."

Even as her mother spoke, Diana climbed the stairs to the stifling second floor. Her entire body was slippery with sweat.

"You're breaking up," Kerry said.

Diana dropped the receiver into the laundry hamper in the bathroom. Then she peeled off her underwear.

The bathroom had white penny tiles on the floor. There was a shower curtain printed with yellow rubber duckies, a small sink with a square mirror over it, a glass shelf cluttered with acne wash, toothpaste, and a jar of toothbrushes, combs, and scissors. Diana's blue bathrobe hung on a hook on the door, but it was too hot to wear. For a long time, Diana stood in the cold shower. She stood there until she couldn't stand it any longer. Then she stepped out, shivering.

Even she was surprised by the girl in the mirror. She wasn't thin, but she was sturdy, muscular from so much running, her breasts pink-tipped, her eyes fierce, her hair dripping down her back. She didn't recognize herself at all.

She took a comb and raked all her hair forward so that it covered her face. She could barely see herself in the mirror through black strands. She took the scissors and held it open in her hand, cool blades against her palm. For a moment she wanted to feel that blade slicing her skin. She imagined her own blood, red-black, spotting the tile floor. She thought about it, but she cut her hair instead.

Deliciously cool to shear off all that heavy hair. She didn't try to cut evenly, just hacked away until she could run her hand through the mop she had left. Her eyes were darker in the mirror, her face paler. She looked almost like a boy.

She dressed in basketball shorts, a sports bra, and a black mesh shirt, but couldn't find clean socks. She glanced at her bed covered with laundry, her dresser piled high with crap. Pencils and rubber bands, marbles and beads, staplers and the wrong-size staples, a broken alarm clock covered in thick dust. She said aloud, "I feel bad for whoever lives here."

In the kitchen she found a stack of paper grocery bags. She took them to her room and threw them on the floor. She announced, "Let's recycle, shall we?" and swept her dresser clean. She picked up all the stray school assignments and receipts and cardboard boxes from her floor and stuffed them into bags. Stripped her bed of its faded princess sheets and stuffed them into a bag along with her pillowcases. She pulled plush animals from her closet. Duck. Rainbow fish. Black horse with a mane matted from the dryer. There was a small bison, which she had called her "dison." "Time to get a life," she told her childhood elephant.

The doorbell startled her. At first she didn't answer. Then she heard the bell again. Her mother? No, stupid, your mother has the key. Except she might have lost it! She rushed downstairs.

Miss Lazare.

Diana held the glass storm door open with her body.

"Diana?"

"Yes?" Forgetting her new look, unconscious of the stuffed elephant in her hands, Diana wondered why Lazare seemed so confused.

"I was so sorry to hear about your brother," Lazare began.

"What do you mean?" Diana felt a surge of dread.

"I heard he's in the hospital."

"Oh." Diana could breathe again.

"I'm sorry," Lazare repeated.

"Thanks."

"I wanted to ask if you're okay."

Diana gazed into Lazare's anxious eyes. "I'm good."

"Because you weren't in school."

"So I hear," Diana said.

"And I have your Discovery Journal." Lazare held out the composition notebook. "And I was wondering . . . I wanted to know if we could . . . You wrote some things that made me think you might want to talk, either to me or to someone at school."

Diana took the composition notebook.

"There were some things you wrote about your brother," her teacher said in that very gentle voice adults used when they wanted to pry something out of you.

Just a step back, and Diana could retreat inside. The glass door would snap shut again.

"You seemed worried," Lazare said.

"Not really."

Diana's teacher took a deep breath. "You say he's playing nonstop, and you don't know if you should tell on him."

"Wow," Diana said slowly, amazed that her teacher would come out and talk to her like that, not only rereading but repeating written words—dragging Diana's dark, unformed thoughts into the light.

"I thought you might want to—"

"Hey!" Diana cut her off. "Are you talking about my family?" Her face was burning. She had never spoken to a teacher in this way.

Lazare said, "I was afraid you wrote about your brother for a reason."

"No, not at all," Diana said. "Only for the assignment. Educational purposes only!"

She stepped inside and the glass door snapped shut. Then she closed the wood door, and locked it too. She was the only one left, and it was up to her to defend the house. Go away, Diana thought. Get the hell away from me.

She ran down to the basement, which was piled with cartons and moldering window shades. She pushed hard and opened a door to the utility room. There, behind the water heater, she had hidden her doll carriage. Inside the carriage under blankets lay Aidan's black BoX. "Stay there," she said, and stuffed her journal deep inside. "Sit tight." She left her elephant on top.

Hour after hour, Aidan slept. The sun had set, but he didn't know the difference. He had been moved from the ICU to a regular room, and in two days he had two different roommates, a little boy and then a baby in a hospital crib. Doctors rounded, nurses came to change his bags and check his drips. Janitors emptied receptacles of trash and sharps and linens. At night they buffed and polished the smooth floors. Children tottered outside his door and their parents supported them, one step at a time. A chaplain came and blessed the baby on the other side of the curtain. Aidan slept on. He saw none of this.

Sitting at his side, Kerry watched pain, fear, longing flash across his face, and she spoke to him. Sometimes she prayed, "Please." Sometimes she whispered, "Aidan. Where are you?"

Even as she sat with Aidan, he fought on. He killed a thousand bats, yet every moment, more attacked. With huge effort he shook them off, and still they flew at him from their caverns until at last he could do no more than kneel, feeling for some tunnel, or some hole in which to hide. If he could get to the river, the great silver river, if he could immerse himself, that dead water would cover him entirely. Nothing could hurt him then.

Kerry roused herself to cheer him on. "You'll be all right. You're breathing on your own. Your body is resting." She asked and answered her own questions. "Tell me, Aidan. Do you know where you are? You're at the hospital. Do you know why you're here? You have meningitis. Do you know what's going to happen? You're going to get better. Can you hear me? Can you squeeze my hand?"

He did hear his mother, not all the words, but most of them. Do you know you're at the hospital? Her voice was both close and far away, like the rush when you pressed a seashell to your ear. Can you hear my hand?

Ten o'clock at night, Kerry dozed in her chair, and Aidan clawed for some way out, trying to escape the bats feasting on his flesh.

"Mom?"

Kerry jumped at the light touch on her shoulder. "Aidan!" For a split second, she thought he'd risen from his bed. She saw him standing before her in his black shirt, basketball shorts.

"It's just me," Diana said.

"What did you do to yourself?" Kerry cried out. "What happened to your hair?"

"I cut it." Diana was gazing at Aidan. Her mother was still talking, but Diana could barely hear.

Sleep-deprived and overwrought, Kerry felt possessed by her twins' strange reciprocity. Even as she'd told herself Aidan needed a haircut, Diana had chopped off her own hair.

"You just went at it with a scissors? Diana. *Why?*"

"I was hot," Diana answered automatically.

"I left you all alone."

Diana just stared at Aidan, with the needles in his hand and tubes and bags.

"Where's Priscilla?" Kerry asked her daughter. "Did she drive you?"

"No." Aidan was shrouded in his sheets, his faintly printed hospital gown. His chest seemed empty as he breathed in and out.

"I don't think you should take the T at this hour of night."

"I didn't take the T. I just ran over. Hey, Aidan."

"He needs to rest."

"It's me," Diana told her brother.

Kerry broke in, "Wait. What do you mean you just ran over?"

"Look at me," Diana said, but Aidan's eyes remained closed. There was something strange about the lids, as though they'd been sealed, gold lashes glued together. His skin was strange as well, almost translucent. Yes, he was breathing, but he wasn't sleeping normally. He was becoming a statue, an icon of himself. She could see the metal in his cheek. "Open your eyes."

He didn't move.

Diana's voice trembled. "Open your eyes because you're scaring me."

He stirred, turning ever so slightly toward her.

Kerry stood next to Diana. "Keep talking."

Diana's voice sounded hollow, as though someone else were speaking. "So now that you're here, I figured it was a good time to cut my hair, flunk my exams, and sell your stuff."

His eyelids twitched.

"Kidding!"

"Go on," Kerry whispered.

Diana told Aidan whatever came into her head. "Remember in fifth grade when we had that field trip and all the mummies kept beeping when we stepped too close?"

No response.

Remember the bodies in their coffins? Diana thought. Remember their gold masks? She could see Aidan's body; she could see his mask.

"Remember when Jack caught that bird?" If Aidan remembered anything, he would remember this. On a different field trip, in Copley Square, Jack had actually caught an obese pigeon with his bare hands. Teachers started screaming, Oh, my God, what are you doing? Don't touch that thing—it's filthy! Drop it! Drop it! The whole time the pigeon kept flapping in Jack's hands.

Nothing.

"Remember when we went on the T into Boston by ourselves and we thought someone was going to kidnap us? Remember when we thought if we clasped our hands together we could cast spells? Remember how I turned into a deer? I ran three miles tonight. I ran across the BU Bridge and followed the signs for Longwood Medical Area. I was like that crazed deer in UnderWorld."

When she said "UnderWorld," Aidan opened his eyes.

"Don't stop," Kerry whispered.

Aidan's irises were bright as coins, expressionless. Looking at him hurt, like staring at the sun.

"Keep talking," Kerry said.

Diana repeated the one word that was working. "I've been playing UnderWorld on your computer. I've been using your account," she added, just to get a rise out of him. "No, actually, I can't log in." She paused. Then asked tauntingly, "Could I have your password?"

Aidan's voice was hoarse but distinct, as he spoke for the first time in three days. "No!"

Kerry was crying. She was so relieved. Her tears were falling all over Aidan's pillow. Diana was embarrassed, because her mother always made such a big deal about everything, and because when she started crying she made Diana cry. "Aidan, make her stop," Diana said, brushing away her own tears, but Aidan did nothing. He had no energy to tell his mother what to do. To tell the truth, if he'd tried a stunt like that, Kerry would have cried even harder.

The nurse came in. Everyone was talking, but Aidan looked up at Diana. The gold was fading from his cheek, and his eyes were human, soft again, slightly amused. Can you believe this? he was asking silently.

"You're awake!" Kerry told him, as if he didn't know.

Then Aidan smiled at Diana and she knew exactly what he meant. Their mother was so crazy. Dying was so boring. As soon as I can walk, I'm outta here. He said all this without words, and Diana understood. Kerry could read her children, but only haltingly. They were her second language. Diana was a native speaker; she came from Aidan's country. When he closed his eyes again, she knew he wasn't going anywhere.

Now the air-conditioning rushed over her, and her sweaty T-shirt chilled her skin. The hairs were standing up on her arms, and she could feel each one individually. She could feel everything from the most enormous, overarching joy down to the jagged middle toenail stabbing the toe next to it inside her right shoe. She wasn't just happy, she was thirsty. Actually, she was starving. She realized all this as she watched Aidan drift off to sleep again. Kerry was still tiptoeing around the bed, but Diana said, "Mom, could we order pizza?" because everything was good now. Aidan had decided to come back to life.

The next day, he began to look about him. He saw his IV, his plastic bracelet, his scanty gown, his uneaten dinner on the swing arm tray. He began to see the colors of the hospital, grays and muted pinks, the red sharps container on the wall.

His eyes were fierce, even as he lay crumpled in his bed. He seemed to Kerry like a rescued bird of prey, one of those injured hawks caged with a few dead mice for dinner. He was quiet and obedient and—he even let her touch him—almost tame. Stay like this, she thought, even as she prayed for his recovery. Stay gentle. Please don't fly away.

Slowly his strength returned. He lost track of days, but every morning he limped along, leaning on his mother in the hall. Through open doors he saw other mothers in other patients' rooms. Beds decorated with helium balloons, windows covered with cards and paper flowers. Wasn't he too big for this? At the end of the hall they stopped at a lounge filled with toys and dolls and children's books. There were shelves of children's movies. "People donate their old stuff," his mother said. There was a play operating table as well, where a large teddy bear awaited surgery. Or was it a rabbit? He couldn't tell. He had to rest, and, sinking into a tiny armchair, he felt childish and unsteady. He was growing younger and more wobbly by the minute, even as his mother glowed, telling all her nurse friends, We're so lucky. Look, we're up and around!

He knew where his mother was going with all this. In her mind, if you were lucky, you were also blessed, and once you were blessed, it was just a tiny jump to everything happening for a reason, and God putting you on this earth for a purpose. He didn't buy any of it, but he didn't argue either. Leaning on Kerry as they walked back to his room, he was simply grateful for his mother, and happy that she didn't have his BoX.

He was thankful in small ways as well. Glad to wear his own pajamas, grateful to lose his catheter. He felt something else too, a strange curiosity as he observed his own recovery. After four days at the hospital, he closed his eyes and he saw nothing, no spots or sparks, no monsters approaching, just darkness. On the fifth morning, he woke empty, as though he'd run out of dreams. Could that happen? Could your imagination actually run out of things to see? Fascinated, he tried to remember where he'd been last. Caverns? Tunnels? Crevasses? Which circle? Seven or Eight? Briefly his gaming history vanished, and he could not remember where he had left off.

Only Daphne stayed with him. The kiss, the shock of meeting her, his intense desire, and his humiliation. He wanted to speak to her, wanted very much to hurt her. He imagined ripping her open with his sword. But his fantasy had little heat. His mind drifted away.

His fingers began tapping. Softly they drummed the edge of the mattress, and he thought he would be a drummer. He would play drums as he had before, in Liam's band. Or he would play keyboard. Scales and sonatinas returned to him as he lay in bed, and he thought, I'll play again.

The next day this conviction faded. He watched the young resident listening to his heartbeat with a stethoscope. For the first time it occurred to Aidan how strange that was, to listen to another life. The doctor was listening intently, as though he could hear distant hoofbeats, and Aidan thought, I will study medicine.

By evening this vocation floated off as well. All his ideas were abstract, all his desires theoretical. He observed, he admired, he imagined, but he wanted nothing—not even UnderWorld.

Maybe meningitis had wiped out his gaming life. He knew that this was what his mother hoped. This was what she really meant by lucky. When she said everything happened for a reason, she was praying that fever burned the games right out of you.

"Aidan." She was sitting on his bed, and the sky was dark outside his window. "I want to ask you something."

"I know," he said. She wanted him to start over, to return from the hospital cleansed of all his sins. Then this ordeal would be a blessing, his meningitis actually an act of God.

"Could you promise?" She looked so thin. Her hair and hands, her arms, were light as straw. All the color had leached out of her, as though she had taken on his illness for herself. Even Kerry's eyes were ghostly blue. "Promise you won't play again."

He hadn't touched a computer in what seemed like years. Looking down upon himself, as from a great distance, his own thoughts seemed strange, oddly colorless, like clouds. Not even clouds, but the shadows of clouds on empty valleys. How still it was, how slow. Delicious to lie back powerless, to drop the threads of all your gaming lives. It was a kind of death, an abdication. His kingdom would carry on without him as he lay in state. He would sleep and sleep. It was easy to say yes.

26

Walden Woods

The heat smothered Collin outside Arkadia's air-conditioned halls. He had been working such long hours, drawing such beautiful and terrible things, that he felt a kind of grief to leave, as though he were giving up his wings to walk the streets. Summer days were white, overexposed. Trees dusty, and all the flowers overblown. Old houses flaked, bricks needed repointing, and you couldn't do the job in one stroke either. You couldn't change colors in an instant, or render different trees, or refresh roses dry and withered in the sun.

Nina was waiting for him in her VW bug, and he eased himself in. "Thank you."

"You're welcome," she said, shyly.

Quiet, careful with each other, they drove past Waltham's office parks. Were those tiny birds filling the air? Like aeroflakes, they scattered and then drew together.

"Where do you want to go?" she said.

"Anywhere."

"Let's get lunch."

"No," he told her. "Let's get out of here."

They drove to Walden Woods, just a few minutes away. She wasn't dressed for hiking, and they had no food or water, but they parked at the trailhead and they went walking anyway, taking the dirt path into the shady trees.

The light was green, the boulders massive. Chartreuse silkworms swayed on invisible threads. Some leaves were bright, some dark and glossy, some dull, some pale, some olive, and all around them, pines grew straight up to the sun.

It was amazing how fast Arkadia dematerialized in this green light. Mountain ranges and wild horses, brilliant sunsets, Whennish alliances, even UnderWorld's silver river faded away. The lowliest leaf, brown and shriveled, brittle-veined, showed more life and detail than anything in EverWhen. The humblest rock displayed more intricate patterns, lichened, mica-flecked, cool and wet on its underside, sheltering a thousand ants.

Collin helped Nina when the trail got steep. He offered her his hand as they crossed a shallow stream. His shoes squelched, his jeans, her skirt wicked water. Mossy stones slipped under them. No flying here, no bounding over rivers. The stream was slippery and refreshing, but their feet were slow, the whole forest heavy with summer heat.

Her sandals weren't good for climbing, so they didn't get far. They found a leafy knoll, and turned off the trail to rest. Higher and drier than the rocky path, carpeted with pine needles, the knoll was shaded by young trees. Collin sat down, leaning back against a maple. Nina sat on his lap, leaning back against him.

"What if we were the size of tiny insects—like mayflies?" he asked.

"I wouldn't want to live for just one day."

"But it wouldn't seem like just a day to us." Collin closed his eyes.

"I would rather be a bird," Nina said.

"What kind? A little one, or something like an ostrich?"

She answered slowly. "Maybe an owl."

"Are you sleepy?"

"Are you happy?" Nina was so quiet, and so close, the question might have been his own.

"I am now."

"I went to see Diana," Nina told him, "but she wouldn't talk to me."

"Of course not. You're a teacher," Collin said.

She turned to face him and she wasn't thinking about Diana. She was thinking about Daphne. "I do jump to conclusions."

He pushed back her long heavy hair. "It's okay."

"Not really."

"Nina," he said, "it was a million years ago."

"A week."

"That's like a million years in EverWhen."

"I don't like her."

He tried to keep it light. "She's not your type."

She settled down again, leaning against him. As far as Collin was concerned, their fight was history, and so Nina's next question startled him. "Do you ever draw her?"

"What?"

"Do you draw Daphne?"

"No!" Collin lied reflexively. Why was she still thinking that way? How could she mention Daphne in this place, under these trees? "She's obsessed with Peter," Collin added.

"So are you."

"Not like that."

"He's got you drawing nonstop. He'll get you to the point where you *can't* stop."

Collin frowned.

Nina said, "He's hard to resist." She was thinking of the way Peter had driven Julianne, recording her for hours. Julianne had been sixteen when she sang those mermaid voices. She had wilted with exhaustion, but Peter would not let up. He kept her working and he kept watching her. "I'm afraid he'll crush you."

"Give me a little credit!"

"Sorry." Nina's face was pink, flushed with heat.

"You're way too serious," Collin said. "What's the opposite of a martyr?"

"A tormentor?"

"No. Someone too good."

"A savior?"

"Yeah, you think you have to be a savior."

She bent her head. "I was out of line with Diana."

"And that's the other thing. You think everything is set in stone. You screwed up with Diana. So what? We had a fight. It's over. Just erase and start again."

She almost laughed.

"You see?" He caressed her until she licked his neck, salty with sweat, rolled up his shirt, so that his bare skin slid against hers. He had her to himself again.

"What was that?" She raised her head.

Children calling to each other on the trail below. The panting, jingling sound of dogs. "Let's go back." She meant to her apartment, where they could be alone.

The children's voices faded away. Someone called the dogs, and they ran off.

They turned toward each other, tousled, pine needles in their hair. "Do you really want to go home?"

"No."

"Then stay."

But already mosquitoes were hovering, grazing their wrists. Nina sprang to her feet and shook them off.

He wished he could draw Nina then. Her white arms. Her waist, where T-shirt and skirt didn't quite meet. He wished he could do justice to her eyes, not gray but silver in the dappled light. Instinctively he felt in his pockets for a bit of chalk, but he had none. He picked up a stick. "Pick a tree, any tree."

"What do you mean?"

"Just choose one."

She pointed to the pine in front of her.

"Too close."

She pointed to a bigger pine farther away.

He flung his stick like a machete, end over end, and hit the pine square on the trunk. "Another."

She pointed to a maple, even farther off.

"That's Peter." He picked up a second stick and she watched it cartwheeling through the air. It struck the trunk dead center and bounced backward.

She chose a dogwood, and an oak, another sticky pine, some trees close, and others far away. He threw and threw, and he hit every single mark.

"How do you do that?"

"Pure talent," he teased, but it was true. He was outstanding at stick throwing. Fence climbing. Stone skipping. "I'm good at all the sports nobody plays."

She kissed him and she felt his warmth.

He cupped his hands around her face, and he admonished himself as well as Nina. "Remember this."

27

Half Magic

If Walden Woods banished Arkadia from your mind, the opposite was also true. At work, the outside world felt like a dream, far away and insubstantial. You earned real money, but you barely had the time to spend it. Collin bought himself his dream bike, an Eddy Merckx AX, but he was too busy to shop for other toys. He could afford a new apartment—except he didn't have a day to look. Maybe it was for the best. He didn't want to be materialistic—and he loved having money in the bank. He could pay for dinner. He could go to a movie without thinking.

Long summer days turned into nights, and he slept at Arkadia on the hellions' black couch. He closed his eyes and imagined his hands on Nina's waist, his fingers unbuttoning her shirt, her hair tumbling down her bare back. He wanted her, but woke to work and play again. He drew horses for hours, and then he turned to EverWhen to stoke his imagination.

There was a cove near the Whennish shore where waves washed into tide pools, and you could search for pearls. There was another place he liked to wander, beyond the tree line on EverRest. The world was white, with craggy peaks of ice, the only shelter crystal caves between the rocks. You had to break your way inside, cutting down icicles, which shattered at your feet. In the deepest cave, a race of Dwarves served a white-haired, white-eyed queen. Her eyes were frosty, her hands translucent, her behavior secretive. You knew that she was hiding a rich jewel. Other gamers told you where. She had a ruby for a heart.

He played so late and worked so long that his own art raced away from him. His horses ran untamed through the Trackless Wood. Lovely onscreen, they overwhelmed you in the round. First you heard them. Hoofbeats coming closer. Then the sound of branches breaking as they tore the underbrush. Magical, unearthly, they surrounded you with tangled manes and flying legs and dark eyes flashing through the trees. Drawing them apart, he developed each horse as a character, the gentle dapple-gray, the chestnut mare with the scar on its right flank, the black high-kicking stallion. No detail was too small to realize, none too difficult to render. Any line he drew might live and breathe in game.

He sat with Nicholas in his black padded office, and they tried out sound prints for each animal. Collin had no control over UnderWorld's soundtrack, but it was magic listening to the possibilities.

"These are for the chestnut." Nicholas clicked a file on his monitor and Collin heard a quick light step, a sleek rustling, a whinnying, a single twig breaking. "These are for the black." Nicholas opened another file, and Collin heard the stallion's pounding hooves, its heavy breath, the rip and tear of brambles in its path.

"What about when they run through water?"

"Yeah, I've got this muddy sucking sound, and splashing."

Even without visuals, Collin could hear the animals fording a stream. "What if one of them slips? One of them could slip scrambling up the bank."

"Yeah!" Nicholas said. "You hear them slide and then they're struggling. You hear them flailing. And then they scream."

Nicholas was at least fifty, a veteran of three major games and countless game expansions. His beard was gray and his hair was thin on top, and a lot of times he had to wear reading glasses, but he played all kinds of guitars and he could sing. He was a vocalist of the Bob Dylan variety, singer-screamer-songwriter. "How's this?" He opened new files: whinnying, running, and footfalls. Clicking on his computer, he adjusted the volume, and suddenly a horse was screaming, thrashing, dying in a ditch.

Collin flinched, and Nicholas said, "Okay. We're doing something right."

"That was like the worst thing I've ever heard."

Nicholas leaned back his swivel chair. "Thank you."

He looked so supremely satisfied that Collin said, "You love it here."

Nicholas thought about this. "Sometimes I hate it," he said at last. "Sometimes I'm burned out—but I try to stay inspired." He held up his phone, flashing a picture of his son.

Of course, Collin thought. You have to support your kid. That changes everything.

"Sometimes I get bored," Nicholas admitted.

Unconsciously, Collin massaged his right hand with his left. "Then what?"

"I keep going anyway."

"You force yourself?"

Nicholas kept clicking at his keyboard even as he spoke. "Yeah, but you keep going with your own shit too. You keep your little projects going on the side."

A sound of bells, no, faint wind chimes, filled the padded room. The sound of wind rustling in the trees, and then soft chords on a guitar, music frayed around the edges, a wordless kind of blues. All this emerged from Nicholas's speakers.

"What's that?"

"That's me," said Nicholas. "That's my stuff."

The music stopped instantly when he closed the file. "Okay, what else you got?"

"I'm drawing the stallion. Again."

That night in the conference room called the Keep, Collin presented his latest stallion to the hellions. He touched his slate and transferred his small drawings to the big electronic board.

In silence, Peter gazed at Collin's creation, a horse scarier than any other, a biter and a kicker with a bold head and hard black eyes. It was crueler than Collin's previous attempts. Each of those stallions had caught Peter's attention briefly, and then, one by one, they wouldn't suit. They had been too heroic or too noble, or simply too beautiful for UnderWorld. Nobody could say that now. The new horse looked like death, with its gaunt body and vicious mouth, its ragged coat, translucent, dirty white.

Peter frowned, and Collin steeled himself.

Peter examined Collin's work in silence. Come on, thought Collin, but Peter didn't speak.

He took the stylus from Collin's hand. Then, wielding the slender rod like his own wand, Peter touched the stallion's eye. It took only a moment, but the effect was brilliant, ghastly. The horse's bright eye filled with blood. Now the stallion looked possessed. Now Collin's drawing became a character, riveting, repellent.

The whole room hushed as Peter stepped back from the board. One touch and Peter had transformed Collin's horse entirely.

"That's sick," said Peter, contemplating his own work.

A team player would have rejoiced. A humbler artist might have thanked Peter for the lesson. Collin did neither. His feelings were confused. Awe mixed with anger, a sense that Peter had destroyed something. And yet Peter had not destroyed the horse. He had revealed its full potential—and made it his own. All eyes were on

Peter, all praise to him. Even Daphne clapped her hands. It's true—you're obsessed with him, thought Collin. You can't take your eyes off him.

But the moment passed and Daphne was herself again. She was warmer to Collin than before, staying late, after everybody left, laughing, commiserating, showing off her work. She drew up a chair and revealed her new project, posting on fan forums as an anti-gaming activist named Christian Wench.

"Listen to this." Daphne read from her tablet, *"Rise up against UnderWorld! It is the work of Satan. Destroy this game before it destroys our children!"*

"What's the point of that?"

"Rallying the troops!"

"More like aggravating them."

"That's publicity," she said. "We got a hundred responses in the first minute." Daphne scrolled through furious comments. "Oh, look. My second death threat. *I'm cuming for u cutting off your . . .*" She seemed amused, if slightly rattled, by the hatred Christian Wench inspired.

"That's not funny." He was reading over her shoulder.

"Oh, come on. I'm trying to cheer you up."

Her words startled him. She had never before acknowledged what he might feel, or admitted any impulse beyond the desire to win.

"I don't need cheering up."

"You looked crushed in there."

"Fuck you."

"Play with me."

"Why?"

"Because no one's here." Her tone was light, but her breath was soft and eager. The building couldn't be empty, and yet for now they were alone. Other hellions had gone home. Their idle work-

stations had passed into dream mode, monitors displaying ARKA-
DIA in stars.

She took both his hands and he let her pull him to his feet. She
reminded him of Noelle when she was high. Eager, sweetly wild. In
the pale starlight, Daphne's eyes took on a strange sheen from too
much gaming, too much everything. "Come on."

He wanted her then. Hands on her hips, he pulled her in, but she
sprang back, teasing, "Duel in EverWhen."

Insulted, he shot back, "No."

"What, then?"

Of course she knew exactly what he wanted. He stepped closer,
but, like a boxer in her hooded sweatshirt, she danced out of reach.

His heart was pounding, but he kept his voice steady. "I want to
draw you."

For once he surprised her. "You've drawn me before."

"I want to draw you like this."

She held still for just a moment. His gaze unnerved and attracted
her. She followed as he wheeled a swivel chair into the conference
room where he had presented the ghost horse that afternoon.
"Here. Now." With a swipe of his hand, he erased the red-eyed
stallion covering the board. "Sit there." He pointed to the chair.

"What if I say no?"

Hands on her shoulders, he seated her.

Now she looked up at him, curious, mischievous, seriously
tempted, but he wouldn't touch her again. He wasn't a child for her
to tease. He backed away to draw her on his slate.

He sketched her short dark hair, her bright face, the soft folds of
her sweatshirt. Fierce, efficient, he drew Daphne's picture, and she
was amused, slightly disbelieving, as she sat for this formal portrait. Boldly she gazed back at Collin, but he controlled the situation. Her expression, sweet and dangerous, belonged to him.

Finishing his first sketch, he showed her the slate, and she was startled by the likeness. Wonderingly she gazed at her own blue eyes, her parted lips, her body floating in the dark. They stood together looking at her picture and he never touched her, but he had left his mark on her. She was impressed.

"Once more," he said.

He never asked, but she saw the question in his eyes. She unzipped her sweatshirt.

He drew her with the sweatshirt open to reveal her undershirt, and the leaves inked on her bare collarbone.

Daphne was serious now, conscious of her emerging image. Her body stilled and her eyes darkened as Collin drew her. Her mood began to match his.

As before, he showed her the slate. "Again?" She let him slip the sweatshirt off her shoulders.

Now he drew her neck, with its intricate design of leaves. He outlined her bare arms inked with stems. With total concentration, he drew her tattooed shoulders and the ribbed cloth of her clinging shirt. He maintained his distance, but he had her in his hands. For her part, she never moved. She never flinched as she gazed back at him.

Collin showed Daphne the slate and then erased it. He erased each drawing and deleted every image for good measure.

They didn't speak. He didn't need to ask. In silence, she locked the door and took off her undershirt. They were alone, and no one could walk in on them. She sat for Collin and her breasts were white, her nipples small and hard. He stepped back and took a breath, but even then, he didn't think that anyone would ever know.

No one walked in, but one person saw. Invisible to them, Peter sat in his office, watching Collin's sketch emerge on his own monitor. He could not see Collin, but he knew Collin's line. Only Collin drew like that, with such detail and speed.

"Careful, Collin," Peter said.

Even as Collin deleted Daphne's image, his drawing remained on Peter's workstation. Line by line, Peter watched the next drawing develop. Daphne's face, her short, tousled hair, her patterned arms and shoulders, her bare torso. "Careful," Peter murmured, but Collin couldn't hear.

28

The Question

Aidan sat at the kitchen table with his thousand-page textbook spread before him. He was sweating it out in summer school, learning cellular respiration. Oxidative phosphorylation. Cast away in the kitchen, without computer, without weapons, without any other voices in his ears, he gazed at the page, and the diagrams meant nothing to him. He waited, closed his eyes, and looked again. It was easy once he got his mind inside the picture. Once there, he could inhabit each cell's tiny factory. The hard part was getting in. Only sheer boredom did the trick. The table was bare except for a bag of pretzels. When those were gone, when he was left with salt dust at the bottom of the bag, he glared at his biology text until, like a sulky cat, his imagination came around again.

His mother said that he had changed, and she was right. She said life was a miracle, and he could see it. Little things like ice cream, or summer cloudbursts. He would think, Here I am, tasting Toscanini's cocoa pudding. Here I am, with rain streaming down my face. I might have missed all this. He watched sparrows hopping into puddles to wash their dusty feathers, and he thought, How sweet they are; I never noticed.

He was hungry again. He devoured dinner and then prowled the kitchen late at night, finishing whatever leftovers he could find. His desire to play grew stronger too. As he woke from sickness, regaining stamina and appetite, he dreamed about his spectral life. Even now, under the table, his right foot tapped nervously—but he held back. Thrill seeker, storm chaser, he couldn't qwest a little bit.

He sat in class three hours a day. He met with the school psychologist, Miss Sorentino, who was pale and strange, with huge eyeglasses and a metallic voice. "Who's better than you?" Sorentino would say whenever something pleased her. Patiently he sat at her desk and stared at her collection of miniature turtles. "This one's soapstone," she told Aidan. "This teeny one's made out of an acorn. This one's marble. This one's glass."

He did his time. He listened to Sorentino talk about his uniqueness and his future. "What do you think?" she asked. Sometimes she said, "It's up to you."

"I get it," he told her, and he wasn't lying. When he thought of gaming, he wrote in the margins of his bio notes, *Not now.* He knew how fortunate he was. Plagiarism was minor. As of yet, no one had accused him of his real crimes, and he knew better than to press his luck.

Even so, he felt the tidal pull of UnderWorld. Like water flowing underground, UnderWorld seeped into his ordinary life. How beautiful, how strange, to see dragons in the shadows, and silver in the Charles River. Phantom visions. He could drown in his own thoughts.

Diana was running down the stairs.

"Where are you going?" he called out to her.

"Where I always go." She had a summer job across the street. Every afternoon she took care of Sage and Melissa's one-year-old, Henry.

"Where's the BoX?"

"What?" She thought that she had misheard him, he asked so casually.

"Where did you put it?"

She stood there in shorts and T-shirt and dusty running shoes. "You said you wouldn't."

"I won't!"

"You said you wouldn't even ask."

"I was just curious." He turned back to his diagram of leaf and tree. "You don't have to tell me anything."

All afternoon, Diana felt uneasy. She took Henry to Hancock Park with a net bag of pails and shovels dangling from the stroller. She helped the toddler into the sandbox and tried to keep his sun hat on his head, and the whole time she was thinking, "You don't have to tell me anything." Was that supposed to reassure her? Or was it some kind of threat? Did Aidan plan to find the BoX himself?

She told Henry, "People as bald as you are should wear hats, or they'll get cancer."

"No," said Henry. It was one of his best words, along with "my."

"He'll never find it," she told Henry.

"No."

"He can't find it."

"No." Henry took off his hat.

"*Yes.*" She put his hat back on again.

He smiled, showing his two teeth, and took off the hat.

Stop panicking, she thought. He can't find it, because I don't have it. "He can look and look," she told Henry, as she pushed the stroller back to Antrim Street, "but I won't tell, and you won't tell."

Henry laughed because the ride was bumpy. He loved the jolts where the sidewalk buckled over tree roots.

. . .

"It's the little things, right?" Diana told Brynna that evening, as she laced her shoes. "Henry gets that."

"You like babies!"

"I like money."

They ran together along the river. At first Brynna complained she couldn't keep up, but six weeks into the summer she had lost what was left of her pregnancy weight. Diana burned—she was fair and freckled—but Brynna's body loved the sun. She tanned and her thick hair flew out behind her, streaked with gold.

"I think I might switch religions," Diana said.

"You can't switch," Brynna panted. "You're Catholic."

"I know, but . . . not really."

"You go to church," Brynna pointed out.

"My mom goes."

"What would you switch to?"

Diana glanced at the wind-ruffled river. "I'd be pagan."

Brynna snorted. "No, you wouldn't."

"I already am."

"Last year you were Wiccan," Brynna reminded her.

"That was different. I was younger then!"

They stopped at the light at the Eliot Bridge, and Brynna bent over, laughing. "Yeah, and now you're almost seventeen."

"I hate you," Diana said, although the opposite was true. When she was with Brynna, her uneasy feeling disappeared. When the light changed Diana took off again and her friend followed. Diana said, "I would be a pagan god."

Brynna didn't have the breath to answer.

"I'd be the god of secrecy," Diana said. "No one could get anything out of me."

"How much farther?"

"Just Fresh Pond."

"No way," protested Brynna.

Still, Diana pressed on, and Brynna followed.

They cut away from the river and ran up Brattle Street, and then up Sparks to Huron Avenue, past fancy stores like Graymist, which sold Nantucket baskets, and Marimekko, which sold umbrellas covered with enormous poppies. "You got this far," Diana encouraged her, but when they got to Formaggio Kitchen, Brynna sank down on the old-fashioned park bench out front.

"Please!" Diana begged. "We're almost there. I'll let you take the bus home."

Diana knew her friend could run all the way, but Brynna didn't. Brynna's cheeks were scarlet, and her shirt clung to her, soaking wet. Diana had to coax her into the store for air-conditioning and water.

"Wow." Cool air prickled the hair on their arms as they stared at all the treats. Ripe apricots, pluots, and nectarines. Strange pears. Tart cherry scones. Marble tables displaying slabs of sheep cheese, goat cheese, runny cheese, unpasteurized cheese. Brynna said, "Isn't that against the law?"

There were boxes of Belgian chocolate and Italian nougat. Salted caramels from Seattle. Candied violets. Amaretto truffles. You could buy chocolate-covered grapefruit peel. "Oh, my God, look," Brynna said. "Wild strawberries."

Tiny berries trailed over green pint-size containers. "This place is incredible," Diana said, in a hushed voice.

Brynna checked the price per pint. "And everything costs a bazillion dollars."

You couldn't even buy regular water. You had to buy spring water untouched by man. They burst out laughing as they escaped with their single purchase.

Diana took a long swig and handed the bottle to Brynna. "This water bubbled up through natural aquifers in a volcano."

Brynna splashed water on her own face. "How does that work?"

"Come on." Diana pulled her by the hand. "This is the best part of the day. See? The sun is going down."

"Next time." Brynna untied and retied her hair. "I have to take care of Angela."

"Please."

"Come back with me," Brynna offered.

Diana shook her head.

Alone, Diana ran up Huron Avenue to Fresh Pond, the reservoir, hidden in trees. There was a good trail there all around the pond, and a water fountain where you could splash yourself and dunk your head. Older ladies strolled along, deep in conversation, and every once in a while one of them would look at the water and say, It's so beautiful—look how still the water is. It's like glass; it's like a mirror. Look at the mist! And for a split second they would stop and look, and then they'd go right on talking. Joggers brought their terriers, and big black Labs and goldens, and Irish setters straining at the leash. But if you knew where to go, you didn't run into people so much. There was another pond, a smaller one, all choked with water lilies. The big pond was fenced, but at Little Fresh Pond, you could run right to the edge.

Diana knew a fallen tree, an oak that looked like it had taken its own life, keeling over and trailing its branches in the water. She ran to this tree, pulled off her shoes without unlacing them, and peeled off her sweaty socks. Broken bottles lay scattered on the ground. Frowning, she collected a few of the big shards, but the shore was littered with little jagged pieces. She gave up and climbed the toppled trunk to dangle her legs and soak her feet.

The sun had set. The first stars began to show themselves, but it wasn't dark. The evening was bright, and the trees stood black against the sky. Diana stretched herself out the length of the tree trunk, her back against the bark. It was good to rest; it was good to be alone, to test the edge of your own loneliness. When she looked up at the night sky she saw how impersonal it was, how big, how changeable. Everything was moving, trees, moon, stars. You tried to keep up, but you couldn't run fast enough.

A scuffling, growling sound.

She started up and then held still as possible, as she saw two pit bulls, racing through the trees off-leash. Their master called to them, but they scented her immediately and ran for her, barking, red-eyed.

"Anton!" she screamed when the dogs' master appeared. "Get your fucking dogs away!"

He ordered them to stay and then to sit. He clipped leashes to his dogs' collars, but they never took their eyes off her, and they growled deep in their throats, even as they obeyed. Anton didn't speak, but he stared as she scrambled off the tree trunk and retrieved her shoes and socks. His eyes traveled down her shoulders, and over her breasts, down the front of her wet shirt to the waistband of her shorts, then lightly over her bare legs to her feet.

"I didn't recognize you," he said.

"I'm the same," she told him flatly.

"No, you're not."

"You wouldn't know." Probably she should have been afraid of him, but she felt a confused kind of power.

"Did you run here?"

She didn't answer.

"I'll drive you back."

"Yeah, right," Diana said. "Is that what you told Brynna last year?"

"What happened to you?" Aidan asked when she got home. She was dirt-streaked, blistered, carrying her shoes.

"Are you playing?" Diana demanded. Aidan was sitting just

where she'd left him, with the open biology textbook, but she saw that he'd got ahold of their mother's clunky old desktop computer.

"No," Aidan said. "Why're you in such a bad mood?"

How to answer? My feet are bleeding. I had to fight off wild dogs. I'm scared for you.

She limped upstairs and saw that he had searched her room. Her piles on the floor had toppled. The clean clothes on her chair had shifted. Her closet door was ever so slightly askew. "Aidan!" she screamed. She wanted to run downstairs and knock the chair out from under him, but her legs were so sore that she couldn't move. *"Aidan."*

No answer.

She threw herself onto her bed and opened her phone.

WTF, she texted him.

?? he replied, as if anybody else would have searched her room.

You know what u did dont deny it. what is wrong with you??

calm down, he wrote.

NO

Its been 6 weeks

Idc

I have like one week of summer. By this he meant one week between the end of his summer course and the first day of school. He had seven days of freedom, and he wanted to spend it with his BoX. That would be Aidan's vacation. A week of caves and red-eyed vampire bats. You promised you wont play, she typed.

Instantly his answer appeared. I promised mom not you.

29

The Kiss

In the last days of summer Aidan got his class assignments for senior year. Physics, calculus, Spanish, European history, American literature again because he'd plagiarized. He talked his mother into computer access too. Kerry had given him her ancient desktop—safe, she thought, because it was too primitive and slow for gaming. Aidan couldn't play, but he scanned fan forums all day long, following the news. He couldn't enter games, but he could dream about them. He stood in the center of his room and closed his eyes and he could see the leaden river, and the Gates, the dark caverns all around him. He clenched his fist and saw his arm changing to silver. He drew his sword—and yet no caverns rose up around him, no tunnels opened up. He had to live outside of UnderWorld.

Official beta testing was beginning, but he had not been chosen. The BoX was to go on sale in the winter, but he couldn't wait until December. The situation maddened him because he had a BoX, but couldn't get his hands on it.

He searched every room, every closet and cabinet. On Labor Day weekend Diana found him hunting in the basement. Carrying her laundry bag downstairs, she found him rummaging in dusty cartons labeled CHILDREN'S BOOKS; HUMIDIFIER; TENNIS; WINTER CLOTHES.

"Just stop!" Diana said, acutely aware of the doll carriage in the boiler room.

"Tell me where it is."

"No."

"I finished summer school," he said.

"So what?"

"I did what I was supposed to do."

"You gave it to me," Diana said. "You said keep this for me."

"Not forever."

She set down her laundry bag as if to stake her claim. "Yes! Forever. You gave it to me when you were getting sick."

"I wasn't getting sick! I got sick later."

He was always correcting her on that, but in her mind, his illness and the black BoX went together. "You said I could have it, and now, guess what, Aidan? You don't get it back again. It wasn't like a long-term loan."

"I want it."

Diana snapped, "What makes you think I kept it?"

He dipped into the tennis box and hurled a yellow ball at her.

Shielding her face, she caught it. "What the hell is wrong with you?"

Aidan didn't answer.

Just an hour later, Diana sneaked into the boiler room, retrieved the BoX, and stuffed it into her backpack. Then she ran across the street.

For a moment she stood looking up at the third floor of Maia's triple-decker. All she could see were the tomato plants in Sage's window boxes. She had the key from babysitting, but she felt some trepidation as she slipped inside and climbed the stairs. Sage and Melissa had taken Henry to the Cape, and she felt like a trespasser.

Stifling hot without AC, airless, dusty, deathly clean, Sage's apartment scared Diana. No, that wasn't true. She brought her anxiety with her, and she was afraid to touch anything, almost afraid to touch the floor.

She set her backpack on the couch and took out the BoX, so heavy and compact. No lights, no buttons, no electric ports. Not even the words MADE IN CHINA. Just a perfect cube, smooth and mute. Diana felt it now, the strange desire to touch this thing, to open it. She opened the hall closet instead, rooted behind ice skates and hockey sticks, and heaved the BoX in.

Done. She tried to leave, and yet she felt no relief. Hiding the thing was not enough. She took up her burden again, carrying the BoX out in her backpack. Slowly, she walked around the block. Once around, and she felt the BoX hard against her back. A second time, and she felt the weight between her shoulder blades. The third time around, she met Lois returning from the gym with her furled yoga mat. "Excited about senior year?" Lois asked.

"Not really." Diana was watching for her mother's car.

"It's a transition," Lois said, all teacherly.

"Mom!" Diana saw her mother drive up. "Mom!" Diana sprinted across the street.

"What's wrong?" Kerry called through the open car window.

"I have to give you something."

"Okay." Kerry was drenched in sweat. Her car's air-conditioning had broken long ago. "Just let me get inside."

"No. Not inside. Here." Diana blocked her mother's way. "This is Aidan's." She unzipped her backpack and unwrapped the BoX.

Kerry flinched. "What is that?" she asked reflexively, but she knew. She seized the BoX, even before Diana finished explaining.

"Don't bring it in," Diana pleaded, as Kerry marched up the steps. "Don't let him see."

Kerry took the BoX into the kitchen and set it on the table. "Throw it away! Get that thing out of here," Diana begged her mother. She was afraid to see it in the open.

Kerry was rummaging in the broom closet, but Diana hovered over the black BoX. She had done the thing she'd sworn she'd never do. She had betrayed her twin, and her younger self as well—the girl who'd promised, chanting along with Aidan, We won't tell no matter what.

"What are you doing?" Diana cried out when her mother returned with a hammer in her hand. "Wait, not in the house."

Kerry didn't hesitate. She took her hammer and she struck again and then again. She hit so hard the salt and pepper shakers jumped. She struck a third time and a jagged hole opened in the smooth black cube.

A cloud of aeroflakes flew up to the ceiling, shrouding the light fixture, clouding the air. Kerry didn't even look. Harder and harder, she kept hammering down blows. This was for UnderWorld. This was for Arkadia. This was for night shifts. For lack of time. For lack of money. For unanswered prayers.

Kerry smashed the BoX to pieces, even as Aidan ran downstairs. He watched in silence as the walls of the black BoX shattered. Disoriented, unfocused, the little motes faded, faint as watermarks on the kitchen walls.

"Stop," Diana said, as Kerry hammered pieces into powder.

With a long, shuddering sigh, Kerry set down her hammer and sank into a chair. Diana was the one who sponged the plastic shards into the trash.

All that afternoon, Aidan kept himself locked upstairs. Diana heard him pacing. She heard him moving furniture. His desk? His bed?

She knew better than to knock. She texted him just once. I had to.

He did not respond.

Her mother tried to comfort her. She sat with Diana on the couch and she kept murmuring, "You did the right thing."

"Yeah, I can tell," said Diana, "because I feel like shit."

"Don't punish yourself like that."

Diana buried her head in the cushions. "Just get away from me, okay? The only one punishing me is you."

In the heat of the evening, the afterburn of the long summer day, Diana ran all the way down Magazine Street to Cambridgeport to bang on Brynna's door. "No!" Brynna protested. "My feet still hurt. I can't."

"Please, please, please," Diana begged, and even as she asked, she kept moving, jogging in place, hopping from one foot to another. "I need you."

"What happened?" Brynna asked.

"Nothing, if you'll come with me," Diana said. Her face was tearstained, her body eager, strong.

Together, they ran along the river. Diana charged ahead, and the sullen breeze riffled her dark hair. Brynna followed, protesting, "Wait up. You're way too fast."

Diana was too upset to wait. She was still too close to home; she had to get away. All she wanted was to run faster, to outstrip the setting sun and plunge into darkness. She wanted to feel nothing, remember nothing, be nothing.

But even she couldn't keep up this furious pace. Gradually the girls found their rhythm, running up Huron Avenue. Diana wiped the tears from her eyes, and Brynna stopped complaining, gathering her strength, saving her breath until they reached Fresh Pond, the reservoir, fringed with trees.

"Rest," Diana said.

They stopped at the fountain near the water treatment plant and splashed their faces.

Brynna sighed. "That feels so good."

"Wait. I'll show you something better," Diana said.

She led Brynna to Little Fresh Pond and showed her the half-drowned tree. "Watch out. There's glass." Together they picked their way around the broken bottles, and climbed up on the fallen trunk. They pulled off their running shoes, peeled off their sweaty socks.

Night fell, sky and water deepening. Barefoot, Diana walked along the fallen tree to the point where the trunk dipped into the pond. She sat there trailing her legs in the waterlogged branches. She reached for Brynna, who hesitated. "No one's here." Diana stretched out her white arms. She was persuasive, confident. Even her voice seemed lower, whispering. She was a different creature in the dark.

Brynna followed Diana and sat next to her. Water lapped the backs of her knees, green-black leaves felt like seaweed on their feet. "Are you still hot?" Diana's voice was so soft, Brynna wasn't sure whether Diana was asking her, or talking to herself.

Diana took off her sweat-soaked shirt, balled it up, and tossed it onto the bank. Brynna hesitated a moment and then took off hers. They faced each other in shorts and jogging bras. Fair Diana, and darker Brynna with her hair tied back. The air was heavy, the summer weighed upon them, humming with mosquitoes. They could hear the frogs and the cicadas, the scrabbling claws of unseen animals, the rustling trees.

A branch snapped.

Brynna started. "What's that?"

"Nothing." With her thumb, Diana smudged out a mosquito on Brynna's neck.

"We'll get eaten alive," Brynna said.

"Come swimming then."

Brynna glanced at the dark trees. "We're not supposed to."

"So what? I swim here."

"When?"

"I run up here and swim at night."

As they sat side by side, their bare arms were almost touching. Brynna said, "Isn't that dangerous?"

"When you were younger—" Diana began.

"You're always saying, 'When you were younger,'" Brynna said.

"Okay, before you had the baby, you wouldn't ask."

"I'm not so different."

"Yes, you are."

"Because of Angela?"

"Because of Anton, obviously."

Brynna said, "I never even see him anymore."

"Good."

Brynna sighed. Her breath brushed against Diana's ear. "Do you swim in your clothes?"

"No," Diana whispered. "I take them off."

"Would you now?" Brynna asked.

"If you come with me."

Brynna held still, absorbing the suggestion.

"Do you want to?" Diana asked, as she unhooked the back of Brynna's bra.

"Yes."

Brynna's breasts were full, her nipples dark. Brynna's heart was racing underneath Diana's hand. "I just want to touch you," Diana whispered, and Brynna didn't pull away. Her skin was soft under Diana's tongue.

They slipped into the water, and Diana had no twin; she had no mother. She had Brynna alone. They were standing waist-deep, and Brynna glanced back at the water's edge. "What if someone sees us?"

For a moment Diana thought of Anton and his dogs—but no

one had followed them. "No one sees us," Diana murmured, as she stroked Brynna. "No one's here." The darkness and the water concealed them.

She touched Brynna's face. She kissed Brynna's lips and she forgot everything but Brynna's soft mouth. She forgot Aidan and she forgot herself. It was happening. She was becoming someone else.

30

Poetry Inaction

Aidan would not forgive his sister. He wouldn't even look at her. Exiled in the hospital, he had been too weak to care. Now he was strong and restless, and resentful. He had endured days and weeks of summer school, and this was his reward. He had trusted Diana, or so he told himself. He had counted on her to keep his black BoX safe, and then just when he needed it—just when he'd earned it—she turned on him and gave it to their mother.

His mother had taken back her desktop, and so he had rehabilitated Liam's old laptop to play while she was at work. The laptop was easy to hide but almost useless, because it was so flat and slow. His BoX had spoiled him. As color eclipsed black and white, as computers supplanted typewriters, so OVID overshadowed all the gaming platforms that had come before. Onscreen graphics seemed old as picture books to Aidan. All he wanted now was gaming in the round.

He tortured himself, inhaling articles on UnderWorld's paradigm-shifting technology. He read about the millions waiting for BoXes in December, and it killed him to think he'd held his own BoX in his hands. i've been inside, he typed on UnderWorld's fan forum. no way, the other Everheads shot back. whats it like? your full of shit. prove it. pix! But he had no proof.

Those last days of summer he swallowed his pride and texted Daphne, he messaged her on fan forums, he emailed her at her official Arkadia address, but she did not reply. At last he did what he should have done first. He logged in to EverWhen and searched for Riyah. He wandered the Trackless Wood and hunted by the shore, he journeyed past the tree line on the slopes of EverRest. The night before school started, he sat in bed wearing his old headset and fell asleep trying to find her.

The crunch of autumn leaves, the rush of water.

"What's up, Tildor?"

He opened his eyes and heard Daphne speaking to him, although at first all he could see was his screen saver.

He touched his trackpad, and there she stood on a rough boulder before a thundering waterfall. She was wearing her thigh-high boots and scant bodice of black leather. Her eyes were huge, her blue hair flowed down her back, but her avatar was just that to him, because he'd seen her for real.

"Sleeping?" She touched his Elf lightly on the shoulder.

He shook himself awake. "I need another BoX."

"Sorry. One per person!" Riyah folded her arms across her chest.

"Wait. Listen. My mom took a hammer and destroyed mine."

She threw back her head and laughed.

"Go to hell," breathed Aidan.

"Excuse me?" said Daphne. "Which of us can't get there?"

She repulsed him. Much as he'd admired her when they'd met, honored as he had been, qwesting in her company, he hated her now. He knew Daphne was a schemer and a marketer, neither Elf nor ordinary gamer, and he didn't want her anymore. He had one desire. "I have to play."

"Oh, well." Riyah jumped down from her rock and began searching for jewels in the crystalline pool beneath the waterfall.

"I'll make a deal with you," Aidan said.

"I can't." Riyah waded deeper into the water. She looked like a tiny dominatrix, but she sounded like an irritated teacher. "You have to wait like everybody else."

Tildor splashed after her. "I won't wait."

"You have to."

"I'll tell everybody you're breaking the law."

"Vandalizing property?" Riyah said. "That would be you."

"You made me."

"Hey. Stop right there." She drew her sword.

He drew his shining weapon and advanced. Steel on steel, the two of them were fighting, waist-deep in the water. "You tricked me!"

She struck and slashed his arm. "I never tricked you. Think about it."

In a fury, he forced her back toward the roaring waterfall. White water reddened with his blood, but he would not let up. "You said I could play."

"You did play."

"You promised."

"I kept my promises."

"I need to play now."

"Grow up."

"You owe me!" He knocked her down into the water and with one massive stroke sliced off her head. The pool was black now with her blood, the water churning with her headless body.

"Okay, game over." Still bleeding, Riyah picked up her head and leapt onto a rock.

He panicked. "Please. Just give me a new BoX and I promise you'll never see me again."

She stood there holding her head as casually as a fencer holds her helmet after a bout. "You won't see me either." Riyah replaced her head and turned her back on him.

"Come back," Aidan called out.

Already she was out of reach, leaping from rock to rock.

"I did everything you wanted."

"You did what *you* wanted." Those were the last words Daphne ever said to him.

He was in a killing mood that night. He rampaged through the Trackless Wood, murdering animals, one by one. He slew a wild boar, hacking the beast until he was knee-deep in blood. He tracked a golden fox and shot it through the eye. Charged a two-headed dog and killed it twice. A few people from his old company texted, Tildor u back? Or Qwest now? He hunted on, alone and furious.

In the starlight his Elf shot down a phoenix with a gold arrow. The bird flamed like a falling star, but all Aidan could think was how much better the fire would have been in UnderWorld, with sparks showering down upon him.

In the distance he could hear Diana rustling across the hall. Far away he heard her knocking at the door. "You know what day it is, right?"

He took off his headphones but he didn't answer. He waited until she left the house to log off and walk to Emerson. Let her wonder whether he'd show up the first day. Let her think he had forgotten. Angry as he was at Daphne, he was angrier at his sister.

School smelled like paint. A few days before, a troop of City Corps kids had descended on the building to spruce it up. Scuffed floors were lemon-fresh, walls bright with new bulletin boards. A purple banner hung in the lobby blazoned POETRY IN ACTION.

People were embracing. Girls were calling to one another like long-lost sisters. Everyone was supercharged with energy. The shoes alone were blinding. Aidan wanted to turn around and leave.

"Good morning, Aidan." Miss Lazare pursued him up the stairs. "Welcome back!"

What was that about? Aidan ducked into his math class and out of range. Lazare was such a lethal mix of concern and hopefulness.

If I were Mrs. West, thought Nina, I would have demanded a response. "Excuse me, young man. You look me in the eye and say, 'Good morning,' when I greet you." Next time, Nina thought, even as she added a new resolution to her mental list: Don't compare yourself to Mrs. West.

Her list was long. Start off strict and set expectations high. Mean 'til Halloween, as Mr. Allan said. Insist on homework. No lost books, no missing papers, no unexcused absences. Keep track of time. Finish lessons before the bell. She was wearing Collin's old-fashioned watch.

This year will be different, she thought, as she stepped into her classroom. I'll get it right. I won't fail you, she promised her kids silently, as she shut the door.

"Good morning," she said.

A few kids answered, "Good morning."

"I'm Miss Lazare, and this is American Literature," she announced, just in case someone had wandered into the wrong room. "I'll take attendance before we get started, and I'll just say," she added as a couple of boys walked in, "I need everybody here on time. Colleen. Matisse. Jared. Australia . . ." She tagged each student in her mind with a mnemonic. Colleen, with the eyebrow piercing. Rachelle, with hennaed hair. Candace was chewing gum. "Take out the gum, Candace. Take these poems. Pass them down."

She watched her photocopied handout ripple from hand to hand. "As a class we'll study American poets and writers. As a school, we have a new initiative this year. You may have seen the banner." She paused and felt a little dumb. The banner was a good twelve feet long and hard to miss. "Our school will be participating in the national recitation competition."

Groans and laughter. Confusion about what recitation might entail. Scuffling in the back.

"Miss?" Candace held up the extra photocopies.

Keep it moving, Nina thought. "So we'll start the year with two American poems. Do I have a volunteer to read the first?"

Silence.

"Anyone?" Nina volunteered a girl named Zena, who had been whispering. "Right here." Nina interposed herself between Zena and Colleen.

"*I hear America singing,*" Zena began, "*the varied carols I hear, / Those of mechanics, each one singing his as it should be blithe and strong . . .*"

As Zena read aloud: "*The carpenter singing his as he measures his plank or beam . . .*" Nina opened a fresh box of chalk. Was there anything more perfect than new chalk? "*The mason singing his as he makes ready for work, or leaves off work . . .*"

"How would you describe the mood here?"

"Ummm," Zena said.

Nina waited. Unconsciously, she played with Collin's watch. It was so big, it kept flipping over, buckle up, facedown, rubbing the inside of her wrist.

"Mmmm." Zena considered the words before her.

"Happy," called out a boy named Trey.

"Okay!" Nina wrote "happy" on the board.

"Cheerful."

"Yes." Nina wrote that too.

"Full of it," Australia suggested, and Nina heard the class cackling behind her.

"No, that's good. Why do you say that?"

Australia did not explain.

"Does anybody else think Whitman's full of it?"

Natalie and Mikayla raised their hands.

"He's too happy about everything," said Mikayla, but Natalie forgot what she was going to say.

"It will come back to you," said Nina. "Let's see how Langston Hughes responds to Whitman. Trey, read the second poem aloud for us."

Trey began reading, *"I, too, sing America . . ."* but a snickering undercurrent accompanied him.

"Hold on," Nina interrupted, and she waited for silence. "Okay, go ahead."

"I am the darker brother," he read, and the other kids burst out laughing, because Trey's skin was darkest in the class.

In second period Nina repeated the two views of America, Walt Whitman's and Langston Hughes's. Once again she mentioned the recitation contest, which kids were already calling Poetry Inaction. Every student had to choose and memorize a poem from the contest website to recite in class. Then the class would vote for a winner to compete in front of the whole school.

Students shifted in their seats.

"What if I have no memory?"

"Is it graded?"

"Whose idea was that?"

Nina almost said, "You can thank Mrs. West."

Instead she held still, as she'd seen Collin do when he visited as Shakespeare, cool and distant.

Kids paused in their conversations when they realized she was no longer talking. They looked up, curious.

Lazare had a reputation now. She had a mad-hot, cross-dressing boyfriend, but she was so strict she corrected grammar when you were only talking. Total mind reader, she could tell whether you'd plagiarized just by looking at you. She was confusing. One minute she was all intimidating, and then when people didn't listen, she got emotional, so you couldn't hate her without feeling bad. That was the worst! On the other hand, she was fun to watch. She had a photographic memory, and if you were lucky she'd stop teaching and show what she could do.

At the end of each class, Nina closed her attendance book and left it on the desk. Then she looked each student in the eye and came up with the right name. "Darsy, Lalitha, Jean-Albert, Theresa, Cameo, Susannah, Tyrell, Joanna, Sebastian, Yasmin, Aria . . ." Without a single mistake, she had identified each kid in her first class, but she faltered now in second period. "Becca, Jameson, Nico," she began. "Shana, Rafael, Siddhartha, Miles." She named each kid correctly until she got to the back of the room. "Aidan."

The boy shook his head.

"I'm sorry. I mean Ethan!" Aidan was missing, although she'd just seen him on the stairs.

All this happened in a moment, but when Nina turned to the next student, her memory failed her. She looked at the girl's round face. Black eyes, smooth hair, gold hoop earrings, tight shirt. Nina looked into the girl's dark eyes.

Anxious—was she unmemorable?—the girl stared back.

Siddhartha called out, "It starts with an *S* . . ."

"Sofia," Lazare said at last. Gold hoops quivering, Sofia sank back with relief.

Nina texted Collin after the bell. I did it! Then, a little later, when he hadn't answered, Are you there??

31

Joy Street

Blood in his eye, the Ghost Horse raced through caverns, wheeling, screaming, rising up on his hind legs, then crashing down, a beast possessed.

"Okay," Peter said.

They were sitting in the sound booth. When Nicholas stopped the demo, Peter rose to leave.

"What about the rest?" Collin asked.

Peter glanced at the second monitor, where Collin's wild horses streaked across the screen. The Ghost Horse belonged to Peter now, but the herd was Collin's joy. The gray, the chestnut, the palomino, shining pale gold. They stretched their necks and ran together. You could see them close, coming down upon you. On a third monitor you could see them from above, and their tails streamed behind them so they looked like shooting stars. All the time you heard the hoofbeats and the hot breath of those horses.

"No," Peter said.

Nicholas clicked once and the room was silent. The horses froze. Peter said, "We won't use these."

At first Collin couldn't even hear. He could not absorb the words.

He had worked for months. He had spent the entire summer on these horses.

Peter turned back to the horses caught in midair. "They're pretty." Peter bent and clicked on the palomino, highlighting the horse in blue, isolating the creature's body, its slender neck, its little ears and feet. Suddenly the horse *was* pretty. Peter clicked again and vaporized the animal. Now he touched the chestnut, with its soft eyes and flowing tail. Clicked once, clicked twice. It disappeared.

Shocking how cold he was as he killed each of Collin's steeds: the velvet black, the gray.

Collin said, "You wanted them before."

"No, they aren't right."

"What isn't right about them?"

Peter looked at Collin, and in that moment he smothered Collin's protest. "They're like illustrations in a children's book."

He spoke with experience and authority. He spoke with his uncanny insight. The chestnut, the palomino, and the gray were nothing more than wild ponies, lovely, gentle, sweet. They had no edge, none of the Ghost Horse's snarling cruelty. How had Collin been such a fool? He had been too in love with his own work to understand. These horses did not belong in UnderWorld.

"They're just not interesting."

Collin nodded; he could not argue.

"You'll be okay," Nicholas counseled after Peter left. "It happens all the time. Not everything gets used."

Collin nodded, but the verdict cut deep. He had never been sentimental about his art. He had erased his own work with freedom and with joy, but this was different. He had worked so long on these bright horses, invested so much of himself—and he had not been the one to wipe the board.

Phone in hand, he stood that evening in the parking lot and texted Nina, Im fine working late. He was okay, just as Nicholas had said, but he couldn't talk to her. He had to absorb the shock, along with his new assignment.

He would work on UnderWorld's Flamethrowers, evil Amazonian women guarding treasure in UnderWorld's Sixth Circle. Testers had reported that these characters looked too much like elves. Collin had to make them scarier.

"Condolences," Daphne told him the next day. It was as if he'd been demoted to a janitor, cleaning up other people's work.

"I don't care."

She pretended to believe him.

With numb determination he drew the Flamethrowers and their fiery arrows. His heart wasn't in it, but he forced himself, working for weeks to make the women nastier, sharpening features, drawing snarling faces. He even tried Peter's trick of bloody eyes. Peter rejected every iteration, and responded to the red eyes with contempt. "You're painting by number now, and that's just desperate."

Discouraged, Collin took his slate and scrolled through his old work. He saw all the faults that Peter found and more. Crude Flamethrowers and pretty horses, thoughtless cartoons. He was a copyist, just as Peter had predicted. His art was superficial, glib.

Nina said, Don't let Peter mess with you. Her uncle was harsh, unreasonable. She pleaded, Don't believe him. None of this meant anything to Collin. In fact, her exhortations made him feel worse. He would rather talk to Nicholas, who said, Shit happens. He would rather play Daphne, dueling late at night with broadswords. For the first time, Collin avoided Nina. He used work as an excuse, and when she asked about Arkadia, he picked a fight or pushed her away. He said, Don't tell me what to do.

Offended, Nina drew back. Her own days weren't easy. Her kids were rowdy, and she had her evaluation coming—observations and online surveys of her students. She wanted to confide in Collin as she had before, but she held back because he had so much going on. This too will pass, she told herself. She would teach and he would find his way. Therefore, she didn't offer help, nor did she come with Collin to the hellions' Halloween party. She didn't trust herself to see Peter without losing her temper, so she stayed home.

Collin's roommates were not so reticent.

"Take us with you!" Emma said, as Collin set out for Peter's house.

"It's hellions only."

Darius handed him a stack of Theater Without Walls postcards. "Disseminate!" The company was staging *The Importance of Being Earnest* at South Station, with the audience convening on one platform and then departing on two different trains.

Collin shoved the postcards into his jacket pocket.

"Seriously. Pass those around."

"It's the least you can do," Emma pointed out.

Collin said, "People at this party don't care about plays."

"What are you talking about?" Darius exclaimed. "Videogames are us. Games *are* plays."

Collin began wheeling his bike out the door.

"Don't be jaded," Darius said.

"I'm not jaded. I'm late."

Darius called after Collin, "If they need actors for UnderWorld, we're available!"

Collin jumped on his bike. "They already recorded all the voices."

Across the shining river, through the looking glass to Boston, Collin sped toward Joy Street. The wind was harsh, but it felt good to travel to a new place, neither Cambridge nor Arkadia. He was nervous but curious as well, crossing the bridge into Peter's city, with its gas lamps and cobblestone streets.

Peter lived in a pair of townhouses, catercornered. One faced

Joy, and the other faced Myrtle, and they shared a basement, like conjoined twins. There were two sets of windows, and two front doors, but the windows were all curtained, and both doors closed. Locking his bike to a lamppost, Collin eyed the Myrtle Street entrance. A bouncer stood on Peter's steps. He was a massive man with short arms and a little derby hat.

"Name?"

"Collin James."

Officiously, the bouncer scrolled down on his tablet. "You're not on the list."

"Yes I am. I'm from Arkadia."

"You aren't here."

Collin felt a prick of anxiety. Then he said, "Were you looking under *C* for *Collin*, or *J* for *James*?"

The bouncer opened the door, releasing a tidal wave of sound.

Walls pulsed with laughter and with music, and it was dark, the entryway cavernous, shrouded in mist.

As his eyes adjusted, Collin found himself at the foot of a grand staircase with a body splayed across the bottom. A woman in a ripped ball gown lay quite still, her body painted white, blood trickling from the corner of her mouth. Nimbly, caterers stepped around her. In the next room, guests posed for pictures with another dead body languishing on Peter's velvet couch.

The furniture was dark and battered, fantastic, unrestored. Velvet upholstery split at the seams, leather crazed and cracked, rough to the touch. A pair of gilt clocks on Peter's mantelpiece stood motionless, hands stopped, but the effect was lively, nothing like a morgue. The whole place thrummed with song and shouted conversation, bartenders in every corner. He saw the Dresden Dolls, the actual Dolls, in matching corsets, pounding drums and electric keyboard.

Animators crowded the dance floor—colleagues Collin saw each day at meetings, solving problems, scrumming together. They looked ghostly now, in slippery black gowns and feathered masks, black lipstick, fangs. The pudgiest programmers seemed ethereal in flickering candlelight. Like night-blooming flowers, they came into their own, singing together—*"Coin. Operated boy. Coin. Operated boy"*—louder and louder, with pedantic glee.

Drink in hand, Collin scanned the crowd for Peter, but couldn't find him. Maybe he didn't come to his own parties. Maybe he just wound them up and hid somewhere to watch.

A tarnished mirror leaned against the wall. Collin recognized that mirror, the model or dilapidated cousin of the Magic Glass in EverWhen. When Collin touched the surface he half expected it to dimple and then melt, a watery portal to the Trackless Wood.

Peter was everywhere, even when you couldn't find him. He had changed each room into a theater. Aeroflakes transformed the paneled library into a forest of shifting autumn leaves, and Obi and Akosh were gaming there. Obi was a Fire Elf breaking a path, cutting through underbrush with his ax. Akosh was a falcon. Like a dancer, he gestured with his hands and wrists, flying his avatar above his head. At a little distance, Collin discovered Peter watching every move.

"Welcome." Peter turned to Collin as if he were sharing a particularly lovely view. "What do you think of falcons in the round?"

Together they watched the falcon soaring and dipping between trees. Collin kept thinking Peter would leave, but he was in a rare mood, gazing at the colors haloing Akosh and Obi.

Collin ventured, "What if Akosh could do more than fly? What if he could see like a falcon too? He'd have this incredible vision where suddenly every detail was magnified twenty times. The whole game would shift to his point of view."

Intrigued, Peter glanced at Collin, who seized the moment. "You'd be swooping through the air but you could see your prey

down on the forest floor and every clue, and every crevice. You'd
see it all so fast."

"That would be terrifying," Peter said.

He could be gracious, acknowledging your contribution. He
could be generous. He had opened his grand home, draping windows with the softest, darkest velvet, adorning his marble mantel-
pieces with prosthetic limbs, filling each room with a different food
or drink, a raw bar in the parlor, a dim sum station in the breakfast
room. He had staged this party with corpses that looked real, and
flowers that seemed artificial. He'd filled great urns with protea—
blossoms spiky green, and curling coral, and deep pink fringed
with feathery black.

"That's beautiful," Collin murmured as he watched night falling
in the game.

"You think so?" Peter pounced. "What's beautiful about it?"

Collin gazed at the deepening shadows. Lavender, lilac, indigo.
"The colors."

"They're boring," Peter said. "They're just what you'd expect."

Of course Collin saw his mistake. Once again, he'd made the
easy, sentimental choice.

Peter kept his eyes fixed on the game. "Let me give you some
advice."

Collin waited.

"Don't rely on clichés. You aren't good at them."

Dappled forest light played on Peter's face, but he looked at Collin now. "That's why you can't get the Flamethrowers right. Are
you tired of them?"

You know I am, Collin shouted inwardly, but he said, "What
would you suggest?"

"Use your sketches of Daphne."

In all that noise and all that shifting light, Collin stood perfectly
still. Peter spoke without rancor. He made his suggestion without

heat, but Collin didn't for an instant take Peter's words as artistic advice. He heard them as a casual display of power: I know about your drawings; I know everything about you.

"You do better when you draw from life," Peter concluded as he walked away.

The party was raging all around, but Collin heard only his own heartbeat. I know you, Peter had told him without words. I know you and I know that you've been drawing Daphne.

But how did Peter know? Gazing through the doorway where Peter had gone, Collin saw a flash of white. Three steps and he had caught Daphne in the hall.

She had no idea what was wrong as she laughed up at him. Her blue eyes were dark, almost black in the black shifting light. She was barefoot and she wore a sheer slip of a dress.

"Come here," he said.

"Why?"

Hand on her back, he steered her away from the dance floor.

"I'm not drunk enough for this."

He hurried her out to the dark entryway.

"It's cold." The stone floor chilled her feet.

Collin didn't listen. "You told Peter."

"What?"

"You told Peter I drew you."

"I did not."

"Of course you did."

"I never told him anything!"

"Tell the truth."

Playground-sincere, she said, "Cross my heart and hope to die."

Her mockery infuriated him. Either she had told Peter, or she had let him watch. He took her by the shoulders and demanded, "What is wrong with you?"

"Nothing!"

His hand tightened on her shoulder. "He saw us and you knew the whole time, and you never warned me."

"You're hurting me."

He heard the fear in her voice and he let go. She saw her chance and slipped into the dark.

The party burst apart. The corpse in the ripped ball gown sat on the stairs with a plate of calamari. The man impaled near the bar took to the dance floor with his ax protruding from his chest. Other cadavers mingled, dancing, laughing, rolling cigarettes.

Hellions crowded the dining room with its massive table and carved chairs. As Peter spoke, those material objects began to change. Above the table a Japanese lantern waxed into a full moon in the gathering mist. Dead water pooled where Peter's table had been. Stalagmites replaced chairs, and UnderWorld's white bats swarmed overhead. In the confusion, it took a moment for the assembled animators to perceive a dead knight lying in the water.

Collin edged closer to hear.

"Those would have been our maggots." Like a surgeon demonstrating in the operating theater, Peter pointed to the corpse with a red-tipped laser. Tiny silver worms were writhing in every open wound and orifice, consuming flesh inside ears and eye sockets, underneath the skin. "These would have been our rats." Peter announced with grim satisfaction. He pointed to a crevice where a blind rat devoured her own pups.

At first Collin didn't understand. Then, gradually, he saw that Peter was displaying outtakes, gorgeous horrors he had cut from UnderWorld before the launch.

A thundering of hooves, a crashing avalanche of stone, and all bats scattered as Collin's horses broke through virtual stone. Watching his horses run together, Collin felt his heart shift. He was watching his horses and they weren't pretty. They were earth shakers, storm raisers. How had Peter stolen Collin's confidence? He had messed with Collin's mind. He was messing with Collin even now.

"These would have been our horses. We had to choose just one."

The herd raced past, tails streaming.

"Look," Akosh exclaimed. "There must be some way to use them."

"Murder your darlings," Peter said.

"Asshole," Collin whispered. Fucking vampire. He pushed his way out of the dining room, past hellions deep in conversation. He skirted the dance floor and crossed virtual fields, stubble white with frost. He dodged dart games and turned away from tables of good food. He would not touch any of it. He took narrow stairs into a dark passageway. He kept moving away from the music. Suddenly, he realized he'd passed through to Peter's other house.

This twin house was grand, but empty and undecorated, dimly lit, with plaster peeling, windows covered with brown paper, floors bare and scuffed. In one room Collin saw mattresses upended and leaning against a wall, in another an old couch draped with a white drop cloth. Doors opened into empty rooms and narrow passageways. Desolate, confused, half dreaming, Collin imagined snow behind those doors, a lamppost in a wintry wood. Instead, he found dark closets and brick walls.

"Are you looking for the way out?"

He turned and saw Daphne sitting all alone in a small straight-backed chair. He had never seen her so quiet or so still. "I didn't tell him," she added.

"How does he know, then?"

"He has the sketches. He has everything."

"I deleted them. They don't exist."

"Deleting doesn't help. The system backs up every image. You know that!"

Her words chilled him. He had known, but he had imagined some vast dump, electronic compost no one sorted. He had not pictured Peter collecting his discarded work. Every image, every version, every line.

"I thought you didn't care."

Peter hadn't just heard about the drawings. He hadn't just glanced at them. He owned them.

"What's going on?"

She wouldn't even look at him.

He knelt down at her feet so he could see her face. "Tell me."

"Nothing to tell."

"Then why are you crying?"

She glanced down at her own elaborately inked arms, and it seemed to him that her tears magnified and blurred her leaves.

"Come on." He took her hand. "It's late."

Her words were lively, but her voice was sad. "No, it's not. It's early."

"You know what I mean. Let's go."

She shook her head.

"I'll take you home."

"That's just it," she said. "I live here."

32

Two Rivers

Fear mixed with anger as Collin fought his way through passages and crowded rooms to push open the front door. Confused images flashed before his eyes. His horses and Peter's face, and Daphne's tears. She lived with Peter. She was no longer obsessed or tangentially involved. Nor was she wild or independent, as she pretended. She lived in Peter's house. She belonged to him.

How different Peter's past behavior seemed. Not just critical, but jealous. Not just impossible to please, but punishing. He had punished Collin with advice. I've got you. That's what he'd been saying. I know what you have and I know what you want.

There he was even now. Standing outside on the steps, Collin opened a message from Peter on his phone. Subject: Flamethrowers. Attachment, a huge cache of sketches. Not just three or four, but every sketch of Daphne. Dozens of drawings, quick and slow, dressed, undressed. Peter had them all. He had been collecting them.

Collin whirled around to stare at the closed door on Joy Street.

This was a threat. This was Peter saying, I have your art—not just your art, but your ideas—and I can send them anywhere. He could send the sketches to Nina. He might have sent the file already.

Collin sprang onto his bike and raced away. It did not occur to him that Peter would protect his niece from these pictures. Collin sped across the bridge with just one idea. He had to get to Nina first.

Cold knifing his throat, legs burning, Collin didn't stop to rest. He had to catch her before she left for school.

He used his own key, took the elevator up, and rushed into her dark apartment.

The rooms were still. At first he thought he was too late. Then he heard her stirring in the bedroom. "Collin?" She appeared in her big Hill School shirt. "What's wrong?"

"I thought I'd missed you."

"Why?"

"Aren't you supposed to be at school?"

"It's Saturday."

He sank onto the couch, and pulled her down next to him. It was the weekend and he hadn't even realized. They had the whole morning, but she was wide awake now, and her laptop lay there on the table like a bomb.

"What is it?"

He wanted to say, Nothing—I just missed you; instead he forced himself to tell the truth. "I drew some sketches and I never showed them to you."

"Sketches of what?"

"Peter got them, and he says that I should use them."

Nina looked at him and said, "You drew her, didn't you?"

"The thing you have to understand—"

"Show me."

"I just wanted to tell you . . . they're rough sketches. They weren't . . ."

She wasn't having that. He didn't get to talk about his drawings in the abstract. She handed him her laptop.

Guilty and indignant, hating himself, but hating Peter more, he logged in and opened Peter's message.

The first image emerged, a line drawing of Daphne in silver. Next, a sketch of Daphne slouched down on the shuttle bus. Daphne leaning over, playing pool. Daphne drinking at a bar. Daphne gaming like a dervish with her arms outstretched. One by one, each image filled Nina's field of vision, and she saw Daphne with her wide eyes and her laughing mouth and her cropped hair. She saw all this and she saw the time Collin and Daphne spent together. Daphne drunk and funny, messed up, impudent.

Then she saw Daphne sitting just for him. Full color, fully shaded, Daphne in her hooded sweatshirt, Daphne unzipped, Daphne in her undershirt, Daphne undressed.

"How could you draw her like that?" Nina gazed at Daphne's arched back, her breasts, soft and white, in contrast to her patterned torso, her black-inked collarbone.

"They're just studies."

"Studies of what?"

"They're not important," Collin said. "That's what you have to understand."

Nina said nothing.

"I didn't even keep them!"

She was remembering the summer day they'd spent together. The pine trees and the heat, the taste of salt. She had asked him, "Do you draw Daphne?" And he had lied to her, even at that moment. He'd lied to her then.

Now he told Nina, "I was practicing. I was just experimenting, and I erased them all."

"I can see why."

"No, it wasn't like that! They were just like chalk drawings. I wasn't trying to keep them from you. I didn't even keep them for myself."

"Is that why you said you didn't draw her?"

"I said it because . . . it wasn't important. And it didn't matter."

She closed the laptop and hugged it to her chest.

He struggled to explain. "I want to be open with you. That's why I'm showing you the sketches."

"You're showing them because you're afraid of Peter."

"No! I'm showing them because I won't let him hold this over me—or us."

Over days and weeks Nina had dismissed Daphne from her mind; she had fought against distrust. Now all she saw was Daphne's body and her inked arms and her kissed mouth. All this had happened. It was still happening. Collin spent every day with her. "You see her all the time. You'll see her today."

"No, I won't. I don't want to see her."

He could talk as much as he liked. His drawings drowned him out. They weren't ordinary. They weren't occasional. There were too many.

"I'm being honest," he protested.

"You *have to be* honest!" she shot back. Peter had Collin's art, and Peter had Daphne, and now Peter had Collin too. Because of this, Collin had confessed what he'd been keeping from her. He could say that these were only sketches. He could insist he didn't take them seriously. She knew better. After all, he'd drawn her too. She read a whole relationship in these studies, a second life entirely, overlaying theirs.

"Nina," he said softly.

"Just get away from me," she said. "Just leave."

• • •

He left in frustration, but arrived home guilty. There were no little lies for Nina. There was no action without meaning. Wasn't that what he loved about her? Now he had hurt her; he'd misjudged her. He reached for his phone without a plan, without any motive but apology.

Too late. Nina didn't want to talk. She didn't want to see him. When he texted and he called, she didn't answer. All Saturday, he left her voicemails. He wrote emails. He kept starting them, anyway. *Dear Nina, This is such a mess . . . ; Dear Nina, I realize . . .* They weren't any good.

Darius said he had to stop. On Saturday night, he took Collin to The Plough & Stars and said, "Believe me, the only thing worse than cheating is going on and on about it."

"I didn't cheat!" Collin burst out.

"Whatever," Darius said. "Stop talking about it."

He began writing on a yellow legal pad. *Nina, I shouldn't have kept those drawings from you. Please believe me when I say they didn't matter. The sketches aren't important. I don't think about them. I think about you.*

His words were colorless. They could never capture what he felt. After all, what could he say? I lied. I should have told the truth when you asked. But also—you're different from anyone I know. A bunch of drawings, a few late nights, a girl taking off her clothes. What did any of it matter? Noelle had worked as a model at the Museum School. Collin never took it personally—but Nina looked inside art, uncovering intentions. She had seen his curiosity, his pleasure, his intense attraction.

Late at night, Collin anguished over Darius's words. He considered his own denials and felt guiltier than before. To be honest, he would have cheated. He would have slept with Daphne, but she didn't let him, so he drew her instead.

Loving Nina didn't mean he'd changed; he was the same guy as before. The same except for his remorse, his growing understanding as the hours passed. She had trusted him. She had risked her heart with him. Why had he taken it so lightly?

How could you? he kept asking himself. And at the same time that other voice grew stronger. The voice demanding, Why are you surprised? She's way too good for you. You knew it all along and now you've proved it. This was inevitable, his conscience told him. Give up. You don't belong together. He told himself all this, and yet his heart jumped every time he got a message. If only he could reach her.

Nina turned off her phone. She left her computer closed on the table. She couldn't bear his explanations and apologies, abject but self-serving. His images possessed her, multiplying in her mind, and she filled in the blanks, imagining where his art would lead. Collin was undressing Daphne, touching her, caressing her.

She didn't eat or drink. She had lessons to prepare, but when she looked at Emily Dickinson's poetry, the words seemed foreign. *It was not Night, for all the Bells / Put out their Tongues . . .* What did that mean? She had no idea. Only when she was calm and happy had she understood those lines about despair.

At some point Sunday night, Nina's alarm clock began beeping. She struggled to open her eyes, and did not remember falling into bed. She did not remember anything in those first moments between sleep and waking. Then her disappointment came crashing down upon her. Pinned, she looked out at her shadowy room and saw her laptop blinking, her stacks of papers, Emily Dickinson facedown on the floor.

Monday, she thought, and then, I can't. She had nothing to say, and nothing to give. *I believe that each of you has a unique contribution to make,* she had typed on her syllabus. *Therefore, I expect you to come to class prepared. I understand that you are very busy,* *but I am asking you to make this class a priority, as it is a priority* *for me . . .* Had she really written that? God, how insufferable she had been.

She forced herself to shower. Threw on some clothes, gathered papers, remembered to run a comb through her wet hair. When she took the elevator down, she was surprised to find her car keys in her hand.

It was street-cleaning day. When she arrived at school she saw the trucks, Phil's Towing—WE MEET BY ACCIDENT—hitching up and pulling the parked cars away. Raindrops beaded on her windows as she drove past the school, looking for a legal space. Then her windows fogged. She was driving in a cloud.

Slowly, she climbed the stairs with the last stragglers. She had had no coffee; she hadn't even brushed her teeth. She hugged her thick copy of Dickinson to her chest. The bell was ringing, but a crowd stood outside her classroom door.

"Miss! Miss! Check this out," her students called to her. Her class was standing room only. As soon as she saw her blackboards, she knew why.

Her double boards had been transformed. Black no longer, they had changed into a pair of landscapes—two views of the Eliot Bridge over the Charles, one in winter, one in summer. The winter river glimmered white. Snow outlined the bridge, bare bushes, and park benches on the icy bank. The world was cold, the sky pale, with just a hint of red suggesting the early-setting sun. Next to this winter scene, the summer river showed the same bridge and trees, but here the dark water danced under a bright sky. The bridge was ruddy, the bank thick with grass and tender leaves. The pictures were huge, but also detailed. In winter you could see a lost mitten on one snowy bench. In summer, a family of ducks clambered up the riverbank.

"Who *did* this?" Trey asked.

Rachelle wondered aloud, "How'd they get in?"

"Is this, like, vandalism?" Tentatively, Candace touched the summer riverbank, smudging the grass. "It comes off."

"Stupid," said Trey. "You know it's chalk."

"All right, everybody in my class sit down," Nina said. "Everybody else—go where you belong."

Reluctantly, students from other classes backed out the door. They couldn't take their eyes off those pictures. No one could. Nina gazed at the blackboards and saw the Charles sparkling in white stillness, as it had that first snowy winter night. It hurt, but she could not look away. She saw the scene as if no time had passed, and she was there with Collin and without him, looking at the same river twice.

Meanwhile her kids were taking pictures with their phones. "Okay," Nina said softly. "You know the rule."

Reluctantly her students shoved their phones into their pockets and their backpacks. They found their seats, but couldn't settle down.

Zachary echoed Trey. "Who did this?"

Nina took a quick attendance. Colleen, Matisse, Jared, Australia, Candace, Rachelle . . .

"Because he's, like, a genius," Zachary said.

"How do you know it's a guy?" Australia demanded.

From force of habit, Nina turned to write, *DO NOW*, on the board. She stopped. There was no room, and the rivers were too beautiful to erase. Setting down her chalk, she began her lesson. "Dickinson leaves space for your own imagination. She leaves a space around each word so you can think about it. *"Memory is a strange Bell* . . . What do you associate with the word *bell*? *Memory is a strange Bell—Jubilee, and Knell*. What's a *jubilee*? What's a *knell*?"

The kids shifted restlessly. She called on Sebastian, and he just stared at her. She was heartless in her students' eyes, standing with her back to this amazing art.

Australia was pointing to the footings of the chalk bridge and asking Trey, "That's the place where the geese live, right?"

"No!"

Several kids corrected her at once. "The geese live at the BU Bridge."

"We're looking at *Memory is a strange Bell*," Nina said, but she was distracted too. How had he gotten in? How many hours had he spent on this? Amazed, she thought, You must have worked all night. Affronted, she thought, And you think that you can color over everything. "All right, listen up."

Nobody paid the least attention.

"I'll wait," Nina announced, but she thought—how? How could she get through this lesson and four more classes as well? "I'm ready."

"Shut up, Liam," Tanya responded to some unseen slight.

That did it. Nina yanked open the file drawer of her Steelcase desk and found her water bottle. At last her students hushed as she unscrewed the cap.

Silence as Nina poured out the water, wetting her industrial-size eraser just as she had seen Collin do. A long horrified sigh as she swiped the center of Collin's winter river. "Miss," they murmured. "Ohhh," they exhaled, as she ruined Collin's beautiful illusion, sweeping it clean. She felt almost criminal, but she didn't stop.

When she turned around to face her kids, they sat chastened in their metal chairs. For the first time, they were afraid of her, because her eyes were filled with tears.

She was faster than her students when the bell rang. First out and down the stairs. She would have fifteen minutes to wash her face, to soak paper towels and press them like a rough compress against her closed eyes. She got to the staff restroom, and realized that in her rush, she had forgotten the key.

She glanced behind her, but she saw Jeff coming. She turned and ran down the hall, took the back stairs to the basement.

In the therapy room she could close her eyes. She could shut herself inside—but someone else had come down here as well. She saw him at the end of the dark corridor, typing into the keypad on the wall, disabling the alarm.

"Stop!"

The boy shrank back, trying to disappear. Too late. Nina threw herself between Aidan and the door. This is how you do it, she thought. This is how you skip out in the middle of the day. What do I tell him? How do I keep him here? What can I do? The questions tumbled over one another, as her mind woke. Now. Now. Today of all days. "Aidan!"

He turned back, trying to avoid her. He wanted to walk back to class, pretend nothing had happened, but she had caught him and she wouldn't let him go. He knew he was in trouble. She knew this was her chance.

33

Busted

He was unreachably tall, eyes fierce, head crowned with tangled golden hair.

"You know you can't leave school."

"I'm not leaving."

"You have class," she said. "You've got *my* class now."

Silence. He didn't move, but she braced herself against the door. "I know what's going on."

That irritated him, her sad-and-disappointed look.

"I know you're smart. I know you're capable . . ." Standing with her back against the door, she remembered Maia's advice. Be funny. *But I'm not funny.* Be desperate. Now Nina told Aidan, "I've seen your work."

That surprised him. He had not turned in many assignments.

"On walls."

He stared in disbelief. She didn't know. She couldn't know. Her accusation made no sense. He searched her pale, tear-streaked face. What was wrong with her? Lazare wasn't an adult anymore; she looked like a kid his age.

Even so, she spoke as his teacher, with authority. "I know what you've been doing."

"What have I been doing?" he asked coolly.

"Playing UnderWorld with Daphne. Tagging the school."

Then he went cold. Lazare was a mind reader, just like people said. No, she'd seen him. She'd watched him somehow—at school or in the park. How did she know? He understood, of course, that she was Viktor Lazare's daughter. Neither in school nor in the neighborhood had she flaunted that connection, but it was creepy to consider now. "You talked to my sister," he said in a hushed voice.

"She didn't let me."

"You came to my house."

The bell was ringing. She was going to be late. "I haven't told anyone else yet."

"Wait."

She interrupted. "You have a choice. Meet me in my classroom after school and we'll start working. Or meet me in the office with Mr. DeLaurentis." She turned to go.

"What do you mean—with DeLaurentis?" Now he was following her through the basement, up the stairs.

"You know what I mean."

He trailed her to the classroom, where the other kids were waiting. Head down, he slipped inside and sat in back.

All through her lesson, she sensed Aidan slouching in his chair, but she never spoke to him. She taught around him, calling on Becca to his left and Siddhartha to his right. Becca, could you read aloud? Siddhartha, why does Dickinson use the word *abyss*? Aidan looked up once, but she was careful not to catch his eye. She almost had him, and she wouldn't press her point.

"Look at Dickinson's dashes," she told her class. "What does she use them for?"

"Punctuation," said Miles.

"Yes," Nina said. "What else?"

"Instead of commas?" Miles asked.

"Look at these lines." Nina wrote them on her chalk-smeared board.

> There is a pain—so utter—
> It swallows substance up—
> Then covers the Abyss with Trance—

She repeated her question. "Why do you think she uses dashes?"

Shana said, "To show where you should breathe?"

"Good! Say more."

Shana hesitated and Nina had to resist the impulse to rush in and flood the room with questions. Did the dashes allow space for imagination? Could they be like rests in music? A nod to ambiguity? A way to honor the unsaid?

She said none of this. She held back, calm and quiet. When kids talked in class or rocked their desk chairs back, when they flirted or they fought, she stood between them and pointed silently to the correct line on the page. After her disastrous morning she began to right herself, slowing down and teaching her lesson, class by class. She had thought the day would be impossible, her lessons incoherent. In fact, she made a lot of sense. She saw it in her kids' faces. Less prepared than usual, she didn't try to cover so much ground. She kept it simple, giving students time to think.

"Thank you," she told her fifth-period seniors, right before the bell. Her students looked puzzled, but Nina couldn't tell them what she really meant. Thank you for crowding into my room. Thanks for whispering behind my back. Thanks for reading with me. She was grateful even when her kids refused her. I don't get poetry. I still don't understand. They took all her energy, and all her heart.

When the last bell rang, her students thundered down the stairs, and Nina stood alone. Her windows were dusty, but her room glowed in the gold November sun. Washing down the last of Collin's rivers, she thought, I taught more than one hundred kids today—and some of them were listening. She thought, I'm getting better at this. At the same time, she was deeply sad.

"How do you know Daphne?"

Aidan was standing at her desk.

"Have a seat."

He remained standing. "How did you . . . ?"

She dragged over a chair. "I don't want to talk about her. You're here so that we don't have to talk about her. Please." She gestured to the chair.

Wary, Aidan sat down.

Nina took her grade book out, along with her weekly planner. "Okay. You owe me six vocabulary sheets, three journals, and two expositions. Then for next week you have your analysis, and your poem."

"What poem?"

"For Poetry in Action." She studied the planner. "Start with the exposition. You can choose a Dickinson poem to analyze and memorize it at the same time." She looked up. "You'll need to come in every day."

He stared at her in disbelief. First of all, he had never heard of meeting with a teacher every day. Detention, yes. Private tutoring? Nobody did that. And he had work. He was bagging leaves after school. He had begun with his mother's yard. Then he'd cleaned up Maia's place. His mother said that she was proud of him. His sister said nothing. She suspected him, but he ignored her. He wasn't angry with Diana anymore. He barely thought about her.

He lived alone, he worked alone, raking yards on Fayette and Amory and even as far away as Kirkland Street. He had filled forty giant bags with the fallen leaves of a giant copper beech. His arms were hard, his hands rough and cracked, because he didn't wear gloves, but he was more than halfway to a new BoX.

"I have a job."

Nina met his gaze with her gray eyes. "Adjust your schedule."

He said, "I have to do my—"

"Sorry."

He persisted. "I have a lot of—"

She interrupted, "I don't care."

Nina wasn't sure that Aidan would return the next day. Even when he showed up in class, she doubted he would meet her after school again. He looked so distant leaning back, his legs stretched out before him. His body told her, I'm here temporarily.

After school, she regretted telling him everything at once. She had surprised him, but he wouldn't stay surprised for long. She had presented a stark choice, but on consideration he might not care. If he called her bluff, she would have to go to DeLaurentis. A whole investigation would follow. She would have to explain why she had never mentioned Diana's journal before, and she would have to answer questions about her own behavior, her impulsive visit to Diana, her threat to Aidan, her flouting student privacy. There would be consequences for her as well as him. She stood in her empty classroom and she waited, but Aidan didn't come.

At last, Nina started loading her bags with student papers. She was about to leave when she saw Aidan's face in the window of her classroom door. Quickly she dropped her bags behind her desk and ushered him inside.

"You're late."

He didn't answer.

"Take a seat."

They sat together at two student desks, and she handed him a vocabulary worksheet, the first assignment that he'd missed.

He looked at her uncertainly. Was she planning to sit there while he did these? That seemed to be her intention. She actually watched him fill in blanks with *misanthrope, jocular, protean, lassitude, inchoate.*

"You know the words."

"Why wouldn't I?"

She heard the challenge in his voice and countered, "I didn't know that you had time to read."

He looked up and she saw a flash of fear in his blue eyes.

"Just keep working," Nina said.

Every day after that, they met in her empty classroom after school. They sat together at her desk and read Dickinson. She had him type his analysis on the classroom computer, where she could see him. *"I heard a Fly buzz—when I died" is an eerily calm poem about death. The narrator is detached from the situation . . .*

"What are you saying here?" She pointed to his opening paragraph.

Aidan searched Nina's face for clues, trying to find the words she wanted, hoping to fulfill his obligation fast.

"You're not interested in any of this."

"Not really."

She was sitting with her elbows on her desk, her chin resting in her hand. She was very serious, and very beautiful. "What if I say you have to be?"

"You can't make someone interested," he pointed out.

She ignored this and handed him his analysis. "Go ahead and read it to me."

"Aloud?"

He caught the hint of a smile and he thought, Oh yeah. Otherwise she couldn't hear me. But when he started reading, she challenged him.

"Are you sure you want to say death doesn't bother her?" she asked. "How do you know? How can anybody know?"

"True." He considered his own words. "I'll say it seems like death doesn't bother her."

He kept reading, and she bent her head to listen. It amazed her that he had plagiarized a paper. He wrote clearly, choosing his words well. He was more than capable. What was it then that had compelled him? Gaming in itself, or Daphne?

Tears welled up, but she didn't think that Aidan noticed.

He saw more than she realized. He saw her sadness. He saw her ink-smudged hand, her forearm where her sleeve fell back, her small wrist. He saw her head dip slightly. She was exhausted.

At first he watched for those moments when she let her guard down, the split second when she almost fell asleep. He willed her to lay down her head so he could rush outside.

Gradually, however, Nina drew him in. Shaking off sleep, she had such an edge about her, an intense concentration. She reminded him of someone, and he kept searching his memory. Who was it?

"Remember the speaker," she said of the Dickinson poem. "Who is speaking?"

"Someone dead."

"And what does that sound like?"

"Calm," Aidan said. "Numb."

Nina was leaning forward, intent on every word. When she pulled back, he caught the resemblance. She was like the doctor at the hospital, listening to his heart.

Day by day, Aidan began to catch her moods. Sometimes she was sleepy, sometimes miserable, sometimes bored. He forgot about escape. Her determination fascinated him. Her eyes closed for just a moment, but she never put her head down. She sat up straight and she was Miss Lazare again. "Here," she said, "I think you overstate your case."

Her knowledge scared him. Not her knowledge of literature, but her knowledge of his secret life.

"You need to memorize the poem." She passed him her thick book, the complete Dickinson, its paper jacket printed with blue and green leaves.

"I can memorize it now." He read the poem rapidly to himself and then turned the volume facedown on the desk.

"Don't do that! It's old. You'll break the spine." Protectively, she gathered her book up again.

Startled, he blurted, "Sorry." Then, trying to appease her, he recited the poem rapidly all in one breath, *"I heard a Fly buzz—when I died— / The Stillness in the Room / Was like the Stillness in the Air— / Between the Heaves of Storm— / The Eyes around . . ."*

She waited until he'd finished and then she said, "No. Say it like you mean it."

"But I don't mean it," he answered, sullen, because she was not impressed.

She looked at him steadily, without anger, without reproach. She could have snapped at him. She could have walked out, but she said nothing, and she stayed.

Gazing back, he saw his teacher's patience, vast and still, spread out before him like an inland sea.

At last she ventured, "You're a good student when you're in school."

"How do you know?"

"I've read your transcript, obviously."

She wanted more than anything to bring Aidan down to earth, but that was not the effect she had on him. She seemed to him enchanted, dangerous, a mermaid in the Whennish Sea.

When she was dissatisfied, she barely looked at him. When he worked harder, she nodded, as though she'd promised herself she wouldn't praise him. Her determination drew him to her. Lovely and difficult to please, she sent him off to prove himself in thorny fields, and set new tasks as soon as he was done.

She said, "When you recite, you have to slow down and think about the meaning of the words." But when he recited again, *"I heard a Fly buzz . . ."* he was thinking about her. He was imagining her elusive smile.

" *'I heard a Fly buzz—when I died' is an eerily calm poem about death,"* she said, quoting his essay back at him. *"The narrator is detached from the situation."*

Briefly, he felt it. Detached from the situation, he watched Miss Lazare sitting at her desk. He saw himself, looking into his teacher's eyes.

34

Bird on a Wire

Collin felt as though his world had changed to black and white. He had known magic. Nina had touched his life with gold. Now he could not reach her. He could not get back to where he'd been.

In games you could redeem yourself with points or jewels. You could trade gold for freedom, or even give an extra life away. In EverWhen you always had some recourse. Collin envied Everheads counting down to Launch Day in their ordered companies, their banners rippling overhead. He wished that he could run away and take his place among them. He wished that he could quit his job and disappear. Such was his guilt, his increasing sense of shame. Then he thought, No. Quitting was just what Peter wanted.

Monday morning, Collin walked to the bus stop, although he thought more than once of turning back. Waiting, he remained uncertain, but when Arkadia's shuttle arrived, he boarded. He would not give up. He had seen his horses thundering through the dining room. He had seen them with his own eyes, and they weren't pretty. They had silenced everybody.

The other hellions on the bus were quiet. How much did they

know? Had they seen him confront Daphne at the party? She was not riding the bus, but had they spoken to her? Maybe they thought he was a coward, crawling back. I can't win, Collin thought suddenly. He's got me to the point where I look like a quitter if I leave and a punching bag if I return.

Collin hunched down alone in a window seat. Just do your job. Just do your work and you'll get paid. He told himself this, but he thought of Peter. His harsh words, his frown, his cold dissatisfaction.

When the bus stopped, he roused himself to follow the others, stepped off with furious determination. To do what? He hardly knew. He wanted the impossible, the life he'd had before—his work, his love, his happiness.

Exiled from Nina, Collin found himself alone at Arkadia as well. In the next days and weeks, Peter reorganized pods so that Collin worked with all new people on background—texture and detail, condensation on rock faces, mists and shadows, damp stains on stone.

Collin was not the only artist reassigned as the launch approached. Even so, Collin sensed that Peter was isolating him. No one disabused him of the notion. Obi, Akosh, Tomas, and Daphne kept a friendly distance. They smiled and even played Ping-Pong with him on occasion, but they kept the conversation light. No gossip, no commiseration.

Daphne approached with cheerful caution, never once alluding to the drawings or the party or her tears. Only once was she at all real with him.

Collin passed her desk and startled her. She cleared her screen with a quick swipe of the hand.

"What was that?" Collin said. "Was that your new marketing plan?"

"New project," she admitted.

"For UnderWorld or something else?"

"You don't want to know."

Of course new projects cropped up all the time. Stealth mode was common, but Collin understood that he had been excluded once again.

"You'll get through this," Nicholas told Collin in the sound booth.

"Maybe." Collin had been rendering stalagmites in Under-World's caverns, and dragon bones, and mountains of slick guano. He was beginning to wonder if he would ever draw a face again, and yet he toiled on, sometimes bitter, sometimes laughing at himself. He was drawing bat shit, after all.

Work got even worse. Peter moved him to color correction. For days he didn't draw at all. He studied sequences at his workstation, analyzing the tint and continuity of dragon scales in the dim light, underground. His hands hovered over the keyboard, and, like a caged panther, his imagination turned and turned upon itself.

He stood and stretched his arms. He spun around and he saw dragon scales on every surface. Every cubicle glowed silver. He had never been so tired or so bored, and he wanted to bust out of there. Pride prevented him. Don't give up now, he told himself. Don't let Peter win. He forced himself to work, imprisoned in his chair. The days stretched out, hour after hour.

On Launch Day Collin watched news reporters arrive, trailing long black cables. He watched the hallways fill with virtual mist, an atmosphere of mystery advertising aeroflakes. From a distance, he watched Viktor speak.

"Today we are announcing that OVID will support all Arkadian games. Not just UnderWorld, but EverWhen as well. We are opening portals for world-jumping so that players can move seamlessly from one game to the next."

The metallic kiss of cameras.

"A world without edges," Viktor said. "No screens, no frames. You go where your imagination takes you."

I wish, thought Collin.

He wandered through the building, and there was food, and there were kegs. There were demos. Reporters standing at the Gates and dueling in the halls. Bright as a harvest moon, a virtual clock was counting down to midnight. The illusion caught Collin's attention, but he could not forget the maze of cubicles beneath.

He paused for a moment at his desk. On impulse, he pocketed a black pen and five packs of sticky notes. Then he headed outside.

The wind hit hard. The evening was bitter, and he was glad. It was quiet outdoors. No speeches, no demos, but as he rounded the corner of the building, he heard voices.

"Hey, hey, ho, ho. UnderWorld has got to go." Shoulder to shoulder, members of Christians Against Gaming Exploitation were marching in the west parking lot, a dozen young men and women carrying hand-painted signs. CU IN HEAVEN! JESUS PLAYS FOR KEEPS.

Collin stared at the picketers bundled up like carolers in their knit hats and Christmas sweaters. One in particular, a paunchy guy in rectangular glasses, called out to Collin. "Hey, man, listen!"

Collin studied the protestor's round face.

"The Lord tests the righteous, but His soul hates the wicked and the one who loves violence."

Wearily, Collin said, "Hi, Darius."

"Repent!" cried a young woman in a reindeer sweater. Her long hair spilled out under the brim of her candy-striped hat. Her eyes were bright, her nose and lips and eyebrows ringless.

"Hey, Emma," Collin said.

He took the early shuttle back to Cambridge, but it was dark when he got off in Harvard Square. He stood for a moment on Mt. Auburn Street, just watching the students, and the construction workers, and the homeless veteran, and the people carrying rolled yoga mats. He glanced at Grafton Street and the Harvard Book Store, where Nina used to meet him.

His heart rebelled against his loneliness. His body ached from hunching at his desk, and now his fingers flexed. He walked across the Square to Grendel's. He hurried down the stairs to the old dive, and all the green lamps on the tables welcomed him.

"Collin!" Sam cried out as he approached the bar. Tiny, sharp-eyed, hospitable, she brought a pint without his asking. "You never call, you never write."

"Hey." Kayte was still waiting tables. "How's Nina?"

Collin didn't answer, and she didn't press.

He sat at the bar and watched Sam mixing drinks as Grendel's music pounded all around him.

"What's it like there?" Sam asked.

"It's just work."

"Come on, give us some dirt," Kayte called out as she passed through to the kitchen.

"I got nothing," Collin said.

"Empty-handed," Sam said.

"No." He felt in his jacket pockets and pulled out the sticky notes. He lined them up on the bar along with the pen.

Sam said, "Oooh, exciting. Little pads of paper."

"Pick a color. Any color." They were all pale office shades. Pink, blue, green, yellow, white.

"Green."

He drew a leaf on a green sticky note. A simple maple leaf, outlined in black pen.

Sam said, "You quit your job."

"No." He turned back the first sticky note and drew the leaf again. On every page he drew the maple leaf in a slightly different position.

"So you like it there."

Like is not the word, thought Collin. Liking the job didn't enter into it.

"Nice," said Kayte, who was looking over his shoulder.

He sensed several people watching. Two girls sitting next to him leaned closer as he drew another leaf.

"Oh, I get it," one girl said, as he drew the maple leaf for the twentieth time, edges curling in an imaginary wind. Her name was Emily and her friend was Kira and they were going out for Kira's belated birthday. Emily was bright-eyed and heavy. She had blond hair but dark eyebrows, and she wore a low-cut shirt. Kira was heavy too, but softer and quieter. Her eyes were dark with eyeliner and she had beautiful black hair all down her back. She looked like the girls Collin had known in high school. He drew a leaf on the last sticky note and gave the whole pack to Kira. "Happy birthday."

"Oh, wow," said Kira, uncertainly.

Emily said, "It's a flip-book."

Kira held the pack of sticky notes and flipped them with her thumb. The maple leaf drifted, rising and dancing and falling to the bottom of the last page. "It's so pretty," Kira exclaimed. "How did you learn to do that?"

"You're terrible," Sam told Collin.

He was already drawing a flip-book for Emily. This one wasn't nearly as beautiful. It was just an ice cream cone melting in the sun. "You're so good," Emily exclaimed.

"No, ice cream is boring." Collin gave up halfway through. "I'm doing something else."

The two of them waited quite seriously, and a few others stood behind them. Even Sam leaned over the bar.

"Okay, let's try this."

He took his black pen and drew a line across a blue sticky note. A line sagging ever so slightly. A telephone wire. Then he drew a bird on the wire. A black bird, alone and hunched. He turned the page and drew the bird again. He turned each page and drew the bird spreading its wings.

When Collin finished and thumbed through the book, his audience watched the bird take flight, soaring and swooping in the air until at last it flew off the page.

"It's yours." He gave the book to Emily, and she showed it off to everyone. At one point Kayte came over with her phone and filmed it.

The girls bought Collin another drink. They invited him to a party later on that night.

He enjoyed the attention, and then, suddenly, he was tired of it. He started glancing at the door. Actually, he explained, he was waiting for someone. Nobody believed this, but he wasn't lying. He was waiting for Nina, although he knew she wouldn't come.

35

In the Hall

Gold showered down. Autumn leaves so bright that for a moment Aidan covered his eyes. He wasn't used to this anymore, the dazzling colors, the shifting light and shadow. Opening his new BoX, he felt like a figure in a snow globe, wind blowing, leaves swirling all around.

He heard cheering, tramping in the Trackless Wood—the remnants of his company. Of his sixty-one Elves, only twelve remained. Centuries had passed since they had qwested together, scores of battles had been waged and won. Giants of the dark cliffs had forged an alliance with the Gnomes who toiled underground, and together they'd built an enormous fighting force, the Nord, who had begun raiding Elvish strongholds in an attempt to launch themselves against the Keep.

We've been waiting, Aidan's comrades said. In real life, the company was scattered in living rooms, bedrooms, and basements all around the world. Some guys were fat, some had bad knees, some were just kids wearing pajamas, but in EverWhen they were all Water Elves, tall and elegant, with flowing hair. They wore chain mail and they carried swords. "You're late, Tildor," chided Dracon, Aidan's second in command.

Even as he spoke, the forest darkened and the wind picked up. No, not the wind. Aidan threw himself to the ground as dragons tore through the wood, blackening every living thing. Moments later it was over, but his ears were ringing with the dragons' screams.

Shaking off ash, he struggled to his feet. Close by his side, Aidan's old qwesting friends debated what to do.

"March on!"

"No. Hold back and wait."

Already, moss crept up blackened tree trunks. Ferns sprang up from the ashy forest floor. Withered branches spread and multiplied, sending forth new twigs. Pale folded leaves opened into oak, or maple leaf, or elm, filtering the light and showering charred earth with every shade of russet, gold, and green. The others were appealing to Aidan for orders, but he gazed at the changing leaves, the ever-shifting light, and he thought, How beautiful. How strange the way the woods surrounded you.

"Let's go," Dracon urged him.

Aidan lifted his arm and Tildor held his sword aloft. "Follow me!"

He led his Elves to a thousand-year-old beech, a cosmos of its own, with its vast canopy of leaves. The whole company, linking hands together, could not span its massive trunk. "This is the place." Aidan scored the smooth gray tree trunk with his sword, opening a seam that darkened with a sickening sound of splitting wood. "This is the way," Aidan called out as the others followed him inside the tree to UnderWorld.

All that night, he qwested with his company. They fought their way to the silver river and took a ferry to the far shore.

"Cover me!" Aidan shouted as he attacked the Iron Man, striking welded joints and eye slits. Battle-tested, he knew how to move, and how to leap, how to manage spectral weightlessness. He could fend off white bats, and navigate labyrinthine passages carved in stone. Even so, the way was difficult, increasingly complex.

They came to a cavern he had not yet seen, a crypt where they found Elves disfigured and leprous with mold. Aidan saw cauliflower ears and wobbling jaws, noses melting like candle wax. "Stand together," he commanded.

"Put up your swords. We have no power," a living corpse with blackened fingers said.

Wonderingly, Aidan asked, "Who were you?"

"Fire Elves."

"Who did this to you?"

The ruined Elf pointed through the archways to a dim-lit chamber, where a rustling creature stirred. Taller than Aidan, a praying mantis whirred, and clicked, and cleaned its folded legs on a dark throne.

"Watch out," the moldering corpses shouted as Aidan approached the insect king. "Don't let him bite," the blackened Elf called after him.

"Wait here," Aidan told his company, and all obeyed, except for Dracon, who followed him.

Like a dying fire, the chamber faintly glowed. The praying mantis turned, and Aidan saw the insect's mandibles working, outer eyes wide-set and swiveling.

Aidan drew his sword. "Reverse your spells."

With a dry, rattling sound, the mantis rose up gigantic on its hind legs.

"Reverse your spells, or come down and fight."

Instantly, the mantis pounced. Aidan sprang back just in time, slashing at the insect's hard body, its whirring limbs, and pointed face. He sliced one antenna. Instantly, the quivering organ grew back. He stabbed the mantis in its thorax and the insect lost its balance, staggering back for just a moment. Then, like a boxer, the mantis rose up and pounced, toppling Dracon with a single blow.

"Get up. Get up!"

Too late. Dracon lay on the throne room floor, his neck pinched in the insect's mandibles.

Aidan's company rushed the room, even as the mantis bent over its prey.

"Stay back," Aidan shouted, but they didn't listen and mobbed the insect, attacking with their useless swords. Each blow glanced off the insect's back, and the mantis fed until Dracon's body began to swell. His flesh turned white, his face began to curdle.

The other Elves tried to drag away the body. Fenuel seized one lifeless arm, Lorimar the other. Suddenly these friends were stricken too. Their hands withered where they had touched Dracon's white flesh, their fingers blackened as with frostbite.

Aidan knew death in battle. He himself had been dismembered, impaled, decapitated, but that was just a nuisance and a loss of points. After a few minutes, anyone who died in EverWhen could jump back up again. This was something else, a wasting disease. "Don't touch him," warned Aidan as his Elves crowded Dracon.

Once again, the clicking, rattling sound. The mantis? Alarm clock. "I have to go," Aidan told the others. His mother was still at work—no danger there—but he was on every kind of probation: academic, disciplinary. He had to get to school.

A moment later, he was diving for clean clothes, racing to the bathroom, stumbling down the stairs. After his all-nighter, the house seemed warped and thrown together, the ceiling dangerously low. At the breakfast table, Diana was a headless body. It took Aidan a few seconds to see that she'd buried her head in her arms.

Gradually, the kitchen began to right itself. The sink, the chairs, the window, the apple clock, Diana sitting there with bloodshot eyes.

Was she crying? At first it was hard to tell, and then he saw her tearstained cheeks, and it was hard to look. Long ago Diana would cry when their father hit Aidan. Then Aidan would start crying too. He would shut his eyes and turn away, do everything he could to stop, but once he saw her tears, he could not force back his own. "What happened?"

She pushed her chair away from the table, but she didn't speak.

She had lost Brynna. Not in a day, not over weeks, but gradually, as the days grew shorter, as rain turned to snow, and snow hardened into ice, Brynna had pushed Diana away. At night she went to parties, while her parents watched Angela. She stayed out with Anton and his friends, Khalil, Dmitri, Sevonna. She was actually seeing Anton again.

Late at night Diana had confronted her by text. What ru thinking? Cruelly Brynna had replied, Ur only jealous. After that Diana couldn't sleep. She'd lain awake all night, listening to Aidan qwesting.

Light-headed, Aidan watched his sister dematerialize into dots. He gripped the edge of the table and she was herself again—but much smaller than he'd remembered. He had just put away his sword and there she was, slipping on her parka, shouldering her worn-out backpack. She looked so defeated, he forgot her tattling. After all, it didn't matter anymore. He had his new BoX and he loved Diana again. He had never stopped loving her—but she should have known that.

He didn't speak, but he felt for her as she stepped into her snow boots. Those boots looked so heavy, they could have been stone.

Diana kept her head down and her coat on once she got to Emerson. Her jacket's hugeness shielded her as she made her way upstairs past couples kissing, girls gossiping, guys chest-butting like demented stags. Brynna approached, and Diana looked up, hoping for an instant. Her former best friend swept past her.

Anton arrived, and his blond hair was short and spiky, his eyes hard. He'd nicked himself shaving, so you could see a spot of blood on his neck. Diana tortured herself, watching Brynna drift toward him. She looked so soft and gentle, her thick hair wafting over her shoulders. She was nothing like Anton, and yet she stood with him by the lockers. Hands in each other's back pockets, they were practically married.

"Congrats," Diana said as she walked by.

Brynna pretended that she didn't hear, but Anton snarled, "Dyke."

A moment later, Anton's head smashed into the metal locker doors. It happened so fast even Diana was surprised. She barely understood what she had done when he surged back and seized her shoulders. His fingers clawed through her down coat.

Voices all around her, cheers, and catcalls. Mr. Allan yelling, "Whoa. Walk away. Walk away." She didn't walk. She kicked and scratched. Like a creature shedding her second skin, she slipped from Anton's grasp. Lithe and strong, she left her puffy jacket in his hands.

He dropped the jacket and she flew at him as he fought her off, ignoring Mr. Allan's threats and Brynna's pleas. The bell was ringing, the hall flooding with students. Teachers were struggling to pull Diana and Anton apart, but it was Aidan who charged between them. He had followed her to school, shadowing her all the way upstairs.

"You touch my sister and I'll fucking kill you." Aidan's cheeks were blazing. He was white light, he was the dazzling sun.

Ten minutes later, Aidan and Diana sat together at the round conference table in DeLaurentis's office. Anton sat at a little distance on the other side.

Mr. DeLaurentis spread his hands. "Can we work this out?"

The three of them sat silent. Anton stretched out, with his chair pulled back from the table. Aidan stole a glance at Diana. Her eyes were bright, her tears gone. She looked taller, as though she had thrown off a crushing weight. And it was strange, but he felt taller too. He had not realized how heavy her sadness had become.

Mr. DeLaurentis told Diana, "We don't tolerate bullying."

She pointed straight at Anton. "He bullied *me*."

"As for you . . ." DeLaurentis turned to Aidan.

"He didn't do anything!" Diana interrupted. "He was protecting me."

"This conflict didn't happen on its own."

Aidan settled back, preparing for the onslaught. It was always like this at school. The actual fight lasted just seconds. The discussion afterward took hours.

Diana was still stuck in the principal's office when DeLaurentis ordered her brother to return to class. Aidan felt guilty about leaving, because he knew exactly what would happen next. She would have to see Miss Sorentino, who made you talk until you would admit anything. You were bored at school, you were tired of your life. She got you to the point where you confessed feelings you didn't even have.

Slowly he made his way to English, arriving in a tide of whispered speculation.

"Where's Anton?" Sofia whispered to Aidan, as soon as he sat down.

Rafael asked, "What did you do to him?"

"Was he expelled?"

"Okay, let's concentrate." Miss Lazare handed Aidan a ballot for Poetry in Action.

Lazare was calling on each kid, one by one. You had to stand

and recite your chosen poem from memory, after which the class would vote for one student to represent them in the school competition. Unless you were into theater like Becca, the whole thing was a nightmare until your turn was over. Then you could sink down and watch other kids rock back on their heels, and forget their lines. Miss Lazare said, "That's okay, just take a breath," and it was torture, but she never let you give up. She made you stand there. Naturally people chose the shortest poems eligible. "Fog" by Carl Sandburg. William Blake's "The Sick Rose." "Do *not* vote for me," they whispered to their friends.

"I need your attention," Miss Lazare told the class. Nico was reciting Roethke's "My Papa's Waltz." *The whiskey on your breath* . . . But Aidan was the center of attention; even those who hadn't seen him challenge Anton had heard about the brawl.

"Did you really break his nose?" Sofia whispered.

"Would I be here if I'd actually hurt him?" Aidan retorted, enjoying his notoriety.

"Aidan," Miss Lazare said, as soon as Nico had finished.

He waited for the reprimand. Don't talk in class.

"Get up there."

Oh. In the excitement, he'd actually forgotten.

"Your turn."

Aidan remembered nothing. He had prepared, of course. Lazare herself had practiced with him, but when he stood in front of the blackboard, he could not recall a single word of Dickinson.

Curious, his fellow students stared at Aidan. Their ballots fluttered all around them.

He glanced at Miss Lazare, who waited in the back of the room with her clipboard in her hands. He didn't care about the others, but he hated himself for letting her down.

No. He had to think. Back before the lecture in DeLaurentis's office. Before the fight, before Diana at the breakfast table and the long qwest underground. He had to tunnel through all the battles he had fought and won and lost. Mantis king and Iron Man, silver dragons and three-headed dogs.

The moment stretched too long. Not a moment, but an entire day, a year. The class grew restless, but he closed his eyes and fought to uncover words small as insects, black and quivering.

"I heard a Fly buzz—when I died." His voice was deep and deadpan, eerily calm, even as he searched his memory.

"The Stillness round my form / Was like the Stillness in the Air . . ."

The whole class hushed in horror and in sympathy. No one had heard the poem quite that way before. He was struggling but he would not give up. "The Eyes beside—had wrung them dry . . ." Searching for each word, he seemed to be improvising on the spot.

There had never been such silence in that room. Not a word, not a breath. "I willed my Keepsakes—Signed away / What portion of me I . . ." Long pause. "Could make Assignable, and then . . ."

He was like a diver. They could barely see him anymore as he swam deep underwater to retrieve each phrase. His classmates watched as he held his breath and sank into the abyss.

In a trance, he swam down to his own death, his own body on the hospital bed. "There interposed a Fly . . . With Blue, uncertain . . . stumbling Buzz." His voice was strange, not his at all, but cold and numb. "And then the Windows failed—and then / I could not see to see."

Silence again, and then everyone was clapping, because he had found the words, and brought them back alive.

Nina could not stop smiling. All traces of the teacher vanished from her face.

Look at Miss Lazare, kids told each other. Total joy! The little jump you always hoped for, but hardly ever got to see.

36

World-Jumping

"I knew it," Nina told Aidan after school. She had known instantly that he would win the class election. She'd seen it in the students' faces. He would represent them in the assembly.

"That's crazy," said Aidan. He had no interest in reciting for the school, but Miss Lazare's response captivated him. She seemed like an entirely new person, her eyes alight.

"It's incredible," she said. "Fantastic."

She gave him all the credit, and, at the same time she felt that teaching him was the best thing she'd ever done. Bright, dreamy, obsessed with fantasy, Aidan was a natural, seizing language for himself, inhabiting simile and metaphor. He was born for poetry.

Was it that ability, or was it fear? Was it simply practice? Understanding what she was looking for? He was using what she gave him, making connections, drawing inferences. If she spoke to him about one image—death as a fellow traveler—he found a complementary example: *The Carriage held but just Ourselves— / And Immortality.*

"He listens," Nina had told Jeff at their weekly lunch meeting.

"Of course he does. He has your undivided attention. The bigger question is how you want to use your time."

"I don't think I'm taking anything away from the other students."

Jeff warned, "You don't want to play favorites."

"I'm not!" she protested. "He's a student at risk."

"He's not alone."

"But he really learns this way."

"Everybody does."

She knew what he was thinking. Another white-middle-class success story. "I just feel like I'm finally doing something."

"You see him every day; you're spending five hours a week with him. That's an entire class of one."

Waiting for Aidan after school, Nina opened her copy of Dickinson on her desk. Jeff cared about metrics. He believed in trying for the greatest impact possible, and by impact he meant reaching the many, not the privileged few. Nina had privileged Aidan, lavishing her time and her attention on him. It was not her mission to run private tutorials at a public high school.

But what if this was the way she taught best? What if this was how she made a difference? Test scores didn't matter to her in the aggregate. I'm not big-picture, Nina thought. I doubt I'll make an impact on a hundred kids—but I'm teaching one.

She didn't care what Jeff said or how he warned her; she knew that she was getting something done at last. Listen to Aidan recite. Look at his written work. She had his essay marked good and wonderful, lying right there on her desk.

Even so, her influence was limited. She could hold Aidan's attention for an hour, but she could not control his life. When he was late she worried that he wouldn't come. He arrived exhausted after school and she could only wonder, Are you gaming? Are you running out at night? When he seemed distracted, she imagined he was giving up. Most days he focused, but some afternoons he gazed into the distance and she thought, I'm losing him. I will never change anybody. She had not changed Collin. She had left him as she'd found him, gifted, adventurous, devoted to the chase. She had not changed him, but she missed him.

Sometimes she wondered, What if I was wrong? You weren't wrong, Lily assured her. Sometimes Nina thought, He lied to me, but does that mean he'd cheated too? Obviously, Julianne said.

And yet Nina doubted herself. She thought, He was not what I had hoped, but I assumed the worst. He disappointed me, but I set him up. What did I expect, bringing him to that place? She wavered and then stopped short. Collin had decided what to draw and how to act.

"Miss?"

"Oh!" She hadn't seen Aidan come in.

He apologized for startling her. He didn't know how glad she was to see him. He shook her from her thoughts. He handed her three completed vocabulary worksheets.

She said, "Good, and I've graded your essay. We'll go over it."

He looked at her expectantly.

She thought, You know it's excellent. You can't wait to get it back.

"Okay, first of all, let's hear your poem."

"*I heard a Fly buzz—when I died.*"

She wanted to hear him recite again as he had in class. She craved that magic once again.

"*The Stillness in the Room / Was like the Stillness in the Air . . .*"

"Hold on. Slow down."

Embarrassed, Aidan stumbled over *Heaves of Storm.*

"Why are you rushing?"

He thought, Because you're distracting me. She was lovely and he longed to please her—to see pure joy on her face, to surprise her once again. He fantasized about her all the time, but not in the way that he had Daphne. Those visions had been violent. He had chased

Daphne into the real world to pin her down. With his teacher, just the opposite. He took her deep into his dreams and gave her his sword.

When he remembered his lines, they rushed out all at once, too glib, too fast. Nor could he make his voice cold when Nina was his only audience.

"The poem has a kind of mordant wit," she told him. "Very dark. Very wry. Remember how you did it before?"

He didn't feel mordant. He was the one buzzing. He was the fly, and there was no corpse, only his final paper on Dickinson. His three-to-five-page essay with the final comment, *Aidan, I'm impressed*. He kept glancing at the graded essay on her desk. Her words on his, her pen and his typed paragraphs practically touching. How could he remember dying? He said, "I think it was a onetime thing."

"No, that's not true!" She would not accept excuses, nor could he distract her long. "Slow it down. Slow down even more."

He closed his eyes to concentrate. He tried to find that slow and empty place, to become again the diver underwater.

"Yes! Better," she exclaimed. "But look at me. Look at the audience. Don't look away."

He said, "I need to practice that."

He practiced all the way home, stepping slowly, brimful of words. *The Stillness round my form . . .* He saw Nina's eager look, her shake of the head. He saw her listening to him, and the winter afternoon seemed new and strange. The bare trees standing like upended brooms. Small birds darting together, turning all at once, swooping and gathering in an instant, playing with the wind.

"Hey," Diana greeted him. He didn't even stop for a second as he ran up the stairs. *The eyes beside—had wrung them dry— / And Breaths were gathering sure . . .*

Diana couldn't hear the poem clamoring in his ears. She had to listen to Kerry berate her on the phone, while Aidan paced his room above her head. *For that last Onset—when the King / Be witnessed—in his power.*

"It's one day. Just a one-day suspension—and I wasn't even fighting! I barely touched the guy," Diana insisted.

Aidan threw himself onto his unmade bed. *With Blue— uncertain—stumbling Buzz . . .* He saw Nina's face, intent and serious, her slender arms. The chalk dust on her shirt. *Between the light—and me . . . Between the light—and me . . .* Over and over, he imagined her.

A rattling sound roused him, an insistent scratching. He started up, sensing someone rapping, trying to get in. His room was dark, the winter sun had set. He must have drifted off. He turned on the light and saw a bare tree branch rattling against the windowpane. Checking his watch, he was shocked he'd slept so long, past five o'clock.

Shit. He'd promised he would meet his company. He hesitated for a minute, then, scrambling to his feet, he opened his BoX.

"Where is everybody?" he demanded as his Elf shape materialized. All he saw was poor, half-crippled Dracon standing on a stone bridge. Vast caverns, vaults of a subterranean cathedral surrounded them.

"Everybody else gave up," Dracon said. "You were supposed to be here two hours ago."

"Okay, we'll reschedule."

"No. You said the qwest was on."

Annoyed, Aidan kicked the bridge, dislodging a pebble that fell pinging and ricocheting into the ghostly river far below. "Dude, I have to study."

In her bedroom, Diana heard muffled voices through the wall. *I have to study?*

A car door slammed, and her first thought was, Oh no, Mom's coming home to punish me.

No. Just a delivery person. She heard someone clomping up the front steps, ringing the bell, dropping a package on the porch. More footsteps, another weight dropped on the porch. Somebody was tramping up and down.

She slipped into Kerry's empty room and opened the shades to see the street. She found no delivery truck. Only a station wagon in the winter night. She ran downstairs barefoot, wearing her flannel pajama bottoms and a white T-shirt printed DANA-FARBER CANCER INSTITUTE. When she opened the door, she found Jack, with ten battered cardboard cartons stacked up at his feet. "What are you doing?"

He answered in his even way, "I brought you something."

She glanced at the cartons and then looked away. He must have heard. "Aidan's upstairs."

"I came to see you."

"I'm busy."

"Doing what?"

She thought of Sorentino. "Processing what happened—supposedly."

Politely Jack said, "Cool, what did you come up with?"

When she glared at Jack, he didn't even blink. She said, "You feel sorry for me."

He ignored this. "Hold the door."

"Why?"

He hoisted two cartons. "Because they're heavy."

She held the glass storm door open with her hip. "You stole some lame educational props from your father, didn't you?"

"Maybe."

"Wait. Are those fireworks? Because my mom's coming home in like an hour."

Jack knelt on the living room floor, and opened the boxes to reveal thousands upon thousands of black and white tiles.

"Nooo," Diana groaned. Scienceman's birthday party dominoes.

Jack looked up at her. "Come on. You know you want to."

For the next two hours, they dominoed the house, lining up their tiles, spaced at perfect intervals, across the floor and down the hall. They lined up their tiles in all the dusty places, outlining window-sills and baseboards, snaking behind the couch, circling the old upright piano.

"Who plays?" Jack asked.

"Nobody," Diana said. "I mean, Aidan used to."

Above their heads they could hear Aidan's shuffling, stamping feet. He'd put off studying after all.

Like black ants, those tiles marched across that poor piano. They covered the entire living room out to the entrance hall, and then Jack said, "We still have more."

Diana sat back on her heels. "Let's do the kitchen."

They extended their line onto the kitchen floor, around the kitchen table. They built domino formations on the kitchen counters, an array of black tiles from the toaster oven to the old microwave.

"I used to think you had a sad, pathetic life," Diana said.

"Why?"

"Because you're an only child."

One by one, Jack placed his dominoes along the counter. "I like being an only child."

"Obviously." Diana was thinking that being an only child was all Jack knew. "It's worse when you become an only child later."

Jack finished his row and then leaned against the counter, considering her.

"What?" she demanded.

"Is it true?"

"What do you mean?" she asked, although she knew exactly what he meant.

"Do you like girls better?"

"Yeah! Don't you?" He was making her nervous. "Actually, I go by the person."

"So you don't know . . ." Tile by tile, he was encircling Kerry's coffeemaker.

"I don't know about you."

Footsteps. Their miniature world began to rattle. Aidan was like a giant heading to the bathroom overhead. Every move, a step of doom. They heard the toilet flush, the water running in the sink. They held still as he returned to his room. Their dominoes wobbled as walls and floorboards creaked. Then he slammed his bedroom door.

The old house absorbed the shock, and all the domino chains tumbled in the kitchen down below, whole regiments collapsing on their bridges, folding onto countertops and floors. Jack and Diana doubled over, laughing.

"Earthquake!" Aidan shouted, deep in game, but of course Dracon felt nothing on his side.

A flurry of white bats descended.

"Help me!" Dracon tried to fight them off one-handed.

Aidan drew his sword, but he wasn't fast enough. Already the bats began to feed.

He pulled Dracon into a cave, reached for his diamond flask, and sprinkled hatchling's blood on Dracon's wounds.

"What are you doing?" Dracon protested even as his own flesh healed. "There's ten more infections in the company and now you've used up the flask. You've wasted it!"

"We'll find another dragon's egg," Aidan promised.

"When?" Dracon asked bitterly.

"When we get the company together."

Now Dracon lost patience. "You no longer have a company." Sword in hand, Dracon turned his back.

"Where are you going?"

"I'm qwesting elsewhere," Dracon said with dignity.

Furious, Aidan said, "I'll go myself."

He stood alone in the dark cavern and lifted his arms so that the bats descended, feasting. They ate his arms to bloody nubs, and bit his body to the bone. They devoured his face, and his knight fell writhing to the cavern floor. Aidan was unafraid. He had trained for transformation, and he chose this metamorphosis, stretching out his torso, trading sword for a long tail. He saw his hind legs lengthening, his bloody flesh resolving into silver scales. Two dark patches on his back began to swell. Black wings opened wet and heavy, then fanned out, shedding sparkling drops of water. His skull had changed to silver, his tongue unfurling with a lick of fire. He lit the cavern as he took flight, exploding through stone walls into the Arkadian sky.

Aidan spread his wings and he was soaring, his spectral dragon rising over mountains, flaming over trees and frozen lakes. Now he saw the contours of the Trackless Wood, the distant towers of the Keep. He had jumped worlds to EverWhen.

Gliding softly in familiar skies, Aidan saw Elves lying where they had fallen in the snow. Hundreds of qwesters, too weak to move. Had the contagion spread to EverWhen? How many qwesters had jumped worlds before him, carrying the disease? Grimly he turned toward EverSea.

Flying low over crashing waves, he took his place among the other dragons nesting on the coast. He folded his great wings as he slithered into the low cave. Quiet now and smooth, his body undulating, he shed his dragon body. His serpentine form coiled and disappeared with a sucking sound like water down a drain.

A knight again, he crept between mountainous dragons. Clutching his needle sword, he felt his way inside their rocky nest. Softly, laboriously, he carried out an egg the size of a watermelon. The egg was speckled white and brown, and hard to handle, slipping constantly, so he had to stop and readjust his grip. Over rocks, and tide pools, past the open mouths of caves, he carried this burden, until, exhausted, he set it on the sand. He would strike the egg with his sword, and kill the hatchling. Fill his diamond flask with blood, and then . . . What next? One flask wasn't enough to heal his whole company. He would have to steal another egg and yet another, and even then, all of EverWhen was infested. Working alone, he could not move fast enough. The game was impossible. Not just difficult, but hopeless. He struck the eggshell with his sword, and the fissure widened. Green fluid leaked onto the sand. Chipping at the shell, prying it apart with his bare hands, he found the hatchling curled within. The monster didn't snap or bite. He pulled open the creature's wings, but they fell back, inert. He pried open the dragon's eyes, but they were white and empty.

"No!" Aidan shouted. The thing was dead.

He could not extract elixir, nor could he restore his company.

He kicked the broken egg and all its contents into the sea. Hurled his sword like a javelin into the waves.

The surf rose in a fury, swallowing the egg and then the sword. Rising higher, ocean consumed the rocks and drowned Aidan in darkness.

The shore was gone. The waves had disappeared as well. There was no ocean left. His bed appeared where there had been cliffs and caves. His silent desk displaced the raging surf. His painted ceiling blotted out the stars.

He had killed the game. For a moment he stood in shock, convinced his anger had destroyed it. His BoX lay inert, an old toy on the floor.

He felt for his computer, tapped the keyboard, clicked the mouse. A message appeared on his computer screen.

DUE TO TECHNICAL DIFFICULTIES, WE ARE RESETTING ALL ARKADIAN WORLDS. WE APOLOGIZE FOR ANY INCONVENIENCE. PLAY WILL RESUME AS SOON AS POSSIBLE.

37

Contagion

At first Collin thought the problem was a power outage. Monitors went dark, the great screens on the wall faded and died. The whole building seemed to dim, games ceasing and illusions dissipating, but the problem was not electrical. Viktor had stopped play altogether, ordering a hard reset of all Arkadian games.

"Two days. Three days at most," Viktor told reporters.

He spoke of the human factor, rogue behavior by a few who spread disease. The UnderWorld infection, designed as a gory interlude, easily reversible, had become a raging epidemic. World-jumpers carried the contagion to EverWhen and EverSea, where unsuspecting players sickened and lost power. Some trained in healing arts had attempted cures. Others had begun spreading the disease on purpose, lying in wait to lay hands on each fresh Elf or Gnome. Millions died, and in many cases, they stayed dead for days. Unaccustomed to disease, the dead logged off as they grew frustrated, waiting for resurrection. Viktor posted a concise explanation on fan forums. "The epidemic was not a problem we could solve in real time. We thank you for your patience."

As players faced blank screens, Arkadians swarmed their cubicles like frantic bees. Viktor spoke to the media, while Peter rallied the troops in the Atrium. Like militia awaiting orders, hellions mustered among the corporate palms.

How strange the way an imaginary disease became a real threat, rogue gamers a financial liability. Collin stood among the hellions and the moment seemed to him bizarre, ridiculous. You won't believe what happened, he imagined telling Maia—but he could never explain how surreal this was, the loophole in the game, the sudden rift in the Arkadian cosmos. He could never convey how he felt— bemused, alone, confused. This was what happened when a game consumed itself, the system crashing down. This was the ouroboros devouring its own tail. He saw it now, and all he wanted was to talk to Nina.

"We have to change the game," Peter explained to the assembled. "We want controlled chaos, not total anarchy. The goal is *simulated* tragedy." Together, they would curtail and streamline UnderWorld's plague so that the disease would run its course with Arkadian speed. The whole cycle, from wasting away and dying to resurrection, would take minutes instead of days. Equally important, hellions would ensure the leprous blight could not travel from one game to another. Contagion 2.0, as Peter called it, would remain in UnderWorld. While artists worked on symptoms, programmers would adjust settings so that if a player jumped to any other realm, the plague would lose its power.

And what will I do? thought Collin. The answer came quickly, because every minute counted, every hour offline eroded audience. Collin would have a chance to draw again. He worked with his own pod, and the whole thing was weird, the whole exercise was strange, but the work was so absorbing, that Collin forgot all that. No one shaved, and no one showered, no one went home. Caught up in the collective effort, Collin began to feel like himself again. It was such a relief to do his job.

Past problems seemed to disappear, as hellions worked together.

Viktor had food delivered at all hours. Nicholas set up an earth-shaking sound system, rocking the building with heavy metal, techno, classic rap. Even as programmers tapped furiously at their keyboards, Daphne reached out with hope and reassurance on fan forums. Sometimes she posted as an impudent insider, Reconnect with family and friends while you still can, because UnderWorld is almost baaack. Sometimes she played fangirl, sometimes she became a spy. Often she assumed her favorite role, the activist who went by "Christian Wench" and argued that the contagion had been sent by God to destroy Satan's handiwork. As EverWhen is visited by plague, typed Daphne, so shall the world. Repent! Turn away from darkness. Fast and pray!

News reporters understood by now that the Christian protest against Arkadia had been a hoax, but Daphne continued posting anyway. She did this to entertain UnderWorld's fans, who loved to hate their Christian enemies—even when they knew they were imaginary. At the same time, Daphne's message boards began to draw in real anti-gamers. It seemed that actual mothers were now posting complaints. I have a 13 year old child I hope and pray that UnderWorld is gone forever. Daphne tried to answer every comment. Amen, Amen, she typed, or May it be thy will.

She was doing her best work, and she was not the only one. Collin felt a surge of energy. His spirits lifted, even as he drew a crumpling nose, a blackening ear. He caught Peter gazing at his monitor, examining a series of degenerating eyes. Pupils gradually enlarged, eyeballs clouding, one lid dropping, pendulous, elephantine.

Peter said nothing, but Collin didn't care. He no longer waited for a verdict, a word of praise or blame. He no longer worried if Peter would use his work. The fact was, his art was necessary, and it was good.

He showed off to Obi and Akosh, entertaining them. When they sprawled out on chairs or on the floor exhausted, he drew a couple of flip-books, a dragon hatching, an exploding face.

"No way," Akosh told Collin.

"What?"

"No way are you still drawing now."

He felt alive, awake again. He drew constantly, almost effort-lessly. He did more than his share, accomplished even more than Peter asked. When the crisis ended, he was surprised to realize that he had been working three days straight.

When Arkadia went live again, Tomas recognized Collin's work, high-fiving him. Collin stood like a hero with his pod, as Viktor climbed atop a desk to speak.

"May I say?" Viktor held up a hand to stop the cheering. "Can I just say? It isn't curing cancer, but it *feels* that way."

Gamers flooded EverWhen and UnderWorld. They returned in a great wave, like migrating birds. Caverns rang with players and their avatars, and most Arkadians went home to sleep—but Collin went to O'Riley's with his pod. The pub was warm and crowded, alight with televisions. He kicked back with Akosh and Obi. Even Nicholas came this time. Daphne challenged Tomas to a game of pool, and Peter paid for everyone.

Drunk and almost happy, Collin drew another flip-book at the bar. Careless, he just drew what came to him. Wild horses with necks outstretched and flying feet.

"Stop." Daphne touched his shoulder with her cue. She was try-ing to warn him, but he didn't understand.

"I dub you Sir Collin." She was chalking up his shirt.

"Let's have a game." Nicholas offered Collin his own cue.

But Collin had caught Peter's attention. The ink drawings were simple, streamlined, but the horses unmistakable. There was the little gray, the chestnut with the scar on her back. Peter darkened as he watched Collin's pen. "Where did you get those?"

"What do you mean?" Collin looked up, surprised.

He doesn't even notice, Peter thought. Collin sat and sketched and people gathered around him as if he were jamming at the piano. He was like a musician sitting down to play by ear. An endless riff, a raw feed of images.

But Collin spoke out. "I didn't get these horses from anywhere. They're mine."

Daphne held her cue upright, tapping it against the floor.

"We're using them," Peter said. "They're ours."

"These sketches? These horses in particular?"

"We're using these horses for a new game. Elysium."

Collin's cheeks burned. This was the game in stealth mode; this was what Daphne had said he didn't want to know. He turned to look at Akosh, and Obi, Tomas. Nobody spoke. Nicholas was playing nervously with his phone.

"Why didn't you ask me?" Collin said.

"Because we didn't have to ask."

"I mean why didn't you include me?"

"We had what we needed."

Right, thought Collin. As usual, you were collecting my work. "You said my horses were pretty," he reminded Peter. "You said they just weren't interesting."

"There was work to do."

"You really are a shit," Collin said slowly. Even in the crowded bar, he sensed the hellions hush around him. He felt Nicholas's hand on his arm and he looked at the sound engineer and wondered, Are you still warning me? Are you really so afraid? Collin feared nothing at that moment. He said the thing no one was allowed to say. "My work belongs to me."

Of course this wasn't true. Collin had signed a contract. Peter said, "Your work belongs to Arkadia, as you know."

"I drew those horses," Collin countered. "I have them in my hand. How can they be yours without me?"

Peter didn't deign to answer this.

"You try to draw them." Collin held out his pen. "You show me what you know. Show me. Show me now!"

The others tried to talk to Collin, but he wouldn't listen. "Look, we're all tired," Nicholas said in his conciliatory voice.

Collin wanted to fight. He wanted to write all over Peter's face, but he would gain nothing by it, except immediate satisfaction. Peter owned his work; he could use it forever, and Collin could not get his drawings back. All he could do was make new art. His fists clenched, but he did not touch Peter. He turned around and left instead.

He had no ride back to the city, but he didn't care. Snow fell lightly, but he brushed it from his eyes and kept on walking, oblivious to slush and cold.

"Collin!" It was Daphne coming after him. She was holding his coat.

"He knows what's good," Daphne pointed out. "You could take it as a compliment."

Collin shot her a look.

"Okay, yes, he was a shit in there," Daphne conceded with her impudent smile.

But Collin did not believe in Daphne's disobedience.

"Here." He took his coat and pulled his slate from the pocket. "Take this back to him."

He went home and slept until eleven in the morning, and when he woke, he felt entirely empty. He started rummaging for food. Emma and Darius were out, and the refrigerator was nearly empty. Collin ate all of Emma's leftover bulgur wheat salad, although this would infuriate her. He didn't care. Nicholas had texted, but he didn't answer. There were other messages. There were piles of junk mail on the floor, a note from Dawn about people coming to look at the boiler.

The bulgur salad tasted like nothing. The piles of mail were indecipherable, like relics of some other person's life. He felt numb until he took a shower. Freezing water jolted him awake. That was when he decided he would bike to Emerson.

"Collin, honey? Is that you?" said Mrs. Solomon from behind her desk.

He took off his helmet and signed in. Under "purpose of visit" he scribbled, *Meeting*.

He wanted to catch Nina at lunch, but Mrs. Solomon said, "Oh, no, you can't do that. She has her evaluation!"

Upstairs in the Resource Room, Nina was sitting down with Jeff and Mrs. West, and Mr. DeLaurentis. They were meeting at a wood-grain table and Jeff was looking sympathetic—always a bad sign. He offered Nina a bottle of spring water.

"No, thanks," Nina said.

"Our goal is objectivity," Mr. DeLaurentis explained, by way of introduction. "This is why we stress the online evaluation system. By looking at the numbers we build a strong foundation."

Nina gazed at her printed results.

"One of your strengths would be your knowledge base," said Mrs. West. "As you can see in column one, almost ninety percent of students feel that you show knowledge of your subject area. On the other hand—a full eighty-two percent of students feel somewhat, very, or extremely uncomfortable asking for help."

Numbers blurred on the page. Could this be true? Nina's students called her all the time. *Miss? Miss?* They wanted this, they wanted that. Were they actually afraid of her?

"Before we dive into the details, I want to look at a couple of other issues," Mrs. West continued. "On page two in classroom management, forty-five percent of students feel somewhat or very distracted by their classmates, which is concerning. Sixteen percent characterize the atmosphere as chaotic."

"Wait," Nina said.

Mrs. West looked up. Everybody waited.

"The students are distracting each other and now they're report-ing it?"

Jeff said, "They're reporting on your classroom management."

"We've supplemented the questionnaires with classroom obser-vations," said DeLaurentis.

"I've provided all my notes," said Jeff.

"The question of favoritism," Mrs. West said. "Look at page three."

Everyone turned to page three. "Sixty-four percent of stu-dents feel that you occasionally favor some students over others. Twelve percent feel that you often do." Mrs. West paused. "That's high."

Now Nina's cheeks began to burn.

"Are you aware of this perception?" Mrs. West asked.

Nina wanted to say no, but at that moment she was acutely aware of what she had done. She was not only a rookie, but a rule-breaker as well—singling out Aidan, protecting and manipulating him, forcing him to learn.

Mrs. West did not mention Aidan. She made no specific accusa-tions. She crushed Nina with simple moral force. "*All* our students need us. All the time."

As Nina tried to catch her breath, Mrs. West marched on, pluck-ing startling numbers she had highlighted in yellow. "Let's turn to the last page."

Trembling, Nina turned, and yet even then she hoped for some-thing decent, at least average. What she saw was a composite score of 69 out of 100, and the verdict, FAIR.

"You look surprised," said Mr. DeLaurentis.

"I just thought . . ."

"You've made progress," Jeff consoled her. "Seriously."

She looked at him and wondered—progress from what? Total disaster?

Mr. DeLaurentis said, "Shall we look at your self-evaluation now?"

No! Nina screamed inwardly. She couldn't bear the comparison. The process was so humiliating. "I imagined I was doing better."

"That's why we look at the quantitative results," Mr. DeLaurentis repeated.

She didn't cry. That was her one comfort as the meeting ended: She hadn't let them see her cry, although she had come close. How had she deceived herself all year? Had she mistaken her slow progress for success? Had she imagined knowledge and goodwill would win the day? She was reaching some students. Apparently that was not enough. She had connected with a few, but that was favoritism. She couldn't win!

These were her thoughts as she walked past Collin in the hall.

"Nina," he said.

Startled, she turned toward him. Was something wrong? Something must have happened. She hadn't seen him in so long. She was concerned and affronted by his presence, but mostly confused.

"Could I just talk to you?"

The bell was ringing and eighty-two percent of Nina's students were afraid to ask for help. Concentrate, she told herself. Do you even remember your lesson?

"Just for a minute?" Collin said.

"I can't." She shut the door.

Handing back her students' work, she thought, I'm just a know-it-all. I came here to bestow my knowledge and I've failed classroom management. Even now her kids were talking. Twice she had to tell them, "Settle down." Some quieted. Others kept on talking.

Nina shouted, "What do I have to do to get your attention?"

Silence. She had never raised her voice like that before. For a moment Nina felt powerful, then she realized that she had miscalculated yet again. Cold and offended, her students gazed up at their desperate teacher. They were not accustomed to this treatment—not from her. Conversations continued in a whisper.

Wearily, Nina began passing back vocabulary quizzes. "Let's start again."

Her kids had done well on their tests. Most of them had learned the words. Before her evaluation she would have delighted in these scores. Now she dwelt on her mistakes, current and cumulative. She presented a fair lesson on Walt Whitman because there wasn't anybody else to do it. She tried to spark discussion of *Song of Myself*.

Fiercely, she taught to the last bell, and as her students streamed out into the hall she called after them, "Final drafts due Monday! Revise and *proofread*! Don't forget!"

Just outside her door, Collin saw her long hair curtaining her face as she picked up a paperback *Twelfth Night*. For a long moment, she seemed a stranger, tall, elegant, the girl from far away.

She drew back when he stepped inside. How long had he been watching? She retreated behind her desk.

Hurt, he said, "Don't worry."

"I'm not!" She was polite, as though she didn't know him.

The distance seemed to stretch between them. Collin near the door, Nina behind her Steelcase desk. "I just want to talk to you."

"What do you want to talk about?" The question sounded like, What else is there to say?

He approached her desk. "I know you don't want explanations."

"Collin," she said. "I can't think about this now."

"I just have to tell you something."

She studied his face. He looked so nervous.

"I miss you," he began, but then he stopped. "That's it," he told her. "That's the whole thing. I miss you. I need to be near you."

She said nothing.

"I was stupid. I was overwhelmed."

"Don't say that," Nina burst out. "Don't say you were overwhelmed and so you had to hurt me."

"I didn't think that I deserved you."

"So you went out to prove it?"

He didn't know how to answer that. "I've never known anyone like you," he said at last.

"I don't play games," she told him. "I can't play games with you."

"Remember when we went sledding? Remember when we walked down by the river?"

She did remember skimming down the hill and walking in the cold. She remembered his hands in her coat pockets.

"All of that was real."

"It was real at the time."

He wanted to say, No, that day will last forever—but if happiness could last, what of anger? Pain?

"Remember when I knelt in front of you right here and embarrassed you?"

Her anger flared. "How about the time you covered the blackboards with chalk pictures and ruined my lesson?"

"I was trying to apologize!"

"You picked a hell of a way to do it." She turned her back to gaze at the dusty board.

"I was arrogant," Collin admitted.

Almost inaudibly she said, "Me too."

He walked over to her side of the desk. She didn't turn toward him, but she didn't ask him to leave either. She blinked back tears, and he pretended not to notice. He just leaned against the desk and they gazed at the board with its vocabulary list. *Trill, defile, nimbus, manifold.*

"I'm sorry," he said at last.

She closed her eyes.

"Nina?"

She leaned against him ever so slightly. Subtly, almost imperceptibly, he felt her weight shift.

He said, "You were right about Arkadia. It's crazy there, and I've made such a mess."

Her eyes opened. "What happened?"

"I quit."

"Well," she said slowly, "you can still do the thing you want to do."

"Unpaid?"

"You can say that you're an artist. I can't say I'm a teacher."

"Yes, you can."

Not next year, she thought. Not if I'm looking for a real job. "My evaluation was so bad." Her voice broke a little and she almost laughed, because she had worked so hard and cared so much and failed in so many ways—and it was such a relief to tell him. "Either they like me and they don't respect me, or they just hate me." Softly she admitted, "I'm just not good at it."

"But that takes years and years."

"Maybe."

"You'll get old like a real teacher. You're already bitter—and you're getting strict. I could hear you from the hall."

"Oh, God. I lost my temper."

"What's wrong with that?"

"No, you don't understand."

Actually he understood pretty well. When she'd lost her temper, she'd done it for real. She didn't know how to lose it theatrically, how to shout and scream and stamp her feet and keep her sense of humor. And now she told him, "I was terrible."

Instinctively he touched her arm, but she shrank back. He began to speak and stopped. What could he tell her? I love you. I worship you. Those were words anyone could use. He wanted to give her something of himself. He pulled a flip-book from his pocket.

"What is it?"

He showed her how to flip the pages with her thumb.

The drawings were black ink, sharp, and stylized. A horse running riderless, fast and faster, ears back, neck outstretched. The moving picture was so fluid, the running horse so elegant, that without thinking Nina flipped the book again. "Is this for a new job? Who is it for?"

He was surprised she had to ask. He gave her another flip-book, and said, "Just you."

This time the horse approached a fence, coming at it flying, mane and tail streaming. In one fluid leap he took the jump and landed on the other side. Nina flipped the book again and yet again. The tiny animation was so beautiful, the horse leaping, the line drawing come to life. She felt absorbed in this brief story. Each time the horse swept her away, flying at the jump. "I like this better than the Ghost Horse."

Drawing closer, Collin watched her face. "You're glad I left."

She glanced up quickly. "Not if it's on my account."

"Don't worry." He was so close. His lips brushed hers. "I would never do anything for you."

He nearly kissed her, but she pulled away. "Oh, wait! I have a student coming."

Too late. Aidan had already spied them through the window in her classroom door. Collin talking, Nina listening. Although they had their backs to him, they were standing too close for ordinary conversation. Aidan could tell they were together, so he kept on walking down the hall, downstairs, and out into the winter day. Zipping his old ski jacket, he started walking home.

Alone in his bedroom he dumped his backpack on the floor. Heavy-hearted, he sat at his computer, and checked his news feed and message boards, U.S. politics, and Arkadian alliances. He followed the news, real and imaginary, but he had not been qwesting since the contagion. His dream life with Nina upstaged all others.

Dracon sent bulletins from his new company, but Aidan didn't join them. Hey we're in 8th circle, Dracon wrote in chat. Old and experienced, Aidan replied as Tildor. Watch for scorpion.

A new message flashed on Aidan's screen. Nina Lazare.

What r his powers? Dracon typed.

She had never sent a private message before. Subject: Apologies. Dear Aidan, she began. Dear! To his eyes the opening was intimate, not standard. He didn't get letters, and his friends' messages did not begin like that. I'm sorry we missed our appointment this afternoon—especially because it was our last meeting before the assembly. I wanted to show you these performances by other kids in last year's nationals. Here's the link. They're really excellent—but so are you. He read that last phrase twice, and then twice more. He read it even as he opened the link to the Poetry in Action website. *So are you.* He heard her say it as he watched clips of kids reciting Billy Collins, Gerard Manley Hopkins, H.D., Robert Frost.

Dracon was typing, r u there?

Aidan minimized Dracon's chat box.

Here was the mission statement of Poetry in Action. The list of past winners. A list of eligible poems. Seasonal poems, nature poems, most viewed poems. He clicked through categories on the website, and hundreds of titles appeared. Love poems. Short poems (under twenty-five lines). Poems about animals, poems about illness, poems about loss.

Clicking on LOVE, he scrolled down through page after page of titles and first lines. *How like a winter . . . How sweet I roam'd . . . I carry your . . . I went out to the hazel wood . . . Sing me a song of a . . .* One line jumped out at him, two sentences: *No, No! Go from me. I have left her lately.* He clicked on those words and an entire poem materialized, the story of a knight worshipping a noble lady. *I will not spoil my sheath with lesser brightness, / For my surrounding air hath a new lightness; / Slight are her arms, yet they have borne me straitly / And left me cloaked as with a gauze of aether . . .*

He sat back in his chair to stare at the fourteen lines onscreen. Message boards crowded against the poem's white space. Discussion of Arkadian weaponry, shortcuts to the Keep, new mods for EverSea. He hardly noticed. He felt so strange. How did the author know? How did "Ezra Pound, American, 1885–1972" write so specifically about his life? The poet had it all down—her slender arms, her fair skin, his new lightness, even his sword. These lines scared him. *Oh, I have picked up magic in her nearness.* He felt haunted. A stranger had been telling his secrets, publishing his dreams before he was born.

38

Win, Lose, or Draw

"Okay, listen up!" Mr. DeLaurentis announced. "Take your seats. We need your full attention." Last period, last day before winter break, 450 students filled the auditorium to over-flowing. "Nobody in the aisles. Everybody in a seat." The chairs were hard and loud. They dropped open with a satisfying bang.

DeLaurentis planted himself center stage. Square-shouldered, massive in his suit, he looked out at the student body, a sea of legs and arms. "We're starting now. Shhhh. Settle down. People in the back! Let's move along."

Behind him, in folding chairs, sat twenty-one contestants, a daunting number for a competition scheduled to last an hour. Mrs. West had instructed the competitors to sit in rows, to stand and walk to the front as soon as their names were called. That way they could recite, one after the other, without wasting time. On a white screen above their heads, Mrs. West would project title and author as each student recited. She was sitting on one side of the stage to judge the competition along with Mr. Allan and the school librar-ian, Miss McGahn.

"Let me start by welcoming all of our guests and visitors." Mr.

DeLaurentis looked out at the parents peppering the audience. "And let me express our gratitude to Mrs. West, who brought Poetry in Action to Emerson High School and spearheaded this unit. Let me thank our three judges." The judges looked up briefly from numbered printouts of each poem in competition. "And all our language-arts faculty for taking time out of their busy schedules to hold classroom recitations. Each and every one of our students has memorized and performed a poem this year. I'm waiting . . ." he broke off, as the roar of students drowned him out. "Shhhh. The winner of this competition will go on to represent our school at the district level. But let me say this. Every one of our students up here onstage is already a winner in our book. Win, lose, or draw, you are all, each and every one of you, *victorious,* for everything you did to get up here and everything we know you will accomplish today. And now, without further ado . . ."

Mrs. West announced the first contestant: "Keisha Mori."

"Go, Keisha!"

Scattered applause and whistles as the first contestant took the stage. Mrs. West had to stand up. She took off her reading glasses and said, "People. We have a lot of poems to get through in a very short time, so please hold your applause until the end."

Keisha wore a black skirt and blazer and high heels. In the middle of the auditorium, where she sat with her tenth graders, Nina saw that several of the contestants had dressed like that, as if for church. A couple of boys wore dress shoes. Xavier even wore a tie. These kids were performers, the best in the school. Several sang a cappella in the Emertones. At least five were actors in the drama club. Nina recognized the Stage Manager from *Our Town.* The contestants sat up straight, gracious in the spotlight. All but Aidan, who leaned back in his chair.

He was wearing jeans and a black sweatshirt that looked too small, and he was stretching in the second row, eyes open, but unseeing. Was he listening to Keisha recite Mary Oliver's "The Summer Day"? He didn't even glance at her.

Khalil stood up, shook out his dreadlocks, and recited Rudyard Kipling's "If—" A girl named Natalie performed Shakespeare's Sonnet 106: *"When in the chronicle of wasted time . . ."* and tripped up, stumbling on *the blazon of sweet beauty's best.*

"The blazon of . . . the blazon . . ." She stood for a moment in distress.

"Go, Natalie. Go, Natalie," kids chanted in the audience, as though she were standing in the gym, preparing for a free throw.

Natalie swallowed hard. Once again, Mrs. West had to stand up and shush everyone before the poor girl could finish.

Even then, Aidan leaned back, as in a trance.

Ismail Brown gave everything he had to "Mending Wall." Daniella Kovatcheva performed "Ozymandias."

They're good, Nina thought, as students jostled restlessly around her. *"My name is Ozymandias, King of Kings . . ."* Regally, Daniella commanded, *"Look on my Works, ye Mighty, and despair!"* and Nina sat up, entranced. This girl from Emerson owned Percy Bysshe Shelley. But Aidan could do just as well—or better—if he wanted. That was the question. What did he want? He was still staring into space.

She began dreading Aidan's turn. Other students excelled with Sharon Olds, Robinson Jeffers, Wilfred Owen. Wake up, she pleaded silently. The other kids were known quantities. They smiled, they ran cross-country. They went to prom. They did what teenagers were supposed to do. Aidan was the one in doubt. He could capture the audience if he wanted. He could astonish the entire school—or he could slip away.

She kept her eyes on him as a girl named Jacqueline Ing recited Amy Lowell. *"I walk down the garden paths, / And all the daffodils / Are blowing."* For the first time, Aidan straightened in his chair.

He seemed to gather himself. Jackie's voice was soft but intense with repressed emotion. *"I too am a rare / Pattern. As I wander down / The garden paths."* Almost imperceptibly, Aidan's right foot jiggled. *"And the splashing of waterdrops / In the marble fountain / Comes down the garden paths."*

Aidan gazed out into the audience and found Nina. In all those hundreds of people, he found her eyes. She smiled at him, hopeful, encouraging, and for a moment he gazed back at her, as if he were starting on a journey and he had to memorize her face.

Elegant, tremulous, Jackie painted a word picture with her recitation. She paced her patterned garden in her patterned brocade dress, waiting for news of her lover, who was fighting *in a pattern called a war*. But even this poem couldn't last forever. Just a few moments left, as Jackie built slowly to her anguished cry, *"Christ! What are patterns for?"*

Scattered applause, despite Mrs. West's injunction, as Jackie returned to her chair. She sat down, ducking her head modestly.

Now Aidan unfolded himself and pulled down his sweatshirt, too tight, too short.

EMILY DICKINSON flashed on the screen as Aidan ambled to the front. He took his time, adjusting the microphone. He was easily a foot taller than Jackie.

Halfway out of her chair, Mrs. West gestured for him to move along. "Whenever you're ready."

"No," Aidan shot back.

The entire student body gasped in admiration. "What are you doing?" Nina murmured in despair. Mrs. West sat down in shock.

"No, go from me," Aidan said. *"I have left her lately. / I will not spoil my sheath with lesser brightness . . ."*

Now all three judges were flipping through their printed poems in confusion. Where was Dickinson? This was not "I heard a Fly buzz—when I died."

"Slight are her arms, yet they have bound me straitly . . ." The lines were tender, but Aidan delivered them with a hard, defensive edge. Voice defiant, he seemed to stand alone onstage against his audience, against the world. *"Oh, I have picked up magic in her nearness / To sheathe me half in half the things that sheathe her."*

Nervous laughter. He ignored it. Whispered conference of the judges.

Nina stared at him in disbelief. Why, Aidan? Why choose this poem no one knew?

He looked out into the audience and kids gazed back, awed by his intensity.

At the back of the auditorium, Diana's hands clenched as she watched her twin. Her heart was pounding, she was so nervous. She heard rebellion in his voice; she saw him flouting the competition, breaking rules, and she was proud and embarrassed. Her brother was so fierce, so serious. Her palms were sweating. She was afraid everyone would laugh at him.

"No, no! Go from me. I have still the flavour, / Soft as spring wind that's come from birchen bowers."

Strange, archaic, the words came naturally to Aidan, direct as ordinary speech. *"Green come the shoots, aye April in the branches."* What a relief to tell his teacher how he felt, to give up his secret in this safe place, an auditorium full of people. The words weren't his, but he gave them breath and life, repatriating them like looted artifacts. Thrumming with the poem's subtle pitch, his body swayed. *"As winter's wound with her sleight hand she staunches, / Hath of the trees a likeness of the savour: / As white their bark, so white this lady's hours."* He stopped, and everybody waited. No one knew what would happen next.

Even Diana sat back, mystified. Aidan ambled to his folding chair and Diana felt a pang and then relief to watch like everybody else. He was speaking a language incomprehensible, even to her.

Aidan didn't see his sister in the crowd. He hardly noticed any-one. All he knew was that the ordeal was over. He knew he wouldn't win. He'd never won anything before, and Mrs. West hated him for having plagiarized.

When all the recitations were done, Mrs. West was the one who led her fellow judges offstage to confer, while competitors shifted in their chairs onstage, and the student audience surged, noise level rising, clock ticking toward dismissal. West was the one who took the microphone to tell everyone to settle down so that she could announce the winners. She raised her hand for silence. "People? People. Listen up."

When the other judges filed back onstage a few kids applauded, and one guy whistled in the back. Teachers tried to hush the audi-ence, but the auditorium rustled with impatience and hilarity. Only the contestants' parents gazed at the stage with perfect concentra-tion. Among them, Kerry sat transfixed as she watched Aidan.

"First, let's have one more round of applause for all of our con-testants," said Mrs. West. "We are so proud. We are so very proud of you." Once again, Mrs. West made a show of donning reading glasses as she unfolded her list. "Please come to the front when I call your name. Honorable mention. Claryce Williams for 'Har-lem.' Come on up, Claryce. Khalil Watson for 'If—.' Yasmine Singh, for 'Do Not Go Gentle into That Good Night.' Congratula-tions! You three, stand right over here. Now." She paused. "We have three more outstanding performances—and let me just say, we had some debate."

Were they debating me? Aidan could not suppress the question.

"This was such a close competition. Third place. Ranazia Don-yon for 'Jabberwocky.'" Hoots and whistles, applause and foot stamping—not just for the performance but for Ranazia herself, since she was so popular. "Come here. Take your prize." She handed Ranazia a book, a glossy anthology of poetry.

"Second place," Mrs. West continued. "Daniella Kovatcheva for

'Ozymandias.' " She got almost as much applause as Ranazia as she took her book.

"Finally. Our winner. The student who will represent us at the district competition. A student who chose a difficult poem . . ."

Difficult! Aidan thought.

"Which was also very powerful."

Powerful!

"A student who went above and beyond." Mrs. West paused, and everybody in the auditorium thought, Oh come on, but Aidan experienced a private agony of expectation. "Jacqueline Ing, for 'Patterns' by Amy Lowell," said Mrs. West. "Congratulations!"

Okay, thought Aidan, as Jackie walked to the front, and applause rained down.

He hadn't won. He stretched his arms above his head and stood up, joining the others crowding off the stage. He hadn't won and he was glad. He was sure of that. The disappointment he felt, the quiet comedown, could not be real. He had never wanted any prize. He didn't take this competition seriously—hadn't then, and didn't now. Therefore, he was more than fine with losing. Only his heart dissented: But you were good; you were really good.

Students stampeded for the doors, but parents stuck around. His mother appeared, and although he'd known she was coming, he was surprised to see her there. She stood right in front of the stage, stretching out her arms to him. Looking down from the stage, he almost laughed because she reminded him of swimming lessons, those afternoons when she stood in the shallow water, urging him to jump. He took the stairs instead, but he could not escape her. She latched on, pinning his arms to his sides in her embrace.

"Mom?" She held him so long that he started worrying about her. "You're okay," he said, extracting himself, and Kerry smiled through tears. Who was this child? So tender and so patronizing? "You're gonna be okay."

While Kerry went to shake hands with DeLaurentis, Mrs. West

was congratulating all the contestants as they milled around on the floor below the stage. "I'm proud of you, honey," she told Xavier. "Good job, sweetheart," she told Khalil.

"Aidan."

"What?" Aidan doubted Mrs. West would say, "Good job," to him.

"Hey, hold on. Come back."

That wasn't Mrs. West calling him. He spun around and saw Nina standing in her white parka. She had been waiting for him! She was standing underneath the EXIT sign.

"Aidan! First of all—you were amazing. Second of all . . ." For a split second, she took him by the shoulders, as if to shake him. "What am I going to do with you?"

Don't stop, he thought, overwhelmed by her brief touch.

"You realize that the judges disqualified you for switching poems."

"Okay," he said.

"What were you thinking?"

He met her eyes, and of course she knew what he'd been thinking. She had known it all along, but she had pretended otherwise, convincing herself that her student was in love with poetry.

Instantly he saw the change to adult concern, a teacher's worried face. Missing her, he couldn't help fishing. "I'm sorry if I disappointed you."

She shook her head with her old warmth. "I wasn't disappointed. I was proud. You silenced everyone!"

She didn't say how much she'd wanted him to win. Oh, he could have shown DeLaurentis and the whole school—even Mrs. West.

Snow was falling when Nina left school. Cement steps, black wrought-iron fence, schoolyard—all turned pure and white. The last few students were leaving the building. The big painted doors slammed behind them.

"Hey, Shakespeare!" she heard one of the kids shouting. "Bard of Avon!"

Collin was waiting for her. He opened the gate, and when he saw her face, he opened his arms as well.

His snowy collar brushed her cheek. He clasped her shoulders, and she rested in his embrace.

"That bad?" he asked, taking her bag.

"It wasn't bad," she said.

"What was it, then?"

She tried to find the words. "Exciting, and difficult, and . . . surprising."

He kissed her ear and when she turned toward him, he kissed her lips. His kiss was sweet and eager, but he was laughing at her too. "Yeah, that's exactly how I remember assemblies in high school."

They drove to Maia's place to bake gingerbread and move furniture around. Collin set up Maia's little white lights to frame the windowsills. Nina saved the empanadas from burning, while he ran out for paper napkins and more wine.

As the winter light began to fade, Maia's guests and neighbors came bearing brownies, latkes, trays of stuffed portobello mushrooms, for the solstice party. Melissa and Sage arrived. Sage carried a bowl of bulgur wheat salad with dried cranberries. Melissa led Henry by the hand. Lois brought caramel corn. Dawn came with steamed artichokes.

Maia set the food out on the table, and listened to her neighbors ask Collin, Hey, bud, how's Arkadia?

"It's good," said Collin.

Maia said, "He designed the new game. UnderWorld!"

"What?" Lois exclaimed. "Collin. Is that true?"

"Not exactly!" he called over his shoulder as he carried coats to Maia's bedroom.

Kerry arrived, and Aidan followed, carrying an enormous chocolate cake dusted with powdered sugar. "I tripled the recipe," Kerry said.

"He was one of the designers," Maia told Lois. "I don't know if you've seen it yet, but you stand in the center, and the whole game showers down on you like fireworks."

"Fireworks! You worked on that technology?"

"I was a concept artist."

"What?" Maia's ears pricked up at the past tense.

Meanwhile, Kerry found Nina in the kitchen, ladling punch. "This one is spiced," Nina explained, "and this one's spiked."

Kerry told Nina, "It was so strange hearing my own child recite."

Dawn said, "Remembering all those lines?"

"No, just hearing him say so many sentences together. I'd almost forgotten the sound of his voice! I was so surprised."

"I was surprised too," Nina told Kerry.

Kerry set her glass down on the counter and touched Nina's shoulder. "Thank you."

"He did all the work. Not me."

"I know that isn't true. You tutored him!"

"I mean he did his own thing," Nina explained. "He learned one poem and then at the last minute he just—switched." Stop right there, she thought, but she couldn't help adding, "I think he could have won."

Maia swept in, looking fierce.

He's told her, Nina thought, as Maia unwrapped a tray of baklava.

"Nina says Aidan could have won," Kerry told Maia.

But Maia was distracted, thinking about Collin. Was he really giving up Arkadia, and all that money, and all that magic, to look for work in Somerville? Was he really looking for some indie-animation thing?

"I really think he could have done it," Nina told Kerry.

"It doesn't matter," Kerry reassured her. "For me it wasn't about winning."

"I know." Nina couldn't help sounding wistful. "But he's so talented. It's a little hard."

"Just wait 'til you have kids," Maia interjected, blessing and cursing Nina, both at once.

As night pressed against the windowpanes, a new girl slipped inside the door. She wore a silky black shirt, black tights, black boots. She was strange and beautiful, her face pale, her hair and lips dark, her eyes outlined in black. At first, nobody recognized her—not even little Henry. When she bent down and said, "Hey! Remember me?" he shrank away from his former babysitter, frightened by her red-black lips, her huge dark eyes.

Lois was the first to greet her. "Diana, honey! How are you?"

"Good."

Alert and narrow, a greyhound of a boy, Jack appeared behind Diana. "And what have you been up to?" Lois inquired, but she had been seventeen once, and she thought she knew.

Maia was playing African music, flamenco music, tangos by Astor Piazzolla. She rolled back the carpet and danced with Greg. The china cabinet rattled; the whole apartment began to hum.

Nina had abandoned her post to sit with Collin. No one was watching in the kitchen, so Jack and Diana served themselves spiked punch. Jack had two cups, and Diana had almost three. They laughed together and Diana leaned against the counter.

He said, "I know where we should go." They got their shoes and slipped out the kitchen door.

In the living room, Sage was on her knees dancing with Henry, holding both his hands. Collin and Nina sat together on the couch and watched, while, at a little distance, Aidan watched them. Nina rested her head on Collin's shoulder, and Collin stroked her hair. How casual he was. He didn't even need to look at her.

Maia's windows steamed up. Her kitchen overflowed with neighbors in their stocking feet. The front door stood like a green island in a sea of boots. Everyone was drinking, everyone was warm and loud as Aidan slipped outside. It was snowing when he crossed the street to his own house.

He knew Diana and Jack were in there. He could see their footprints on the steps. They were up in her room, tipsy, kissing, laughing. He hesitated, wondering if he should venture in or return to Maia's house. He didn't want to watch Collin stroking Nina's hair, and he really didn't want to listen to Diana and Jack.

Hesitating, he noticed a padded envelope stuffed into the mailbox. He pulled it out and read two words in handwriting he knew. *For Aidan.*

He picked up the box and studied the curve of his own letters in Miss Lazare's writing. How strange to see his name there out of school. He stared at the words and then in a rush he ripped open the envelope and felt the thick book inside.

Oh. He knew what she had done. She had bought him his own poetry anthology because he was a winner too.

He almost threw the thing away. He didn't need anthologies, and didn't want to be consoled. Even so, he pulled the book out, hoping for a card.

Now he discovered something else entirely. This was Lazare's own Dickinson, the one she had carried in the classroom and the hall. The very book he'd turned facedown on the desk. *Don't do that! It's old. You'll break the spine.*

He found no card, no explanation, except for an inscription in blue ink. Not Miss Lazare's compact handwriting, but some other penmanship, pale and spidery. *For Nina Lazare, in recognition of excellence in public speaking, and with kind regards from her teacher, Lawrence B. Rousse* ... She had given Aidan her own prize. She had won it in school, and now she was giving it to him.

He closed the volume and weighed it in his hands. Then he took a flying leap off the porch. The bare trees tilted, neighbors' Christmas lights flickered around him as he almost fell, but he caught himself and landed on his feet.

Clasping the book with one arm to his chest, he raced up Antrim. He had no goal in mind, no destination. All he wanted was to run.

He stopped at the corner and looked once more at the treasure in his arms. Then, winded, he retraced his running steps, walking down the street again. He was not religious, but, like his mother, he believed in mysteries. Now he realized that Nina had sent him a sign, as Elvish queens bestowed a diamond flask, a gossamer handkerchief, a ring of gold. She had sent him a message with this poetry. He was noble, and he was magic. He was a champion and a prince.

No, none of that. Not really.

He saw the lights of the party. He had returned, but he stood out on the sidewalk, too shy to go inside and thank his teacher. Brushing snow from Nina's book, he felt her distance, magnified by kindness. There was nothing he could do, and nothing he could say. He could not explain what he felt, even to himself, the mix of hopelessness and grace. She didn't love him—not the way he loved her—but she had singled him out. She had given him her gift.

ALLEGRA GOODMAN's novels include *Intuition, The Cookbook Collector, Paradise Park,* and *Kaaterskill Falls* (a National Book Award finalist). Her fiction has appeared in *The New Yorker, Commentary,* and *Ploughshares,* and has been anthologized in *The O. Henry Awards* and *Best American Short Stories.* She has written two collections of short stories, *The Family Markowitz* and *Total Immersion,* and a novel for younger readers, *The Other Side of the Island.* Her essays and reviews have appeared in *The New York Times Book Review, The Wall Street Journal, The New Republic, The Boston Globe,* and *The American Scholar.* Raised in Honolulu, Goodman studied English and philosophy at Harvard and received a PhD in English literature from Stanford. She is the recipient of a Whiting Award, the *Salon* Award for Fiction, and a fellowship from the Radcliffe Institute for Advanced Study. She lives with her family in Cambridge, Massachusetts, where she is writing a new novel.

allegragoodman.com
Facebook.com/AllegraGoodman

ABOUT THE TYPE

This book was set in Sabon, a typeface designed by the well-known German typographer Jan Tschichold (1902–74). Sabon's design is based upon the original letterforms of sixteenth-century French type designer Claude Garamond and was created specifically to be used for three sources: foundry type for hand composition, Linotype, and Monotype. Tschichold named his typeface for the famous Frankfurt typefounder Jacques Sabon (c. 1520–80).